I0819025

Praise for Jenn McKinlay's romance novels

"The characters are fresh and beautifully drawn, and the chemistry is magic. It's the perfect summer vacation."

—Annabel Monaghan, *New York Times* bestselling author of *It's a Love Story*

"A playful breezy read that I couldn't put down!"

—Abby Jimenez, #1 *New York Times* bestselling author of *Just for the Summer*

"A pure delight! Has all the elements of a perfect story: small island setting, a feisty yet vulnerable heroine, and a nerdy hero who stole my heart."

—Jennifer Probst, *New York Times* bestselling author of *The Secret Love Letters of Olivia Moretti*

"McKinlay writes sexy, funny romances!"

—Jill Shalvis, *New York Times* bestselling author of *The Sweetheart List*

"I devoured this clever novel in one sitting!"

—Lori Nelson Spielman, *New York Times* bestselling author of *The Star-Crossed Sisters of Tuscany*

"In turns poignant and amusing, *Summer Reading* belies its title to tackle serious issues with aplomb, exploring essential definitions of self, friendship, family, and love while maintaining a breezy wit and pleasing pace. McKinlay's writing is sure to charm."

—Shana Abé, *New York Times* bestselling author of *An American Beauty*

"McKinlay's fresh spin on a favorite trope is as frothy and pleasing as a piña colada, delivering both laughs and poignant tugs on the heartstrings. Perfect summer beach read."

—Lori Wilde, *New York Times* bestselling author of *The Wedding at Moonglow Bay*

"A delightful romance with characters I adored! Jenn McKinlay takes readers along on a fun and charming adventure in *Paris Is Always a Good Idea.*"

—Emily March, *New York Times* bestselling author of *The Summer Melt*

"McKinlay spins a funny yet poignant tale."

—Jen DeLuca, author of *Well Traveled*

"This book made me laugh and swoon and gave me some serious wanderlust!" —PopSugar

"The must-have summer read of the year." —Fresh Fiction

"With lovable characters and swoon-worthy moments, this heart-warming tale has it all." —*Woman's World*

"This flawless rom-com is sure to delight."

—*Publishers Weekly* (starred review)

"[An] immensely enjoyable rom-com." —Shelf Awareness

"With McKinlay's zingy prose and effervescent wit . . . she deftly pivots from moments of comic absurdity to heartfelt emotion without missing a beat." —*Booklist* (starred review)

TITLES BY JENN McKINLAY

Paris Is Always a Good Idea
Wait For It
Summer Reading
Love at First Book
The Summer Share

Witches of Dubious Origin

HAPPILY EVER AFTER ROMANCES

The Good Ones
The Christmas Keeper

BLUFF POINT ROMANCES

About a Dog
Barking Up the Wrong Tree
Every Dog Has His Day

CUPCAKE BAKERY MYSTERIES

Sprinkle with Murder
Buttercream Bump Off
Death by the Dozen
Red Velvet Revenge
Going, Going, Ganache
Sugar and Iced
Dark Chocolate Demise
Vanilla Beaned
Caramel Crush
Wedding Cake Crumble
Dying for Devil's Food
Pumpkin Spice Peril
For Batter or Worse
Strawberried Alive
Sugar Plum Poisoned
Fondant Fumble

LIBRARY LOVER'S MYSTERIES

Books Can Be Deceiving
Due or Die
Book, Line, and Sinker
Read It and Weep
On Borrowed Time
A Likely Story
Better Late Than Never
Death in the Stacks
Hitting the Books
Word to the Wise
One for the Books
Killer Research
The Plot and the Pendulum
Fatal First Edition
A Merry Little Murder Plot
Booking for Trouble

HAT SHOP MYSTERIES

Cloche and Dagger
Death of a Mad Hatter
At the Drop of a Hat
Copy Cap Murder
Assault and Beret
Buried to the Brim
Fatal Fascinator

The Summer Share

Jenn McKinlay

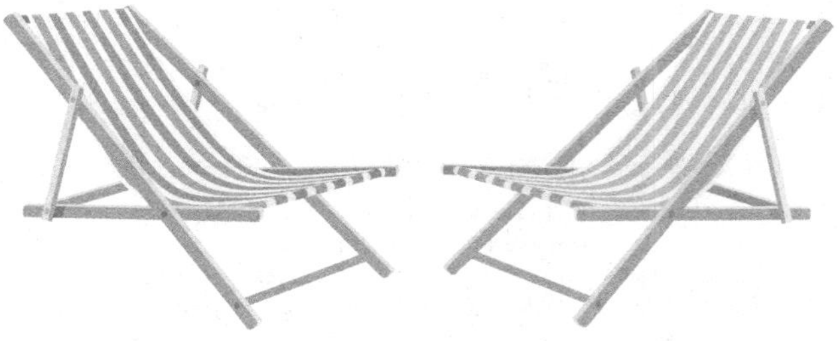

Berkley Romance
New York

BERKLEY ROMANCE
Published by Berkley
An imprint of Penguin Random House LLC
1745 Broadway, New York, NY 10019
penguinrandomhouse.com

Book design by Kristin del Rosario
Interior art: Beach and nautical art © Olga Selyutina / Shutterstock

Library of Congress Cataloging-in-Publication Data

Names: McKinlay, Jenn author
Title: The summer share / Jenn McKinlay.
Description: First edition. | New York: Berkley Romance, 2026.
Identifiers: LCCN 2025050630 (print) | LCCN 2025050631 (ebook) |
ISBN 9780593955468 trade paperback | ISBN 9780593955475 ebook
Subjects: LCGFT: Romance fiction | Novels | Fiction
Classification: LCC PS3612.A948 S88 2026 (print) | LCC PS3612.A948 (ebook)
LC record available at https://lccn.loc.gov/2025050630
LC ebook record available at https://lccn.loc.gov/2025050631

First Edition: May 2026

Printed in the United States of America
1st Printing

The authorized representative in the EU for product safety and compliance is Penguin Random House Ireland, Morrison Chambers, 32 Nassau Street, Dublin D02 YH68, Ireland, https://eu-contact.penguin.ie.

In loving memory of my guncle, Brian L. McKinlay.
You had the brightest smile and the most contagious laugh—
I can still hear it whenever I think of you.
Your wit and wisdom are sorely missed,
but I'll carry my happy memories of you in my heart always.

The Summer Share

Hannah

"Good morning, travelers," I said to the camera on my phone, which was perched in its holder on the dashboard of my vintage Volkswagen van.

Bang! The right-front tire lurched into a pothole on the sorely neglected road.

"Ah!" I took my foot off the gas and swerved out of the danger zone. The van didn't shimmy or pull so we hadn't popped a tire. *Hallelujah.* I'd had enough flats in my career as an online camper van enthusiast to know when Buttercup—yes, my baby had a name—was in trouble.

Dude, my Great Dane rescue, lurched to his feet and shoved his big blocky head in between the front seats—to offer assistance, no doubt, as he was always helpful like that. I reached up and rubbed his soft, floppy ears.

"It's okay, buddy. We're almost there." I tapped the camera off on my phone. Given the poor condition of the road, I figured it was better to record my content for next week after we arrived.

I turned my attention back to the narrow lane. There was

enough room for only one car so I really hoped no one approached me from the opposite direction. Because with vibrantly green grassy marshland squeezing the road on both sides like a too-tight corset, there was no place for me to go except into the brackish muddy water.

I scanned the area, looking for the cottage where my Pops had spent every summer for as long as I could remember. The Outer Banks had been his special place in his later years. No one in the family had ever been invited into his fishing sanctuary. It was just him and his solitary weeks spent on the water. I think we accepted the banishment only because he kept us supplied with enough grouper, red drum, and little tunny for the entire winter.

Now that I was here, my chest felt tight with a fresh wave of loss for the man who had been my number one fan, my champion, and my best friend. Inhaling through my nose, I slowly exhaled out my mouth, trying to control the grief that had been ever present since the moment Pops had passed four weeks ago.

The van lurched into another pothole. "Damn it."

When I was a kid, Pops and Nana brought me to the Carolina shore for weeklong summer vacations. My memories were full of sand between my toes and ice cream cones, marathon Monopoly games when it rained, and generally just basking in the adoration of two of my favorite people.

When they divorced, in a split my dad called the most amicable parting of ways in the history of marriage, the vacations stopped. Nana started dating while Pops continued his trips to the Carolina shore but he went by himself, making this place his own.

Another large divot appeared and I refocused on the road, weaving around the treacherous-looking pit. The marshland fell away as Buttercup rumbled onto firmer ground and the road widened just enough for two vehicles to fit with a fine hair between them.

Dude and I followed the curved lane, passing by several houses tucked back amid a copse of enormous live oaks. The way the modest cottages were nestled under the massive trees with their thick trunks, wide canopies, and arching limbs, it felt as if I'd stumbled into a sort of magical forest. I glanced at the numbers on the homes and knew I was getting closer.

Excitement zipped through me. I was overcome with curiosity to see the place where Pops had spent so much of his life by himself. Separated from the other residences by a stand of smaller sand oaks was a lone white clapboard house with dark green trim and matching shutters, all of which were closed over the windows. I felt my lips curve up. This was exactly the sort of place where I could picture Pops spending his days, fishing and boating, enjoying the quiet after so many years as the local news anchor in Providence, Rhode Island.

The van chugged to a stop and I turned the key in the ignition off. I double-checked the metal numbers tacked onto the side of the house. Eighty-one. This was it. Dude let out a small whimper and wiggled as if he, too, knew that we'd finally arrived. I turned and patted his shoulder. "Let's check it out."

I opened my door and Dude clambered over the seat—all 150 pounds of him—almost knocking me down in his haste to follow me as if afraid I might leave him behind. He trotted forward two steps and immediately lifted his leg on the trunk of a crape myrtle, identifiable by its peeling brown bark and thick clusters of bright pink flowers. I couldn't blame him; a dog has his priorities, after all.

I took a beat to take in the house in front of me. A sense of déjà vu hit me right in the chest. I had been here before. I was certain of it. I remembered thinking in my little-kid brain that this house was a sentient being, that the dormer windows on the second floor were eyes, the front door a nose, and the porch a wide smile. I supposed it might just resemble the house I'd stayed in with Pops and Nana, but I felt certain it was the actual house.

I remembered Pops had let me ride my bike on the wraparound porch and we pretended I was a race car driver doing laps until Nana declared I was making her dizzy. When had Pops bought the house that we'd rented for our vacations, and why hadn't he ever told me?

I marveled at the place that held a decade of summer memories. When Nana returned from her vacation, I'd call her and ask if she knew this was our old rental. I put my hand on the stair railing and studied the place. Upon closer inspection, the house was less charming and more woebegone in appearance. The roof had missing shingles, the gutters were stuffed with leaves, and several of the shutters were missing slats and in a few cases hanging drunkenly from their hinges.

The paint was peeling and green moss was growing thick in the shadows and crevices. Knee-high weeds filled the front yard, covering the crawl space below and curving up onto the porch railing as if intent upon swallowing the house whole. Several tree limbs had fallen in the yard, probably from recent storms.

Given the state of the outside, I hated to imagine what the inside looked like. A month had gone by since Pops had passed and his estate settled. I knew it had been several months since he'd come down here to fish. I had no idea if he had anyone checking on the house or not. I was assuming not. During those months of vacancy, I feared a wild critter or two might have taken up residence and would now claim squatter's rights.

"Do not bite anything in the house, especially if it moves," I said to Dude. He tipped his head to the side as if he found this order confounding. "I'm serious. You don't know their medical history, if they have fleas, ticks, or rabies. No biting." He opened his massive muzzle and yawned. "Oh, I'm sorry. Am I boring you?"

I pulled the key to the cottage out of the side pocket of my beige cargo shorts. The house was much smaller than I remembered, but given that I'd been living in my van for the past five years, it felt like a castle to me. Not for the first time I wondered why—out of all the members in my family—Pops had left his summer place to me. Was it because I presently lived in a van? Unlike the rest of my family, my grandfather had never tried to dissuade me from my current life choices.

Pops had followed me on the socials and actively engaged in my posts. I'd always thought he was proud of me for going my own way when my career in journalism came to an unexpected and tragic end at the same time that my husband announced he no longer loved me and ended our marriage. But maybe Pops had given me the house so I had a safe place to land when I was tired of my nomadic lifestyle. If so, he'd been right. After several years of nonstop traveling—some might say running away—lately I'd been getting the urge to plant myself somewhere and put down some roots, or at the very least take a sabbatical from the daily quest for content.

I climbed up the steps, fully prepared for the boards beneath my feet to give way. They did not. They even supported Dude. The front porch was empty except for two large white flowerpots on each side of the front door that contained the dried husks of what had once been some sort of large plants. Geraniums? Roses? I couldn't tell.

It seemed an unexpectedly cheerful aesthetic for a man's fishing retreat. I tried to remember if Pops had been a plant guy. He'd never remarried after his divorce from Nana, and I couldn't remember any plants in the bachelor residence Pops had maintained down the street from my parents' house in Little Compton, Rhode Island. He and Nana both lived in that neighborhood. When Nana married George, my bonus grandpa, Pops had been the one to give her away.

Another wave of grief hit me. How could a man who had loved his family and friends as fiercely as Pops had be gone? There'd been no warning. No time to say good-bye. The lump in my throat was hard and I tried to swallow it down. Pops hadn't seemed himself the last three months of his life. His contagious laugh, a deep throaty chuckle, was seldom heard and the sparkle in his eyes was dim. Whenever I asked him what was wrong, he pushed away my concerns, blaming it on aging, but it never sat right with me. I should have persisted. Now I would never know what had been on his mind during those last few months.

Guilt and regret honed my grief to a sharp edge. I glanced at the door in front of me. Ever since my dad had handed me the key to the house, I'd pinned a lot of hope on finding solace in this place that Pops had loved so well.

I slid the key into the dead bolt and twisted it until it clicked. I turned the knob and pushed the door open. Well, I tried to push it open. The humidity had swollen the door shut and I had to put my shoulder into it. Dude watched me encouragingly as I used the force of my entire body to ram the door. When it gave way with a groan of protest, I stumbled inside.

With the exterior shutters closed over the windows, the light was weak. I reached for the switch by the door and flipped it on. Nothing happened. No electricity. Great.

I squinted into the gloom and as my eyes adjusted I noticed dust sheets covered the furniture, and the place smelled musty. It hit me then that the last time Pops had been here, he must have closed it up knowing he wasn't coming back. Otherwise, why would he have used dust sheets when he'd popped down here once a month and every summer?

I crossed the front room to the closest window, turned the latch to free the interior sash, and pushed it open and then the screen as well. The clasp to the shutters was on the inside, so I quickly popped it and pushed the shutters wide. I swear I felt the house sigh in relief as I lowered the screen. I did the same with three more windows until there was enough light to see and air moving through the house to push out the musty scent of neglect.

Dude prowled through the living room, the dining area, and the kitchen—his favorite room, of course. His nose was pressed to the ground and he snuffled his way through, looking for any snacks that might have been left behind.

I followed him, taking in the vintage cooking space. White appliances and rounded oak cupboards. Hello, 1994. I recognized the same interior aesthetic from my baby pictures in my parents' old photo albums.

I opened the large window over the sink and unlatched the shutters, pushing them wide. The view from the back of the house boasted a monstrous live oak to one side, a sloping woefully overgrown lawn, and a narrow dock that ran fifty yards through the tall grass to the wide waterway that ran through the center of the marsh. Wooden stairs led up to a small shack on a large platform raised on stilts. That had to be where Pops cleaned his fish and stored his boat during inclement weather.

Below the shack was a lower platform that sat on the edge of the wide channel. I noticed a boat was tied up to it. It was not Pops's boat, as his was moored at the marina in Little Compton. He might have left the house to me but the boat was his pride and joy and had been bequeathed to my dad, his only child. And yet there beneath Pops's fishing shack was a boat . . . and a fisherman.

I'd been worried about critters squatting at the house. It hadn't occurred to me that a person might have done so. Fantastic. The lawyer for Pops's estate was due here at any minute. This was so not what I needed right now.

From this distance it was hard to get a sense of the man. The sun glinted off his thick, wavy, dark brown curls, his broad shoulders were snug beneath his T-shirt, and as he cast his line, his muscled calves flexed beneath his knee-length shorts as he strode along the rocking planks with purpose. He was pale as if he didn't get enough time outside and yet he looked entirely too comfortable on Pops's . . . er . . . *my* dock. I decided I was going to have to go say something. I patted my pocket for my phone, realizing then that I'd left it in the van.

"Come on, Dude. I don't want to confront anyone without the ability to call for backup if things get weird or nasty."

Being a woman, traveling on my own, I had become very savvy about always having my phone fully charged and on hand. If I got a weird vibe, I called someone and started talking about where I was and what I was doing immediately.

I turned, expecting my ginormous shadow to follow. He did not. Instead, Dude nudged open the back door with his nose. Not hard, since it had apparently been left OPEN! Clearly, the trespasser on the dock with the boat had been in Pops's house. The audacity!

"Dude, don't go out there!" I ordered. He went out there. Damn it!

I slipped through the door, hoping the man on the dock didn't notice us, and hissed through gritted teeth, "Stop, Dude, get over here right now." He didn't.

Instead, he let out a deep *woof* of greeting and started to gallop across the yard and down the dock toward the poor bastard standing on the edge of the platform, holding a fishing pole and having no idea what was about to hit him.

Simon

Nothing was biting. How had Gramps spent so much time in his getaway cottage, fishing off the dock when there were no fish? It boggled.

I reeled in my line and cast again, watching the lure plop into the water. I pulled my fishing rod to the side, tugging the lure a bit, trying to entice a fish, any fish, to come and play. There was no action, i.e., no takers.

"Dude! You get back here this instant!" A shrill voice broke the silence, startling a gray heron out of the marsh. He launched into the air, beating his massive wings.

I whipped around at the sound of footsteps behind me and saw a wild-haired woman in cargo shorts and a tank top thundering down the narrow dock on the heels of a black-and-white horse—okay, more like a pony—that was headed straight for me.

I quickly set my pole in the holder on the base of the dock and crouched down, putting up my hands in surrender as if the beast barreling toward me was there to rob me.

"Whoa, whoa!" I cried. The behemoth didn't slow down one bit.

By the time it occurred to him to jam on his brakes it was too late. The beast slammed into my chest like a Mack truck and the next thing I knew I was flailing and free-falling into the channel.

The water was colder than I expected for late June, but what did I know? I hadn't planned to go swimming. Instinctively, I started to kick up to the surface. I popped up to hear the woman, scolding her beastie.

"Dude, what were you thinking? What if there are alligators in there? That man could be their lunch." There was a pause and then her voice took on a harsh warning note. "Dude, don't you do it. Dude!"

I wiped the water from my face just in time to see the horse come flying at me. His feet were pedaling in midair as if he were still running. His tongue was hanging out and his ears flapping in the breeze. I had only a second to take in the sight of him, realize I was his target, and try to get out of the way before he hit the surface like a wrecking ball. I didn't make it.

The monster hit me right in the solar plexus and I plunged below the surface and sank like a rock. The pony had knocked the wind out of me, but I'd spent enough time surfing the Carolina coastline to know not to try to breathe. Still, blacking out was a high probability as everything started to go fuzzy.

A splash disrupted the water near me and I felt someone grab me by the collar of my shirt and haul me in sluggish yanks and tugs back up to the surface. When we broke through, my diaphragm was still locked and I couldn't breathe.

"I think you killed him," the woman gasped. Then she thrashed against me. "What was that? Something brushed my leg. Ah! I bet it's an alligator!"

I would have told her to calm the hell down but I didn't have enough air to form words. Instead, I started to slowly sink beneath the surface again.

"Oh, no, you don't." She yanked me back up. "I did not risk getting eaten by a prehistoric creature just to have you drown."

Something splashed next to me and I recognized the big pink tongue as the pony swam beside us, kicking his long legs and enormous paws, without a care in the world.

I tried to suck in a breath but my chest refused to move. I could feel a thrum of panic surge through me as I flailed to get to the dock.

"It's okay." The woman's voice was a husky whisper in my ear. "I've got you. I won't let you drown."

As if I would! My pride took issue with this but I didn't have enough oxygen in my lungs to protest. My argument would have to wait.

She wrapped her arm around my torso and towed me to the lower dock where my boat was tied. The small horse was already out and bouncing on his feet, wagging as if he was having the best day ever. Jerk.

With a hearty shove, the woman rolled me onto the rough wood and then pulled herself up beside me. "Let's get you on your side." With a grunt she maneuvered me into a fetal position. Humiliating. And then she started to vigorously rub my back. "Try to relax. You just had the wind knocked out of you. Take small breaths. It's all right. I've got you."

I managed a small sip of air and the darkness receded from my peripheral vision.

"That's it," she said. She kept up the circular massage and I felt my diaphragm slowly loosen, allowing me to take deeper breaths.

When I had enough air to be able to speak, I lifted my head and rasped, "I'm all right."

"Thank goodness." She flopped onto her back on the dock beside me and panted. "I haven't been a lifeguard in years. I was afraid I'd lost my skills. Plus, alligators."

I didn't know what to say to that so I said nothing, closing my eyes as I concentrated on inflating my lungs.

"I'm sorry about this. Dude has spatial-awareness issues. He thinks he's a lapdog and I can't seem to dissuade him from that notion. He's knocked the wind out of me a few times."

I held up my hand, opened it and then closed it, hoping that she could grasp the universal sign for *Stop talking*. Then I dropped my forearm over my eyes while I tried to catch my breath in between coughing and wheezing.

She must have gotten the message because she said nothing. When my breathing became normal, I dropped my arm from my eyes and turned to face her.

"Lapdog? I thought he was a pony." I glanced up to see the biggest dog I'd ever encountered standing over us. His ears were perked up and his head was cocked to the side. Was that how he looked right before he ate someone?

I pushed myself up to a seated position. The dog-horse immediately shoved his snout in my face and licked my head from chin to eyebrow. It felt like a very soggy apology but I wasn't sure I was ready to forgive him just yet.

The woman sat up and I got my first eyeful of her. The wild hair I'd seen when she was running toward me was now plastered to her head, revealing sun-bronzed skin, a heart-shaped face, and enormous blue eyes. Her wet clothes were suctioned to her body, revealing a figure that was wickedly curvy. I forced my gaze back to her face, not wanting to be the kind of man who ogled, no matter how tempting she was.

Her eyes were framed with long dark lashes, and she had an upturned nose that sported a spray of faint freckles. Her full lips were presently tipped up in one corner in an expression of exasperation as she pushed her dog away from me. "Dude, manners."

"His name is Dude?"

"Yeah, 'or El Duderino if you're not into the whole brevity thing.'"

Maybe it was the lack of oxygen to my brain, but the *Big Lebowski* reference surprised me and I laughed. "'The Dude abides.'"

"Nice." She held up a fist. I glanced from it to her and back. She was offering me a knuckle bump and a knowing smile. It felt like a truce and I was willing, despite her dog trying to drown me, to let bygones be bygones. I was only going to be here for a few weeks. I didn't have time to hold a grudge with a neighbor. I tapped her knuckles with mine.

I pushed up to my feet and offered my hand. "I'm Simon O'Malley."

She hesitated for just a second before grasping my palm and allowing me to pull her up. "Hannah Spencer."

"And the Dude." I released her hand.

"We're a package deal." She grinned and I blinked. It was like looking directly at the sun.

Hannah twisted the end of her shirt, wringing out the excess water. I decided to let my T-shirt and shorts drip-dry and retrieved my fishing rod. Dude followed me and watched with his head tilted forward on his shoulders as I reeled the line in. He seemed as disappointed as I was to find nothing on the hook. I secured the lure and started to walk back to the house.

"Excuse me, Simon, but where are you going?" Hannah dropped her shirt and frowned at me. She'd said my name very purposefully as if she didn't believe it was mine.

"To my house." I pointed to Gramps's cottage.

A look of confusion creased her brow and she shook her head, sending droplets of water in all directions. "That can't be your house. It's my house."

"This is 81 Old Hickory Road." I wondered if she'd booked a summer rental and had gotten confused about the address. These things happened.

"I'm aware," she said. "I'm meeting my attorney here to discuss my inheritance, which is that house."

"*Your* inheritance?" I shook my head. "That's not possible. The only attorney coming here today is the one planning to speak with me about the cottage—this cottage—that my grandfather left to me."

Her eyes narrowed in suspicion and she assessed me from my sodden hair to my soggy Vans. Clearly, she hadn't planned on having me dispute her claim.

"I don't know what game you're playing, Simon—"

"No game, Hannah." I said her name with just as much bite. To soften my stance, I held my hands out much as I had when Dude had been bearing down on me. "I'm the grandson of Robert O'Malley, the owner of this property, who left it to me."

"But that's not . . . that can't be . . . I have paperwork that says otherwise," she countered.

We stared at each other. A sick feeling twisted in my gut. I studied her face. She was in her late twenties or early thirties. Not a kid—unless I compared her to my grandfather's age of seventy-nine when he passed. Could he have . . . would she have . . . ? Ugh, my mind rebelled at the mere idea of Gramps shacking up with a woman *less than half his age*.

"How did you know my grandfather?" The question came out harsh. I would have softened my tone but knowing how difficult any claim she made on the property would make things for me, I felt a solid offense was my best play.

"I think you're confused," she protested.

"I assure you, I'm not."

"I'm here because—"

"Ms. Spencer. Mr. O'Malley." A voice called from the deck on the back of the house. "Good afternoon. I'm Vincent Cosmo from Cosmo, Stuart, and Kline. Sorry to have kept you waiting. I was stuck in court."

The middle-aged white guy wore an impeccable navy suit, clearly bespoke, and a haircut so precise even the summer humidity couldn't curl the silver buzz cut. He waved down at us noticeably unsurprised to find us both here. I knew in an instant this did not bode well for me or my plans for the house.

Hannah and I turned to each other with matching raised eyebrows and asked in unison, "Your attorney?"

"Yes." We answered together.

"Interesting." She turned and with Dude at her side walked up the dock to the house.

I said nothing, thinking I would have gone with a different word like *bullshit* or at the very least *unexpected*. What the hell had Gramps been thinking to leave anything to a woman he couldn't have known for very long? Could he? She was young enough to be his granddaughter!

Maybe I was wrong. Perhaps it wasn't a "relationship" relationship. Possibly she was his cleaning lady or landscaper. No, I'd seen the inside of the house as well as the outside. If she was either of those things, she was terrible at them. Still, there was no need to assume the worst. Hannah might be an elder-care volunteer or a visiting healthcare worker. It had to be something like that.

The Gramps I knew had only had one love in his life and that was Granny. I glanced back at the water. In my mind, I could picture Gramps sitting in the same nylon folding chair he'd sat in on the sidelines of every soccer game I'd had as a kid. All right, maybe a newer version of the chair, given that my peak soccer days were more than a decade and a half behind me.

I wondered if Gramps smoked his cigars out here while nursing two fingers of his preferred whiskey, served neat in a rocks glass. Before she passed away when I was thirteen, Granny had made a good-natured fuss about his stinky cigars. After she died, I'd frequently see him staring ruefully at the unlit tip of a cigar he had just trimmed and was getting ready to light, as if he missed her chiding concern.

It was shortly after Granny passed that he started taking long weekends here in Cape Split, this tucked-away peninsula on the Outer Banks. He'd said fishing made his mind quiet, which was why he never invited anyone to join him. I suspected that this cottage on the marsh was the place he'd grieved losing his partner of thirty-seven years.

Dragonflies darted above the water's surface, flitting in and out of the marsh, a bullfrog croaked, and the breeze rippled through the grass in a hushed whisper. I took a deep breath and let it fill me up before releasing it. Was this the peace Gramps had found? Being in nature? Embracing the quiet? I could see the appeal.

As I turned to follow Hannah and the Dude, I heard the trill of a Carolina wren. I felt my shoulders drop as if I were letting go of my responsibilities for the first time in a long time. Was that what Gramps had felt here? Was that why he'd never shared his cottage on the water with anyone in the family? Had he wanted to keep this peace to himself? I couldn't blame him.

Having just found out about the surprise inheritance two weeks ago, I had no idea what my grandfather had been thinking and wouldn't until I met with the attorney currently greeting Hannah and her pony with obvious enthusiasm. I picked up the pace and hurried to join them.

Hannah

Mr. Cosmo smiled as he shook my hand as if he was completely fine with this strange man claiming his grandfather had left Pops's cottage to him. Someone here was confused, misinformed, or something even more nefarious because the only explanation that my racing brain could offer was that Pops had a second family under a different name—*O'Malley?*—with a wife and a kid/s and a *grandson*! A secret life that no one in my family had known about. The thought made me woozy. It simply couldn't be true.

"Nice to meet you, Ms. Spencer," Mr. Cosmo said. He held out his hand for Dude to sniff, which I thought was rather brave. Most people steered clear of Dude because of his massive size. Also, Dude looked like he'd be happy to shed and drool all over the nice man's suit, but that didn't seem to concern Mr. Cosmo in the least.

"Good boy, now go play in the yard." I patted Dude's head. His ears rose as if he didn't like the idea of leaving me alone with strangers. "It's all right."

With a warning bark at Mr. Cosmo and Simon, who joined us

on the deck, Dude turned and ran down the steps to the sloping lawn, where he promptly flopped into the tall grass and rolled onto his back, scratching his itches with gusto.

"Beautiful dog," Mr. Cosmo said. He gestured to Dude's black-and-white markings. "A harlequin?"

"Yes, and thank you." I felt myself soften a bit. "He's a rescue."

"I work with the local shelter." Mr. Cosmo beamed at me. "Rescues make the best pets."

I could feel a rapport between us happening and took it as a good sign that he would set things straight.

"Mr. O'Malley." Mr. Cosmo reached out and shook hands with our uninvited guest.

"Call me Simon."

"And I'm Hannah." I forced a smile, not wanting to lose the connection I'd forged with the lawyer, especially if I needed his services to clarify things with this interloper. Yes, that was the word I was looking for. *Interloper.* I shot Simon a sideways glance and found him studying me with an equally suspicious gaze.

"Excellent. Please call me Vincent. I'm glad you both could make it." Vincent gestured to the house. "We have much to discuss and I think we'd be more comfortable inside, yes?"

Simon nodded so I did, too, even though, on principle, I resisted agreeing with him on anything at the moment.

"If it's not too much trouble, I'd like to change into something dry." I gestured at Simon. "I had to jump into the water and save him when he had an unfortunate accident."

"*Save* me?" Simon repeated, looking outraged. "For the record, I did not need saving."

"Really?" I asked. "You sank like a sack of cement."

He pressed his lips together as a red flush appeared along his jawline. "I feel compelled to point out that I wouldn't have needed any assistance if your pet pony hadn't knocked me off the dock to begin with."

Vincent's head swiveled between us as we volleyed accusations back and forth. I sucked in a gulp of air for my rebuttal when the lawyer said, "I do have another meeting to get to, so perhaps we can put a pin in this discussion and you two can revisit it when I leave?" His tone was bland but it was also all business, letting us know we were going to get charged his lawyerly rate and maybe squabbling like children was not the best use of his time or our money.

"Of course." Simon and I spoke together—again—which I found incredibly annoying.

Simon disappeared down the hall and came back with a bath towel around his neck and held a second one out to me. "Will this do or would you prefer to change?"

"It'll do." I took the towel and was determined not to say anything else but my manners were too ingrained to be ignored. "Thank you."

He inclined his head and whisked the sheets off the furniture in the living room so that we could sit down while we listened to whatever Vincent had to tell us.

I'd hoped the living room furniture would be less aged than the kitchen, but no. The chairs and matching sofa were upholstered in a rough fabric of turquoise and gray with a decided southwestern flair in the matching triangular throw pillows.

I wrapped the towel around me, wishing I had taken the moment to change, but I suspected it was just me wanting to stall because this meeting had taken a sharp detour into the unknown, for which I was completely unprepared.

How was I going to explain to my family that Pops had a secret life? He and Nana were divorced. Was this why? Did she know? Had they been protecting my dad from Pops's other life all these years? And if so, why hadn't Nana at least warned me? Ugh, I did not want to be the one to tell my dad his father had a second family under a different name tucked away in the Outer Banks.

I cast a side-eye at Simon, noting his square jaw, full lips, and sharp nose. Did this mean we were related? I supposed we must be. If we shared a grandfather, then I assumed we were cousins? He turned toward me as if aware of my scrutiny, and looked at me with one eyebrow raised in equal suspicion. Well, that took some nerve.

"What?" I demanded.

He shook his head and shrugged as if he was trying to dismiss the dark thoughts he was having about me. Obviously, his family didn't know about my family, either. How had Pops pulled that off?

Simon was clearly trying not to engage, but he couldn't stick to the script as he cast me a considering glance and said, "I don't care what sort of relationship you had with Gramps, you're not inheriting this house."

"Excuse me?" I drew back. "What exactly is that supposed to mean? And what are you to me anyway? A cousin? A half cousin?"

"Cousin?" he barked as if offended by the mere idea. "How do you figure that, bonus grandma?"

"Bonus grandma?" I choked. "What—and I cannot emphasize this enough—the hell is that supposed to mean?"

Vincent flinched. I couldn't blame him. My volume was cranked up to a solid seven and I wasn't a gal for swearing but . . . *bonus grandma?!*

"If I could interject," Vincent said. His voice was as calm as the water in the channel. "I think there's been some confusion."

At that moment, Dude trotted in through the open back door and plopped his butt onto the couch next to me. He rested his head on my shoulder and it was like being comforted by a bowling ball. Vincent smiled at him adoringly before he continued.

"I tried to convince your grandfathers to give their heirs a heads-up, but they were resistant and insisted you would understand and manage the property together just fine." The dubious expression on Vincent's face made it clear what he thought of that. "Hannah, your grandfather has left you his share of this cottage and the property on which it sits."

I slumped back against the sofa, trying to process. What did he mean when he said "grandfathers"?

"Wait." Simon held up a hand. "*Her* grandfather?"

"Yes, William Spencer," Vincent said.

"But this cottage belongs to my grandfather, Robert O'Malley," Simon said.

I glanced between the two men. Vincent cleared his throat. "Half of it does, which he left to you."

"Half." I sat up, my back rigid. Pops had never ever mentioned that he shared ownership of his cottage. Were there other owners? Was this some sort of time-share nonsense that I could never get out of and was going to regret for the rest of my days?

"Yes, your grandfathers, plural, each owned fifty percent of this house and this property," Vincent said. "And you have each inherited *your* grandfather's half."

"So, we're co-owners," I clarified.

"Precisely." Vincent beamed at me. Then he grew serious. "They made no restrictions about what to do with the house and property, so that is entirely up to you, but they did stipulate that you both must reside in the house for the duration of one summer, approximately two months. After that, whatever you decide to do with the property must be consensual. If you decide to sell or one of you buys the other out, you'll have to sign an affidavit that it's a mutually-agreed-upon outcome."

"That's easy," I said. "We're not selling." At the same time Simon said, "Of course we're selling."

We turned to look at each other and the *Excuse me?* tension between us had enough bite that Dude put a ginormous paw over his eyes as if he couldn't bear to watch what was going to happen next. Vincent must have felt the same way. He pulled some papers out of his briefcase and plopped them onto the coffee table.

"It's all explained in here. I'll give you some time to process the situation." He grabbed his briefcase and bolted for the exit. "If you have any questions, don't hesitate to call."

The front door slammed shut behind him as Simon and I silently watched him escape.

"Well." We said it together and then glowered at each other.

"I'm not selling," I said at the same time Simon asked, "Why would you want to keep this place? It's so old, it's probably haunted."

"It is not!" I protested. As if to mock me, the front door that Vincent had closed behind him slowly creaked open as if letting in a ghost.

"You were saying?" Simon's tone reeked of *I told you so*.

"The house has simply been neglected. It's obviously been months since anyone was here." I crossed the room and closed the door, giving it a nudge with my hip for good measure. "A little effort will make it habitable again."

"Effort?" he scoffed. "I hope you mean with an excavator and a dump truck."

I could feel my temper start to bubble to the surface. I had barely set foot inside the house that Pops had left me, a place that held some of the happiest memories of my childhood, and this guy wanted to demolish it. Nope. Nuh-uh. No way. Nohow. Not on my watch.

While I wanted to lash back, I'd learned in my years as a journalist that arguing rarely worked when trying to get a subject to talk to you. I took a deep breath and gave Simon a serene smile.

"You are more than welcome to do whatever you want with your *half* of the house," I said. "But I plan to live in mine."

"You're serious?"

"As a heart attack."

"You'll give yourself one if you try to repair this fixer-upper." He glowered and I might have been intimidated but it lacked heat.

I didn't know what Simon's relationship with his grandfather had been like, but Pops and I had been close and I wanted to know why he'd entrusted his special place to me. Whatever Simon O'Malley had going on was not my business, and I wasn't selling to accommodate him or his issues.

"Considering I've been living in a van for the past five years, this house could fall down around me and it would still be a palace in my eyes."

"You've been living in a van?" His eyes went wide with horror. "For five years?"

I nodded. "I travel the country in it posting online about my journey. It's what I do for a living."

He opened his mouth, closed it, then opened it again but no words came out. Well, obviously, that shut him up. I tried not to look too pleased with myself. I failed.

"Well, that's—" Simon stopped talking and shoved off the couch, rising to his feet, as if he needed to take a beat to think about things. "I'm going to go and secure my boat."

I watched him stride out the back door and made a quick grab for Dude's collar so that he didn't follow him. One dunking incident for the day was enough. As soon as the door shut behind Simon, I went to retrieve some dry clothes from my van.

It was muggy outside and I could feel a sheen of sweat coat my skin as I pulled open Buttercup's sliding door. I glanced up at the sky and noticed several dark gray, bottom-heavy clouds rolling our way. Rain was coming. I glanced back at the house. Rough weather inside and out. It was going to be a fun night!

I riffled through the clean clothes I stored in a built-in cupboard. My wardrobe was utilitarian so I chose another pair of cargo shorts and a fresh tank top and underwear. I glanced at the house and wondered if we had running water and how long it would take to get the electricity turned on. I knew a house was going to bring more responsibilities than my van, but I hadn't anticipated a reluctant roommate being one of them.

My disappointment at the complication of a joint ownership of Pops's cottage was immense. I'd so been looking forward to having a place to myself to unplug, detox, and figure out my life. How the heck was I supposed to do that with six foot two of resentful hot guy underfoot? I tried to look at the bright side. At least he wasn't my cousin.

Simon

Small mercy that Hannah wasn't my bonus grandma. I felt my mouth curve up slightly as I remembered her outraged expression and the fire that had shot out of her blue gaze when I had suggested as much. Admittedly, in hindsight it had been a pretty dumb assumption, but how was I to know Gramps owned only half of a cottage? He'd never mentioned that he and a buddy shared the place. This news was definitely going to cause me some major problems.

I needed to sell this place for economic stability. I had too many responsibilities to indulge in owning a vacation home or even half of one. If Hannah insisted on living here, the cost of fixing up this place would just become a money pit for me. I couldn't have that, and even though it might make things simpler if I explained my situation to her, I wasn't comfortable discussing with a complete stranger the dysfunction junction that was my family.

I glanced back at the cottage from my vantage point on the dock. It was well situated and the property was a substantial size, allowing for the building of a very large vacation home or several townhomes. We could make so much money if we sold it. Not that there wasn't a sentimental part of me that wanted to hang on to the place, but it simply wasn't an option.

My original plan had been to come and inspect the property while I packed up Gramps's belongings. I'd assumed I'd be here for a month—giving myself some time to fish, surf, and get away from the office grind for a while—but now I had to scrap that plan and figure out what to do about Ms. Hannah Spencer. An image of her soaking wet from jumping into the channel popped into my mind. I blinked, trying to dislodge it. But then the sound of her husky voice saying "I've got you" echoed in my ears. I shook my head. I couldn't let this woman get under my skin so easily.

All my plans had been crafted with me as the sole owner of the cottage. My future and the future of my brother, whom I provided for, were at stake. Even though I was now looking at making half of what I would have in a sale, the thought of the potential consequences of not being able to sell the cottage made my anxiety spike. Charlie needed round-the-clock care, and I was determined that he would have only the best. I owed him that. I'd think I was overreacting, but the probability of being able to sell the house, especially given the fact that my co-owner had been living in a van for five years, was in jeopardy. It seemed highly unlikely that she was going to sell the first home she'd had in years, especially when it was free.

I glanced out at the marsh and noticed that it had gone quiet. It was almost as if the birds and critters knew that my plans had just imploded and they'd scattered to higher ground to avoid my primal screaming. A chill wind blew, ruffling my hair, and I glanced up to see the blue sky being overtaken by rain clouds. If my life were a movie, I'd call it foreshadowing.

All was not lost, I told myself. It could be that the realities of taking care of a house, especially one that was falling down, would get old really quickly for Hannah. All I had to do was step back and let her take the lead on dealing with the problems, and she'd see how much work this place was and by the end of our mandatory two months together, she'd agree to sell.

Another gust of wind chilled my damp clothes and I shivered. I needed to get the boat, my only mode of transportation presently, out of the coming rainstorm.

I maneuvered my boat onto the lift and hoisted it up into the boathouse. I had motored down here from my sister, Lorelei's place in Kill Devil Hills. Thankfully, neither my sister nor my brother cared that Gramps had left the cottage to me. In fact, Lorelei had said she hoped that I kept the cottage for myself and used it to get away from work. It was a nice sentiment but we both knew that I had other responsibilities.

As I secured the boat, I wondered why Gramps hadn't mentioned that he shared this property with someone. Was William Spencer a friend? An acquaintance? From a financial perspective, a house share made sense. Houses in the Outer Banks were not cheap and this one was located right on a marsh with access to the ocean, but it wasn't as if Gramps had been hurting for money. So why the secrecy?

With the mandatory stay of two months that the attorney had stated was a condition of our inheritance, I figured I'd have plenty of time to figure it out. Just like I had the summer to get to know my housemate and see if I could talk her into selling.

My brief impression of Hannah Spencer was that of an impulsive—she'd jumped into the channel to save me—fearless—again, the jump—person who didn't think things through before she acted. I could work with that. I'd have to play it cool and let the cottage's sad state dampen her enthusiasm for staying while I got to know her. Then, when I knew what she wanted out of life, I'd dangle the possibility of achieving it and convince her that selling was her best option to reach her goal, whatever that might be.

I stared up at the sweep of lawn and the cottage as the rain clouds barreled toward it. How many times had Gramps stood in this spot in the place he'd called his sacred space? I had expected to feel something when I arrived at the cottage, mostly loss and grief. I hadn't expected confusion with the arrival of an unexpected housemate, and, in the form of a small pony, chaos.

I had so many questions and I desperately wished Gramps were here so I could ask him. His loss hit me low and deep. Gramps had been gone for four months and while I'd accepted his passing, mostly, the missing of him and his gruff affection frequently hollowed me out at my core and I found it hard to breathe.

Big drops of rain started to splat on the boathouse roof. Enough brooding, I needed to get back to the house. I turned and glanced out at the water. I felt my lips compress into a thin determined line.

"All right, Gramps, I'm going to trust that you knew what you were doing and try to make the best choices I can for this place."

A fish jumped in the channel, and I had the fanciful notion that it was Gramps giving me his approval. I turned to jog back to the cottage before I drowned in my own sentimentality or the downpour that had just begun.

I was soaked through . . . again . . . before I reached the back door. The rain was surprisingly frigid and the late afternoon became shrouded in a gloomy gray. A perfect reflection of my current dark mood.

Hannah was closing the last of the windows to keep the rain out. She crossed back to the living room, sat on the couch, and dried her hair with the towel I had given her. Dude was on the floor at her feet, watching her with a worshipful look in his eyes. The papers Vincent had left us were on the coffee table exactly where he'd put them.

"So . . ." I grabbed the towel I'd used before and sat on the edge of one of the recliners while I dried off my arms, legs, and hair. "It looks like we have some things to discuss, Ms. Spencer."

"Do we, Mr. O'Malley?" she retorted as rain hammered on the roof.

"Clearly, neither of us knew about the shared situation of this cottage." I met her gaze. She pursed her lips and slowly nodded. "You came here expecting to have the house all to yourself and to settle in and stay, correct?"

"Yes." There was a bit of pout in her voice that should not have been as charming as it was.

"And I planned to sell the place as soon as possible," I said.

"Why?" She cocked her head to the side in confusion. "Why would you sell something that your grandfather left to you?"

I frowned. How much did I want to tell her about my personal life? About my brother, Charlie, and his care? My instinct to protect my brother roared in my chest just as it always did. I went for a diversionary tactic. It was time to lean into the house's state of disrepair. "Have you looked at this place? Really looked at it?"

"Yes." She crossed her arms over her chest. "It's fine."

At that moment a water drop plopped onto her forehead and ran down the length of her nose to drip onto her shirt. I had never believed in cosmic intervention until that exact moment. We held each other's gaze for a beat before Hannah tilted her head back to see where the water had come from.

I followed her gaze and saw the bubble of paint right over her head. There had to be a leak somewhere, and the only things holding the water back were the many layers of paint the ceiling had gotten over the years. Another drop plopped onto her head.

"Bucket! We need a bucket!" Hannah cried.

I started to stand but stopped myself. It took some effort to remain seated as my normal inclination would be to help but that would defeat my purpose in convincing her to sell. I relaxed back into my seat while she raced from the living room to the kitchen, where I heard her banging around in the cupboards until she returned with a large steel spaghetti pot. She placed it under the bubble and stepped back as the drops from the water bubble began to *ping* into the pot.

"There." She brushed her hands together.

"Not really a solution, though, is it?" I asked.

She looked me over with an annoyed expression. "It'll do for now." The drops increased in speed and Dude's ears perked up as he watched.

"If you say so." I took my phone out of my pocket and started to scroll, checking my messages. Sure enough, there was one from Charlie. It was a funny video, featuring a hamster eating a tiny burrito. I decided a response could wait.

The gloom outside increased and I checked the weather app to see how long the rain would last. It looked like another hour. Excellent. I was eager to see what the next calamity to hit the house would be.

Hannah sat down and tapped the papers on the table. "We should probably read through this. Vincent left a copy for both of us."

She picked up one navy blue folder and handed it to me. It had the law office's name embossed in silver on the cover. I flipped it open and turned on the light app on my phone so I could read in the gloom. I glanced at the chair where Hannah sat and noted that she was doing the same.

We were both quiet. While I was painfully familiar with insurance contracts, I'd never read a will before. It was jarring to see Gramps's formal name, Robert Augustus O'Malley. I forced myself to keep reading. It was very straightforward. Just as Vincent had said. We shared the house equally and were to live in it for two months, either at the same time or individually, before making any decisions. If we chose to keep it, we were to invest in its care and maintenance equally and if we sold it, the profit would be split. If one of us was to buy the other out, it would be for half of the current market value. Well, shit.

I glanced up at Hannah over the edge of the folder. She was reading her copy. A small frown marred her forehead and I wondered if she was reading the same section I'd just read.

"What do you suppose half of the current market value is?" she asked, confirming my suspicion.

"More than either of us should spend on a house that is falling down." I tossed my folder onto the table.

My phone chimed in my hand. I flipped it over to see that it was Charlie . . . again. I knew my brother well enough to know he wasn't going to stop messaging until I called him as I did every evening. "Excuse me, I have to make a call."

Her eyebrows lifted but she didn't say anything. Dude had fallen asleep on the floor at her feet and was snoring. I tapped Charlie's name in my contacts list and strode into the kitchen to make the call in as much privacy as the house offered.

"Hey."

"Did you get my message? Why didn't you respond? Are you okay? Is something wrong? Is there a problem?"

I glanced through the door to see Hannah reading the will while absently rubbing Dude's belly.

"No, no problem," I lied.

Hannah

Simon's voice was a low grumble in the kitchen. I had the distinct feeling he didn't want me to overhear his conversation. I wondered if it was a romantic partner. Probably. It went against the laws of nature that a man that good-looking was single, unless of course he was a jerk. The jury was still out on that verdict.

I tossed my folder onto the table just as Simon had. I had no idea what half of this house would cost to buy but I doubted I had enough money to make an offer to Simon unless I wiped out my savings and retirement, and took out a loan. The thought was depressing. I'd worked so hard over the past five years to pull myself out of medical debt and have a stable financial position. But there was no getting around the fact that given our different feelings about the house, the simplest solution to our problem would be for me to buy him out.

I stood and stretched, clasping my hands together over my head and arching back as far as I could. We'd had a long drive to get here from Asheville today and I was tired. Dude was clearly exhausted, judging by his snores.

I wandered around the room, listening to the rain. It should have soothed me but it didn't. Potentially, it was because I could hear Simon on the phone. His answers were monosyllabic and there was a strain in his voice that made it clear the conversation wasn't going well. Perhaps his partner was upset to find out he was here with an unexpected female housemate. I couldn't say I'd blame them.

The afternoon's watery light wasn't helping the mood in the cottage. This was all so different from what I'd expected. I'd imagined Dude and I arriving at a quaint little cottage by the sea, opening the door and being welcomed by the essence of Pops. Instead, we were here with a brooding hot guy who seemed more than a little put out by my presence. Sorry, not sorry, my guy, but it's my house, too.

I made my way into the dining room and admired the hutch. Behind the glass doors was a full set of Lenox white china with silver edges, and on the top of the walnut cabinet with rounded corners was a row of Pops's local Emmy Awards from his news anchor days. He'd brought his awards here? How strange. He never put them on display in his house in Rhode Island. Maybe here he was freer to celebrate his accomplishments. I reached up and took one down. It looked just like the Emmy Award they gave out in Hollywood and it was heavier than I expected.

There was something hanging off the back of the globe. Thinking it was a dust bunny, I went to wipe it away. My fingers brushed a warm furry body and I screeched. The little thing flapped its wings and I yelped and jumped, dislodging the bat—*a bat!*—from its perch. As it fluttered up toward the ceiling, I dropped the statue, crouched low, and ran out of the room, still screaming.

"What the hell, Spencer?" Simon appeared in the doorway to the kitchen. "Are you being murdered?"

"Bat!" I panted. "There's a bat. In there. Alive."

He squinted at me. "You sure? It's pretty dark in there."

"It. Flew. At. Me." I gritted out each word around the pounding of my heart.

"Did he, though?" Simon asked, his voice filled with doubt. "I'm sure you scared him more than he scared you."

I glared at him and shook my head. "Nope. Not possible."

Dude had lifted his head but upon seeing me unharmed, he rolled over and promptly went back to sleep. So helpful.

Simon glanced past me into the room. "I don't see him."

"I think he went back up onto the hutch," I said. "There are some statues up there that make good perches, apparently."

Simon glanced from the top of the hutch to me and back. Then he nodded and retreated back to the safety of the living room, exactly where I wanted to be.

"Let me know when you get him out of there." Simon sat down on one of the recliners and began to thumb through his phone.

"Are you serious right now, O'Malley?" I wanted to kick him. "Might I remind you that this is your house, too, so if there's a bat in here—"

"There's probably a colony of bats in here."

"What?" I instinctively covered my head with my hands.

"A group of bats is called a *colony* and there's probably more than one, don't you think?" Simon glanced from his phone to me and then back down to his phone. "I mean, the place has been empty for a while, right?"

"The last time Pops was here was four months ago," I said.

"And it was longer than that for Gramps." He nodded. "Yeah, there's probably a colony."

"We have to get them out!" I resented the slight note of hysteria that crept into my voice.

"Do we?" he asked. "I mean, if we were to sell . . ."

“I’m not selling.” I fisted my hands at my hips. I had the sudden urge to wring his thick neck.

“Even if there’s a bat infestation?”

I was unable to stop the shiver that racked my body from head to toe. “There isn’t. It’s just one little guy who took a wrong turn down the chimney or something.” I pointed to the small fireplace in the corner.

“You’re likely right.” He continued scrolling through his phone. “Good luck with that.”

I was definitely going to kick him. Fine. Be that way. I could handle a bat on my own. He’d just startled me. I would catch him and set him free. Easy-peasy.

I snatched the towel I’d used earlier to dry off and returned to the dining room. I hesitated for just a moment, but knowing O’Malley was watching me, I pushed through it. I was doing a good deed, I told myself. The little bat needed to be outside to survive and thrive. He was probably lost and alone and stuck in this house. I would rescue him. I would be a hero. Newly motivated, I stepped into the room.

The gloom of the rainy day was not helping me see into the shadows and I didn’t want to scare him by shining my phone flashlight. I assumed he had gone back to his perch above the hutch as there weren’t any other hiding spots in the small room.

As quietly as possible I moved a chair from the dining set to the hutch. I clutched the towel in my hands and stepped on the seat of the chair. Slowly, I straightened until I was standing and could see over the edge of the wooden cabinet. I squinted into the shadows, trying to find my new friend. I wondered if I should just throw the towel over the trophies and hope I got him, but I didn’t want the little dude to be impaled by one of the golden angels’ lightning wings.

I scanned the shadows, trying to see if the wee bat had found a new perch. My heart was racing and my hands were sweaty. It wasn't that I was afraid of bats; it was that I was terrified. Not fair to the bats, I know. But once when I was a kid, my friends and I found a bat on the sidewalk on its back and Blake Tedeski poked it with a stick and the poor thing flew right at me just missing my hair. I hadn't felt easy around bats ever since.

But this was just a tiny little fellow not much bigger than a mouse, and Dude and I had handled plenty of mice, especially that one spring when we'd been caught in a surprise snow at Glacier National Park and the little ones had found a way into the van to keep warm. If I could wake up with three mice curled up on the pillow next to me, I could handle one little bat. Right? Right.

I thought about insisting Simon help me as it was his house, too. But I didn't want him to mistake me for some fragile female who needed a man's help with anything that scurried. Also, I got the distinct impression that he wouldn't, and I didn't need that sort of rejection right now. He'd looked irritated by my shriek but I suspected that hadn't been what annoyed him and rather it had been whatever phone conversation he'd had.

A jealous girlfriend? Annoyed boss? Who knew what he had going on. He was, after all, completely unknown to me.

I focused on the task at hand. Lifting the towel up, I waited to see if my little friend would make an appearance so I could grab him. There was a shift in the shadows and I stifled my yelp, closing my eyes for a second to calm myself before moving the towel closer to where I'd seen the movement. I closed in, leaning over the edge of the hutch while raising the towel. I was certain the little guy was hanging off the statue in back. If I could just drop the towel on him I could scoop him up and get him outside.

"Okay, count of three," I muttered. "One, two, ahhhh!"

The bat dropped off the statue and flew straight at me. Straight. At. Me. I dodged out of the way, forgetting I was on a chair, and the next second I was windmilling to catch my balance as the bat flew out of the dining room, around the corner, and up the stairs. I braced for the impending fall but found myself plucked out of midair by a pair of strong arms. Simon.

He staggered a bit under my weight, which I liked to think was more my momentum than my pounds, but he steadied himself within a couple of steps and glanced down at me with a beleaguered look that I was beginning to think was his permanent state.

"Really, Spencer? I'm embarrassed for you." He removed his arm from beneath my knees, dropping my feet to the floor and stepping back as if he couldn't wait to get away from me. Rude.

"He flew right at me." My voice was justifiably defensive. "And then he flew upstairs."

Simon rolled his eyes and tipped his head back as if he couldn't believe what he was hearing. Granted, it was not my finest moment but I was confident that if the bat had flown directly at him, the result would have been the same.

"Are you going to go upstairs and get him?" Simon asked.

"No." I turned and walked out of the dining room. "As far as I'm concerned, the bat and I are done. I just won't go upstairs. The second floor belongs to him now."

With an incredulous look Simon followed me. "You can't just let him have the upper part of the house."

"Why not?" I argued. I sat in the chair that faced the stairs. I wanted to see the bat if he decided to cross back over the border to downstairs.

"Because that's not a solution?"

"Says you. It works for me."

"Where are you planning to sleep?"

"Right here. You can sleep upstairs."

He looked at me in horror. "With the bat?"

"You're not afraid, are you?"

"No. Don't be ridiculous." He didn't meet my gaze and sat on the chair beside mine, also facing the stairs. "Afraid of a bat? Pfft."

Dude's snoring was the only sound to be heard as the rain had lightened to a gentle patter on the roof. "It's going to be dark soon."

"Should we open the door and hope he goes outside?" Simon asked.

"I don't know about the door," I said. "We might be inviting something even worse inside."

"How about a window?"

"Okay, but upstairs."

"As in, we're going where the colony is?" He looked at me as if he expected me to balk.

I narrowed my eyes at him. "Are you mocking me?"

"Whyever would you think that?"

There was a knock at the door and I jumped. Dude rolled out of his slumber onto all four paws and started barking in alarm as if the door had been kicked in. There was no way the bat would be coming downstairs now.

"I think that's for me." Simon rose from his chair and crossed the room. He did not glance at the stairs, leaving me to conclude that he had no fear of the bat and he *had* been mocking me.

"Easy, Dude." The barking stopped but Dude stood at alert should his assistance be required.

I heard Simon speaking to someone outside so I leaned forward to see who it was. A twentysomething guy, carrying a brown sack and an umbrella was taking a cash tip from Simon, who thanked the young man for coming out in this weather.

The guy nodded and departed. Simon entered the house with a bag of what my nose identified as Chinese food. My stomach rumbled in response. How long had it been since I'd eaten that gas-station breakfast taquito this morning?

"You ordered food?" I didn't mean to sound accusatory, but in my defense I was seriously hangry and that paper sack smelled amazing.

"Since we don't have electricity, I figured cooking was out. There's plenty for you and Dude, so long as he likes pork fried rice."

"I don't know," I said. "Dude has a very discerning palate."

As if to emphasize my point, Dude dropped to the floor to lick an itch in the area of his nether region. Simon glanced from him to me and his lips twitched when he said, "Clearly."

Simon unpacked the bag, setting the white cartons on the kitchen counter. I didn't want to interrupt—because food!—but we still had a problem. "What about the bat?"

"We can deal with it after we fortify." He pushed a carton of orange chicken at me. I was too hungry and tired to resist.

We ate out of the cartons at the kitchen counter. Dude had a small portion on top of his kibble, which I'd retrieved from the van. As soon as he was finished, he returned to the couch, leaving the recliners for Simon and me.

"Are we going bat hunting now?" I wiped down the counter and tossed the empty containers in the trash.

"If by that you mean we're going to open a window for him upstairs, then yes."

"Does it have to be we?" I asked. "Couldn't it just be you?"

"No." He shook his head. "It'll be better with two sets of eyes. The sun sets at half past eight. It'll be dark soon. We should get it done while we still have a little light."

I glanced at the windows. The rain had stopped and the sun came out just to give us a little heat with the humidity. I could practically feel my hair frizzing in response.

"All right," I said. "Dude, stay here." A snore was his only response.

Simon led the way upstairs. We both had the flashlight app on our phones on, shining it into the dark corners as we went. My entire body was clenched, ready to fly back downstairs at the first sign of our winged houseguest.

The doors to the rooms upstairs were all open. A quick glance and I noticed there were two bedrooms of equal size separated by a bathroom. Simon paused on the landing and I stopped beside him, hunkering down a bit in case the bat appeared.

"There are no windows up here except for the ones in the rooms," he said.

"We could just shut the doors and trap him in the rooms."

"But then he'll stay inside. We need to give him an out." Simon headed for the bathroom.

I followed, almost pressing myself against his back as we went.

It was a small space with a shower-tub combination, a sink with a vanity, and a toilet. Like downstairs, it was vintage '90s with wallpaper that was sailing ships and lighthouses. The toilet, shower-tub combo, and counter around the sink were all in a shade of country blue to match the wallpaper, no doubt. I quickly shone my light around the room. No bat.

The lone window was beside the toilet, and Simon unlocked it and raised the sash and then the screen behind it, leaving a large enough gap for the bat to escape through. I tried not to think about more bats coming in through the window.

"All right, on to the bedrooms." Simon turned and I had to

jump back so he didn't plow into me. He gave me a curious glance and then stepped around me. I hurried after him.

He went into the bedroom on his right. I could make out only the shape of the furniture with my flashlight as the drapes had been pulled across the windows. Simon chose the first window and pulled back the curtains. Twilight illuminated the room in a soft violet glow.

The hair at the back of my neck prickled and I felt as if I were being watched, which was ridiculous because even if it was the bat, there was a reason for the expression "blind as a bat." Or was that inaccurate? I made a mental note to research facts about the eyesight of bats later.

"A little light here, please." Simon pocketed his phone and pushed aside the curtain, looking for the latch.

"Got it." I raised my flashlight to help him locate the window latch. As the beam moved over the wall, the light picked up a fluttering motion to the right. The bat! I didn't think. I just reacted. I tackled Simon while yelling, "Get down!"

He landed with a heavy thump onto the carpeted floor and I landed right on top of him. He let out a low groan and said, "That's gonna leave a mark. What the hell are you doing, Spencer?"

"Saving your life, O'Malley." My face hovered just inches over his. He scoffed as if I'd just said the most ridiculous thing he'd ever heard. So I doubled down. "Do not mock me. It's the bat. It's right there!"

"Where?" Simon's gaze darted around the room.

I moved the beam of light across the ceiling to pick up our little furry friend. And there he was, hanging off the curtain rod. When the light hit his little face, I could swear I saw fangs dripping blood. With a yelp, I crawled right over Simon, kneeing him in the chest in my haste to get out the door.

"Oof! Where are you going? You're taking the light!"

I heard a scuffling noise behind me and thinking it was the bat, I scurried triple time toward the hallway. It wasn't the bat. Simon had overtaken me and was right beside me as we both tried to squeeze through the door at the same time. We got stuck. Lodged in the doorway because of his broad shoulders and my generous hips.

"Back up!" I ordered.

"I'm trying but you're kneeling on my shorts."

I lifted my knee but he still couldn't move. I tried to wriggle past him but a fluttering noise sounded overhead.

"Bat!" Simon cried, and dropped to the floor, taking me with him. "Shine the light."

"I'd love to," I grunted from under 180 pounds of male. "But my arm is trapped under me, which is under you."

"Oh, sorry." Simon lifted his body a few inches off mine and I managed to get my arm out with my phone in hand and flashlight still on. I directed the beam up and we saw the bat flutter into the opposite bedroom.

"Damn it," I muttered. "Now what do we do?"

"We follow it." He rolled off me and gestured for me to lead. When I stared at him and didn't move, he said, "You have the light."

I switched the flashlight app off.

"Really, Spencer?"

I crossed my arms over my chest. "I've already had the bat fly at me twice. It's your turn."

"Fine," he sighed. He took his phone out of his pocket and switched the light on. He aimed the beam in the direction of the room and crawled across the upper landing commando style toward the other bedroom. I scuttled behind him like a good little follower.

Simon started to enter the room when the bat flew out, dive-bombing Simon on the way. I opened my mouth to scream but a shriek was already disturbing the peace. I shut my mouth and covered my hair with my arms.

"It's okay," Simon whispered, sounding breathless. "He went back to the other bedroom."

I lowered my arms. We were lying belly-down in the hallway and when I turned toward him, our faces were mere inches apart.

"Did you just scream?" I asked.

"Me? No." Even in the dim natural light, he looked appalled.

"Well, somebody did and it wasn't me," I said.

"I shouted," he clarified. "As one does when a bat is about to attack."

"It's a little brown bat," I said. "I don't think they bite people."

"And yet, here we are hiding from it on the floor," he countered.

"Hiding? So, you admit it," I said triumphantly. "You're afraid of bats."

"Not afraid," he corrected. "Just cautious."

"Judging by that shriek—" I began but he interrupted me.

"Shout." He pushed up from the floor to a seated position.

"Right, that 'shout.'" I sat up, too. "You're just as scared as I am, so there's only one fair way to see who goes into that room to open the window."

We glanced at each other and at the same time said, "Rock, paper, scissors."

"Fine," Simon said. "But it's one and done with none of that two-out-of-three nonsense."

"Agreed."

We each made a fist with one hand and tapped it onto our open palm three times. Simon counted down. "One, two, three, shoot."

I threw down a rock, keeping my fingers curled into a fist.

Simon, however, had opened his hand into paper and covered my rock.

"Off you go, Spencer." Simon nodded at the door. "I'll be here if you need me."

"That was uncool," I said. "Why do I feel like you knew I was going to choose rock?"

"Because I did," he said. "Statistically, rock is the most common first play in RPS, making paper the obvious countermove."

"How do you even know that?" I asked.

"Everyone knows that." He shooed me with his hand. "Stop stalling."

Despite his ridiculous good looks, I decided I didn't like Simon O'Malley. Not at all. I switched my flashlight app on and crept to the door. I paused in the doorway, sweeping the room with the light. I glanced over my shoulder to see Simon grabbing a towel from the bathroom.

"What are you doing?" I asked. It was a heck of a time to take a shower.

"When you scare the bat out of the bedroom, which you will, I'm going to catch it in the towel," he said.

"You're not going to smother it, are you?"

"No! I'm not a monster."

"To him, we both probably are," I said.

He nodded and I felt the energy shift. Simon moved to stand behind me. "Let's save him from us, then."

Feeling less on edge, I entered the room. "Hey, little fella, I'm not here to hurt you. I'm just going to open the window so you can get out there and eat some tasty bugs. Sound good?"

"That's it," Simon coached from the doorway. "Just move nice and slow."

I reached the window without baby bat flying at me, which I

took as a positive sign. Then again, maybe the poor guy was just scared out of his little bat mind and exhausted from trying to escape us.

I reached for the latch on the nearest window and turned it. Then I lifted the inner sash and the outer screen. I locked them both into an open position, giving the bat several inches to navigate his escape. Then I started to back away. This was good. I'd just shut the door behind me and Mr. Wee Bat would fly out into the night.

I knew better than to celebrate wins early. I did. I'd had enough practice in my life watching the basketball circle the rim and then inexplicably pop out, all my numbers come up in bingo only to have the last one never get called, or the mother crusher of them all, thinking that the second line on the pregnancy test would appear only to wait and wait and wait but it never showed, forcing me to accept my infertility.

Still, like a big dope, I was supremely confident that with the window open, the bat would flutter to freedom and our problem would be solved. I was so wrong. I had almost reached the door when the little bat fluttered down from who knew where. He was swooping in between me and Simon when suddenly a towel landed over my head, trapping the bat inside the towel with me.

"Ah!" I let out a shriek and smacked the towel off my head, freeing the bat.

"Oh, shit! Sorry!" Simon yelled. "I was going for the bat. Ah!"

I shoved my hair out of my eyes to see the bat had landed on Simon's head. Simon went to swat it, but I grabbed his hands, stopping him. "Don't hurt it!"

"If it bites me and I get rabies . . ." Simon's eyes were looking up as if he could peer through his own skull.

"Here's what we're going to do." I suppressed a shiver when I saw the little bat's head pop up out of the thick waves of Simon's hair. "We're going to walk to the window and you are going to stick your head out and shake him free."

"His little feet . . . paws . . . claws . . . whatever . . . are digging into my scalp." Simon's voice was strained.

"It's just a few steps," I encouraged him. "Trust me."

"You're not the one with a bat on your head," he said through gritted teeth.

"Not for your lack of trying," I countered.

"Accident."

I let it go. As soon as we were close to the window, I helped him crouch down on his knees and angle his head through the opening of the window.

I directed my phone's light onto the bat. He seemed quite content, nestled in Simon's hair, taking in the growing darkness.

"He's not moving, is he?" Simon asked.

"No," I admitted. "Maybe shake your head."

Simon jostled his head slightly.

"With more vigor," I suggested.

Simon shook his head like he was headbanging to some heavy metal, and the little bat fell off his perch and immediately fluttered out into the night.

"There he goes!" I cried, kneeling beside Simon.

Simon glanced up, catching sight of the little fella before he disappeared into the safety of the trees. Then he collapsed back onto the carpet and put his hand over his heart. "I do not ever want to be that close to a bat ever again."

"Let's hope there isn't a colony, then. In fact, we should open the windows and close the doors up here in case there are more." I crossed the landing to the other bedroom and opened the window, shutting the door behind me. I did the same with the bathroom. If there were any more bats in the upstairs rooms, they had tonight to get their furry little butts out of my house. I returned to the bedroom to find Simon still lying on the floor.

I knelt down and said, "I'd better check your scalp and make sure he didn't scratch you or poop."

"Gah!" Simon sat up and tipped his head in my direction.

I aimed the light beam at his scalp and ran my fingers through his hair; it was ridiculously soft. I swallowed hard as I checked the area where the bat had been perched. The ends of Simon's hair twined around my fingers in the most beguiling way. I snatched my hand away. "You got lucky, no scratches or poop."

When I leaned away from him his deep brown gaze was studying me with an awareness that mirrored my own. His voice was low when he said, "Thank you, Spencer."

He was so appealing in his dishevelment, I almost leaned in. But his use of my surname checked me. Nope, nope, nope. I had no interest in making a complicated situation worse.

"I'd better check on Dude." I all but ran from the room.

When we arrived downstairs, Dude was still snoring and the cottage was almost fully dark. I shivered. I wondered, What should I do now? Curl up with Dude? Sleep in one of the chairs? On the floor? Or go out to my van, where I had a bed? That was the most reasonable option, but I suspected Simon would consider me weak for fleeing the house, and I didn't want to give him any ammunition to argue in favor of selling the house. Despite the bat, I wanted to stay. Maybe just downstairs until I knew there were no more critters, but within the house all the same.

I glanced over at Simon. In the darkness, I could see he had reclined his chair to the fully sprawled position. His ankles were crossed and his arms were folded over his chest. I was about to ask him if he planned to sleep there when I heard the faint sound of deep breathing accompanying Dude's snores. The man was out.

Fine. I reclined my chair as well, pulling the crocheted throw that had been draped over the back of it across my body. I snuggled down into the seat, assured that if Simon put one toe out of line, Dude would protect me.

The smell of coffee roused me and I opened my eyes, startled to find I wasn't in the bunk in my van with Dude on his dog bed on the floor. It took me a second to remember that I was in Pops's house, sleeping in the living room because . . . *bat!*

I popped up and scanned the room. The recliner next to me was empty as was the couch. Daylight illuminated the room and I glanced toward the kitchen, where I heard the distinct thump of a tail wagging.

I pushed aside my crocheted throw and staggered to the kitchen. Seated at the counter was Simon and beside him was Dude. It appeared they were sharing a breakfast of eggs and sausages. My stomach growled but I couldn't keep letting Simon feed me. It made the balance of power uneven if I didn't provide my fair share.

"Sit." Simon's tone of voice didn't invite a discussion. I sat.

"I went out for a run this morning and picked this up on my way back. Eggs, sausages, biscuits, gravy, and hot coffee." He loaded up a plate and pushed it toward me along with a large paper cup full of coffee.

"Are you trying to win me over through food?" I forked up some of the fluffy eggs.

"Would it work?"

"No, but I am grateful."

A small smile tipped the corners of his lips. "Eat. We can talk after."

He didn't have to tell me twice. I ate as if I hadn't seen food in a month. I didn't know if it was the fresh air, the bat caper, the anxiety of sharing a house, or if I was cruising up on that time of the month, but I was starving.

When I finished, Simon took my plate and said, "We can talk now."

I cupped my coffee in both hands. "All right."

Dude settled down on the floor once he was certain no more food was forthcoming. Simon sat on the stool beside mine.

"I want to make you an offer," Simon said.

"An offer?" I repeated.

"For your half of the property," he clarified. "I want to buy you out, Spencer."

Simon

"I thought you said the cost would be more than either of us should spend on a house that was falling down." Hannah tossed my words back at me.

"Yeah, well, I crunched some numbers during my run this morning and I think I can make it work," I said. The truth was I'd have to cash out some investments and move around some savings, but it would be worth it if I could flip the house and make back the money—and then some—that I'd lose in buying out Hannah at half the market value.

Since Gramps had passed, my role changed from helping with the financial support to becoming the sole provider for my brother, Charlie. It was a responsibility I didn't take lightly. When I had inherited the house from Gramps, I had known right away that I would sell it and bank the profit so that Charlie would always be financially secure. Having my mother pass away when I was a teen had taught me that no one is guaranteed a long run and I needed to make certain that those who depended upon me were set for life should anything happen to me.

Hannah sipped her coffee, studying me over the rim. I couldn't tell what she was thinking but with every sip, her blue eyes got brighter, as if the sleep was being forcibly removed from her brain by the caffeine. She sat up straighter and said, "I'm not interested."

I frowned. "You haven't even heard my offer."

"I don't need to." She tipped her chin up. "Pops left me half of this house and I'm staying."

"You're not being at all reasonable." I took a deep breath through my nose while I tried to manifest some patience.

"I might say the same about you. We haven't even been here for twenty-four hours and you're expecting me to agree to sell my inheritance when you know we have to live here for at least two months. I haven't even had a proper look at the place yet," she said. "I think this might be the same house that Pops and Nana rented when I was a little kid. We used to come to Cape Split for a week every summer, but then after the divorce, we stopped."

She looked sad. Oh, this was not good. Hannah had vacationed here in this house as a child? The sentimentality quotient was going to be hard to beat. Maybe it wasn't the same house. Either way I wasn't ready to give up. Like Dude with a bone, I was going to stay on mission. "I feel like we got a pretty good look at it while running for our lives from the bat last night."

"Maybe you did, but I was entirely too busy freaking out." She glanced at me over the rim of her paper cup. "Have you been upstairs yet to check the rooms?"

"For the colony?" I clarified. "Um . . . no."

She gave me a closed-lip, knowing smile, almost a smirk, to be honest, and I felt the need to defend myself.

"I am *not* afraid of bats," I said, fully aware that I had shrieked like a little kid last night in the hallway.

"Whatever you say." She sipped her coffee.

"I know what you're doing and it isn't going to work." I crossed my arms over my chest.

"What am I doing?" She blinked her wide baby blues at me and I could almost feel myself giving in. No. I was not falling for it.

"You're trying to get me to prove that I'm not afraid by going upstairs and checking the rooms," I said.

"But if you're not afraid . . ."

"I'm not. I'm cautious, which is why we'll go together," I said. "Then you'll see that this place is more of a fixer-upper than you want to deal with and you'll agree to allow me to take it off your hands."

Her mouth compressed into a straight line. "The house is not that bad." She pointed to the ceiling. "Even the paint bubble from last night's storm is gone."

"Because I popped it this morning," I said. "Next time it rains, we'll likely have a flood in here."

"If the house is so horrible, why do you want to buy it?" she countered.

"Because I want to sell it and you owning half of it is making that impossible," I said. It was mostly true but she didn't need to know that.

"Why not let me buy you out?" she asked.

"Don't you live in your van?" I asked. "How do you think you'll come up with that kind of money?"

She looked annoyed. "First of all, you have no idea how much money I have and second, I could always take out a loan."

I shook my head. "No."

"No?" Her eyes were wide.

"I won't let you put yourself in debt to buy this place. It's a money pit and my conscience can't abide sticking you with it."

"But you're fine with me sticking you with it." Her eyes narrowed. "Something doesn't add up, O'Malley."

She wasn't kidding. For a second, a nanosecond really, I thought about telling her about my brother, but after years of keeping my private life private, I found I couldn't talk about Charlie with a near stranger, even one as seemingly nice as she was.

"Listen, I'm just looking out for you." I wasn't. "Even if you could get a loan to buy the house from me, how would you manage to pay for all the repairs that are needed?"

"What repairs?" Her gaze flitted from the ceiling to the front door.

"For starters, a new roof, which is estimated at fifteen thousand. You'll need a tree-removal service, there's a monster live oak on the north side that's just waiting to come down in a storm, probably taking a chunk of the house with it. That can be another couple thousand. And the wraparound deck has rotted-out planks and supports that need to be removed and replaced, costing another thousand or so, assuming you get a good deal. That's just the exterior. Should I continue?"

She looked pale and I felt like a heel for dumping on her, but she needed a reality check and if that caused her to consider selling to me then I could live with it.

"Why are you willing to take all of this on?" she asked. "You have to know that an inspector will tell any prospective buyer about the issues and you'll be lucky to sell it for any profit, especially if you buy me out first."

I sipped my coffee. I didn't want to lie to her but if I told her my plan was to flip the property, she might balk or she might want to go in on it with me, which was not a part of my long-term financial plans for Charlie.

"You're going to sell it to a developer, aren't you?" Her eyes flashed with accusation.

My plan was to sell it to a potential resident but if a developer wanted to buy it for a small fortune, was I really in a position to refuse the sale? No, I was not. I decided to avoid answering.

"If you sell your half to me, it really doesn't matter what I do with it, does it?" I asked. My voice came out harsher than I intended, no doubt because I was smarting under the accusation in her gaze.

"You're right," she said. "It wouldn't be my business." She rose from her seat and started riffling through the kitchen drawers until she came up with a roll of masking tape. "But since I will never ever *ever* sell my half to you, it seems that the only logical step is to divide the house in half. How about you just stay on your side and I'll stay on mine?"

Shit. This was the last thing I'd intended. Clearly, I'd struck a nerve. Big-time.

"Listen, Spencer, it doesn't have to be like this." I tried to sound cajoling but judging by the heated glance she sent my way, it had come out as condescending. "I didn't mean to offend you by pointing out there's a lot of work to be done."

"I wasn't offended by that." She ripped a huge strip of tape off the roll and started to mark off the kitchen. She pointed to one side. "Your half, O'Malley."

"I clearly pissed you off," I countered, ignoring the tape. "Listen, whatever I said, I apologize."

"Oh, that seems sincere," she scoffed. She continued taping into the living room and the dining room and even around the counter where I sat. "Neutral areas are the appliances and the doors since I can't really deny you access to those things."

"What about upstairs?" I asked.

She held up the roll, which was much smaller than when she had started. "I need more tape but I'll get to it."

"Spencer, you can't be serious about this," I said. "What did I say that was so bad?"

"Oh, I can assure you, I am very serious." With that, she used the last of the tape to mark off the path to the front door. She stood and put her hands on her hips, staring me down with a look that at any other moment would have been smokin' hot. "And just so you know, I have spent the past five years visiting national parks, raising the public's awareness of them. You want to know who the enemy of our national parks is?" Her upper lip curled ever so slightly. "Developers."

Ah, now it was coming into focus. I had unwittingly aligned myself with her personal enemy. Well, hell. Without another word, she stomped into the bathroom, slamming the door behind her.

I figured she'd get tired of the tape divider by the end of the morning. She did not.

In fact, she packed up Dude and disappeared for the day.

The house seemed ridiculously empty without her and Dude, mostly Dude, underfoot. I wondered as I spent the day fishing off the dock if she'd gone to see our attorney, Vincent Cosmo, to see if she could get rid of me. I wasn't sure how I felt about that. Not good, I decided.

When she arrived back in the evening, she didn't greet me with a smile. Just a terse comment thrown over her shoulder: "I'll go pick up some dinner to make up for breakfast this morning and dinner last night."

"You don't have to do that." I felt weirdly resistant to the idea of her leaving again when she'd been gone all day. She waved me off so I tried to stall her departure. "Just so you know, I checked the upstairs and we are bat-free."

She paused and turned to face me. "Thank you, O'Malley." She sent me an indifferent glance. Ouch.

I turned my attention to the Great Dane, finding I'd missed him, too, today. "Hey, Dude."

Dude, at least, seemed to still like me. He barreled across the room and shoved the top of his head into my palm. "How was your day, buddy?"

Hannah gave him an annoyed look but said nothing. She carefully stayed on her side of the taped line, working her way around the room to sit on the edge of the recliner next to mine, all while staying within her taped-off perimeter. "I did some thinking today, O'Malley."

"I'm listening." I leaned forward, finding I was eager to hear what she had to say. There was something about Hannah Spencer that pricked my interest even though we were at odds over the house. It wasn't personal. I just had obligations that I couldn't ignore.

"I propose six months–six months," she said.

"Meaning?"

"I have the house for six months and then you do, and we alternate," she said. Dude left me to go to his favored spot on the couch.

"But I don't want to live here for six months," I said. "I want to sell."

"But why?" she cried. "Do you know what I did all day?"

"Obviously, no." I didn't mention that I would have loved to know if she hadn't shot out of here this morning like I carried the plague. I felt I showed great restraint in not saying as much.

"I've been revisiting some of the local sites," she said. "The Wright Brothers National Memorial and the Cape Hatteras lighthouse. It's so beautiful here. I have a list of places I want to get reacquainted with and you should check them out, too. How can you want to sell?"

"It's not a matter of want," I said. It was as close to the truth as I was willing to share. "It's about being practical."

She pursed her lips, and her eyebrows lowered.

"I understand that you have an attachment to this place, I do." And I did. I hoped she could hear the sincerity in my voice. "But making a long-term decision based on emotion . . ."

"It's only partly that, it's also—" she started to answer but a crack of thunder overhead drowned out her voice. We both jumped and Dude let out a pitiful wail and dove from the couch to the floor.

The enormous dog belly-crawled under Hannah's legs, wedging himself between her and the chair. Then he put his head down and covered his eyes with his paws. She glanced at me. "Dude doesn't like storms."

"Poor guy. I saw it rolling in when I was on the dock. This one's gonna be a banger."

The wind whipped the branches of the trees against the side of the house. Hannah opened her shoulder bag and took out a small pouch of treats. She gave one to Dude while she stroked his head and crooned reassuring words to him. Dude didn't move the paw from his eyes but his shivering eased a little.

"He'll be okay," she said. "That was a calming dog chew. It should kick in soon."

"Lucky dog."

"I could give you one, too," she offered. Her prior irritation was replaced by a wide smile and her eyes crinkled in the corners. I glanced away, refusing to acknowledge the warmth I felt in my chest when she smiled so big and bright. At least she didn't seem quite so peeved with me and was smiling at me instead of growling.

A shutter slammed outside and I wondered if one of the loose ones had been torn free. Excellent! If this storm produced enough damage, it might sway Hannah to let go of her sentimental attachment and sell her half to me. A guy could hope.

"Listen," Hannah said. I met her gaze. Gone was her mischievous smile and in its place was a look of determined resolve. "I don't want to be contrary but I've made up my mind. I'm not selling my half to you or anyone."

Well, hell.

She patted Dude's head and then reached up and finger-combed her windswept hair, releasing the faint smell of a coconut-lime shampoo. It made me think of the summers of my youth—surfing the waves, flirting with pretty girls, and mistakenly thinking the freedom of those days would never end. It had been a long time since I'd enjoyed a summer like that and a wave of nostalgia washed over me.

Hannah used the hair band she wore on her wrist to tie her hair up in a high ponytail. She was wearing a tank top and a pair of shorts with boots, the sort made for hiking. I wanted to hear more about what she'd seen on her adventure today, but I wasn't quite ready to put the topic of her selling the house to me to bed just yet.

"Okay, but if you should change your mind . . ."

"I won't."

Our gazes met and held. The divide between us was much wider than a flimsy piece of masking tape.

"Looks like we're at a stalemate." Hannah broke our eye contact and glanced around the room, taking it all in—the art on the walls, the tchotchkes tucked in among the books on the bookcase and on the table beside her where there were several framed photographs.

I watched as she picked up the picture on the end. It was of two men standing side by side, each holding up their catch of the day and grinning at each other. I recognized Gramps immediately. His baseball hat was pushed back on his head, revealing his receding hairline. He was wearing his favorite fishing vest over an eye-wateringly colorful Hawaiian shirt that was not his usual utilitarian style. When Hannah paused and stroked a finger down the face of the other man, it confirmed it was her Pops.

A soft sigh escaped her and she sniffed as a tear slipped down the curve of her cheek. She brushed it away with a fingertip and closed her eyes as if willing away the grief that was presently consuming her. Ambush grief. I knew it well. I waited, not wanting to intrude. Instead, I returned my gaze to the photo she still held.

The man beside Gramps appeared to be about the same age and sported a head of thick white hair and aviator sunglasses. He wore a blue golf shirt and baggy shorts. The photo captured his fish in mid-wiggle but it was clearly bigger than Gramps's. Given how competitive Gramps could be, I found it surprising that his grin was so wide. Had I ever seen Gramps look that happy?

Gramps had been the backbone of our family, taking over the raising of us when my mom passed away and my dad dipped out. Gramps was a tough-talking, whiskey-swilling, cigar-smoking man's man of the first order. He worked hard, played harder, and devoted himself to his family. I had always thought he was happy with his life but this picture of him made me question that assumption.

Time spent with Gramps made up some of the best memories of my childhood. He taught Charlie and me how to drive a boat, fish, and camp. When Lorelei insisted that she be taught these same life skills, Gramps had included her, unable to say no to the force of nature that was my sister. He loved us fiercely and never missed any of the big or small moments in our lives, but again, when I saw his smile in the picture, I knew I had never seen him that full of joy.

I had a strange feeling in the pit of my stomach that I was seeing Gramps in an entirely different way, sort of like the difference between seeing a lion in captivity and one out in the wild.

Hannah's eyes opened and she turned to me with an apologetic glance. "Sorry. Sometimes, the grief just sneaks up and flattens me."

"There's nothing to be sorry for," I said. I envied her ability to grieve so openly even in front of a stranger. I had yet to shed a tear for Gramps. I felt that if I didn't allow myself to grieve then I could deny that he was actually gone, which was ridiculous and I knew it, but still the tears didn't come.

"Why do you suppose they didn't tell us or anyone about their friendship or their shared ownership of the cottage?" My voice was strained with the grief I was unable to express. If Hannah noticed, she didn't show it.

"I have no idea," she said. "But I'm going to find out."

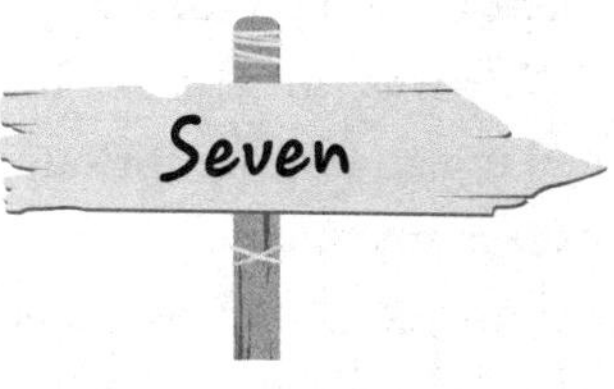

Hannah

I could feel my dormant reporter skills crackle to life as if they were Frankenstein being zapped by the lightning that flashed intermittently as the storm moved closer. I had never wanted to stop being a journalist, but the industry had changed drastically from my first day fourteen years ago at the Cronkite School at Arizona State University to now.

I had done a five-year tour of duty as a beat reporter at a major newspaper in Washington, DC, but when times got tough and reporters were laid off en masse—as a new hire, I was one of the first to go.

With no job prospects, my marriage dusted and done, and no home to keep me in DC, I decided to buy Buttercup and take a year to travel around the country visiting national parks. I started posting my adventures and suddenly I was a #vanlife influencer. What was supposed to be one year became five. While it was a surprisingly remunerative career, I still missed chasing down a story as a journalist.

Being here in the cottage with the scent of a story filling my nostrils like wildfire smoke, I felt as if I owed it to myself and Pops to learn everything I could about why this cottage on the Outer Banks was so special to him. I mean, I knew it was the one he and Nana had rented when I was a child, but we'd rented a few others over the years, too. Why was this the one he'd chosen to buy? Was it intentional? Or had it just gone up for sale when he was looking? And why had he never mentioned it?

"How do you plan to start?" Simon asked.

I put the picture back on the table and glanced at him. His hair was a tousled mess of thick waves with curly ends, and his square jaw was set, not in stubbornness but rather with what seemed to be well-practiced patience. I wasn't sure if I was being patronized but since we'd just met and his good looks were frankly distracting, I decided to assume he wasn't being condescending until proven otherwise.

"First, I'm going to scour every inch of the cottage looking for any clues about Pops's life here." I paused and picked up a wood carving of a bluebird on the table. It was crudely done but the little bird had a distinctive personality. It looked puffed up and irritated. It made me smile. I turned it over to see who the artist was. Carved into the base was the name O'Malley.

I held it out to Simon. "I believe your grandfather did this."

He frowned, his eyebrows lowering over his deep brown eyes. "Gramps wasn't a woodworker."

"Well, unless you know another O'Malley who came here, I think it has to be him." I turned the carving and pointed to the name.

Simon reached across the space between us and took the bluebird from my hand. Our fingers brushed and I noticed how warm his skin was compared to mine. I pulled my hand away and patted

Dude as another roll of thunder sounded. He let out a small whimper and pressed harder against my legs.

Simon studied the name and then the bird and then the name again. "I don't understand. How could I not know this about him?"

I gestured to the cottage interior. "It seems to me there is a lot we don't know about both of our grandfathers. Aren't you curious to learn about the life your Gramps enjoyed here?"

He glanced up at me and I could see by his expression that he was conflicted. I knew he wanted to sell the place, but I thought that he, like me, had to be wondering about the life his grandfather had led here. How could Simon not want to know more?

"Of course I'm curious, Spencer." He glanced around the room, taking it all in. "But it's simply not practical. I have . . . time constraints."

"Job?"

"Career." He corrected me but his expression was subdued as if this career of his wasn't something he enjoyed.

While it had never been my dream to be an online persona, I genuinely enjoyed traveling to new places and meeting interesting people. The thought of spending my life doing something I didn't enjoy was unimaginable to me. I wondered if that was why Simon seemed overly serious. Maybe that was just his personality? That didn't seem very promising for our co-ownership of the house. I studied Simon, trying to guess what he did for a living.

He was rocking a pretty generic bruh outfit of baggy shorts and T-shirt attire. I decided to commence a gentle interrogation.

"Wife and kids, O'Malley?" I asked just to confirm what I already knew. He wore no wedding ring and if he had a wife and kids they'd be here with him. Who would miss a trip to the Outer Banks as a family?

"No." He shook his head.

"Dating anyone?"

"Not at the moment." There was a slight pause before he answered and I wondered if it meant he'd just broken up with someone or he was reluctant to tell me he was single in case I decided to make a play for him. He should be so lucky. Or was he always this thoughtful when questioned because he was checking for conversational land mines? Interesting.

"Are you an attorney?" I narrowed my eyes, squinting to see if I could picture him in a suit in a courtroom. It was a stretch.

"Oh, gross, no. How could you think such a thing, Spencer?" He grimaced.

My eyebrows flew up. That seemed like a harsh response. Before I could fire another question at him, he asked, "Are *you* married?"

"No." What I didn't say was *not anymore*.

"Dating?"

Did I have to admit it had been years? My life on the road had not been conducive to anything more than the occasional week-long fling, which suited me just fine. I decided to repeat his answer back to him. "Not at the moment."

He nodded. A small closed-lip smile tipped one corner of his mouth as if my answer pleased him. Maybe he thought I'd be easier to convince to sell the cottage if I didn't have anyone in my life with a vested interest in having me keep the place. He clearly had no idea how hungry I was for the first real roof I'd had over my head in ages. I was not about to give it up easily.

Whatever Simon had been about to say was cut off by the sound of a horrendous crash from upstairs. We both jumped and Dude let out a mournful howl that I was certain was the doggy equivalent of "We're all going to die!"

“Wait here!” Simon bolted across the room and up the stairs to check it out.

Without Simon to talk to, the wind seemed to take on more menace than it had before and the gloom that had been dimming the natural light seemed to get even darker. Hopefully, we were in the apex of the storm and it would start to mellow. I sincerely hoped so because Dude was shaking so hard my entire chair was vibrating.

The rain pelted the roof and sides of the house, flashes of lightning lit up the room so frequently it was as if we were having an impromptu dance party with a strobe light, while thunder rolled overhead with a mixture of rumbles and booms that were practically deafening. The noise of the storm was so loud I couldn’t hear anything from upstairs.

What if the roof had collapsed and Simon was trapped under it? Maybe a part of the building had fallen off and the storm had washed him out? Maybe there was a power line down and he’d been electrocuted. My heart was pounding in my chest as my unsubstantiated fears ratcheted up into a solid case of panic. I had to get up there and see what was happening.

“Dude, I’m going to need you to be brave.” He quaked as if he knew what was coming next. “I have to run upstairs.”

I stood and pulled the cushions off the couch and began to pile them on top of him until he was cocooned in his very own cushion fort. I added the wool throw that had been on the back of the couch for extra protection. I couldn’t see my big baby boy, but this dog could hear the cheese drawer in the van’s fridge from a quarter of a mile away, so he could most assuredly hear me now.

“I have to see if everything is okay,” I said. “Stay. Don’t move.”

A melancholy yowl was his only response. I stepped away from the couch and ran up the stairs. Other than my time hunting the bat, I hadn't been upstairs, as I'd spent my day gathering material about the Outer Banks for my online content.

When I stepped onto the landing, I noticed all the doors were open, which made sense given that Simon had said he'd checked for any more bats. Judging by the feel of the wind blowing into the hallway from the bedroom on the right, I knew that was the location of the situation.

"O'Malley? Are you all right?" I shouted over the wind as I hurried into the gloomy room.

Simon was standing beside the bed trying to yank the quilt off. He was soaked through and his T-shirt clung to his muscled chest. Not the worst look. "I'm doing better than you, at any rate. This was going to be your room."

"Ha! Very funny," I retorted as I joined him.

A tiny smile, barely discernable in the dimly lit room, tipped up one corner of his mouth. I was about to call him out when the bedroom curtain billowed on a gust of wind and I gasped. As the sheer drapery lifted, I could see that a tree had punched through one window and then shot out through the one diagonally across from it, leaving the trunk stuck inside the house! Rain was pouring in both smashed windows while Simon struggled with the blanket.

Glass crunched under my boots as I took in the damage.

"Where's Dude?" He raised his voice to be heard over the storm.

"Safe in a pillow fort." I moved around the bed to help him tug the blanket off.

He nodded as if that made any sense and then said, "I'm going to tie the corners of the blanket to the curtain rod to try and block out as much of the wind and rain as I can."

I nodded. He took one end and I took the other. The blanket was wet and heavy and it was tough to maneuver it over the tree. I was too short to be able to tie it from the ground, so I hopped up onto the bed. It felt like I was wrestling an alligator as the wind kept smacking the sodden blanket back into my face.

"Here." Simon tied his end then came around the bed to my side. He reached over me to fasten the corner of the quilt around the curtain rod. His chest was pressed against my back and I tried to focus on the crisis at hand and not the warmth of his body against mine.

"That should do it." His voice was low and deep and just inches from my ear.

I nodded and he backed up, giving me room to hop off the bed. Together, we tucked the end of the blanket around the tree and into the bottom of the sill.

We repeated the task on the second window with another blanket from the bed. This part of the tree branch was smaller so it was easier to maneuver the blanket around it. As soon as we stepped back, Simon gestured to me to lead the way out of the room. He shut the door behind us once we were on the landing.

"That'll have to do for now."

"How does a tree javelin its way through two windows?" I glanced down and noticed that I was once again soaking wet. It was beginning to feel like a permanent condition.

"It could have been a microburst or a baby tornado."

"Tornado?" I yelped and ran for the stairs. There was a tornado and I'd left Dude alone? I was a terrible dog mom. "Dude! I'm coming!"

When I reached the first floor I hurried to the lump that was my dog. A quick peek inside his fort and I could see he was still there, shivering and with his paws over his eyes. I reached in to pet him but he was inconsolable and would be until the storm had passed.

I felt Simon hovering behind me so I turned around and said, "He's all right. He'll be fine once it's over."

As if Mother Nature was mocking me, the interior of the house became almost blackout dark as the storm seemed to have stalled over us, and our meager shelter was relentlessly buffeted by the wind and rain. A banging noise sounded and I wondered if the tree upstairs had been jostled loose. It sounded closer than that.

I remembered opening the shutters when I'd arrived and figured one of them must have gotten loose. I pointed to the dining room.

"I think that noise is one of the shutters I opened yesterday. Can you sit with Dude? I don't want to leave him alone in case he freaks out."

"I can check the window," Simon offered.

"I think I know which one it is," I said. "Also, Dude might feel better with a bigger person beside him."

"Permission to cross the line?" He quirked up an eyebrow and pointed to the tape.

"Granted."

Simon sat on the floor beside Dude. He leaned in and talked to my boy, describing the tree that had gone through two windows upstairs. Dude took his paw off his eyes just long enough to let out a long high-pitched complaint about the storm, then he licked Simon's wrist and covered his head with his paws again. Simon smiled at me just as the shutter started to slam against the side of the house in earnest.

"Be right back." I hurried across the room. It sounded like the third window. I threw up the sash and the rain pelted me through the screen, pushed by the fierce wind. I raised the screen and reached outside to grab the shutter. The wind tried to rip it out of my rain-slick fingers, but I didn't let go and managed to latch it more firmly this time. I quickly lowered the window, figuring I could deal with the screen tomorrow.

I grabbed a towel out of the linen closet to dry off my face and dab my clothes as best as I could before I used it to mop the floor. I returned to the living room to find Dude half out of his fort with his upper torso lying across Simon's lap and his head wedged between Simon's side and his arm.

"Don't let his astraphobia fool you. He really is a ferocious watchdog," I said.

"Astraphobia?"

"Fear of thunderstorms."

"Ah, of course."

I took Simon's seat in the armchair. The room was getting darker by the minute. I reached over to switch on the lamp. Nothing happened.

"Nuts."

"Power is still out?" he asked.

"Looks like it." I tried to turn on the television with the remote. Nothing. "Confirmed."

"This happens every summer," Simon said.

"You've been here before?"

"Not here specifically. I grew up in Raleigh, and we spent our summer vacations on the Carolina shore, up until . . ." He paused. "Until we didn't."

I wondered what he'd been about to say.

"Is that why you have that North Carolina drawl?" I asked. "You were born here?"

"Yeah." He nodded.

I did not add that it was an extremely attractive drawl because that would be inappropriate at best and extremely awkward at worst given that we were virtual strangers sharing a house. But it was. I particularly liked the way he said "Dude." It came out low and deep and with an extra syllable wedged in there. Judging by Dude's current imitation of a weighted lap blanket, he liked it, too.

"I have some camping lanterns in my van," I said. "When the storm eases up, I'll go get them. For now, I'll check the kitchen for a source of flame." I gestured to the candle on the coffee table. It would have to do.

I used the light from my phone to see inside the drawers, where I found some matches from a local bar. I returned to the living room and lit the fat white pillar candle. It gave off the scent of fresh linen and I smiled. Pops's house in Rhode Island had always smelled like that.

I sat on the floor on the other side of the table. The flame flickered, highlighting Simon's sharp cheekbones and strong brow. He should have looked demonic in this light, instead he was melt-a-gal's-undershorts hot, because of course he was. I glanced away.

"I have a question," Simon said. His big square hand was making lazy circles on Dude's back.

"Fire away." I gestured to the storm outside. "It's not like we're going anywhere."

"Why did you think I was an attorney?" He sounded appalled.

Simon

I had no idea why I found this so offensive, but I did. Me? A lawyer? Did I seem like the litigious type? Maybe it was because I was so beaten down by the corporate rat race I'd been living in for the past eight years.

I'd attended the Savannah College of Art and Design, majoring in illustration, with the plan to be a children's book illustrator primarily. I'd had big dreams to change the world through collaborations of story and art, but instead I'd been thrown a curveball and had to ditch the art career in favor of a steady paycheck with benefits and a 401(k) situation. Gramps had gotten me in at the insurance company he'd founded with a friend. I was an insurance salesman and I loathed everything about it.

At the time, I'd assumed I'd be able to pursue my art as a side hustle, that the job was just temporary until my art paid me enough to survive and provide for Charlie, but somehow there was never time for that.

"You say 'attorney' like it's a bad thing, O'Malley," Hannah said, bringing my attention back to her.

I tipped my head to the side. "You essentially called me an ambulance chaser. How could that be construed as a good thing?"

"I did not!" she protested, yet her grin was wide and her eyes glinted with mischief. "How was I to know you had such preconceived negative feelings for attorneys? Maybe I'm one."

"Didn't you tell me you live in your van and post about it online?" I asked. "That doesn't seem like a successful law practice."

"Nice to see you're a good listener." She propped her chin on her hand. "I truly meant no offense."

Thunder boomed. Lightning flashed. I wondered if it was the universe calling her out in a fib and would have said so but Dude started to wail and shiver and my attention was diverted. I wrapped my arms around him, trying to soothe him. Poor guy. Hannah left her spot and joined us. She sat beside me, so close that the coconut-lime scent of her shampoo flirted with my nose.

She was deliciously curvy and the press of her soft body against my arm caused my brain to fritz. How long had it been since I'd dated a woman for more than the occasional hookup? Longer than I could remember. Well, that was depressing as hell.

Dude wriggled across my lap until he was on Hannah's as well. We held him tight and whispered soothing words. His shivering eased but as the storm overhead raged, he let out a beleaguered moan that pulled at my heartstrings.

"I think we should sing him a song," Hannah said.

I lifted my eyebrows. I refused to get bamboozled by the riot of dark curls that surrounded her heart-shaped face. With her big eyes, upturned nose, and wide smile, she looked guileless in the candlelight, but I wasn't fooled. Hannah Spencer was the sort of woman who snuck into a man's heart by inches and the next thing the poor guy knew he was smitten and doing all sorts of dumb things, like singing to a dog in the middle of a housebreaker of a storm.

I opened my mouth to flat-out refuse but what came out instead was, "Does Dude like rock and roll or is he more of a pop guy?"

Hannah's grin about split her face in two. "He loves Taylor Swift."

"Of course he does." I rolled my eyes. I didn't believe her for a hot minute. Still, I accepted it for the challenge it was, cleared my throat and sang about rain in the bedroom, as it seemed appropriate, and everything being wrong.

"Ah!" Hannah cried. "That's from 'Forever & Always'! O'Malley, are you a Swiftie?"

"No, absolutely not. However, my baby sister is and she has been since *1989* came out. Anything I've picked up is entirely her fault because I was in a hostage situation driving her to and from school, but given our current circumstance, it seemed on point."

Hannah laughed and then leaned down and crooned the song in its entirety into Dude's ear and damned if he didn't relax against us, making him even heavier and cutting off the circulation to the lower half of my body, which, given how it was responding to Hannah's nearness, wasn't a bad thing.

From that song, we stayed with the rain theme and moved on to "Here Comes the Rain Again" by the Eurythmics, "Purple Rain" by Prince, "Umbrella" by Rihanna, and "November Rain" by Guns N' Roses. It was quite an eclectic mash-up, and when we didn't know the words, we hummed until Dude met our duet with a deep snore.

We glanced at each other with our mouths open in a silent whoop of success. Hannah leaned closer to me and whispered so softly her breath stroked my ear. "We did it, O'Malley. Also, I think his gummy kicked in."

It was impossible not to smile at least a little. My life had offered me a lot of challenging moments, but singing a Great Dane to sleep with this woman in the middle of a storm was one of the better ones. I found myself softening toward her but immediately checked the feeling.

"I think the worst of it has passed." I shifted, putting some space between us. "You can take the bedroom upstairs. I'll sleep on the couch."

"How do I know you're not hoping another tree will hit the house and take me out?"

I put my hand over my chest in mock pain. "You wound me."

A small smile curved her mouth but it disappeared as her gaze narrowed. "Just so you know, I have a gun and I'm not afraid to use it."

I looked her up and down. Over the years, working in insurance, which did not bring out the best in people, I'd come to read my fellow man and woman pretty well. Hannah gave off a *be kind* vibe the likes of which I rarely met in my line of work.

I scoffed. "You don't have a gun."

"All right, fine. It's a T-shirt cannon that a friend gave me for protection, but I do know how to use it."

That was unexpected. I blinked and then an actual huff of amusement came out of me, causing Dude to snuffle and snort in his sleep. Hannah kissed his head and said, "I'm going to grab some stuff from the van. Will you stay with Dude?"

"Sure." It was still raining but the thunder rumbles and lightning strikes were few and far between. "Do you need help?"

"Nah, I'm just grabbing some dinner for Dude. Speaking of dinner, how do you feel about peanut butter and jelly?"

"PB and J? Huge fan," I said. "Of course, right now I'm hungry enough to eat belly button lint and toenail clippings so . . ."

She gagged. "Sorry, I'm fresh out. You'll have to make do with an Uncrustable with apple slices on the side."

"My taste buds will endeavor to adjust."

She wiggled out from under Dude and strode for the door. As it closed behind her, I rubbed Dude's soft ears and thought about how different the past few days were from what I'd expected. I'd thought I'd be alone dealing with the cottage and my grief. Instead, I had a Great Dane in my lap and a feisty woman offering me PB and J sandwiches.

Dude let out a satisfied yawn and his eyes rolled back as I continued to rub his head in small soothing circles and crooned nonsense words of comfort to him.

I glanced at the carving of the bluebird on the table and the bird's expression was so like Gramps when he was feeling particularly cantankerous that I felt a sharp stab of missing him spear my chest. I knew without a doubt that he would laugh his ass off at me, sitting here on the floor of his cottage with Dude while trying to manage a wild-haired woman who was not at all on board with my plan for the house.

I was about to heave a beleaguered sigh when the door banged open and in strode Hannah. Her arms were full and I pushed Dude off and rose to help her. She had two camping lanterns and a bag of groceries that had two enormous dog dishes poking out of the top. I had no idea how much Great Danes ate but judging by the size of these bowls, it was impressive. I grabbed the bag.

Hannah set one of the lanterns down on the coffee table and switched it on. "Let there be light!"

The entire room was immediately bathed in a soft yellow glow. It was then that I noticed the rocket launcher she had strapped to her back.

"You were serious?" I gaped.

"I never joke about my T-shirt cannon," she said. She swung it around and pointed it at the ceiling while she braced her other hand on her hip, striking a pose like a military leader calling out maneuvers. With her curls framing her face and her tank top hugging her impressive curves, she was seriously the hottest thing I'd seen in a very long time. I shook my head, trying to clear her image from my mind. Nothing good would come of me being warm for the form of my new housemate.

"I will maintain a healthy perimeter." I raised my hands in a *surrender* gesture.

"I'm sure you will." She grinned and set the cannon down, propping it against the back of the couch. "Come on, Dude, it's dinnertime."

Dude glanced from his safe space to her, obviously feeling conflicted. She patted her thigh and coaxed him with encouraging words but he didn't move until she said, "Sirloin tips."

He rose and pressed up against her side, pushing her toward the kitchen while maintaining contact with her at all times.

"Not to be a complainer," I said as I followed with the bag of groceries. "But why does he get sirloin tips while we're having PB and J?"

Hannah reached into the bag I set on the counter and pulled out a can of dog food. "I'm sure Dude wouldn't mind sharing if you'd like."

The can was a gourmet brand of dog food that was labeled "sirloin tips in gravy." My stomach actually growled. I would have been embarrassed but I was too hungry to care.

"Here." Hannah handed me a box of premade sandwiches with the crusts cut off. "Eat before you become faint with hunger."

She didn't have to tell me twice. Still, I had manners. While she found a can opener and prepped Dude's food and water, I scrounged plates and divvied up the sandwiches and sliced the apples, trying to make a meal out of what I would normally consider a sad kid's school lunch.

When Hannah patted Dude on the head and left him to his bowl of chow, I handed her a plate. She glanced at the arrangement of apple slices around the sandwiches. "Oh, fancy, O'Malley."

Inexplicably, I felt my face grow warm at her teasing. "It's all about presentation, Spencer."

I led the way back to the living room. We sat on the recliners and used the coffee table to hold our plates. Hannah doubled back to the kitchen and returned with two bottles of water.

The storm continued to rumble intermittently overhead. I picked up one of the round crustless sandwiches and took a bite. I managed to devour it in two and had to admit it was tasty. I held up the second one. "Where have these been all my life?"

"They're my go-to when I just don't feel like cooking dinner," Hannah said. She went to take a bite of hers and out of nowhere an enormous maw opened and snatched it out of her fingers.

"Dude!" she cried, holding her hand in the air as if she couldn't believe that it was empty. "That is completely unacceptable behavior, mister."

Dude lowered his head, looking abashed even as he tried to work the peanut butter off the roof of his mouth.

Hannah pointed to his pillow fort. "You're in timeout."

The big boy skulked around the coffee table to the mound of pillows and used his snout to nudge one aside so he could belly-crawl under it. Thunder boomed and he scooted faster. Because he was next to me, I reached out and patted his hindquarter, letting him know I was here for him.

"Don't let him snooker you," Hannah said. "If he's brave enough to snatch my dinner, he's not that scared."

She picked up her remaining sandwich and took a bite. I split my second in half and plopped it onto her plate. She smiled at me and said, "Thank you."

"No need." I polished off my half. "Without you, there'd be no dinner or dessert." I bit into an apple slice.

"I suppose we're going to have to figure this all out." She tapped the stack of papers Vincent had left.

"Maybe we'll have a clearer picture of what we want to do when we survey the storm damage tomorrow," I suggested. What I did not say was that I planned to make it as discouraging as possible.

"That's fair." She nodded. We finished our apples and I took our plates to the sink. Given the lack of light, I figured they could wait until tomorrow.

"You can have the bedroom upstairs," Hannah said. "I don't think I'm going to be able to get Dude out of his pillow fort until after the storm passes."

She said it pleasantly enough but I knew when I was being dismissed. As a woman alone in a small house with a strange man, I imagined she figured it was best to keep me contained on the upper floor while she and her dog and her T-shirt cannon staked out the room closest to the exit. I could respect that. Survival of the fittest and all.

I checked the time on my phone and discovered it was later than I'd thought. I took the lantern Hannah offered to light the way upstairs. I was halfway up when Dude let out a mournful moan. I stopped and spun around.

Hannah shook her head. "He'll be fine."

As if to mock her, thunder cracked overhead at a sonic-boom level and Dude let out a howl that rivaled the storm. "Okay, okay, I'm coming back."

I jogged down the stairs. Dude wagged his tail so hard it thumped against the couch, doing triple time. Hannah looked at Dude and then at me. "Flip you a coin for the couch?"

Hannah

It was heads. I'd chosen tails. I have no idea why. I never chose tails. I supposed it was only fair, given that Simon was so much taller than me. His head rested on one armrest while his feet hung over the other. How he was going to sleep like that, I couldn't imagine.

As for me, I took the cushions off the armchairs and made a mattress out of them on the floor. I'd definitely slept on harder ground at some of the campgrounds Dude and I had visited when the summer heat made sleeping in the van impossible. With my dog pressed up against one side and my cannon on my other side, I felt confident that I was safe. Maybe I was an idiot, but Simon struck me as a solid guy despite his shortsightedness in wanting to sell the house.

He'd been offended that I'd called him a lawyer but the storm had interrupted us before he'd told me what he actually did for a living. I didn't know how to bring it up now without it sounding like I was doing a background check. Not that it was any of my business. The truth of the matter was, we'd both inherited this house and he had just as much right to be here as I did.

This brought me back to thinking about Pops and how much I missed him. I wanted him here with me now so I could ask him the million questions that were swimming through my head as I listened to the rain—the thunder and lightning had finally stopped—like, Why hadn't he ever invited me here to see this place of his? Yeah, sure, I'd been busy with my career, my marriage, my divorce, the end of my career, the reinvention of myself in the aftermath of all that destruction, but I would have found time to come here to Pops's special place.

Would I have, though? If I were totally honest with myself, I didn't know if I'd have gone out of my way to visit Pops here. The brutal truth made me feel terrible about myself and my priorities. I wondered if Simon, who seemed to have been as surprised as I was to find out the cottage was a shared property, was feeling the same sort of guilt.

I was about to ask him when I heard a soft snore coming from the couch. It seemed Simon was not suffering from the same curiosity I was or Dude's neediness had worn Simon out. Either way, I took it as a sign to get some shut-eye myself. Snuggling up to my T-shirt cannon, I closed my eyes and let the sound of the rain on the roof lull me to sleep.

Dude barked right in my ear. It was his "stranger danger" bark so I bolted awake, expecting to be in my van but found myself on a living room floor instead. The cushions had separated and my butt was on the hard ground. I pushed the blanket I'd found in the linen closet off and sat up.

I glanced at the couch to find Simon there, with his head sandwiched between two pillows, obviously trying to muffle Dude's barking. Good luck with that! As I pushed to my feet, Dude charged the front door, barking all the way.

I wondered if it was the attorney, Vincent, stopping by to see if we'd murdered each other in a property dispute yet. Wouldn't he be shocked to hear that we'd had a sing-along to comfort Dude instead?

I opened the door to find a man, wearing a tie-dyed T-shirt and a baseball hat with a fish embroidered on it, holding a chainsaw. I let out a yelp and slammed the door.

"O'Malley!" I ran into the living room with Dude on my heels, still barking. I yanked the pillow off Simon's head. "There's a man *with a chainsaw* at the door!"

Simon opened one eye. "And?"

"And what?" I stared at him, wondering how he'd missed the important part. "Chainsaw!"

"Did you ask him what the chainsaw was for?" Simon rolled into a seated position and scrubbed his thick hair with his fingers as if trying to wake up his brain.

"Um . . . no," I admitted. "I saw the chainsaw and freaked out."

He pushed to his feet. He was wearing the same shorts and T-shirt he'd had on last night, both of which were rumpled from his sleep on the couch. I glanced down and noticed I looked equally disheveled.

Dude was dancing around our feet, clearly needing to go outside. The knock on the front door sounded again, sending him into another frenzy of barking.

"I'll put him outside and we can answer the door together," Simon volunteered.

"Thanks, I'm not really functional before coffee." I waited while he opened the back door and Dude bolted out.

It wasn't that I was scared of a stranger wielding a chainsaw, but I was relieved to have Simon with me when I opened the door again.

"Mornin'." The man tipped the brim of his hat at me. "Sorry if I startled you, miss. I'm Zach Pomeroy, I'm your neighbor down the road."

"Oh . . . oh!" I felt my face get warm. "I'm sorry I shut the door on you. The chainsaw startled me."

Zach looked confounded by this. He glanced at the chainsaw and then at me. "You've never seen one before?"

"No, I have . . . I just . . ." I could feel Simon shaking behind me. I didn't have to look at him to know he was silently laughing at me. "I'm Hannah and this is Simon."

Zach shook my hand, then Simon's.

"Nice to meet you, Zach." Simon gestured to the chainsaw. "I take it you saw our remodel."

Zach frowned in confusion and then caught on and let out a chuckle. "Hard to miss." He gestured to the side of the house. "That's why I stopped by. I thought you might need a hand."

I blinked. It had been a long time since I'd had neighbors of the neighborly sort. In my old apartment building in the city, I knew exactly two of them by sight. In the few minutes he'd been here, Zach and I had just exchanged more words than I had with either of those neighbors, and I'd resided there for five years.

"We definitely do," Simon said.

I nodded in agreement. "Aside from the tree, our power hasn't been turned on yet."

"Wouldn't matter if it was. The whole Split is out. I've got a spare generator you can borrow," a voice piped up behind Zach. It was an older man, who had the same beaky nose and warm brown eyes as Zach.

"This is my dad, Roland," Zach said, introducing us. "Dad, this is Hannah and Simon."

I shook Roland's hand and Simon reached around me to do the same. Roland stepped onto the porch just as Dude came bounding around the side of the house, barking like a fool.

This was Dude's "Hi! Hello! I'm so glad you're here! What did you bring me?" bark, so I wasn't worried, but a stranger wouldn't know that and I fully expected Roland to dart into the house to get away from Dude. He did not.

Instead, he went back down the steps and held up his hand in a stop gesture and stared at Dude in what looked like a meeting of minds. Dude skidded to a stop in front of Roland and sat with his tongue hanging out of his mouth and his ears perked.

"How did you do that?" I marveled.

"Dad's a dog whisperer," Zach said. "And a cat soother, raccoon guru, opossum mentor, you name it, and Dad can tame it."

"Impressive." I gaped at Dude, who had never followed a command from me without a bribe being involved.

"We all have our gifts." Roland shrugged.

"Backyard, Dude," I said and to my surprise he trotted back around the house to his new domain. I glanced back at our neighbors. I wanted to ask if either of them had known my grandfather but I didn't know how to finesse that into the conversation just yet.

"Roland, Zach, I see we all had the same idea to welcome the new neighbors." I glanced past the two men and saw a very pregnant woman, carrying a tray of fresh fruit and pastries, with a man behind her, holding a carafe of coffee and looking like he planned to catch her if she teetered too far in any direction.

"Mornin', Bebe, Luke," Zach said, returning her greeting with a smile. "Per usual, we bring the power tools and you bring the pastries."

The men stepped aside to let Bebe through and Roland clapped Luke on the shoulder as he walked by. It was a genuinely affectionate vibe among the four of them and I knew Pops would have loved that sense of community.

"Hi! I'm Bebe Abraham and this is my husband, Luke." Bebe's hair was styled in rows of braids that were pulled back from her face, accentuating her high cheekbones and large brown eyes.

"Hi, I'm Hannah Spencer and this is Simon O'Malley."

"You two must be related to Billy Spencer and Bobby O'Malley then," Bebe concluded.

"Billy?" I said at the same time Simon said, "Bobby?"

As far as I knew no one had ever called Pops Billy. He'd always been William. No nickname of any kind. I was guessing by the surprise on Simon's face that his grandfather had never been called Bobby, either.

"Billy and Bobby were just the sweetest. Total relationship goals, you know?" Bebe continued without taking a breath. "Are you their children or grandchildren?"

"Grandchildren," we answered together, and I sent Simon an annoyed look.

"When you said 'relationship goals'—" I began but Bebe handed me the fruit and pastries and waddled past me into the house.

"So sorry to impose, but I've got to use the facility." Bebe danced a little on her feet so I could tell it was an emergency.

"Oh, absolutely, I'll show you . . ." I stepped aside as did Simon.

"No need," Bebe cried as she hurried past. "I know the way."

Luke smiled in bemusement. He ran his free hand over his close-cropped hair and said, "Sorry about that. My wife's body is no longer her own."

"Understood." There was a time when the sight of a pregnant woman would have caused a pang in my heart, but I'd had five years to come to terms with my infertility and that my dream of having a husband and children of my own was never going to happen. I was okay with it . . . mostly. I waved Luke into the house. "Come on in."

"Roland and Zach, can I offer you some coffee or pastries?"

The father and son sent me matching grins. Roland nodded his head while Zach said, "We never say no to coffee. How about we look at that remodel of yours first, just to make sure my chainsaw can do the job?"

"That'd be great," Simon said. "I haven't had a chance to see what sort of tools are in the shed so this is a huge help."

Luke and I watched the three men trudge up the stairs. I could tell Luke was curious, so I said, "Go ahead and have a look. I know I've never seen anything like it."

"Thanks." He set the carafe on the counter and hurried up the stairs behind the others.

I was pulling plates out of the cupboard when Bebe reappeared.

"Do you have a dog?" She sat down on one of the stools at the kitchen counter. "I thought I heard one barking. I love dogs."

I pointed out the sliding glass door to the yard where my big boy was lying in the grass with his belly in the air. "That would be Dude."

Bebe gasped and clapped her hands together. "A harlequin Great Dane? He's beautiful. I'll have to bring my Frank over. He loves other dogs."

"Thank you," I said. "He's mine but my . . . er . . . housemate Simon put him outside so he didn't knock you down with his usual exuberant greeting."

"Housemate?" Bebe rested her hand on her chin in a *tell me more* pose. "Is that why there's tape on the floor? Setting boundaries?"

"Just measuring rooms." I was too mortified to admit I'd taped off everything in a snit. How could I possibly explain this extremely unusual situation?

I unwrapped the pastries and fruit and set the tray on the counter for easy access. I put out the plates with a stack of paper napkins I'd found in the pantry, then the coffee mugs, most of which had pithy fishing expressions on them like "Gone Fishing" or "Sorry I missed your call, I'm on the other line." My mouth turned up in the corners as I could not picture Pops, a man who loved his Churchill Blue Willow, drinking out of one of these but given the contents of the cupboard, he must have.

"Your pastries look amazing."

"Thank you." Bebe smiled, clearly pleased. "I bake when I'm emotional." She patted her belly. "Which has been most of the time lately."

"And it's the reason I'm rocking a baked goods belly to rival her baby belly." Luke walked into the kitchen, patting his belly through his T-shirt. "You have to help a guy out, Hannah."

"Well, when you put it like that . . ." I grabbed a cinnamon swirl Danish off the tray and took a bite. Crunchy on the outside, chewy in the middle, with thick ribbons of cinnamon and raisins spiraling into the center. It was Nirvana in the form of pastry. "Oh, wow, this is really good. Come over anytime."

Bebe laughed and then grew serious. "Luke and I were so sorry to hear about Billy's passing especially so soon after Bobby's death."

It was jarring to hear her call Pops "Billy." I simply couldn't wrap my brain around it. Then her words made me pause. "I'm sorry, did you say he passed shortly after Bobby?"

She tipped her head and a crease formed between her brows. “You didn’t know?”

Simon entered the kitchen. I glanced at him, wondering how much he’d heard. He met my gaze and I knew as surely as my middle name was Belinda, after my Nana, that he’d heard us.

“Neither Hannah nor I knew that our grandfathers were co-owners of this cottage until the day before yesterday, and between chasing down a rogue bat and the damage from last night’s storm, we haven’t had much time to figure things out.” Simon turned to me. “Gramps passed away four months ago.”

“Pops was a month ago.” I turned to Bebe and Luke. “The estate attorney told us that we each inherited our grandfather’s half of the house and the property. We’re supposed to live here for two months before we make any decisions regarding the place.”

“That must have been a surprise,” Luke said. He picked up a cheese Danish and took a healthy bite.

“A bit,” Simon agreed. “Our grandfathers apparently shared this cottage as their fishing getaway and never told either of our families about the arrangement. It makes sense, though. Outer Banks property is pricey. They likely were trying to offset the expense by being co-owners.”

Luke and Bebe exchanged a considering glance. Simon snagged a cinnamon-raisin pastry and bit into it. A smile of delight passed over his face, making him even more annoyingly handsome.

“I don’t know about Hannah, but you can unload your baked goods on me anytime,” he said. It was exactly what I’d just said. Our mind meld was beginning to concern me.

“I’ll fight you for them.” I turned and met his gaze. I was just teasing but his eyebrow ticked up and I remembered we were at odds about what to do with the cottage. Maybe joking about fighting wasn’t my best play.

Despite the fact that our grandfathers had been friends, I had to remember that Simon was a relative stranger to me and I didn't want to get myself into a situation where I was the woman remembered as "one who lit up every room she entered" in a news story about a house share gone wrong.

Bebe turned to Luke. "I like the new neighbors already."

Neither Simon nor I corrected her assumption that we were moving in permanently. Although I fully intended to live in the cottage, I had no idea if Simon would. And even though we had managed the bat and the chaos of the storm last night, I wasn't sure how I felt about sharing a house with a man I'd met less than forty-eight hours ago.

I poured out mugs of coffee while the low hum of the chainsaw sounded from upstairs.

"Zach and Roland are going to get the tree out of the house," Simon said. "I offered to help but they turned me down."

"That's just as well," Luke said. "Roland can be very particular about the way things get done."

Simon and Luke started talking about fishing, football, and the weather while Bebe and I discussed the cottage. She was polite enough not to remark on the ancient '90s interior so I did it for her.

"I think that carpeting was designed during the Cold War to survive a nuclear winter," I said.

Bebe snorted and pressed her hand to her nose as if to keep the coffee she just drank from leaking out. Then she laughed. "I didn't want to say anything to you, but I used to tease Billy and Bobby about their twentieth-century vibe."

"It's totally fresh," I said, and we both snickered.

"Fresh?" Luke looked doubtful.

"It was the only '90s reference I could think of to describe the decor." I held my arms wide to encompass the living room.

"It does look frozen in time," Simon said. "But I thought Gramps bought the cottage about twenty years ago."

"Do you think they bought it furnished?" I couldn't remember what the interior had looked like when I'd been here as a kid.

"They must have," Simon said. "It's not like there's a big demand for vintage '90s furniture."

"Weird." I glanced around the open floor plan and then at Bebe and Luke. "I still don't understand why they didn't tell us about each other or that they shared the cottage."

Bebe drummed her fingers on the counter. She frowned and said, "I don't want to overstep and speak out of turn, but . . ."

"But what?" Simon prompted.

"Billy and Bobby were . . . a . . ." She spread her arms wide as if this conclusion was obvious.

Simon and I stared at her.

"A couple." Roland finished her sentence as he appeared in the doorway.

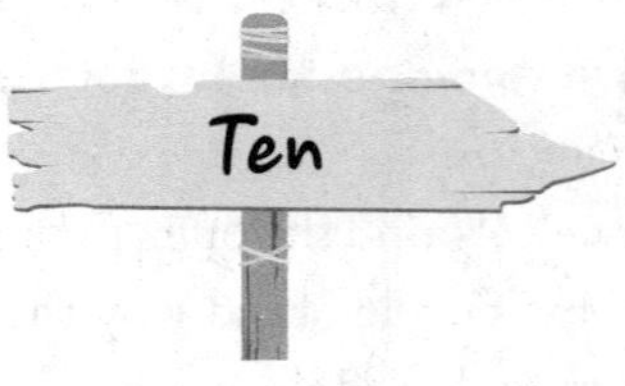

Simon

A laugh burst out of me. "Yeah, no."

Hannah pursed her lips and tapped her chin with the tip of her index finger as if she was actually considering the possibility.

I glanced at Luke to see what he thought and he met my gaze and his voice was gentle when he said, "They were together-together, you know?"

"In what way?" I asked. My voice came out more demanding than I intended and I cleared my throat. "I mean, in what way did they present as together-together?"

"They held hands," Roland said. "Oh, not in town, but here in the neighborhood, when they took their evening walks, they were usually hand in hand or Bobby had his arm around Billy's shoulders."

Bebe nodded. "It was sweet."

"Again, no, that's impossible. Gramps was a lot of things but 'sweet' wasn't one of them," I said.

They were all staring at me with something like pity. I glanced at Hannah. Surely she didn't believe that our grandfathers were in a secret relationship. Her brow was furrowed and she was chewing on her bottom lip. Unlike me, she was not arguing with the people who had been our grandfathers' friends and neighbors for two decades.

Bebe pushed the plate of pastries toward me. "I'm not saying their relationship is why they didn't tell you about each other or their co-ownership of the house. I'm just offering it as a possibility."

"Gramps involved with a man?" I shook my head. "That doesn't track. I mean, he was married for thirty-seven years, he had a kid, and grandkids—one of which is me. He was a widower for twenty years before he passed away." They were all staring at me and I could feel myself start to sweat and it wasn't the morning humidity.

"Pops was married, too," Hannah said. I felt my shoulders drop. She understood. There was no way our grandfathers were a couple. "He and my Nana divorced twenty years ago. Right about the time your grandfather was widowed."

We stared at each other. I could see the cogs and gears turning in her brain trying to make sense of the fact that our grandfathers had cohabited in a cottage for the last two decades of their lives and never invited us—any of us—into their shared world.

It would explain so much but it would also send shock waves through my family that I was not prepared to deal with. My father, Gramps's only child, would absolutely have a stroke at the mere idea that Gramps was in a relationship with a man—if he was to hear about it. Fortunately, this was unlikely as Dad had booked it to Florida after my mother died, leaving us in Gramps's care and he'd never returned other than an obligatory visit every summer.

Of course, his abandonment hadn't stopped him from turning up at Gramps's funeral four months ago. He'd insisted on taking over the planning of the service, a coup attempt my sister shot down with gusto. I'd suspected Dad was mostly there for the reading of the will. When he was left nothing, surprising no one but him, he tried to take away the conservatorship of my brother from me. Thankfully, Gramps had done his legal due diligence making certain that I was the conservator of Charlie's financial affairs and if anything happened to me, it would fall to Lorelei. When my father failed to gain access to Charlie's money, he scuttled like a cockroach back to his new family in Florida. Good riddance.

"Well, we should probably go." Bebe rose from her seat. "Come on, Luke, per usual I think we've overstayed our welcome. Roland, are you and Zach finished?"

"We are." Zach appeared in the doorway, carrying his chainsaw. "I just got the last section of tree back out the window. Ooh, pastries." Hannah held up the tray to him and he snagged a jam-filled one. "Thanks."

"Hannah and Simon, there's a potluck barbecue at the Fisks' house next week," Bebe said. "Monica told me to invite you and that you don't have to bring anything. It's the pale blue house at the end of the road."

"We'll be there, too," Roland said. "Davis makes the best brisket."

Bebe led the way to the front door with Luke, Zach, and Roland following her.

Hannah and I walked them to the door.

"You all right, Simon?" Luke clapped me on the shoulder.

"Yeah, great . . . good . . . hanging in there." I nodded, aware that I sounded as frazzled as I felt.

"Hey, I know a window guy who can replace the windows upstairs. If you want, I'll text you his number," Zach offered.

"That'd be great," I said.

"And Zach and I will get that spare generator set up for you until we all get our power back," Roland said.

"Thank you. You've all been so kind. I can see why Pops loved it here so much," Hannah said. Clearly, she was the one with the polished social skills.

This seemed to ease the awkwardness I had unwittingly created with my surprise that Gramps had been in a relationship. A relationship that I knew nothing about. I didn't care that it had been with a man, but I was absolutely rocked that he hadn't told me about it. I'd thought we were close. If he'd told anyone, it would have been me—but he hadn't.

Hannah closed the door after our neighbors while I doubled back to the kitchen and stuffed another emotional-support pastry—salted caramel, yum—into my mouth. Before Hannah joined me, I opened the sliding door to let Dude inside. I needed the distraction. Being ever helpful, Dude bounded right over to the counter and propped his chin on it, staring at the baked goods as if he could will one to slide off the plate and into his mouth.

"Dude." Hannah's voice was stern but Dude didn't relax his pastry vigil. He simply glanced at her out of the corner of his eye and she sighed. She found a plain croissant amid the variety and broke it in half.

Dude emitted a happy growl and sat on his haunches with his gaze fixed on the flaky bread. Hannah held it out to him, and said, "Gentle."

Dude leaned forward, tentatively opening his mouth just enough to take it from her hand. He was clearly concentrating on being as delicate as possible and I had to admire him for it. These pastries were enough to make me bite a finger if it got in my way.

Once she let go, he swallowed the entirety of it. "It would taste even better if you chewed it." Hannah ruffled his ears. She squinted at me and asked, "You okay, O'Malley?"

"Was my internal freak-out that obvious?" I asked.

"That was internal?" She gave me a pointed look softened with a small smile.

I rubbed my face with my hand.

She reached over and patted my shoulder. "Don't worry. It wasn't that bad, but, yeah, it was clear you were knocked off-balance." She slid onto the stool Bebe had vacated and I took the one beside her.

I felt compelled to explain. "It's not that I care who Gramps was involved with, it's that he didn't tell me. All this time and I had no idea."

"Hmm." She sounded doubtful.

"Gramps was . . . you'd have to have known him to understand." I ran my hand through my hair, pushing it back from my face. Images of the lovable knuckle dragger who had been my Gramps filled my mind.

"No indication of homosexuality then?" she asked. "Assuming there is such a thing."

"Listen, I know it's easy to assume I'm being an asshole and that my upset is about the gender of Gramps's partner but that isn't it." I reached for a chocolate donut that was coated in powdered sugar but had deep fudgy cracks in its surface. "I'm aware that it sounds ridiculous, but the fact is I just feel betrayed."

"Why? He didn't do anything to you. His relationship with Pops changes nothing about your relationship with him." Hannah fed Dude the other half of the croissant. He didn't taste that one, either.

There was something in her voice. A hurt that mirrored my own. Hannah was not nearly as cool with being shut out of her Pops's life as she pretended. "Who are you trying to convince, Spencer, me or you?"

"I'm not trying to convince anyone of anything." Hannah didn't meet my gaze.

"Sure. Are you telling me you don't feel anything about being left out of a significant part of Pops's life? It doesn't bother you at all that he didn't trust you enough to tell you? That maybe you weren't as close as you thought you were."

"You know what, O'Malley, I don't have to assume. You are being an asshole." She pushed off her stool and stormed out, slamming the back door as if it were my head.

Dude stared at me with a reproving gaze.

"Whatever. She knows I'm right."

Dude continued to stare.

"Fine. She's your person. What do I do, go after her?"

The Great Dane's floppy ears twitched, which I took as the dog equivalent of "Duh."

I shoved the last of the chocolate donut into my mouth to fortify myself and then headed out the door. The day was heating up but there was a breeze making it bearable. I scanned the overgrown backyard until I spotted Hannah, sitting on the edge of the dock with her feet dangling in the water.

I remembered how fearlessly she had jumped in after me even though she'd been terrified there were alligators. For a second, just a nanosecond really, I thought about slipping into the water and pretending I was an alligator by grabbing her ankle, but given that she was already pissed at me, I rejected the idea.

Pissing her off was not how I was going to get her to agree to sell the house at the end of our two-month residency. I needed to repair the damage I'd just done and get us back to the us we'd been when we were singing Dude to sleep. I felt a warmth unfurl in my chest at the memory and immediately felt guilty that I was trying to maneuver her into selling the cottage when she'd been very clear she wanted to stay.

I shook it off. I had nothing to feel guilty about. I was doing Hannah a favor by convincing her to sell. It was clear that this place was a lost cause and given that she was living out of her van, how did she expect to pay for all the work that needed to be done to make this place habitable?

Newly reaffirmed of my priorities, I strode down the dock with every intention of making peace. I should have known it wouldn't be that easy.

At the sound of my footsteps, Hannah held up her hand without turning around and said, "Go away."

This did not bode well for my plan to smooth things out. "I wanted to apologize."

"Why? Didn't you mean what you said?"

"I did," I said.

She whipped around to look at me with an expression of outrage.

I held up my hands and continued, "But I meant it about me. I projected my hurt feelings and confusion about my relationship with Gramps onto you and your Pops. That was unfair and I'm sorry."

She turned away from me and I braced myself for rejection. Maybe I had gone too far. Perhaps questioning her closeness with her grandfather was an unforgivable offense. I was about to leave when she spoke.

"Don't be sorry. You weren't completely wrong."

I pondered the back of her head, admiring the way the sun glinted on her hair and highlighted the different strands, from light honey gold to dark coppery brown. Wait. I wasn't wrong?

"Are you saying I was right?"

"No, I said you weren't wrong."

"Which means I was right." Why was I persisting? She was softening and I was arguing semantics. Idiot.

She turned back to me with one eyebrow raised. "Really? You're going to keep pushing?"

"Nope." I shook my head. "No, ma'am. 'Not wrong' is perfectly acceptable."

She turned away again. I could see in the curved line of her shoulders that she was sad and I felt like an absolute dick. Her grandfather had passed away only a month ago whereas I'd had four months to grieve for Gramps. She was still in the thick of it and there I was making her feel like shit about how much he'd actually loved her.

I moved forward and sat down beside her, leaving a foot of space in between us so as not to crowd her. I took off my shoes and plunked my feet into the water beside hers. The cold woke me up but it also felt refreshing.

"Listen, I was wrong," I said. "I have no idea what your relationship with your grandfather was like and I had no right to say what I did. I was angry about Gramps keeping something so important from me and I lashed out. You didn't deserve that. I was incredibly out of line."

She stared out at the freshwater channel that cut through the marsh. The current was moving at its usual lazy pace, swirling around our feet before continuing on. The tall grass on each side of us was rippling with the breeze, and the chatter of birds could be heard over the hum of the insects.

"You weren't." She shook her head. "You were honest about your feelings and if I'd been honest about my feelings instead of trying to find a positive take and pretend I was fine, I would have admitted to feeling a bit tender about Pops never mentioning Gramps—you don't mind if I call him that, do you?"

I waved my hand, indicating she was welcome to.

"And for the same reason," she continued. "I thought we were so close. I can't believe he wouldn't tell me about a relationship that was clearly so important to him. I want to call my Nana and ask about all this but she and Bonus Grandpa George are on a month-long cruise with my parents. They all wanted to get away after Pops passed. I could have gone, too, but cruises aren't my thing, plus that whole fifth-wheel thing."

"I hear that." I nodded.

We were both silent while we pondered why our grandfathers had shut us out. Judging by the way her lips turned down in the corners, she was feeling more than tender. She looked hurt, which I inexplicably found completely unacceptable.

"Hey." I nudged her with my elbow and in a teasing voice, I said, "If you sell to me, you can walk away from this cottage and never have to deal with all of these conflicting feelings."

"Is that how you plan to manage it?" she countered. "Just sell it and walk away?"

"There's nothing for me to manage. Finding out about Gramps and Pops or Bobby and Billy—still trying to wrap my head around those nicknames—changes nothing for me." I shook my head. "I decided to sell the second I found out I'd inherited."

"But how can you just leave when there's so much we don't know about their life here?" She swatted at a bug that hovered in front of her face.

"If Gramps had wanted me to know, he would have told me," I said. "I think he left the house to me knowing I would sell it and not reveal his secret life."

"That makes no sense." She shook her head and I had the feeling she was disappointed in me. "He could have just left his half to my

Pops and then Pops would have left it to me and you never would have known about his life here. I think he wanted you to know."

She made a good point but I wasn't going to be swayed. "I'm selling."

She met my gaze and said, "I'm not."

The impasse remained. I glanced back at the cottage, where I could just get a glimpse of the vintage bright yellow Volkswagen van parked in the driveway. She'd mentioned that she lived in her van, traveling around the country as a sort of online travel persona. How disappointed she must be to have thought she was finally going to have a home, only to discover that she had to share it with someone.

"This situation has to be extremely uncomfortable for you," I said. "I'm sorry about that."

"Not any more for me than for you." She pulled her feet out of the water and held her legs straight, letting the water drip off. "Dude seems okay with you. He likes you . . . unless of course you give him a reason not to and then he'll go into protector mode, which is a lot."

"Has he ever needed to protect you?" The thought of her in peril with just Dude to provide backup made a surge of protectiveness rush through me. Also, I had a feeling with Dude at her side, she wouldn't need me or anyone. Suddenly, I wished Dude was here so I could pet his big blocky head and remind him we were pals.

"Once." She held up one finger. "A man in a campground tried to break into my van while we were sleeping. Dude let him know that was a terrible idea." She paused before adding, "I heard they found his missing . . . appendage the next day."

I felt my jaw drop. I barely restrained the shudder that wanted to ripple through me. It was then that I saw the glint in her eye and the smirk she was visibly trying to squelch.

"Appendage? Really?" I asked.

She cackled. It should have been off-putting but instead it was such a burst of pure amusement that I found myself smiling and shaking my head.

"Well played."

"Thank you." She grinned. "Truthfully, there was no appendage lost or found, but the man realized the error of his ways the second Dude popped up in the window and growled at him."

"Because Dude could actually make an appendage go missing?"

She shrugged. "The Dude abides, until he doesn't."

"For the record, you will absolutely never have to worry about that with me. I would offer to rent another place while we figure this out, but I doubt there's anything available this late in the season."

"It's no problem." She shrugged. "Like I said last night, between Dude and my T-shirt cannon, I feel perfectly safe."

As if he knew we'd been talking about him, the big galoot appeared at the end of the dock and began to run toward us as if we'd been apart for days instead of minutes.

"What are the odds that he's any better at stopping today?" I asked.

"None." Hannah rolled over and flattened herself, belly down on the dock. She glanced at me and cried, "Get ready!"

I turned myself into a human pancake just as Dude was upon us and surprising no one, he tried to stop too late and went sailing over us, landing in the channel with a giant horse-dog-sized splash. Hannah and I were both hit by the wave and stared at each other in shock, with our hair matted to our heads and water dripping down our faces, as the wave doused us head to toe and set the dock to rocking.

"Your face!" we said together, and then shared a laugh.

Dude took this as a sign he had done something right and he clambered back onto the dock and shook himself muzzle to tail, sending more water raining down upon us. Then he ran back up the dock to the house, having committed his havoc quota for the moment.

Hannah braced herself on her elbows and wiped the water from her face. "Do you think there will ever be a time when we're together that we're not wet?"

I pressed my lips together, thinking anything I said was going to be deeply inappropriate. Hannah glanced at my face and immediately turned bright pink with embarrassment. She slowly lowered her body back to the dock, gently thumping her forehead on the wooden planks. I could just hear her when she muttered, "That came out so wrong."

"Simon! Hannah!" Zach Pomeroy was standing in the side yard, next to the remnants of the tree, with Dude bounding around him. "We have your generator. We'll set it up in the back."

I glanced at Hannah but she was still facedown on the dock. She did lift one hand to give me a thumbs-up and I turned back to Zach and yelled, "Perfect! Thanks!"

"Come on, Spencer, it wasn't that bad." I crouched down beside her. "Although I want props for not saying anything."

She lifted her head and squinted at me. "Such as?"

It was not nice of me but I just couldn't resist trying to make her blush again. I leaned closer and lowered my voice until it was a low rumble. "I could have said, 'No, there won't ever be a time when we're together that we're not . . . wet.'"

Much to my satisfaction her eyes went wide and her face turned a mottled shade of red. She opened her mouth and closed her mouth, clearly speechless, which was incredibly satisfying. I stood and reached down to help her up. To my surprise, she took my hand without hesitation.

She rose to her feet, leaving her fingers wrapped in mine for just a beat. Then she glanced at me from beneath her lashes with a calculated look and said, "Promises, promises . . . oh, wait. No, it wasn't." She sighed long and deep as if disappointed. Well, hell.

She turned and sauntered up the dock, leaving me to appreciate the view of her curvy backside swinging back and forth as she walked away, and it felt as if the upper hand I'd just achieved had been used to slap me. I laughed loud enough for Hannah to stop and glance at me over her shoulder. Her smile was pure amusement without a bit of malice and damned if it wasn't sexy as hell.

I followed her all the way up the dock and across the lawn until we reached Zach and Roland. They were moving the generator with Dude's "help," so I hurried forward to give an assist. I stepped around Hannah and Dude, who was busy rekindling his bromance with Roland, judging by the way he was pressing his head up into the man's hand. I tried not to be offended that I was so easily replaced in the dog's affections.

The three of us maneuvered the generator to the back of the house and then returned to where Hannah was standing with Dude beside the tree Zach had cut up.

"Hey, Hannah, this is going to sound nuts, but you're not Van Life Girl on social media, are you?" Zach pushed his baseball cap back on his head, revealing a head of thick, light brown hair.

She looked surprised. "As a matter of fact, I am. Are you one of my followers?"

"No, but my wife is," he said. "I told her a woman named Hannah, with a yellow van and a harlequin Great Dane named Dude, inherited Billy and Bobby's house, and Taylor freaked out and said it had to be Van Life Girl."

Hannah grinned and held her arms wide. "She's right. That's me."

I glanced from Hannah to Zach and back. I got the distinct feeling that Hannah's prior description of her occupation was a very tempered version of what she actually did. I was tempted to pull out my phone and do a quick search but I resisted.

"So, you're an influencer?" I asked.

"I prefer *creator.*" Hannah pursed her lips. "I'm not trying to influence anyone but I do create content about the places I visit, which is what I was doing yesterday. Consistency is key. I can't wait to do more about the area."

I nodded, hoping I didn't look as ill at ease as I felt. How big was her following? How far was her reach? If she shared anything about Gramps and Pops and the cottage and my father saw it, his reaction would make last night's monster storm seem like a summer shower.

Hannah

Simon's expression was not impressed. In fact, he looked disturbed. I knew I was being oversensitive, but the discomfort on Simon's face reminded me of every judgmental person I'd had to deal with since leaving print journalism. Online content had been an adjustment for me, too, but it was always people in traditional careers who struggled the most to grasp that online media was actually a valid way to disseminate information and make a living.

"How did you fall into that?" Simon asked. Both Roland and Zach leaned in, obviously wanting to know as well.

"Well, I started by doing cute little dances and then I did makeup tutorials, one thing led to another, and here I am." I did another enormous overly exaggerated hair toss, which should have clued them in to the fact that I was slinging enough horseshit to clean a stable, but all three of them missed it.

"You're not planning on filming anything at the house, are you?" Simon's voice was strained as if he was trying to sound objective but failing miserably.

I stared at him. I could see the panic on his face at the mere idea of having his life posted online for all the world to see. I understood that. I curated my content very carefully. Other than Dude, I shared nothing personal online. In fact, I posted about locations only after I left them because I didn't want to be intercepted by any overzealous followers. It was my way of maintaining some healthy boundaries. It hadn't occurred to me to share anything about Pops, the house, or my personal reasons for being in OBX, but where was the fun in admitting that to my new housemate, who was clearly freaking out?

"Well, of course I am," I said. "I have to let my fans know every single thing I eat or wear, think or feel, don't I?"

I might have gone too far with that one. Simon's brows lowered and his eyes narrowed. "You're messing with me."

I held my thumb and index finger about an inch apart. "A bit."

Zach laughed and Roland let out a relieved wheeze. "On that note, we'll hook up your generator." The two men returned to their project. Simon watched them go and then faced me.

"I suppose I deserved that," he said. "Having watched a few of my friends suffer the consequences of oversharing on the socials, I try to avoid social media like it's an aggressive venereal disease."

That shocked a laugh out of me. "The metaphor is not entirely inaccurate."

"How did you actually end up being an influ . . . a creator?" he asked.

"I was a journalist whose newspaper went under," I said. "One minute I was covering the movers and shakers in DC and the next I was unemployed and the only thing I owned in the world was Buttercup." I didn't mention my divorce or the staggering medical bills I'd been left with from the unsuccessful fertility treatments as the reason I had ended up with just a van. There's only so much humiliation I was willing to share until I knew him better.

"Buttercup?"

"My van." I tipped my head in the direction of the driveway.

"Aptly named." Simon leaned against the side of the house.

"I tried to survive working freelance while looking for a full-time position, but there just wasn't anything available. Before I got evicted, I packed what I needed, put the rest of my things in storage, and hit the open road. I impulsively decided to live off my savings while I toured all of the national parks," I said. "Shockingly, when I started posting about my travels, I gained a following, which gave me an income, and I've been at it ever since."

He cupped his chin with his hand and studied me. "Is that why you don't want to sell? Because now you'll have a roof over your head?"

I frowned. "The van has a roof. I wasn't homeless. I was addressless, which is not the same thing."

He held up his hands in surrender and I realized I sounded a teeny bit defensive.

"But, yes, it would be nice to stay in one spot for longer than a couple of weeks," I conceded.

"If you sell to me, you can use the money to buy a place of your own," he said.

"Or I can *not* sell my half and have a place that's already paid for and has sentimental value." I studied him. "Aren't you the least bit curious about Billy and Bobby? Our grandfathers were a couple, Simon, how can you not want to know more about that?"

"Because it's none of my business," he said. "As I said before, Gramps would have told me if he'd wanted me to know."

"I already told you I disagree. And I have to ask—Why are you so hot to sell? Is it because you're desperate to get back to that 'career' you love so much?"

His mouth tightened and I knew I'd struck a nerve.

Me, being me, I had to push. "What is it that you do?"

"I work in insurance."

"Oh." I had not expected that.

"Yeah, it's a real soul suck of a job but it pays the bills," he said. "I'm lucky that most of my work can be done remotely, otherwise I'd never be able to live in the cottage for the stipulated two months."

It was easy to see Simon wasn't happy. It was the sort of misery that came with the Sunday scaries of having to spend his weeks doing work that he didn't find fulfilling. I tucked that information into the file labeled Hot Housemate, er, Simon O'Malley in my brain.

"As I mentioned, I have my reasons for wanting to sell," he said. "And I'd rather do it sooner than later."

I wondered if selling would give him enough of a financial cushion to leave his job. But there was no way to verify this without being incredibly rude. I decided to wait and see what I learned about him over the next two months.

"Pops died a month ago," I said. "I've barely had time to process the loss and I haven't had much time to look around. I want to understand this place from Pops's perspective. I want to get to know this section of the Outer Banks and fill in the gaps in my knowledge of Pops's life here, one of which is his relationship with your Gramps."

He frowned. "Why?"

"Because it's important to me."

"Why?" he persisted. "Your grandfather is gone, Hannah, and learning about his secret life here isn't going to bring him back."

I blinked in surprise. Something was clearly eating at Simon. This was not the time to press him for more. I decided to focus on my own mission.

"I'm not leaving until I have a better understanding of Billy and Bobby," I declared, making my voice as firm as the Rocky Mountains I had spent a summer hiking. "I want to know everything about them. How they met, how they fell in love, all of it."

"What if you discover things you don't want to know?" Simon protested.

"Like what? That they were into bondage or something?" I said it just to make him flinch, which he did. I pressed my lips together, keeping my laughter in check. I failed and my laugh came out my nose in a bodacious snort.

"That's not funny." He wagged a finger at me but a tiny smile curved his mouth up on one side, giving him away. "And now I can't get the picture of Gramps in a leather face mask out of my head." He shook himself from head to toe like Dude when he came out of the rain, then he looked at me and said, "You're evil."

"I'm not the one picturing my grandfather in a dom getup."

He ran his hand over his face. "You're only proving my point, you know. We might find out things that we're better off not knowing."

"We've only been here for a few days," I said. "We don't know anything yet."

Simon walked around the house to the front. As he had pointed out before, the paint was chipped and some of the boards looked rotten and in need of replacing. The entire porch was worn and definitely ready to be retired. I studied it with a critical eye. There were certain realities to staying here that I had not yet confronted.

"You know, if I do sell—" I began, and his head snapped in my direction. I held up one hand. "That's a *big* if. This place needs to be inspected, which I don't think would go well. The entire cottage is woefully out of date. I'm not a Realtor but I feel like we'd be taking a hit to sell it as is."

Simon glanced around the cottage. "No, it's prime real estate. It's got a dock, the marsh, water access from the channel to the ocean—"

"Windows and a roof that must be replaced, a yard that needs to be landscaped, new paint all over, and that's just the outside. The inside is like a time capsule of the '90s."

"It doesn't matter, Hannah. Anyone who buys this place is probably going to flatten it and build a colossal McMansion," Simon said. I gasped.

"And you're okay with that?" I was outraged. "This cottage was so special to your Gramps that he kept it a secret for twenty years—how can you just let that happen without understanding why he loved it so much?"

Simon glanced away. I studied his profile and noticed that his jaw was tight and a muscle flexed in his cheek. When he turned back to me, his face was set and expressionless. Whatever he was feeling, he was not in a sharing mood.

"I don't need to know why. Gramps is dead and nothing will bring him back. It's time to move on. My original plan was to spend a month here, clean out his things, put the place on the market, and then be done," he said.

"You sound like you're determined to leave it all behind." I studied him but his face betrayed nothing. The man was on serious emotional lockdown. I reminded myself that this was not my problem. "Listen, we have to live in the cottage for two months, how about I stop badgering you about wanting to know more about our grandfathers' life here and you quit lobbying me to sell the house."

Simon heaved a sigh and tipped his head back to stare at the sky. "Fine. No pestering you to sell for two months but no more tape on the floor. I can't live like that."

He was offering me an olive branch, which of course I was going to take. Why would I refuse and make things weird between us? Still, I had to be honest so there weren't any nasty surprises for him at the end of the two months.

"That sounds reasonable, O'Malley," I said. "But I'm not making any promises that I'll agree to sell at the end of two months. In that time, I might decide I want chickens."

"Chickens?" His eyebrows shot up.

"Or maybe baby goats." I made my face as innocent as possible and he blew out an exasperated breath.

"We can debate it in two months." Simon held out his hand and I clasped it with mine.

Immediately, I was aware of everything about him from the calluses on his palm to the warmth of his hand around mine. I noticed the way his brown eyes lingered on my mouth before he jerked his gaze back up to meet mine, and I smiled. The spark of awareness between us was undeniable and was definitely going to make the summer more interesting. I was relieved to note from the intensity of his gaze that Simon O'Malley clearly felt it, too.

Simon

Two months. Two months was nothing. I'd survived years working in an industry that bored me into a catatonic stupor on a daily basis. Two months with the sexy Hannah Spencer and her lovable horse-dog would be a snap—or so I kept telling myself.

Our gazes met and held for a heartbeat or two. She was right. She'd been right all along. There had to be a reason that our grandfathers had chosen us to inherit the house and if it was to belatedly share their relationship with us then so be it. For two months, I could support her in her quest and maybe it would help me find some closure, too.

After we helped Roland and Zach load up the remnants of the tree into the back of Zach's pickup, we boarded up the smashed windowpanes with plywood and cleaned the bedroom of broken glass. Dude was banished to the yard, where he pounced and rolled in the high grass, having the time of his life.

We were sweaty and sticky and I was certain I smelled like something Dude would have liked to roll in when Hannah opened the top drawer of the dresser. She pressed her hand to her chest and sighed. I glanced over her shoulder to see what she'd found. It was a very tidy storage box of cuff links and tie clips, sorted by size and shape.

They clearly meant something to Hannah as her eyes filled with tears. "These belonged to Pops; he was a television reporter in Providence for years."

"Really?" I wondered if that was why she'd become a journalist.

"He was the anchorman, reporting every night at five o'clock and eleven o'clock," she said. "When I was little, I used to think he lived inside the television and would pop out to visit us before going back to his 'house.' My mom said she frequently found me asking for Pops to come out of the television when it was off."

She reached in and picked up a set of cuff links. They were circular mother-of-pearl set in silver. Classy. I couldn't help but recall how Gramps even at the height of his success had always worn his dress shirts unbuttoned at the collar and with the sleeves rolled up to his elbows, revealing the ropy muscles of his forearms. I don't think he'd ever worn a set of cuff links in his life. It made me wonder how he and Hannah's grandfather had found each other.

I glanced around the bedroom, taking in the utilitarian furniture. I hadn't had a chance to really examine it since I'd arrived but now that I was taking it in, I noted that it didn't appear to be lived in. There were no photos or knickknacks. Very different from the living room downstairs. I decided to check out the other bedroom.

There were sheets thrown over the furniture as if the last person to leave knew he wasn't coming back. Hannah had said Pops passed away a month ago. Gramps had died three months prior. I felt an ominous sinking in the pit of my stomach. How had Pops known he wouldn't be back? Had he been sick like Gramps? Or had he been too heartbroken to be here without Gramps and decided to close it up for good?

I supposed Vincent had been instructed to wait until both men had passed to inform us about our inheritance. It struck me then that the men had died three months apart. I'd heard of partners who lived only a few months after their loved one passed away. Had Gramps and Pops been that deeply in love? I wasn't sure how I felt about that when I had assumed Granny had been the love of Gramps's life.

The first stirrings of real curiosity began to unfurl inside of me and I glanced around the bedroom, realizing this had likely been their shared space.

I ripped the sheets off the furniture. The matching side tables had stacks of books on them, the one on the left had a small white-noise machine, while the one on the right had a pair of reader's glasses. I crossed to the side table and picked up the glasses. They were big blocky black-framed nerd glasses. A laugh burst out of me. These belonged to Gramps. How many times had I seen him push these very glasses up his nose while ordering from a restaurant menu? The laugh turned into a hiccup and I felt my throat get tight.

"O'Malley? You okay?" Hannah appeared at my side. Her hand rested lightly on my forearm as if she was trying to reassure me with her presence while not intruding on my moment of grief.

I cleared my throat. "I'm fine." I held the readers up. "Your grandfather was suave mother-of-pearl cuff links while mine was ugly science dork glasses."

Hannah smiled. It was small and sad and pulled at my heartstrings, filling me with an unfamiliar feeling of tenderness. Her eyes still held a sheen of tears and I gave in to the inexplicable urge to give her a side hug and offer her comfort.

To my surprise, she nestled closer and said, "This is going to be hard."

"We'll get through it." My voice was gruff when I added, "Together."

She squeezed me tight and I caught my breath at the uncalculated affection. I wasn't used to someone reaching for me without having a hand on my wallet at the same time. The coconut-lime scent of her hair was intoxicating and she fit up against my side as if she were built for just that specific spot. I found myself leaning into her softness and it soothed me.

"Despite your lack of skills in the bat-removal department, I'm glad you're here, O'Malley." Her voice was teasing but I knew she was feeling the same way I was. Relieved to have someone to go through the house with. If reading glasses and cuff links were this triggering, I could only imagine what the rest of it would be like.

"The bat caught a ride *in my hair*," I reminded her. I suspected she was teasing to keep the emotions light and I was 100 percent on board with that. "I think that makes my bat-removal skills above reproach."

"Meh." She glanced up at me with a glint in her eyes. When she let me go, I had the craziest urge to pull her back up against my side. I didn't. Instead, I just watched her go, thinking I'd experienced more emotions in the past two days spent with her than I had in years. A flicker of unease hit me low and deep but I shook it off. This was just for two months. I could keep my feelings in check and my hands to myself for less than sixty days.

"You want to use a 20-25 test line when fishing," Luke said. "Also go for nylon monofilament."

This was Luke's answer to my abysmal attempts at fishing. Had it really been over a week since I'd stood on Gramps's dock and cast my line before being dunked by Dude? I glanced around the backyard of the cottage where Monica and Davis Fisk were in the thick of hosting the neighborhood cookout.

With three kids under the age of seven, they had the look of bemused parents who had become adept at controlled chaos. The grill was blazing out hot dogs and hamburgers to order, the smoker had brisket, and a picnic table was laden with offerings from the rest of the neighborhood, which included potato salad, corn bread, and other assorted side dishes. A wild pack of children, including the Fisks' three, were running around the lawn in a game of chase that had no defined rules, judging by the arguments that kept breaking out.

I had a cold beer in one hand and stood silently while I was schooled by Luke and three other men who lived on the Split—as they called it—in the ways of OBX fishing. I watched Hannah move through the crowd with Bebe, meeting and greeting everyone as if she'd lived there for years instead of a little over a week.

I marveled at her ease. She tucked an errant strand of hair behind her ear as the summer breeze tugged it loose from the ponytail at the nape of her neck while she laughed at something one of the kids said. She wore a pale pink sundress with tiny strawberries on it paired with a beat-up pair of white Converse sneakers. When the little girl started spinning with her arms flung wide, Hannah did, too. Because of course she did. I couldn't take my eyes off the way her skirt flared and how she tilted her head up toward the sun as if inviting its warmth into her soul.

As I watched, Dude bounded toward Hannah as if he wanted in on the game. She stopped spinning and bent over to give him a hug. I fully expected little hearts to stream out of his eyes. Satisfied, Dude hurried back to his new friend.

Dude had insisted on coming with us to the barbecue and made a new bestie in Frank, Bebe and Luke's black pug. The sight of the harlequin Great Dane and the pug, who wasn't much bigger than Dude's paw, sacked out in the grass while the children crawled all over them was a sight. Dude rolled onto his back so he was belly-up while he basked in the attention as if he was utterly neglected at home.

On the walk over, Hannah and I had agreed that this was an opportunity to do grandfather recon, as in, we were supposed to ask the other guests what they knew about our grandfathers so that we could get a sense of their life here together. Problem was, I had no idea how to initiate that sort of candid conversation.

I was a guy. Conversationally, my areas of expertise were sports, cars, hobbies like fishing, and technology. Relationship stuff, including the familial, didn't even make the top ten, possibly top twenty. I'd rather talk about bowel movements than delve into feelings. Still, I had promised Hannah I would try.

"My Gramps loved a day of fishing." I glanced at the men around me, feeling as if I were baiting my hook.

"I'll say he did," Luke agreed. He nudged Davis Fisk, who was taking a well-earned break from the grill. "Remember when he and Billy caught all of that flounder?"

"Do I? I love flounder as much as the next guy but I started hiding when I saw them coming to my door with a bag. You just knew it was going to be more flounder."

"Billy was a fisherman, too?" I asked, trying to steer the conversation toward the grandfathers without being too obvious.

"Oh, yeah, they were real competitive about it," Davis said. "Billy told me it went back to the first day they met at the Split."

"They met here?" I couldn't keep the surprise out of my voice. I had never heard of Gramps traveling to this tiny peninsula before he bought his "fishing getaway" twenty years ago.

Davis and Luke exchanged a look as if they weren't sure how well I would handle talking about my recently deceased grandfather. I wanted to say it was fine and that they could tell me anything but judging by the pang of hurt that was twanging in my chest, that would be a lie.

"He didn't say much else about it." Davis looked apologetic. "Other than they were teenagers and met when Billy crowded Bobby out of his favorite fishing spot."

I nodded, trying to look as if this news didn't rock me to my core. It totally did and I wasn't sure I had a good enough poker face to not let it show. Gramps had met Pops—or as the locals knew them, Bobby had met Billy—as teenagers. I took a very long swallow of my beer, trying to play it cool when what I really wanted to do was run across the lawn and grab Hannah and tell her what I had just learned. This was *news* and I desperately wanted to be the one to tell her and hear her opinion about it, but I didn't move. I wanted to hold on to this tidbit and tell her when it was just the two of us.

I watched as she took a seat with Bebe and a few other women. When her gaze met mine, I lifted my beer bottle to her. She lifted her fork in return, and I smiled. Hannah's returning grin enveloped me in the shared amusement, making an unfamiliar feeling of contentment fill my chest.

Wanting to imprint the moment on my mind, I glanced up at the bright blue sky and felt the warm ocean breeze ruffle my hair. I heard Dude and Frank, snuffling and snorting as they rolled in the grass. I glanced around at the clusters of friends and neighbors and felt a sense of belonging as if I was welcome, even encouraged, to take up space in this place. I realized I hadn't felt this level of acceptance since my days in art school. It was one of those precious life moments where I wasn't stressed or angry or feeling overwhelmed. If I could have lived in it forever, I would have. Although Davis and Monica likely would have frowned upon me taking up residence in their backyard.

Realizing the conversation had moved on without me, I focused my attention on the men, trying to figure out what they were talking about. I was infinitely relieved when Roland joined our group with some very strong opinions about braided lines versus nylon filament while I finished my beer and pondered what I'd learned.

Hannah

"Are you sure you and Simon are just housemates?" Bebe asked as we stood in the food line.

"Yes, I'm sure," I said. "I just met him a little over a week ago. Why?"

"He's been watching you," Bebe said. "Not in a creepy stalkery way but with a certain sense of . . . what's the word I'm looking for?"

"Bemusement," Stephanie Fisk, Davis's mom, said. She was the supplier of the corn bread as well as several pies and cakes. Apparently, she owned a bakery in town called Beach Buns, a name that I thought was hilarious.

"Bemusement like he's in shock that he has to share a house with me and Dude or like he thinks I'm cute?" I asked. I'd had two glasses of wine and was feeling a bit fearless.

"Cute," Bebe said without hesitation.

"Definitely that one," Stephanie agreed. She handed Bebe and me plates loaded with brisket, a square of corn bread, potato salad, and green beans, which I gratefully accepted.

Bebe led me to a picnic table in the shade. I couldn't help glancing over my shoulder at the group of men Simon was standing with as I took my seat to see if what Bebe said was true. Sure enough, my gaze met Simon's and he lifted his beer bottle to me in a silent toast. Hmm. Having misplaced my glass, I raised my fork in return, which caused him to smile at me. It was a killer smile.

Bebe leaned against me and muttered, "Told you so."

We had come to a truce about the state of the house, so I supposed Simon might be feeling friendlier toward me; whether it was attraction or not, I'd just have to wait and see.

Monica Fisk, our hostess, and Taylor Pomeroy, Zach's wife, joined us while Stephanie remained at the food station, handing a heaping plate to anyone who walked by.

"No one goes hungry on my mother-in-law's watch." Monica tucked into her plate. "I love that woman."

I took a bite of my potato salad. "I can see why."

"I'm sorry but I have to fangirl." Taylor wriggled on her seat. "I have been watching you and Dude online for years. I can't believe Van Girl is here and Buttercup is parked on my street!"

Taylor looked to be in her late twenties. She was wearing a pink halter top and jean shorts. Her dark brown hair was styled in long curls that framed her face. She had a shy smile and a nervous habit of biting her nails.

"Thank you for watching." I always thanked my viewers because without them I would have no income. "I appreciate it."

"The episode where Dude brought you those stray kittens." Taylor put her hand over her heart. "I cried buckets. He was so sweet with those little babies. And then when you found the mama and they were all adopted." She fanned her face as if the tears would start again.

I felt my own heart do a little flip-flop at the thought of the three kittens. "Their mama had been attacked by a coyote," I explained to Bebe and Monica. "Luckily, we found her and she was able to be healed by the local vet. We fostered the kittens until she could take them back and then we got lucky and a nice family adopted the whole litter and mama. Dude was heartbroken when we had to say good-bye."

"And now I'm crying again." Taylor sobbed into her paper napkin.

"Oh, that is precious," Bebe said. "And it explains Dude's love of Frank." She gestured to the lawn and I turned to see Dude picking Frank up by the scruff of his neck and carrying him around the yard.

"Dude! Drop him!" I ordered. Dude turned to face me with his ears perked and his mouth full of Frank. "Dude." I used my sternest voice and still he just stood there, holding Frank, who at least didn't seem to mind the drool that covered his back. I turned to Bebe. "I am so sorry. I'll go get him."

I was halfway out of my seat when Simon approached Dude. "Now, Dude, is that how we play with our friends?" Dude swiveled his head in Simon's direction. "Put him down, buddy."

Much to my surprise, Dude slowly lowered Frank to the ground and gave Simon his *I'm sorry* head hang. Simon scratched his ears and told him it was okay. Why a man being nice to my dog made me want to swoon, I had no idea, but it definitely did. I sank back into my seat with a sigh.

"Is anyone else finding that ridiculously attractive?" Bebe asked. "I'm asking because I can't tell anymore if it's my hormones or not."

"It is. It totally is." Monica ran a hand through her dark chin-length hair. "There's just something about a man being loving to kids or pets that gets me every time."

"Same," Taylor, Bebe, and I said together.

We watched as Frank nipped Dude's toes and got him to chase him around the yard, much to the delight of the children.

"So, are you and Simon together?" Monica asked.

"No." I shook my head.

"She says they're just housemates," Bebe said. "But I can see the sparks between you two all the way from my house."

The others laughed and Taylor said, "It's true. You do seem to have a connection."

I shook my head. "We're just thrown together by circumstance. Even if there are sparks, it would make sharing the house complicated, besides I don't do relationships."

"Why not?" Monica asked. "You're both in your prime. Maybe you were destined to meet, like a cosmic match made by your grandfathers."

"I'm divorced," I said. "And given how badly that went, I don't have any interest in a serious relationship ever again."

"I'm so sorry, honey." Bebe rubbed my back. "Do you want to talk about it?"

"Nah." I shook my head. "Suffice it to say that when I failed to conceive during fertility treatments, my ex traded me in for what he called a newer model that wasn't defective."

"That bastard!" Bebe cursed while Monica and Taylor gasped.

"Yes." I nodded. "Which is why there will be no situationship of any kind between me and Simon."

A squeal of laughter sounded from the yard and we all turned to see one of Monica's littles putting her pink sun hat on Dude's head. Ever accommodating, he lifted his chin as if pleased with his new chapeau.

"Looks like everyone is going to sleep soundly tonight, the kids and the critters," Stephanie said as she joined us.

"Hallelujah." Monica turned to me. "I may borrow Dude to wear out my three when they need to get their wiggles out."

"He's always available," I said.

The conversation moved to the food. I scored several recipes before it then shifted to warning me about the upcoming tourist season as the Outer Banks was about to get overrun.

Knowing I was supposed to be doing grandfather recon, I tried to steer the conversation in that direction. "I'm surprised Pops stayed here in the summer. He's not a big fan of crowds."

"I think that was the only time Billy and Bobby could stay," Stephanie said. "I thought they'd make the move here permanent after they got married, but—"

"I'm sorry, what?" I asked.

"Billy and Bobby got married." Stephanie studied my face. "You didn't know?"

"No." The brisket that had been so delicious now tasted like cardboard.

"Oh, dear." Stephanie blanched. "I shouldn't have said anything. Pretend I didn't."

"No, no, it's fine," I assured her. It wasn't but I was determined to rally.

"It was a ceremony in name only," Monica said. "It wasn't legally binding. If you want to see what the day was like, there should be a wedding album somewhere in their house. It was my wedding gift to them, as I'm a photographer."

"The album should be in the blanket chest in the guest bedroom," Stephanie said.

"How do you know that?" I asked.

Stephanie grinned. "My husband, Mike, made the chest as a wedding gift for them, and Billy told me he put all of his wedding mementos in it. Mike's hobby is woodworking. And, of course, I baked their cake."

"Luke and I did nothing but attend," Bebe said. "It was a beautiful wedding."

"Same with me and Zach," Taylor said. "I cried when they exchanged their vows but I cry at everything."

She'd cried at my grandfather's wedding. I wasn't sure how to feel about that, other than it should have been me. I shoved the thought aside, not wanting to cause any distress to these new friends. Still, Bebe must have noticed I was upset as she put her hand on mine and leaned close.

"We would have told you about the wedding sooner, but it was clear the day we met you that you and Simon didn't know Billy and Bobby were a couple," she said. "Luke and I thought we could ease you into it."

"And there I went, shooting my mouth off and dropping that news on you like a stink bomb." Stephanie winced. "I'm so sorry, honey. Mike always says if you ask me the time, I'll tell you how to build a watch."

Her regret was so genuine, I forced a smile. "It's all right. I'll look for the album as soon as I get home."

I glanced over at Simon, who had returned to his group of men. It took every drop of self-discipline I possessed not to run over there and tell him what I'd just learned. *Pops and Gramps had been married! Holy banana balls!*

I was tipsy on the walk home. I kicked off my sneakers and carried them in one hand, walking barefoot down the dirt road to the cottage. The hem of my skirt twirled as I spun around to face Simon while walking backward with Dude at my side.

"I really, really, really like the neighbors," I gushed. "I got three recipes for potato salad and one for lemon meringue pie. Did you see the peaks on Stephanie's pie? I've never seen anything that glorious."

"Which one was Stephanie?" Simon's forehead crinkled in thought.

"She's Davis's mom," I said. "She owns a bakery in town called Beach Buns."

He let out a surprised laugh. "Good name."

I spun back around and fell into step beside him. As we approached the cottage, I leaned against him and whispered, "How did your mission go, O'Malley?"

"I believe I got some very interesting intel, Spencer, and you?"

I followed him up the steps and when he opened the door and gestured for me to enter first, I strode inside with Dude at my heels. I had promised myself I would wait to tell him but I couldn't. I genuinely thought I would explode if I didn't tell him right then and there. I turned to face him and said, "They were married."

"Who? Wait. What? No way," Simon said. He sounded shocked and his voice went up with each word. I felt as if I were getting a fleeting glimpse of teenage Simon.

"Hand to God." I raised my right hand as if I were swearing an oath. "According to Monica, the photographer, it wasn't a legally binding ceremony but rather one for just the two of them."

Simon staggered past me and slumped onto the couch. I shut the front door while Dude rested his head on Simon's knee.

"Gramps married? What the hell? When?"

I snapped on the side-table lamp, since we'd gotten our power back a few days ago. "Apparently, they decided to do it right after your Gramps was diagnosed with kidney disease. Steph said the wedding album is in the blanket chest that her husband, Mike, made for the grandfathers, at the end of the bed in the guest room. Let's go find it."

Simon leaned more heavily into the couch. Reluctance sharpened his features and a deep frown line appeared between his dark brows. I was not going to let him refuse.

I grabbed his hand and tugged. "Come on. You have to be curious."

"No, I don't." He resisted. I dug in my heels and pulled harder. Dude, assuming this was a new game, jumped to his feet and barked at Simon.

"Even Dude thinks you should come and help me," I said.

"You're not going to give up, are you?"

"Nope, this album is about your grandfather, too," I said. I gave one more hearty pull and he rose to his feet, the sudden momentum almost sending me toppling, but he caught me around the waist and hauled me back. I found my body pressed up against his and it was like leaning against a brick wall. The man was all lean muscle and he smelled amazing, like the sun and sea with a hint of citrus.

He leaned down as he steadied me and his lips were right by my ear when he asked, "Are you all right?"

I swallowed as the feel of his breath against the shell of my ear made my brain fuzzy and I muttered something brilliant like "Uh-huh," or maybe it was "You smell amazing," or more likely I said nothing at all. I couldn't be sure.

I stepped away from him to gather my wits and turned toward the stairs. "Come on. Don't make Dude haul you upstairs by the scruff of your neck like he did with Frank, because he will."

I grabbed my sneakers from where I'd dropped them and glanced back to see Simon give a side-eye to Dude. Correctly interpreting the look, Dude jumped up and licked Simon's chin.

"Okay, fine, I'm coming." Simon surrendered. He trudged up the stairs behind me, the sound of his footfalls heavy on the carpeted steps.

The freely flowing Chardonnay at the potluck had left me pleasantly fuddled and I knew this was the best headspace to be in to see the life Pops had created for himself, the life he had shut me out of. A flicker of hurt tried to flare to life in my heart, but I snuffed it immediately. This was not about me. This was about Pops.

The windows in the guest bedroom were still boarded up with plywood, awaiting the handyman Luke had recommended, but we'd cleared the room of broken glass and tree debris. Still, I slipped on my sneakers before entering just in case. I glanced at Simon to verify that he still wore his sneakers, too. His were pristine as if they'd just been taken out of the box. Again, I wondered if he ever had much time off from that so-called career of his.

I flicked on the overhead light and crossed to the pretty cedar chest at the foot of the bed. The lid lifted and stayed open, the hinges locking into place. Dude stuck his nose inside, giving it a sniff before allowing me to continue.

Simon crouched down beside me and I glanced at him and said, "Here goes."

The scent of cedar was pungent and I noted the neatly folded woolen blankets, some of which I recognized from Pops's house in Rhode Island.

Simon reached in and removed several of the blankets while I searched the interior. About halfway down, wrapped in a cotton sack was a big square that felt exactly like a photo album.

"I think I've got it." I glanced at Simon in excitement.

I sat back on my heels and opened the cloth sack. It was a white leather wedding album with a picture of Pops and Gramps in a circular silver frame in the center of the cover. They wore white tuxedos and the smile on Pops's face was one of such pure joy, it made my heart ache. I cradled it to my chest as if by hugging it I was hugging Pops.

"Let's look at it downstairs where there's better light," I said. I knew I was going to scrutinize this album like a detective on a true crime show.

"All right." Simon led the way.

I was relieved to have him with me. Coward that I was, I wanted company in this big reveal about Pops's life so that I wasn't alone in feeling left out of the event. Of course, that was assuming that Simon felt the same way.

Dude jumped up on the couch as if he was enjoying this game. I nudged him over with my hip so that Simon and I could share the album. Simon switched on every lamp in the room, giving us a much better source of light.

"Are you ready, O'Malley?" I asked as Simon sat beside me.

He blew out a long bracing breath. "Yeah, I'm good. Hit me, Spencer."

"Tempting offer," I teased.

His mouth lifted slightly in one corner. I wondered if he ever smiled any bigger than that. His was a charming closed-lip smile. It was shy and self-conscious, as if smiling was something that he did so rarely that he wasn't comfortable doing it. That thought made me sad and I wondered what had happened in his life to make him so guarded.

Simon shifted on his seat as Dude pushed him toward me with his back legs as my darling dog eased into a full-body sprawl with his belly in the air and his head hanging over the side. A soft snore escaped him, and I assumed he was exhausted from carousing with Frank and herding children all evening.

I tapped my fingers on the cover just below the framed photo, overly aware of Simon's proximity and the warmth of his skin where his forearm pressed against mine.

"What's the holdup, Spencer?" he asked. "I thought you were eager to see all the pics of the wedding."

"I am." I cringed. "But I can't decide if this is an invasion of their privacy or something they wanted us to see."

"Why not both?" Simon asked. "Gramps was a very circumspect man and given that he never mentioned any of this to me, I can't imagine he wanted to share the details of a relationship that was obviously a private affair to him."

"But Pops wasn't a private man, and although he was very cautious to keep his personal life and his professional one separate, he never withheld anything about what he was thinking or feeling from me. At least, I'd always thought he didn't."

"Maybe it's more about timing." Simon gestured to the album. "They left us, you and me, this cottage and the belongings within it. It seems to me they wanted us to know about this place and their relationship—I'm starting to think you're right about that—but not until after they were gone."

I pondered that for a moment.

"That makes sense," I said. "Otherwise, Pops would have gotten rid of everything before he left it to me . . . er . . . us." I met his gaze for a solid beat before I moved the album so that it rested between us.

I watched Simon take in the framed photo on the cover. He frowned and his jaw clenched. I wondered if the sight of our grandfathers upset him. But his voice was low and gruff with emotion when he said, "They look so happy."

I flipped the cover. The opening shots were of our grandfathers standing on their dock under a portcullis loaded with flowers—the colors were neutral with toffee roses, chamomile, and blush butterfly ranunculus. They were facing each other, the sun glinting on their white and silver hair as they grinned at each other with a love that hummed right out of the photo, encompassing us where we sat.

I would have thought I was just being fanciful, but Simon whispered, "Damn." And I knew it wasn't just me.

I flipped through the pages, taking in the beauty of the day. The overgrown lawn that Dude loved to roll in was perfectly manicured and set with white linen–covered tables and centerpieces made of colorful bursts of wildflowers. Our neighbors—Bebe, Luke, the Pomeroys, the Fisks, Davis and Monica, and Stephanie and Mike—filled the shots. There was so much joy in the pictures, I felt a sharp stab in my chest, but it wasn't a joyous feeling.

More pictures of the groom and groom, pouring mason jars of sand into one large jar, strolling hand in hand along the beach barefoot and with their dress pants rolled up to their knees as the surf washed over their toes, and slow dancing as they gazed into each other's eyes in front of a three-piece band. At the final picture, a romantic shot from behind of our grandfathers sitting on the beach looking out at the waves with their heads pressed together and arms around each other's backs, I slammed the cover of the album shut. It was just too much. I discovered I was pissed.

"You okay, Spencer?" Simon stared at me with his eyebrows raised.

"Nope." I tossed the album onto the coffee table and crossed my arms over my chest. "Not even a little."

"I get it." He patted my knee. "You're mad because they didn't ask you to be the flower girl."

I turned and glared at him. I was certain my nostrils were flaring.

"It's understandable. You would have been adorable in a cute little ballerina tutu–style dress and a circle of flowers on your head."

"Are you making fun of me, O'Malley?" I fumed.

"No, never that." He shook his head with a bogus look of innocence.

"You are," I snapped. "That's fine. I get it. It probably seems irrational that I am devastated that Pops left me out of one of the most important days of his life and not just that, but he never mentioned meeting your grandfather or falling in love or sharing his life with someone for *two decades*—someone he loved enough to marry."

"It doesn't seem irrational and I'm sorry I teased you," Simon said. His voice was gentle, which only annoyed me even more. "I'm not trying to make light of your feelings, but I may have a different perspective on things because of what I learned tonight. Although, given how you're feeling, now might not be the best time to share it with you."

"Oh, no, go ahead," I said. "I can't possibly feel any more shut out of Pops's life than I do now."

An expression of doubt flickered over Simon's face. "All right. According to Davis, Gramps and Pops met here."

I nodded. "Well, that makes sense. They were both fishermen, after all. Was it on a charter boat or something?"

Simon shook his head. "No, it was when they were teenagers."

I felt my jaw drop just a bit before I asked, "What? How? When?"

Simon shrugged. "Davis told me that Gramps told him he met Pops when they were teenagers and they got into a tussle over the same fishing spot."

I blinked. They'd met as teenagers? I wasn't sure what this meant. Had Pops and Gramps been in love back then? Given Pops's age, it must have been in the '60s before he went to college, before he became a reporter, before he met and married Nana.

Nana! Had she known? Was this why they divorced? Did she know that Pops had fallen in love and remarried? And those summer trips we took here when I was a kid, was Pops looking for his long-lost love?

"I am reeling." I leaned forward and clasped my head in my hands. "No pun intended."

"I know the feeling." Out of the corner of my eye I saw Simon lift his arm, and after a slight hesitation, he put his hand on my back as if to steady me. I welcomed the comforting touch. "I almost grabbed you at the picnic and told you, but I didn't want to interrupt anything you might discover and I have to say, you crushed it, reporter lady."

"I think your intel is more compelling than mine," I said. "Mine just confirms that they were in love. We knew that. But to discover that they'd met as young men? That's the stuff headlines are made of. Do you think they kept in touch over the years?"

"I have no idea." Simon removed his hand from my back and I immediately missed his touch. He glanced around the room. "If they did, I imagine there must be evidence of it somewhere in the house. Maybe we'll find something when we start going through their things."

I frowned. "You say 'we' but I feel like you mean 'me,' as in I'm going to be doing the searching. Why don't you seem as upset as I am about being excluded from their life?"

"Whoa, hold up there. You don't know anything about me or my relationship with Gramps," he countered.

"So, tell me then," I challenged him.

He looked uncomfortable as if he hadn't expected me to call him out. Seriously? Of course I was going to ask for specifics.

"Gramps was a crotchety, cranky, surly old duff who, despite not being terribly fond of his fellow man, never missed any of the big moments of my life, which is more than I can say for . . . well . . . it doesn't matter."

Although clearly it did.

"So, you were close?" I asked.

"He was the first person I called about anything—from acing a test to getting arrested," Simon said. "And he always always always showed up."

"Getting arrested?" I repeated.

"Ever the reporter." He made a *tsk* noise that should not have been as charming as it was.

"And?"

"I was sixteen and driving without a license."

I stared at him, making it clear I wanted more details.

"It was a double-dog dare, I had to do it."

"Oh, well, of course you had to." I rolled my eyes.

His eyes widened. "That's exactly what Gramps said and in the same exasperated tone, too."

"Why do I feel like there's more to the story?" I asked.

"Because there might have been a girl involved and getting her to notice me was why I accepted the double-dog dare," he said. "She noticed me, all right, but then I got arrested and her parents wouldn't let her have anything to do with me."

"Heartbreak," I commiserated. "So, Gramps was your go-to guy, but you're really not angry that he didn't tell you about his relationship with Pops, his life here, his marriage, any of it, before he died?"

"I assume he had his reasons."

"Ha!" I pointed my finger at him.

"What?"

"There was hurt in your voice."

He pressed his lips together until his mouth formed a straight line and he shook his head. "No, there wasn't."

"I heard it," I insisted. "Gramps was your first phone call, the guy who was always there for you—your North Star if you want to be poetic about it—and you're totally fine with him not telling you that he was in love, shacking up with someone, and marrying him? Come on, O'Malley, own it."

"All right, fine, I do have feelings about it, but I'm not angry," he insisted. "More like . . ."

"Hurt?"

"No, that's not it, either," he said.

"Then what are you feeling?" I asked. "Because I for one am furious at being shut out. I would have been so happy for Pops. He had to know that. How could he not know that? Why didn't he include me in this wonderful life he'd created? It hurts. It hurts so damn much."

My throat got tight and I felt my eyes dampen. I was not going to cry about this. Not in front of O'Malley, at any rate. Not that I thought he wouldn't be sympathetic but a girl could handle only so much humiliation in one day and, frankly, it had been humiliating to hear about Pops's marriage from a bunch of strangers—very kind strangers—but strangers nonetheless.

Simon lifted his hand as if he would touch me again but then he dropped it back into his lap. "I don't think their life together or their wedding had anything to do with us, Spencer. Their relationship was just for them and they kept it that way. I actually respect that."

"You do?" I reared back to study his face to see if he was bullshitting me. His gaze met mine and he sounded genuine.

"Yeah. We live in a world where everyone shares everything all the time. I don't need to know what this person had for breakfast or where that person is traveling for their vacation. I mean, who cares? We should all be living our own lives to the fullest instead of voyeuristically watching the lives of a bunch of online . . ." His voice trailed off and I studied him with a raised eyebrow.

He pursed his lips and glanced away.

"That came out wrong," he said. "I'm not saying any of that is bad, not really. It's just that the two things we've lost as individuals navigating the world largely through our phones are our privacy and our time, and I think our grandfathers decided they were going to keep both their privacy and their time together sacred, so yeah, mad respect for the old dudes."

Dude's ears perked up at the sound of his name, but he didn't move, didn't open his eyes, and a soft snore was his only reply.

I slumped back against the couch. Simon wasn't wrong. How many times a day did I pick up my phone to see how my posts had been received? How often did I check my numbers, views, likes, comments? Yes, it was my livelihood and I needed to treat it like the business it was, but it took constant vigilance to make certain I didn't cross the line into oversharing just to juice my engagement.

Simon's little speech was lovely, but I didn't believe for a hot second that he was okay with having his grandfather, a man he clearly adored, leave him out of something as monumental as re-uniting with his first love.

I caught my breath. I had to know more about how Gramps and Pops had met. There was a story there, I could feel it all the way to the marrow of my bones. For the moment, I was going to do some recon on the grandson.

"I did a search on you," I said.

Simon's eyebrows shot up.

I pointed to myself and said, "Reporter."

He nodded genially but his expression became instantly guarded. "I suppose I should have expected no less. So, tell me, Spencer, what did you find out?"

Simon

"You have no social media presence." Hannah's voice was bewildered as if she couldn't fathom such a thing.

"I know."

"Is that why your grandfather not sharing his Outer Banks life with you doesn't bother you? Because you're just like him? Extremely private?" As she fired the questions at me, I could almost picture her with a pad and pen or a tape recorder in hand. This was definitely Hannah the reporter in action. Her blue eyes snapped with intelligence and I knew that anything I said would be forensically scrutinized to root out any hidden meanings or subtext. She was studying me as if she were a lie detector in human form. This should have been annoying, instead it was kind of hot.

"Just because I respect Gramps's decision to guard his privacy doesn't mean I'm not bothered or hurt or angry," I said. "Honestly, I haven't known about their relationship for very long so I think I might be in shock. It feels as if Gramps let me in on a secret that I have to keep because my . . ." I paused and cleared my throat. "There are certain members of my family who will absolutely freak out if they find out about this."

"Oh." She nodded. "I see."

"Do you?" I asked. "You said Pops got divorced the same year Gramps was widowed. Do you think your grandmother knew about their past? How would she feel about it if she did?"

"Nana has been happily remarried to my Bonus Grandpa George for many years," Hannah said. "And Nana and Pops remained the best of friends after their divorce. If Pops told anyone about your grandfather, it was her."

"Are you going to ask her about it when they're back from their cruise?" I persisted.

"I don't know." Hannah glanced about the cottage. "I suppose that depends upon what I find here."

"And what about your father or his siblings?" I asked. "How would they handle finding out their father was gay?"

"Dad is an only child and he wouldn't care," she said. "He and Pops were very close and while he'd probably be hurt that he was shut out of Pops's life here—like me—I know Dad would just want Pops to have been happy, which he obviously was. That's why none of this makes any sense to me. Why did Pops keep it a secret when he knew we'd all be happy for him?"

She looked so bewildered and sad that I had a sudden urge to put an arm around her and assure her that it wasn't her or her dad or her Nana that had kept her grandfather from telling them about his life here in Cape Split. But I didn't.

"I'm sorry you're hurting," I said, and meant it. I had a theory about why Pops hadn't told her about Gramps. I knew without a doubt that Gramps had kept his life a secret because of my father, and he had likely asked Pops to do the same so that there was no way my father would find out about them.

Gramps disowned my father when he abandoned me and my siblings after my mom died and took off to start his life over. Being an insurance guy, Gramps had made certain that my mother's life insurance went to her children. My father tried to fight it in court and failed. There was no love lost between my father and Gramps and Gramps knew my father would use the information that Gramps was in a relationship with a man against him in any way he could. So, yeah, I wasn't surprised that Gramps had kept it a secret.

I thought about explaining all this to Hannah, but we'd had a hell of a day and I just wasn't up for reporter Hannah's questions, which would rightly be many. I would tell her, eventually, just not today.

Hannah flopped back against the couch and pressed the heels of her hands to her eyes. "Sorry, grief bomb."

"Don't apologize," I said. "I've had a few of those bombs over the past few months. One minute I'm fine and the next I feel like someone kicked my legs right out from under me."

Hannah dropped her hands and met my gaze. "When Pops first died, I'd get random chest pains that hurt so bad I thought I was having a heart attack."

"Yeah, I literally tried to outrun my grief and ended up tearing my meniscus," I said.

"I'm hearing that as 'exercise is bad.'" She smiled but there was a shadow of sadness in her eyes that made me want to hug her. I didn't.

"I don't suppose you'd be willing to help me search the house tomorrow?" Hannah asked.

"What would we be searching for?"

"Anything that would tell the story of our grandfathers," she said. "Memorabilia, letters, a journal."

"And do you think that will help you come to terms with all of this?" I gestured to the cottage. Maybe if I could help her make peace, she'd be more willing to sell.

"Maybe. I'm not sure. I just want to know more." She tucked her legs beneath her and turned to face me. Her eyes sparkled and enthusiasm lit up her face, dispelling the hurt of just a few moments ago. "Just think, if they fell in love when they were teenagers, there might be mementos of their summer fling before they went to college. How romantic is that?"

"Gramps didn't go to college then. In '67 he shipped out for Vietnam. He went to college on the GI Bill when he came back. If they met that summer, it was right before he left."

Her eyes went wide. "Maybe that's why they never forgot each other. It must have been heart-wrenching for them to part that way, don't you think?"

I shrugged. "I have no idea. Gramps never talked about his time in Vietnam. Ever."

"There's a story there, O'Malley," she said. "And as a reporter, I'm just the person to uncover it."

Was this couch made out of rocks? I tossed and turned, tangling my legs in the blanket. I should have slept in the second bedroom, I supposed, but the plywood in place of the windows had given me coffin vibes.

A sheen of sweat coated my body and I shoved off the light cover, letting my skin breathe. I'd told Hannah to take our grandfathers' bedroom upstairs—chivalry was not dead, not on my watch. Also, self-preservation advised that I didn't want to get blasted by her T-shirt cannon if I startled her by getting up to use the bathroom in the middle of the night.

She and Dude had trotted upstairs shortly after our agreement to search the cottage tomorrow. I hoped Hannah was getting a good night's rest because I sure as hell wasn't. Instead, I was too busy sifting through every memory I had with Gramps, trying to remember if he ever mentioned a person named Billy or a summer at Cape Split or anything that might have clued me in to who he really was.

I hadn't been completely honest with Hannah. I did respect that Gramps had been true to himself and found love during his final years, but I also felt as if I'd never really known the man who had been my hero my entire life. And it bothered me. Like pressing on a bruise to see if it still hurt, I kept thinking about Gramps shutting me and my siblings out of this part of his life. Even knowing that he might have made that choice to protect us from my father initially, I couldn't understand why he didn't tell us in his later years.

I switched on the side-table lamp and reached for the carving of the angry bluebird. Gramps's hands had carved this wood and painted its comically snarky expression. I stared at the bird, willing the grief to come but it didn't. I had shut the pain so forcefully out of my life when Gramps passed that I had yet to shed a single tear. I fell asleep with the bird clutched in my fist as if by holding something he'd created, I could feel Gramps here with me.

The smell of coffee roused me as did the sensation that I was being watched. I wasn't clear which of the two interrupted my sleep first but given the hot breath that ruffled my hair, I was betting it was the staring. I blinked my eyes open to find a big black snout hovering just over my face while Dude stood beside the couch, looming over me.

I jumped with a small yelp that got my heart pumping and

pushed up to a seated position. Dude took this as an invitation to join me.

Hannah entered the living room, carrying two cups of coffee. She set one on the table beside me. “Mornin’, O’Malley. I hope Dude didn’t wake you.”

I glanced from the dog to her. He’d obviously been outside already and she’d had time to brew coffee and get dressed. Today’s outfit was a halter top and shorts and her wavy hair was fastened on top of her head in a sort of hair ball with loose strands that framed her face, softening the look. She’d clearly been up for a while.

“When did you get up?” I reached for the mug of coffee.

“An hour ago . . .” she admitted. “I’m just so excited. There’s so much to discover about our grandfathers and their life together. We need to get cracking.”

I stifled a groan. Barely. “Shower first.” I pushed to my feet and took my mug of coffee into the bathroom. I tried to blast the cobwebs from my brain with a cold shower, as I suspected she’d give me fifteen minutes before she started without me.

Hannah was seated at the kitchen counter with a mug of coffee and a notepad in front of her. She glanced up when I entered and pushed a banana toward me. “Fortify.”

“You sound like we’re preparing for battle.”

“I took a quick glance at the closets upstairs,” she said. “There are many . . . many, many, many . . . boxes.”

“Ah.” I nodded and refreshed my coffee from the pot before peeling my banana.

Dude let out a mournful whimper. Hannah shook her head at him. “No, you don’t like fruit, besides you’ve already had your breakfast, a snack, and a second snack.”

In a bout of drama, Dude dropped to the floor and put his head on his paws with the most woebegone expression he could muster.

I lifted my cup to hide my smile. I wasn't sure who was the more dramatic of the two of them but I had to admit it made for some fine entertainment.

I felt my phone buzz in my pocket and glanced at the display. My sister was texting to check in, no doubt worried because I hadn't texted since my first message when I'd arrived. I shot her a quick note back. There were three memes from my brother, which I immediately replied to, but nothing else of any substance. It struck me then how it used to be me texting Charlie when he went away to college, but now I was the one getting the messages in a complete role reversal.

"Ready?" Hannah set her mug and plate in the sink and turned around to face me.

I stuffed the last of my banana into my mouth and grabbed my coffee. "Lead on."

Hannah was so excited she practically bounced up the stairs with Dude at her side, looking as if he thought we were going on an adventure. I told myself this actually worked out well for me given that I now had an extra set of hands and paws to help me clear out all the stuff.

"Which room should we start in?" Hannah asked when we reached the landing.

"The album was in the guest bedroom," I said. "But the windows are being replaced today so we should wait on that room."

She nodded. "Main bedroom it is."

"What about the attic?" I asked.

She turned in the doorway. "Attic?"

I pointed up at the recessed rectangular door in the ceiling. "Given that there's no basement, they probably used the attic for storage. It'll be too hot to check it later in the day."

Hannah considered me and then the ceiling for a moment. "Attic it is."

I reached up and grasped the handle, pulling down the hatch from which a collapsible ladder unfolded. It creaked and squeaked as if it hadn't been used in ages.

"I don't want to even think about the grandfathers climbing this thing while they were living here." She shook her head.

"Maybe they didn't," I offered. "Maybe the people who owned the house before them were the last ones to use the attic."

"Meaning we'll have to dig through a stranger's stuff?" Hannah wrinkled her nose. "What if it's creepy stuff?"

"Such as?" I straightened the ladder and set it on the floor.

"Doll heads."

"That's the first thing that came to mind?"

"Doll heads are creepy."

"What about taxidermy critters with glass eyes that watch you?"

Hannah bounced back a few steps, almost tripping over Dude. "That's it. You win." She gestured to the ladder. "You go first."

"Me?" I protested.

"You," she insisted. "You came up with the critters. You lead."

"Fine." I glanced away, keeping my smile to myself. I was having entirely too much fun teasing her.

I turned on the flashlight app on my phone and stepped cautiously up the creaky wooden steps, hoping they didn't break under my weight. When my head and shoulders cleared the floor, I swept the light across the attic. It wasn't a large space. I doubted I could even stand upright anywhere but in the center because it was packed. Between this and the bedrooms, we were going to be flat-out sorting for at least a couple of weeks.

"How does it look?" Hannah called from the base of the ladder.

"I have good news and bad news." I turned to look down at her, taking in her eager expression and feeling a flicker of guilt that we were at cross-purposes. "The good news is that the attic is not very big."

"And the bad news is that it's stuffed to the rafters?" she guessed.

"Yeah." I climbed down the steps. "But no dolls' heads or taxidermied critters, at least none that I could see."

"Phew." She blew out a breath. "Okay, there's two of us. We can make quick work of it." She didn't sound any more convinced of this than I was but I didn't call her on it.

The reality was we spent the next two weeks working in the attic every spare second we had around our day jobs. Hannah frequently took afternoons off to film snippets for her online content while I caught up on emails and paperwork and client calls. Mornings, the coolest part of the day, were spent hauling items from the attic to the front porch to be sorted into piles of keep, pitch, or donate.

We were making progress and surprisingly, we even had some laughs in the process. It was late morning and we'd been at it for three hours when I crossed the room to examine an old rolled-up carpet. I poked it with the toe of my shoe and then turned to Hannah, making my face deadly serious. "Spencer, what do you suppose the odds are that there's a body in here?"

Hannah

"Not funny, O'Malley." I frowned at him. A hint of a smile lifted his lips and caused a ridiculous fluttery feeling in the pit of my stomach.

How good this man looked with finger-combed bedhead, a pecs-hugging black T-shirt, and faded jeans, should have been a crime. Needing some space, I went in the opposite direction toward a seamstress's dummy that had a vintage dress pinned to its frame. The pale blue satin was dusty and the lace overskirt had gaping holes as if years of neglect or a moth had eaten away at it.

"I wonder who was making this." I examined the skirt gently between my index finger and thumb. I glanced up to find Simon watching me. I smiled and said, "It's not Pops's color."

His small smile flashed and again I felt dizzy from the impact, which was crazy given that it was such a minimal tip to his lips or maybe it was because his smile was so tiny that it seemed to have more impact. It was as if he was on constant emotional lockdown and getting a sign of amusement from him felt like a huge achievement.

Despite his stoicism, O'Malley had a dependability about him that I liked. He was kind to Dude, even willing to sing to him during a storm. And over the past three weeks, he'd been so understanding, allowing me to grieve and process my loss, which was a major green flag for me.

"I think that carpet predates the grandfathers, don't you?" I was relieved. The thought of having more stuff of our grandfathers' to sort through felt overwhelming. It was much easier to deal with a stranger's possessions.

My unspoken plan had been to soften Simon into seeing this house as an heirloom itself. The last place his grandfather had been happy, and hope that it convinced him we shouldn't sell. Of course, if we didn't sell, we'd have to figure out how to share the house and that could be weird. Would we time-share it as I'd suggested before? He'd get it for six months and then I'd get it for the other. Or could we be housemates? I wasn't sure how I felt about that. The man was too attractive for my own good and I did not do relationships—not that he was interested in one with me, but still.

After my marriage had crashed and burned, I had vowed to be done with long-term relationships. I had yet to meet a man I wanted in my life for more than a week or two, tops. After two months of cleaning out and repairing this house, I was positive I would be tired of Simon's tousled hair, soulful eyes, broad shoulders, the citrus-and-sun smell of him, and how great he was with Dude. Yeah, absolutely, 100 percent sick to death of him, no question.

"Spencer, you all right?" Simon waved at me from across the attic.

"Huh? What?" I asked.

"I think I've found something that might have belonged to our grandfathers."

I hurried across the attic. Plumes of dust shot up from the floor and I sneezed once, twice, three times.

"Bless you." Simon moved aside and pointed to an item tucked behind an old bassinet.

The paint was faded and it was missing wheels but the handlebars and seats were intact. "Is that . . . ?"

"A tandem bike!" Simon announced as enthusiastically as if he'd found bars of gold. Then he smiled at me—with teeth!—and a wicked dimple appeared in his right cheek, causing my brain to flatline. Serious Simon was ridiculously handsome but grinning Simon was dead sexy. I turned away before my condition became permanent.

"You honestly think that belonged to our grandfathers?" I asked.

"It could have," he insisted. "I'm surprised they put it up here, though."

"Why? This is obviously the place where things go to die just like those ancient snowshoes." I gestured to the antique pair hanging on the wall.

Simon left the tandem bike frame and moved over to an old army duffel bag. It had been tossed unceremoniously in the corner and he approached it with caution as if he expected a raccoon to leap out—maybe that was just me. He grabbed the handle and another cloud of dust went up.

"Maybe it isn't theirs," I said. Remembering that his grandfather had shipped out for Vietnam just after he'd met Pops made me nervous that it was Gramps's and that its contents might cause Simon to suffer a grief bomb.

Simon flicked the tag on the bag. The name "Private O'Malley" was typed on the thick paper tag that was yellowed with age. "It's Gramps's."

I put my hand on his arm and squeezed. He glanced at me and I could see the same pain in his eyes that I'd seen in my own mirror over the past few weeks.

"It's probably just his uniform." His voice was gruff and he cleared his throat.

"Right." I hoped my voice sounded encouraging and not worried.

Simon hefted the bag out of the corner and dropped it on the ground at our feet.

The top was a knotted drawstring and he worked at the tie, not making much progress as his hands were squared off and calloused.

"Let me try," I offered. He moved aside and I dug my fingernails into the knot, trying to pry it loose. It took several attempts but finally the cord unraveled and I pushed it back to Simon.

"Thanks." He glanced at me and then at the bag. With a bracing inhale, he pulled the top of the bag open. He used his phone to shine a light into the interior. It looked to be neatly folded fatigues. Just a uniform, then.

Simon emptied the bag, setting the clothing at our feet. When I thought he was done, he reached in and pulled out a dark blue, almost black, leatherette case. Simon popped the lid and we both took in a medal hanging from a purple ribbon with a profile of George Washington on it.

"Oh, wow." I glanced from the box to Simon to gauge his reaction. His face was its usual blank canvas upon which no emotion showed. I forced myself to be patient and let him process.

"Gramps was awarded the Purple Heart for a head injury he received by grenade shrapnel while he was serving as a 'tunnel rat' during his tour as a mechanized infantryman," Simon explained. "He never talked about it, but my father did. He searched Gramps's town house, looking for this." He handed the leatherette case to me and glanced around the attic. "And to think Gramps just shoved it in his duffel and tossed it up here."

"I imagine he had many conflicting emotions about Vietnam." I hoped I wasn't crossing a line by saying as much.

"I wouldn't know. As I mentioned, he never talked about it." Simon shook his head. "When I think about how young he was when he shipped out. Eighteen years old seems like a kid to me. I'm almost twice the age he was when he was sent halfway round the world. He and his battalion were just boys."

I handed the medal back to him. "Will you give it to your father?"

"No." There was no hesitation. "If Gramps had wanted him to have it, he would have given it to him."

Not for the first time, I suspected there was conflict in the O'Malley house. I didn't ask. If Simon wanted to share, he would. It wasn't for me to pick at his festering wounds even though I was absolutely racked with curiosity.

I reached into the bag to make certain it was empty while Simon examined Gramps's uniform. My fingers brushed a piece of paper or cardboard. I gently pulled it out. I went to hand it to Simon but paused when I recognized one of the two young men in the photo.

"Pops," I gasped. Simon dropped the fatigues he was holding and leaned close, his side pressed to mine, and he said, "Gramps."

The photo was creased and faded but I'd know Pops's bigger-than-life smile anywhere. He stood on a pier that I'd seen in Cape Split—*here?*—and he had his arm around the shoulders of the man beside him, who had his arm around Pops's shoulders and was grinning just as broadly. They were in bathing suits standing in front of an old building with a sign that read THE SCOOP. They looked impossibly young and innocent.

"This must be from the summer they met." I turned to look at Simon to see if he agreed. He continued to stare at the photo and nodded. I saw it then, the way his hair flopped over his forehead, the square line of his jaw, and the lean but well-muscled physique.

Simon looked so much like his grandfather—even the dimple that had about knocked me out he'd clearly gotten from the man in the photo.

"No wonder Pops fell for him," I said. Simon cocked his head to the side in confusion. "Gramps was a hottie."

"I don't know about that." He looked uncomfortable.

"I do," I scoffed. "You look just like him."

Simon went perfectly still. His gaze flitted to mine and held me pinned in place with the intensity of his stare.

Oh, shit, shit, shit, did I just say that out loud? I tried to save myself. "Of course, I mean that in a purely platonic nonobjectifying way."

Simon's eyebrows shot up and that imperceptible smile curved his lips, making me dizzy. His voice was low when he said, "So, what you're saying is you think I'm hot."

I rolled to my feet and turned away before he could see my face turn red. Judging by the heat I could feel burning in my cheeks, I was going to have the complexion of an overripe tomato in three, two, one.

"No, I said Gramps was hot. You're like third-generation hot." I glanced at him over my shoulder while trying to hide my face behind my hair.

"But still hot," he said with that damn smile barely curving his mouth.

I refused to engage. I stalked across the attic and began searching the rest of the space. Distraction. I needed a distraction *stat.* If Gramps had put that duffel up here, then there must be more. I found a box of books in the corner and squatted down to flip open the lid. Inside was an old set of Louis L'Amour westerns. I plucked one out and held it up. I tried to make my voice sound breezy and casual. Flustered. Me? Nope, nope, nope. "Was Gramps a reader?"

"Yes, but he was more of a science fiction type of guy." He stood and walked toward me.

"Not military thrillers?" I absolutely did not care what his Gramps read, but I needed to make my embarrassment fade and I was certain small talk this boring would do it.

"No, he said he'd had enough of the military to last him a lifetime, but if you threw a space cowboy at him, he was all over it." He crouched beside me.

"Pops only read nonfiction." I stared into the box as if the musty old paperbacks were fascinating. "Biographies, histories on the Civil War, you know, light reading."

Simon still had the photo in his hand and was studying it. He glanced from it to me and said, "Your Pops was a real looker, too."

My breath caught in my chest. I didn't know what to say, so I said the same thing to him that he'd said to me. "I don't know about that."

His small smile gave way to a grin and the same dimple he shared with Gramps deepened when he said, "I do. You look just like him."

I lowered my head. I didn't know if he was trying to make me feel better about embarrassing myself or if he was just teasing me. Either way, there was no avoiding him when he gently cupped my chin, turning my face to his.

"You have his big blue eyes and his smile, Spencer. It's like a blast of sunshine, all warmth and light." He ran his thumb over my lower lip and I stopped breathing.

"Careful, O'Malley, that kind of talk could go to a girl's head and she might . . ."

"Might what?" He leaned closer until we were just inches apart.

"Kiss you," I whispered, pressing my mouth against his.

This was a terrible idea on so many levels and I was about to throw it in reverse and play the whole thing off as silliness, but then he kissed me back. And it was not just him pressing his mouth to mine, either.

He cupped the back of my head and held me still while his mouth wooed mine with gentle persuasion and a tenderness that made me melt against him. Without breaking the kiss, he shifted out of his crouch, pulling me with him until we were kneeling on the floor, our bodies pressed together.

The feel of his muscle-hardened chest against me made me emit a low moan in my throat. It had been a minute since I'd had any sort of close physical contact and I felt positively starved for affection. Simon slid his mouth across mine and I parted my lips, inviting him in while I moved my hands up his chest, across his shoulders, and into his thick wavy hair. It twined around my fingers just as it had the night of the bat incident.

Simon broke the kiss to run his mouth down the side of my neck, which I arched into. The hum of desire between us was making my entire body throb and not even remotely concerned that we were in a very dusty attic.

Just as I reached for the hem of his T-shirt so that I could run my fingers along his skin, a mournful howl sounded from the floor below. I tried to ignore it, but Dude had clearly run out of patience and either needed to go out or just wanted reassurance that we were okay.

Simon leaned back and blew out a pent-up breath. He tucked a loose strand of my hair behind my ear and said, "It's a good thing I love that dog."

"Same," I said. I popped up to my feet and crossed the attic. The man said he loved my dog. I'd never had a guy say that before. Most of my hookups had tolerated Dude—he is a lot of dog—at best. It felt like this was significant but I wasn't sure how I felt about it. I didn't do relationships and I wasn't prepared to get our lives too entangled. Yeah, like owning a house together wasn't entanglement. I scurried down the ladder as if I were making a getaway.

Dude jumped to his feet when I landed in the hallway. He hurried down the stairs to the back door and it was clear he needed to go out. His timing had never been better. We stepped out onto the deck and into the sweet morning air. I was relieved to discover there was a slight chill from the night before.

My skin was hot and I felt all aflutter on the inside. This was not good. I'd known Simon for only a few weeks and we were at odds about the house. Maybe he was just flirting with me to try to get me to change my mind about selling. He had a pretty enough face to sway a girl into making bad decisions. Ack!

"Come on, Dude!" I ran across the overgrown lawn to the dock. If I needed to plunge myself into the water to cool my overheated reaction to such a small interaction with that man, then clearly I had gone without sex for far too long and it wasn't fair to put that on Simon.

As I strode along the wooden boards, feeling the dock sway beneath me, I rested my hand on Dude's back and took bracing gulps of air. I wasn't going back inside until my head was clear and all traces of my attraction for Simon were expelled.

My ex-husband had done a number on me, of that there was no question. It had been more than five years since our divorce and I had yet to have a relationship of any substance. It was definitely a me problem, but I wasn't going to jeopardize keeping Pops's house over regular sex with a hot guy who might be just as manipulative as my ex-husband. Once bitten, twice shy, and all that.

"Spencer!" I turned to see Simon jogging down the dock toward us. The wooden planks rocked under the force of his stride and I braced my feet wider. Dude left my side to run at Simon in greeting. This time, Simon was crafty enough to have brought one of Dude's toys. He flung the hard rubber ball up onto the lawn and Dude sped past him to go after it.

Simon continued down the dock toward me while Dude searched the high grass, pouncing here and there as he tried to find the orange ball. I couldn't decide if Simon's walk was predatory or not. It was definitely determined. He stopped just a few feet from me and said, "Hey."

"Hey." I had no idea what else to say. Were we going to acknowledge what happened in the attic or not? I'd already made things weird by inadvertently calling him "hot" and initiating the kiss. I was not going to risk making it worse. I'd have to throw myself into the channel and hope it pulled me out to sea if I did.

"I'm sorry if I got carried away. I think your compliment went to my head." Simon met my gaze and held it. His shy smile was self-deprecating when he continued, "I shouldn't have touched you. It was crossing a line, but it'd be a lie to say I don't find you attractive, Spencer. That being said, I can absolutely respect your boundaries and you don't have to worry about me harassing you or making you uncomfortable in any way. Again, I'm truly sorry."

"Don't be. I'm not. And besides, I kissed you first." Was that my voice coming out all breathy? Shiiiiiiit.

Simon

It was official. She was trying to kill me. The sight of her with the sun shining on her wavy curls, her big blue eyes framed by thick dark lashes, and her full lips parted as if in invitation, she might as well rip my heart out of my chest and put it in her pocket.

What was I supposed to do here? We were on opposite sides of what to do with this house in which we would be cohabiting for another five weeks. If we got involved, she would suspect I was doing it to manipulate her into selling the cottage. Then again, how did I know she hadn't kissed me for the same reason, to convince me not to sell? I didn't.

Until we reached a mutually-agreed-upon outcome, where we both got what we wanted with the cottage, there was simply no way we could get involved without one of us getting hurt. And only an idiot would lust for a woman in this situation. Clearly, I was an idiot.

I shook my head and said, "I'm sorry, what did you say?"

She turned away from me to watch Dude in the grass. He'd

found his ball and was now lying on his back holding the ball with his paws. He dropped it into his mouth and then grabbed it with his paws and did it again, delighting in the laziest game of fetch ever.

Hannah cleared her throat. Bright splotches of pink filled her cheeks. Adorable.

"What I meant was there's no need to be sorry. I didn't mind . . ." Her voice trailed off and she gestured to her lips. "It was no big deal."

No big deal? Seriously? The feel of her mouth against mine had hit me with enough volts of electricity to bring me back from the dead, and I'd seen her face. She'd had the half-lidded sultry look of a woman who was feeling the same pull I was.

"Okay." I nodded. "Just so we're clear. I want you to know you're perfectly safe with me."

A vulnerability crossed over her face that told me more than any words could that she had been hurt very badly. The expression was gone almost as fast as it appeared but there was a lot more to Hannah Spencer than she was letting on and I had under five weeks to figure out what it was.

"I know that. I do." She gave me a mischievous side-eye and said, "Plus, T-shirt cannon."

I smiled and it occurred to me that I had done more talking with her in a few weeks than I had with any woman other than my sister in a year. I wanted to touch her again but I kept my hands to myself and said, "Last one back to the house mows the lawn."

She yelped and began to run. The dock was narrow enough that if I wanted to pass her, I'd have to knock her into the water. Instead, I held back, enjoying the sight of a pretty girl jogging up the planks ahead of me, determination in every stride. She came in first, but I felt as if I'd won.

"I did some checking on the place called the Scoop where that photo of our grandfathers was taken," Hannah said. It was mid-afternoon, and after a glance at the sad state of our refrigerator and pantry, Hannah and I had agreed to run into town to stock up on groceries.

"And?" I braced myself. I was beginning to recognize Hannah's *I have news* expression.

"It's still there," she confirmed. "The Scoop is registered as a historic landmark, still owned by the Larson family and still in operation. We should go check it out."

She looked so excited, I couldn't refuse. "Okay, but you know that no one is going to remember two teenaged guys from the '60s, right?"

"I know." She nodded. "But they might remember two older gentlemen from the past two decades. I want to see it, O'Malley. I want to see where they fell in love."

She looked so wistful, I felt my chest tighten. I had the foreboding feeling that if we went ahead with this there would be no turning back. Turning back from what? I had no idea, but I knew that the deeper we went, the more we learned, the harder it was going to be to let go of our grandfathers, the house, and potentially each other.

The Scoop was perched at the base of the town pier. Cape Split was modest in size by any standards, more of a village than a town. There was one main road running through the center and if you blinked while driving, you'd miss it, except for the Scoop. Painted an eye-watering shade of bubblegum pink that was in a sad state of chipped and weatherworn, the squat concrete building looked as if it had thugged its way through so many tourist seasons and hurricanes, it would stand until the end of time.

Hannah parked her van—I refused to call it Buttercup—in the first available spot. She climbed out and opened the door for Dude. He clambered out and she clipped his leash, although it seemed unnecessary the way he walked pressed up against her side. I wasn't sure if he was protecting her or vice versa, but everyone on the sidewalk gave the big boy a wide berth.

We passed several tourist shops, a charter boat office, and the entrance to the large marina. There were restaurants—something smelled amazing—and I realized I was starving. Maybe stopping by the Scoop was genius as it would keep me from shopping while hungry, which never worked out well. I bought the weirdest things like a tub of dill pickles or a whole cheesecake when the hunger was on me.

A seagull perched on a nearby piling startled at the sight of Dude and leapt into the sky, calling out a warning to his feathered friends. Hannah's head was swiveling back and forth as she took in the picturesque village. A narrow strip made up the town green, which had a small playground on one end that was filled with families. A group of children were blowing soap bubbles and I thought fondly of the Fisk children, who looked like a band of lovable pirates compared to these demure little tykes.

Hannah glanced at me and said, "Can you picture Gramps here?"

I paused and she stopped beside me with Dude in between us. I took a moment to picture Gramps from his smelly cigar to his battered fishing hat, except he hadn't looked like that in the photo that was on the table at the house. He'd been a bit more polished.

When I'd peeked into the closet of the main bedroom, the one they had clearly shared, I'd noted that the clothes on what I assumed was his side—determined by recognizing a pair of his favorite sneakers—didn't match the man I had known. To me, Gramps was blue jeans, flannel shirts, and serviceable shoes. But here, he had been polo shirts, Bermuda shorts, and sandals. I couldn't help but wonder which one had been the real Robert O'Malley.

I scanned the waterfront, the park, and the pier. I thought about the man in the photograph and I realized, yes, I could see *that* man here. I turned to Hannah and nodded. "I can. Can you see Pops?"

"Easily." She smiled. "This place is totally Pops's vibe."

"I take it he was a cheerful person." We resumed walking.

"Always." She grinned. "He was definitely the 'if life hands you lemons, reach for the tequila' type."

I could see that just in the time I'd spent with his granddaughter. She had the same fierce optimism. "That's interesting because Gramps was more the 'if life hands you lemons, make sure you know whose eyes to squeeze the juice into.'"

Hannah let out a surprised laugh. "He sounds like a character."

"He was." I smiled. "I miss him every day."

Hannah leaned over Dude and pressed her shoulder against mine. Her voice was soft when she said, "I know exactly how you feel." As we reached the pier, she stopped and turned to me. "Do you think that's what they found in each other? Balance?"

"Maybe." I knew I took after my grandfather with an ingrained cynicism and emotional unavailability. I couldn't imagine spending my life with someone like me. Hannah, with her effervescent personality, certainly seemed like an antidote and I suspected Gramps felt the same way about her Pops.

The Scoop offered a dog-friendly courtyard with brightly painted picnic tables. Hannah chose one under an umbrella that was a vibrant shade of turquoise. A waitress with a name tag that read "Kayla" came by with two menus and paused to pat Dude on the head as he lolled on the ground at Hannah's feet.

"They have food here, too, but the ice cream is what everyone raves about," Hannah said. She studied the building and pulled the photograph we'd found in Gramps's duffel bag out of her pocket. "Where do you think they were standing when this was taken?"

I took the photo from her and held it up, trying to match the view of the building in the photo to the one beside us. There was a mural of enormous cones and bowls of ice cream with a cherry on top the size of Dude in the old photo. The faded picture didn't do justice to what the mural must have looked like, and the dormant artist in me wished I could have seen it back in the day. There was no mural on the wall now, just the relentless blistering pink, but the view of the pier and the water was the same.

"I think it was over there," I said. "See how the corner of the building matches."

Hannah took the photo back and studied it. "You're right. It had to be right there." She turned to me and her eyes sparkled. "Isn't this amazing? Almost sixty years later and we're in the same spot where our grandfathers met and fell in love."

Nothing about my trip to the Outer Banks had gone as expected. Certainly not the cottage, not her, and not this alternative life that Gramps had led. It was a lot to take in and, yet, Hannah's enthusiasm was impossible to dismiss.

"It's pretty crazy," I agreed.

"Hi, are you ready to order?" Kayla returned with a wide smile and another pat for Dude, who was clearly smitten with the cheerful teen as he leaned into her touch as if he never received any sort of affection at home. The big faker.

"I'll have the triple-threat hot fudge sundae, please," Hannah said. "With scoops of rocky road, coffee, and butter pecan. Oh, and extra whipped cream." She tipped her chin and cocked an eyebrow. "Beat that."

I straightened up in my seat and turned to Kayla and said, "And I'll have the five-alive sundae with scoops of strawberry cheesecake, pistachio, black raspberry, almond fudge ripple, and banana, also with extra whipped cream and hot fudge."

"Impressive." Hannah raised her eyebrows innocently as if she hadn't just issued a challenge.

Kayla grinned and glanced down at Dude and said, "Would you like a scoop of our special peanut butter frozen treat for good doggies?"

Hannah glanced down at Dude. "Yes, please. I will never be forgiven if I neglect him."

"Excellent. I'll put your order in."

Kayla left and Dude, looking forlorn, watched her go. I patted his head. "Don't worry, she'll be back."

Dude licked my wrist and settled down to wait.

I glanced around the patio and wondered when was the last time Gramps and Pops had been here. Had this been their special place? And given Gramps's poor health at the end, did they know on their last visit that it would be their last? Ugh. That went dark fast. I shook my head.

"What are you thinking about?" Hannah asked.

I thought about not telling her, but realized she was the only person who might understand. "Gramps died due to complications of kidney failure. He knew his time was limited. I was wondering if he knew on his last visit to the Scoop that it would be—" I hesitated but Hannah finished my thought.

"His last?"

"Yeah." We were both quiet for a beat. "What caused Pops's passing?"

Hannah frowned. She glanced down and ran her finger over the brightly painted tabletop. "He didn't have a preexisting condition, if that's what you mean." She glanced up and her eyes were filled with sadness when she said, "During his final months, he just seemed to give up the will to live and then one night, he went to bed and didn't wake up."

"Was there an autopsy?" I felt like a ghoul for asking but I had a theory that I wanted to avoid saying if I was wrong.

"There was and they couldn't find anything wrong with him." Hannah's voice wavered a bit. "They said his heart gave out but they couldn't find a reason for it."

"Do you think he died of a broken heart?"

She glanced up at me, blinking back some tears. "It never occurred to me until I got here. But after learning about his relationship with Gramps, I think maybe he did."

Kayla returned with our ice cream. Mine looked like a fishbowl stuffed with ice cream, making Hannah's seem dainty in comparison. Dude got a paper cup with one big scoop, which Hannah held while he attempted to lick it clean.

I picked up my spoon and tucked into the dish, thinking about Gramps's final days. He'd been failing for some time but refused to give up his weekends at his fishing sanctuary and now I knew why. This was where his real family was. I felt a pang of hurt and recognized it as the same thing Hannah had felt when we looked at their wedding album.

Gramps had returned home to attend one of his former company's parties. It was always a lavish shindig as Pete Billings, his former partner and my current boss, enjoyed celebrating what he called "the company's wins" in his massive mansion in Raleigh.

In the middle of the party, Gramps had called me over to sit with him. I was happy to as other than Charlie and Lor, he was the only person I genuinely liked at the party.

He handed me a stinky cigar and we puffed the pungent smoke out over the veranda as we watched agents and potential clients schmooze their way around the garden like sharks in an aquarium tank, restless, hungry, and looking to make a killing.

"Make me a promise, kid," Gramps demanded.

"Anything," I agreed without hesitation.

Gramps pointed to Pete with the tip of his lit cigar and said, "Don't become that."

"I'm sorry?"

"Don't get me wrong. I love Pete. He and I busted our tails to build this business together, but this isn't for you. You're better than this. Get out. Go back to your art and live the life you were meant to have before I pulled you into this business." Gramps turned and met my gaze with a steely one of his own.

"You didn't pull me in," I protested. "You offered me a career and a steady paycheck."

"You weren't supposed to make it your life," Gramps reminded me. "It was supposed to be temporary."

I'd felt called out. I knew I'd let go of my passion but I hadn't really had a choice, which Gramps knew. "You know why I can't."

"You can. You just have to want it badly enough." Gramps turned away and resumed watching the sharks swim.

After the party, on his way to his room, Gramps collapsed. He was found by the housekeeper and rushed to the hospital, but he never woke up. I wondered now how Pops had learned of his partner's passing. To not be there, to not be the person by his side at the end, had to have been a crushing blow. Even Gramps's funeral had been overseen by me and my sister. Per his request, Gramps had been cremated and placed in the mausoleum beside Granny. I didn't even know if Hannah's Pops had been at the service.

I swallowed a gigantic scoop of ice cream and was immediately punished with a brutal spike of brain freeze. I clapped a hand to my forehead, waiting for the angry throbbing to pass.

"You okay?" Hannah asked.

"No." I shook my head. "Honestly, I feel unsettled about a lot of things."

"Such as?" She licked a dollop of hot fudge off her lip and I almost lost my train of thought.

I stuffed a spoonful of banana ice cream into my mouth to regroup. Then I put down my spoon and described the day of Gramps's death to her. Her brow furrowed and her big blue eyes welled with tears.

"I hate the thought that Gramps and Pops were separated again at the end. I think losing Gramps for a second time was just too much for Pops to bear," Hannah said. "Maybe they left the house to us so that their love wouldn't be forgotten."

"I think you may be right, Spencer."

When Kayla stopped by to check on us, I borrowed the photograph from Hannah and showed it to her. I asked Kayla if she knew the two men and she shook her head. Not a big surprise, given that the photo was sixty years old.

Hannah took out her phone and showed Kayla a picture she'd taken of the framed photo in the living room. Kayla's eyes brightened and she said, "Billy and Bobby? Of course I know them. We all do . . . did." Her face fell and she looked crushed. "I'm sorry. One of our regulars recently told us that they'd both passed. It's just so sad. The Scoop won't be the same this summer without them stopping in for their evening cone."

Hannah put her phone down and Kayla reached for the old photo. "Is this the two of them when they were young?"

"Yes," Hannah said. "We found it in their house."

"Do you mind if I show it to Tim? He owns the Scoop and I think he'd get a kick out of seeing a picture of the place from so long ago."

Hannah waved to her sundae and said, "Go ahead. We'll be here for a while."

Kayla clasped the photo and turned away. I watched as she ducked back into the ice cream shack. I must have looked worried because Hannah reached across the table and patted my arm. "Don't worry. I took a photo of the picture with my phone as a backup."

"Smart." I scooped in more ice cream.

In moments, a tall red-faced man in a white T-shirt with a red apron and a blue baseball cap on his balding head came out of the building. Kayla was with him and pointed to our table. He headed straight for us. At a glance, he looked to be well into his seventies—old enough to have known Gramps and Pops as a youth?

I glanced at Hannah and saw the excitement on her face. She was definitely thinking the same thing.

"Hi, I'm Tim Larson." The man shook Hannah's hand and then mine. "I own the Scoop."

"It's so nice to meet you," Hannah said. "I see Kayla showed you the picture."

"Billy and Bobby. I remember when this photo was taken." Tim glanced at the photo in his hand.

I slid down my bench and gestured for Tim to sit. Dude immediately pressed his head onto Tim's knee and the man rubbed Dude's ears while he talked.

"Summer of '67," he said, his voice thick with nostalgia. "It was the first year my dad let me work full-time and I spent all day every day here. I was trying to save up for a car. Billy and Bobby were two of our regulars. I heard they got into a fight over a fishing spot around the point and the next thing we knew they were inseparable. This place does that to folks."

"Does what?" I asked.

"Helps people figure out what's important to them," Tim said. "For me, it was easy because I was born and raised here and knew I'd own the Scoop one day. For other folks, they come here and find the part of themselves that's been missing. Not to sound like the local chamber of commerce but there's no place like summer at the Split."

"Do you think that's why they came back after so many years?" Hannah said. "To find themselves again?"

"I'd say they came back to find each other." Tim glanced between us as if trying to figure out how we knew Billy and Bobby.

I decided to help him out. "I'm Bobby's grandson and she's Billy's granddaughter."

"You don't say." Tim looked delighted. "I'd heard that they'd both gotten married and had families before . . . well . . . before they came back." He paused and glanced between us and tapped the picture with his finger. "It was a different time back then. Young men couldn't . . . follow their hearts so freely as they do now."

Hannah and I exchanged a glance. Tim was confirming everything we'd suspected. Our grandfathers had been in love in the summer of '67 and they'd had to let each other go.

"I want to give you both my condolences." His voice was gruff when he added, "They were good men and they'll be sorely missed."

"Thank you," Hannah and I said together.

Tim nodded and dabbed at his eyes with the corner of his apron. "I haven't thought of that mural in years. We painted over it in '85 after Hurricane Gloria came through. She blasted it so hard, there wasn't much left."

"It is a great wall for a mural." I nodded.

Tim slowly turned to me. "That's right. You're an artist. Would you be interested?"

Out of the corner of my eye, I saw Hannah's head turn in my direction. I didn't look her way. My art career was in the past and I didn't want to answer any questions about it. Not from her, not from anyone.

"I don't really do that anymore," I said.

"What?" Tim pushed his baseball hat back on his head and a frown wrinkled his brow. "That's a shame. Bobby used to brag about you all the time. He even brought your book around to show everyone."

"Book?" Hannah asked.

"It was nothing," I said at the same time Tim said, "It's a children's book and it won an award."

"What award?" Hannah's curiosity was fully engaged. Shit.

I felt my face getting as red as Hannah's had earlier. I didn't answer but Tim did.

"The Caldecott," Tim said. I would have been impressed that he knew of it if I wasn't so completely caught off guard. I didn't know what rocked me more, that Tim knew the name of it or that Gramps had bragged about it. I felt my lips tip up in one corner.

"You're a Caldecott winner?" Hannah asked. It was clear she knew exactly how prestigious it was.

"Didn't win." I shook my head. "Honorable mention."

She rolled her eyes and said, "Like that isn't huge."

Tim glanced between us and placed the photo on the table. "I won't pressure you. But I've seen your work and you could do amazing things with that space. The wall is yours if you want it, and I'll pay you well."

"You have to do it," Hannah said at the same time I said, "Thank you, but those days are behind me."

Tim glanced between us and said, "Don't make a decision now. Think it over. Think of it as something to do for your grandfather."

Well, hell. He had to put it like that.

"You know where to find me when you decide." Tim tapped the picture on the table and rose from his seat. He started toward the shack. Halfway there, he turned around and said, "Your ice cream is on the house. Any family of Billy and Bobby is family of the Scoop."

Hannah

By the time we left the ice cream stand, I was rocking a solid ice cream baby. Maybe three scoops had been one too many, but I had no regrets. We hit the local grocery store. It was small but carried the essentials—coffee!—with only three brands to choose from, so it made the decision-making simple.

I refrained from grilling Simon about his art career but it was a struggle. I reviewed what I'd learned. He'd illustrated a children's book—maybe more?—it had won a Caldecott Honor—which was huge!—and something had happened because he'd said his artist days were in the past. If it was possible to die from curiosity, I was certain I'd be on life support.

When we arrived back at the cottage, a very muddy, very red Jeep Wrangler with the top off was parked in front and I wondered if our attorney had arrived to tell us this whole thing was a mistake and the cottage belonged to someone else, but I couldn't picture Vincent Cosmo of the pristine suit and haircut driving a Jeep.

Despite my usual optimism, I tended to be cautious when

positive things—like inheriting an actual house—happened and I stayed on alert for the good fortune to be snatched away. I considered it a trauma response from my short-lived marriage and journalism career.

"I wonder who's here." I parked in the driveway and glanced at Simon.

"I know who it is," he said. "That's my car."

"Oh?" I hoped he'd elaborate but he didn't. Instead, he exited the van and strode toward the front porch. A woman was seated on the steps and she hopped up and threw herself at him. Simon scooped her up in a crusher hug and a wave of intense disappointment swamped me.

I thought Simon had said he was single. Immediately, my brain flashed to my ex's cheating, which of course was ridiculous because Simon and I were just housemates, so there was no cheating happening but still. I felt as if I'd briefly been offered something unique and special—the man and I had rescued a bat together, after all, and he'd understood my grief about Pops in a way no one else had, plus, he'd kissed me—only to have it snatched away.

I climbed out of the driver's seat and slid open the back door for Dude. "Be nice. Don't knock the strange lady down." I hoped I sounded like I meant it more than I felt it.

Dude bounded across the yard. Now, I'm not saying I judge people by their reactions to dogs or by the dog's reaction to them, but when the woman tossed back her long dark hair and crouched low with open arms to embrace Dude, well, my annoyance with her dissipated. At least Simon had the good sense to pick a dog lover.

"Aren't you handsome?" The woman immediately found Dude's favorite spot on the side of his neck and while she scratched, his eyes rolled back into his head and he looked like he might pass out. "What a good boy. You're just perfect, aren't you?"

"Please, you're going to give him an ego as big as his paws," I said. I was only partly kidding.

She glanced up at me and grinned. She looked familiar and a second later it punched me in the face that the arching brows, long nose, deep dimple in one cheek, and full lips were exactly like the ones on the face of the man standing next to her. This was Simon's sister.

"Well, he is a perfect specimen so he really can't help it," the woman said.

"Lorelei, this is Hannah Spencer," Simon introduced us. "Hannah, my little sis—"

"Not little," Lorelei interrupted. She *was* on the tall side. "Younger. I'm your younger sister."

"You didn't care about being called younger before," Simon protested.

"That was before I turned thirty," she said. "Now we emphasize 'younger' at every opportunity."

I laughed. I liked her.

"Fine. Lor is my *younger* sister." Simon gestured to the house. "Do you want to come in?"

Lorelei glanced between us, much like the neighbors had, as if trying to figure us out. I realized Simon hadn't told her about me or the shared inheritance and I figured he might want to talk about that with her in private.

"I'll unload the groceries if you want to give your sister a tour," I said.

"I'll help first." Simon grabbed both bags of groceries from the van and headed toward the house. Well, then.

"So . . ." Lorelei and I fell into step on the walkway while Dude "assisted" Simon. "How long have you and my brother known each other?"

"A few weeks," I said.

"Weeks? I'm sorry, did you say weeks? And you're both living here?" Her eyes were wide with surprise.

"Yeah." I didn't add any details, not wanting to step into any family stuff so I nodded and hurried up the walkway, opening the door for Simon and gesturing for Lorelei to follow him inside.

I trailed Simon to the kitchen and said, "I'll unpack. You can show her the dock." He frowned and I stared at him. "You should probably explain." I gestured between the two of us and he made an O with his mouth as he finally caught on.

"Right." He nodded. "Lor, let me show you the dock so you can be assured that I've taken excellent care of your boat."

I reached for a bottle of wine and poured a glass. As Lorelei walked by the kitchen counter, I offered it to her. "It's a Chardonnay."

"Thanks." She took the glass and followed Simon outside. Dude watched them go, looking as if he wanted to join them, but I said the magic word "supper" and he was properly diverted.

I fed Dude and unpacked the groceries. I thought about cooking but wasn't sure if we were going to be setting another place or not, so I paced and sipped my wine and wondered how Lorelei was taking the news that her Gramps had been in love with my Pops. This was assuming, of course, that Simon even told her. I would be sure to take my cue from him when they returned.

Simon hadn't mentioned why he was the only person his grandfather had left the cottage to. Judging by the hug he and Lorelei had shared, there wasn't any animosity there. Not many families would be okay with only one grandchild inheriting a property. But then, what did I really know about Gramps? Simon had said he'd fought in Vietnam and opened a successful insurance company with a friend; maybe he'd left other equally valuable possessions to Simon's siblings so there was no need for squabbling.

Feeling peckish, which was hard to rationalize as anything but nerves after the ginormous sundae I'd had, I began to put together a cheese-and-cracker spread with grapes and pickles and other nibbles. It gave me something to do and Lorelei might be an emotional eater in need of something to nosh when she heard the news.

Simon and Lorelei returned just as it was getting dark. Dude bounded off the couch to greet them and instead of pushing him away, Lorelei hugged him close. Dude was excellent at emotional support despite being the size of a pony.

"Hungry?" I gestured to the tray. Lorelei sank onto one of the tall chairs at the counter.

"I can always eat." Lorelei helped herself to some cheese and crackers and a pickle—solidifying my affection for her.

Simon refilled Lorelei's glass and then mine before grabbing a beer. He raised his bottle and said, "To Pops and Gramps."

"Pops and Gramps." Lorelei and I tapped our glasses to his before we all sipped.

"Simon says you had no idea about this arrangement, either." Lorelei gestured to the house.

"Not a clue," I confirmed. I wondered if he'd told her everything. I pushed my wine away, not wanting it to loosen my tongue and spill the family secrets, and reached for some crackers.

"Given that our father can be a complete prick about the lives of others, it's not really a surprise that Gramps kept his relationship with your Pops a secret," Lorelei said.

Okay, then. I pulled my wineglass back. I glanced at Simon and his face was set in its usual impossible-to-read emotionless expression.

"I'm sorry," I said. "That has to be difficult."

"Mostly for Sim—" Lorelei began but her brother cut her off.

"It's none of Dad's fucking business, and I'm going to keep it that way," Simon said. He took a long pull of his beer as if to cool the flare of temper he'd just let loose. It was the most emotion I'd seen from him and my face must have reflected my surprise as he met my gaze and immediately shifted back to his blank face.

There was a beat of silence before Lorelei reached over and gave her brother a half hug. "Which is one of the many reasons why Gramps chose you to inherit his sanctuary. He knew you'd protect it, and I bet he also thought you needed a safe space from all of the responsibility you insist on carrying all by yourself." Her gaze bored into her brother's. "You know I'm doing fine as a fully realized grown woman, right? And Charlie is doing great, too. You can loosen your grip on things."

Simon closed his eyes. "Sorry for the outburst. Our father, per usual, brings out the best in me. I know you and Charlie are doing fine." He didn't sound as if he knew that at all. "You're the two most important people in the world to me, so you'll just have to cope with my concern for your well-being."

Lorelei shook her head and I got the feeling this was a discussion they'd had many times before. "In other news and speaking of our brother," Lorelei said, "Charlie wants to come see you."

Simon nodded. His expression didn't change but there was something in his eyes that I couldn't interpret. It looked like pain. I checked the urge to put my hand on his in reassurance.

"When?" Simon asked.

Lor shrugged. "On Charlie time. Could be tomorrow or next year."

Again, Simon showed no emotion but I could feel something was off. Still, I didn't move. I was getting so much information about the O'Malley family; I didn't want to draw any attention to myself and break the moment. I needn't have bothered.

Simon met my gaze and said, "I apologize in advance for whatever my brother says or does when he arrives."

I lifted my eyebrows and said, "Should I hide in the attic?"

"No." Lorelei shook her head. "Charlie is okay, he's just—"

"Charlie," Simon interrupted.

"Yeah," Lorelei agreed.

And this time I saw the same pain in her eyes that I'd caught a fleeting glimpse of in Simon's. Having never had siblings, I'd often felt like I was missing out. Now I was feeling pretty good about flying solo for my formative years. It seemed a lot less complicated.

"I'd stay and we could have a sibling reunion, but I have to get back to my patient." At my questioning glance, she said, "I'm a nurse, specializing in elder home care."

"You're spending the night." Simon crossed his arms over his chest.

Lorelei lifted an eyebrow. "Bossy much?"

"It's late. I haven't seen you in weeks, plus you're on your second glass," he said.

"My staying depends upon one thing," Lorelei said.

"Which is?" Simon asked.

"What's for dinner?" she asked.

"I just happen to be making my famous crab boil." Simon gestured to the kitchen. "Which means you two need to vacate and give the culinary genius some room to work."

"Say no more," Lorelei said. "I never miss a boil."

I picked up the bottle of wine and Lorelei grabbed the cheese and crackers. Together, we retreated to the living room, where Dude was delighted to join us.

While Simon banged away in the kitchen, Lorelei told me about her work and why she'd left Raleigh to live on the Outer Banks. It was the wild horses.

"I was a horse girl," she said. "Absolutely obsessed with them."

"Me, too," I said. "I had riding lessons every week for years. It was my parents' compromise for not buying me my own pony, which was on my birthday wish list every year from age six to sixteen."

"So rude of them," Lorelei commiserated. "I had a horse but my father sold him after my mother passed away and we moved into the city. I was twelve."

I felt my chest get tight. To lose her mom and her horse had to have been devastating to a twelve-year-old. Why would her father do that? I wondered how old Simon had been. He must have been barely a teen. I wondered if his mother's death was what caused him to be so emotionally closed off. My heart hurt for him. Bit by bit, I was getting a picture of the O'Malley patriarch that was far from pleasant.

"The lure of the wild mustangs helped fill the void?" I asked.

Lorelei grinned. "Exactly." She told me about working with the rescue outfit and I instantly knew that seeing the mustangs of Carova Beach was a top priority for the travel blog. I had the content from Kitty Hawk and the Hatteras lighthouse for the upcoming week but I needed to make a few more videos if I wanted to maintain my income, unless I sold my half of the cottage and used that money to live on. I glanced around the living room. No, that wasn't an option. I was still holding out hope that I could convince Simon not to sell.

Dude abandoned us once the cheeseboard was empty, opting to supervise Simon in the kitchen. I could hear Simon talking to him. "You don't want to get on the wrong side of that guy. He'll pinch your nose."

Lorelei was watching me and I realized I was smiling like a doofus. I tried to cover it and said, "Simon's really good with Dude."

She nodded and glanced at the kitchen. We could just see a glimpse of Simon through the doorway. "I haven't seen him this relaxed and happy in years."

"This is happy?" I asked.

"For Simon, he's practically ebullient."

I glanced from her to the kitchen, where I saw Simon sneak a chef's bite to Dude. Simon's mouth was curved up just slightly as he took in the dog, who was wagging like a fool, and I felt my heart turn over at the sight of them. Ridiculous.

"Has he always been . . ." My voice trailed off. I wasn't sure how to describe O'Malley in a gentle way to his sister.

"Somber? Serious? Stodgy?" Lorelei offered.

"Somber and serious," I agreed. But when I thought of his kiss, I had to reject *stodgy*.

Her expression became remote as if she was recalling a different Simon, and when she glanced back at me, her eyes were sad. "No, he wasn't but life happened." She didn't say any more so I approached from a different angle.

"I heard he was an artist," I said.

Her eyes went wide. "He told you?"

"No. I heard it from someone here who said that Gramps bragged about it."

Lorelei nodded. "We were all so proud of him, well, most of us were." She glanced at her brother in the kitchen with sad eyes. "He made the decision to walk away from his art and while I understand why I really wish he could have found another way."

Before I could ask any questions, Simon called us to dinner. The crab boil was amazing. With corn and potatoes and Old Bay Seasoning and plenty of melted butter, I hadn't eaten this well in a really long time. Simon and his sister were funny and charming and clearly fond of each other. When Lorelei started to droop at the table, Simon sent her up to his room to sleep. I started on the dishes and Simon joined.

"You cooked, I clean," I said. "Those are the rules."

"Whose rules?" He took the rinsed plate out of my hand and put it in the dishwasher.

"Mine," I said. "Because if I cook, I'm not doing the dishes."

"We had a guest tonight so I think sharing cleanup is only fair."

"I'm not going to fight you over it." I handed him more plates and he loaded the dishwasher with an engineer's efficiency.

We worked silently until the questions bubbling to the surface inside of me demanded release. "Are you as close to Charlie as you are to Lorelei?"

He was silent for so long I didn't think he'd answer.

"I'm sorry. It's none of my busi—"

"In a different way, I suppose I am."

"Oh." I wanted so badly to grill him, but I didn't.

"It could be my perception of things—being the middle child and all. Charlie was the star of the family. The son of my father's heart."

"Then what were you?" I asked, feeling a surge of anger that a father could favor one son over the other.

"The spare," Simon said.

"That sucks." Now I was furious.

"It was what it was. Charlie was smart, handsome, charming, athletic, and he excelled at everything. It wasn't just my father who worshipped him, everyone did, especially me as a younger brother who had none of those qualities."

I stared at him for a beat. "You're joking, right? I see all of those traits in you."

He flashed me a shy smile and said, "Trust me, I was none of those things growing up."

"But you're close to Lorelei?"

Simon shrugged as he arranged the silverware in the rack. "Little . . . excuse me . . . younger sisters are a different dynamic than older brothers."

"Only child here, so you have to enlighten me." I washed the final pot and handed it to him.

"To be blunt, Charlie's life didn't work out exactly as planned and now he's . . ."

I stared at him, waiting.

"He's different." Simon finished drying the pan and placed it in the cupboard below the counter.

"Different?" I repeated. "That sounds relatable."

"Charlie isn't like you."

"No?"

"No, he's unchecked exuberance and no impulse control and he's given me premature gray hair."

I glanced at his scalp. "I didn't see any when I examined your scalp the other day."

"You were looking for guano not grays." Simon bent forward so his hair was in front of my face. Then he pointed to the top of his head. "There. See?"

It was simply too much temptation to resist. I knew how soft his thick dark waves were and I reveled in the feel of them between my fingers.

"Well?"

"Um . . . no . . ." I ran my fingers through his hair and then I saw one. A single silver strand amid the dark brown. Naturally, I plucked it.

"Ouch!" Simon reared back.

I held the silver hair up and said, "I only saw the one and now it's gone."

"That's only because I haven't seen Charlie in a while. He has a gift for turning my hair gray." A shadow passed over his face that resembled guilt.

"Maybe he's changed since you last saw him," I said. "Maybe he won't be such a handful."

"Unlikely." Simon took the gray hair from my fingers and considered it before dropping it in the trash bin.

He faced me and I could see the muscles tighten in his jaw. I had a feeling I was getting only the annotated version of events but that was okay, we had weeks for him to share whatever he wanted about his family, and if Charlie did arrive at the cottage, I would be able to see firsthand what the situation was.

"So, you and Charlie had a 'Prince William and Prince Harry, the heir and the spare' thing going?" I refilled my wineglass and grabbed another beer for Simon. "I had no idea I was in the presence of royalty, O'Malley."

He gave me a mock bow as he took the bottle and said, "I give you leave to address me as Your Highness."

"My lord honors me with his assistance in the scullery." I curtsied and he reached out and grabbed my free hand with his. The warmth of his fingers around mine sent the same jolt of awareness I always felt at his touch.

"My lady." He lowered his voice as he lifted the back of my hand to his lips. "Thou art too fair a maiden to toil in foul dishwater."

I laughed in delight. The fact that the man could pivot from familial angst to converse in mock medieval tongue was ridiculously charming.

I took my hand from his and rested the back of it against my forehead, arching my back in a pose of feminine distress. "Such flattery. Take caution, kind sir, lest I expire in this very spot from a fit of the vapors caused by your flowery utterances."

Simon snorted, and I could not have been more pleased to be the cause of it. He tried to wipe the amusement from his face but he couldn't and instead he reached for one of the white dish towels. "I surrender. Fair maiden has bested me in this battle of witlessness."

I laughed, feeling a rapport building between us that was more than attraction. I genuinely liked this man. It occurred to me that as much as I loved Dude, and I truly did, I had missed this. Having someone to eat with, talk to, and be ridiculous with was . . . really nice. I led the way to the living room and joined Dude on the couch while Simon took the adjacent recliner.

"So, real talk," I said. "Given that I was trained as a journalist, you won't be surprised to learn that I have boundary issues—as in, I don't have any."

"I've noticed." That small shy smile of his appeared and I glanced away before I got distracted.

"Do you love your current career?" I continued.

"I work for the insurance company that Gramps founded with his friend Pete Billings when he got back from Vietnam," he said. "Loving what I do was never a consideration."

"It could be," I said. "I mean, if you don't enjoy it, why not change it?"

"It's complicated," he said.

"In what way?"

"For a variety of reasons, but the main one is that when my mother died, my father ditched us to start over in Florida, leaving us penniless."

I nodded. I knew what that felt like. Simon tipped his head to the side and studied me. "What?"

"Nothing," I said. "I just know how that feels."

He waited, clearly wanting me to continue but the shame of being kicked to the curb by my husband for not being able to conceive wasn't something I wanted to talk about. Not now. Not ever. "Do you ever hear from your father?"

"Only when he wants something," Simon said after a beat. "Gramps became our guardian until Lorelei turned eighteen. We were surviving, we all worked hard for scholarships and Gramps was an excellent provider. We never wanted for anything. It looked like everything was going to be all right. But when Charlie's life derailed, Gramps took on the care of Charlie until I insisted on taking over when Gramps's health started declining," Simon said. "Gramps was ready to retire, so I took a job at his insurance company and have slowly worked my way up. An art career can't provide the steady income and benefits I need to make to care for my brother."

"Is that why you want to sell the cottage?" I asked.

He met my eyes and slowly nodded. "The profit from the sale would guarantee that Charlie was taken care of no matter what might happen to me or, heaven forbid, Lor."

Well, hell. I let out a slow breath. How could I oppose a man wanting to take care of his brother? I understood, I did, but the part of me that didn't want to give up the place my grandfather had left to me stubbornly hoped there was another solution besides selling. I decided to put the topic aside for now.

"What about Lorelei?" I asked. "Does she help?"

"She wants to," Simon said. "But she's still paying off some student loans from nursing school. I told her that we can talk about it when she gets ahead of things. After Gramps died, she threatened me with physical violence if I didn't start letting her share some of the responsibility." He shook his head. "For a nurse, she is savage."

"You're a good brother," I said. He shrugged. "Why do you suppose your father and grandfather are so different? Your dad disappeared but your grandfather stepped up?"

He considered the question and rubbed his jaw with the back of his hand. "Who knows? My father could be a raging narcissist or just an asshole, who can tell? I do know that Gramps was brokenhearted by how his son turned out. In true Gramps fashion, he blamed himself. He said living through the war made him spoil his only child because he was so grateful to be alive to be a father. I don't believe that, though."

"No?"

"No, I think my dad is just a miserable man who is only happy when he makes everyone around him equally miserable. I'd feel sorry for him but I don't care about him enough for even that."

"I'm sorry your father abandoned you." I wanted to hug him but I didn't.

"Meh." He sipped his beer. "What about you? You likely don't want to live in your van forever, so what's your five-year plan or are you a seat-of-the-pants type of gal?"

I laughed. "Contrary to appearances, I am absolutely not a pantser. I am a list maker."

"Really?" He lowered an eyebrow in disbelief. "You're destroying my illusion of you being the sort of person who wakes up whenever you feel like it and decides what to do for the day in the moment."

"I spent too many years as a beat reporter for that," I said. "Deadlines have honed my personality like river water tumbles stones. I have a day minder in paper as well as on my phone because if I don't write it down it doesn't happen."

A comfortable silence fell between us. Normally, I would have felt the need to chatter to fill the silence but with Simon, it was okay to just sit and rub Dude's ears. As baby boy sank deeper into sleep, I shifted and felt the bottom of the couch shift. I did it again.

"O'Malley, I think this is a fold-out couch."

He glanced at me. "Or it's a falling-apart couch."

I roused Dude. "Let's see. A sleeper has to be more comfortable for you than trying to snooze on it with your feet hanging off the side."

Dude reluctantly vacated the couch and sprawled in front of the cold fireplace. Simon dragged the coffee table to the side and we pulled the cushions off. Sure enough, there was a folded-up mattress on a spring frame.

"I knew it!" I reached in and grabbed what appeared to be a handle.

"Let me help," Simon said.

"I got it." I yanked but the frame didn't move. Frowning, I shifted my grip and tugged with all my might. A piercing feeling of pain spiked into my palm and I yelped and jerked my hand away. In the meaty part of my palm, there was a puncture that promptly started oozing blood. I glanced at my hand, which throbbed, and said, "That can't be good."

Simon

"Don't move, Spencer!" I dashed to the kitchen and grabbed a fistful of paper towels. I hurried back to the living room, feeling my heart pound in my chest at the sight of how deep the wound in her palm was. I pressed the towels into her hand then turned to examine the bed frame.

Using the flashlight on my phone, I illuminated the part that she'd grabbed. There was a rusty spring that had broken free from the frame. I had no doubt it was the one that had injured her.

"Sit." I guided her to the recliner, not wanting her to black out if the sight of blood bothered her. I then bolted up the stairs shouting for my sister. "Lorelei!"

"No, don't bother her!" Hannah cried after me. I ignored her.

I charged into my room, where my sister was snoring. "Lor." I shook her awake. "Do you have a medical kit?"

"Huh? What? What's happening?" Her voice was groggy with sleep as she sat up, pushing her dark hair out of her eyes.

"Hannah punctured her hand on a rusty spring on the couch."

"Oh, shit!" Lorelei threw aside her covers, fully awake now. She crossed the room and grabbed a very large medical bag and then charged down the stairs with me on her heels.

Dude had risen to his feet and was pressing his nose into Hannah's hands as if he wanted to act as nurse. "I'm okay, buddy. No worries."

"Kitchen now," Lor ordered, not waiting for Hannah as she charged to the sink and turned on the hot water.

"It's fine, you shouldn't have disturbed her sleep."

"I saw the wound. It's not fine. It looks deep." I cupped her elbow and pulled her to her feet.

Lorelei was scrubbing her hands when we entered and she quickly dried them with a paper towel and pulled on a pair of blue gloves. She took Hannah from me and led her to the sink, where she examined the wound and cleaned it. She wrapped it with thick padding and some bandages and told Hannah to take over-the-counter pain meds if it started to hurt.

"Thank you," Hannah said. "I'm sure it'll be fine. Simon didn't have to wake you."

I would have protested but Lor beat me to it.

"Yes, he did. There are two things you don't want to mess with: animal bites and punctures." She began repacking the contents of her medical kit. "When was your last tetanus shot?"

"I don't know." Hannah shrugged.

"You will tomorrow," Lor said. "Wait here."

Hannah and I exchanged a look while Lor ran back upstairs. She was back down in moments, wheeling what I had thought was her carry-on but now realized was a medical-grade cooler.

She opened it to reveal assorted vials inside. She reached for one and closed the lid. "My vaccine cooler for my home-health visits."

"Ah." I nodded. My sister never ceased to amaze me.

Lor set the vial down on the counter and grabbed a packaged syringe from her medical kit. As she opened the packaging, Hannah stepped back or, more accurately, jumped back.

"No! I mean, no thank you." Hannah's eyes were wide and sweat coated her skin. She shook her head. "I'm good."

"Hannah, the metal you punctured yourself with could cause tetanus," Lor said in an understanding voice that was both pragmatic and patient. "You have to have this shot unless you can remember the last time you were vaccinated."

"No." Hannah shook her head vehemently. She was trembling and sweating and looked like she might throw up. It was clear she was panicking.

"Hey." I approached her, pulling her gaze away from the needle in Lor's hand. I cupped her face with my hands. "What's going on, Spencer?"

"Nothing," she insisted. "I just don't need a shot."

"Lockjaw, muscle spasms, seizures, believe me, you need the shot," Lor said.

"I'm sure I was vaccinated."

"In the past ten years?" Lor asked.

Hannah didn't answer, which I took to mean she didn't know.

"Talk to me, Spencer," I said. Her face was just inches from mine and I could see the sweat beading on her brow and feel her trembling.

"I'm just not great with needles." She lowered her head and I moved my hands to her shoulders. I didn't know if I was holding on to her for her sake or my own at this point. I just knew that I couldn't not hold her when she was so clearly terrified.

"You're afraid of needles?" Lor asked. She put the syringe behind her back, no doubt to keep from traumatizing Hannah.

"Not afraid exactly. I know you're right. I need to get the vaccination. I definitely don't want lockjaw or seizures. It's just . . ." Hannah's voice trailed off and she shivered. "I just can't."

"Do you want to talk about it?" I asked. The fear in her eyes was making my heart hurt.

"Not really." Hannah shook her head. "Can't I just take my chances and do without it?"

"I don't want to be a hard-ass, but as a healthcare provider, I don't feel like this is negotiable," Lor said. "Simon, help her."

"I'd love to. Any suggestions?" I asked. The only thing I could think to do to get her mind off the needle was to kiss her, but that seemed wildly self-serving and incredibly inappropriate, given the circumstances.

"Tell her about one of your really boring fishing excursions, you know, the ones where you and Charlie catch nothing," Lor said. "That should numb her into a relaxed state."

"Hey!" I protested. I glanced at Hannah and felt her shoulders loosen a little bit while Lor and I bickered. This might just work. "Just because you are afraid of the ocean and never come with us—"

"I am not!" Lor protested just like I knew she would.

"Oh, please, who failed lifeguard school?"

"That was not my fault!" Lor argued. "I have a genuine fear of sharks because of you and Charlie."

"How do you figure that?" I asked.

Lor immediately started humming the theme from *Jaws* and said, "Every time I went swimming one of you snuck up behind me and grabbed my leg, pretending to be a shark. It's amazing I can even take a bath, you two freaked me out so much."

I felt Hannah's shoulders shake and glanced at her to make certain she was laughing and not crying.

"That was all Charlie's idea," I said. "Technically, you're not afraid of sharks, you're afraid of us."

"Oh, no, it's definitely sharks, and it all comes from childhood trauma," Lor said. "Just like you're terrified of heights."

I went still. I hadn't really counted on Lor exposing me like that, but as I felt Hannah relax fully, I knew I would have confessed anything to help her through her panic spiral.

"Are you really?" Hannah's face turned up to mine.

"Not afraid . . . terrified." I didn't love exposing my fear, but if it made it easier for her to get the shot, I'd do it gladly. "I've tried everything—cognitive behavioral therapy, medication, all of that stuff—to get over it but the fear remains."

Her gaze held mine and there was an understanding in it that took my breath away. "What happened to cause you to be afraid of heights?"

I felt Lor go still beside me. This was one of those moments where I could bluff it out, pretend it was just a silly thing I couldn't get over, but I didn't want to. Not with Hannah. I knew we were sharing this house for only a little while longer and then going our separate ways, but I still felt the need to be my authentic self with her—because, as I was quickly realizing, I had feelings for her. And I trusted her.

"When I was eight, I was up in our tree house and I missed Dad's call to dinner. Our mom was away, visiting a friend, so Dad was in charge. He was furious that I didn't come when called. I didn't hear him, but he didn't believe me. He came outside and took the ladder away, leaving me up in the tree house all night. I was terrified. I cried for hours. I never went up in the tree house again, so I guess he made his point."

"What a horrible thing to do to a little boy. I'm so sorry, Simon."

Hannah cupped my cheek with her bandaged hand. It was the first time she'd called me by my first name since the day we'd met, and the sound of it in her low husky voice made something in my chest hum. If I were a cat, I'd probably be purring.

"Ouch!" Hannah started, and we both turned to see Lor removing the needle from Hannah's upper arm and swabbing it with an antiseptic wipe. "Sorry, but it seemed like as good a time as any."

Hannah sighed and said, "No, you're good. I barely felt it and I much prefer a little pinch than lockjaw or seizures."

"Get some rest," Lor said. "If your hand starts to get hot or you feel feverish, come wake me immediately."

Hannah nodded. I gave my sister a quick hug and said, "Thanks, you're the best."

"I know." She hugged me back, snapped the lid on her medical kit shut, and dragged her rolling cooler back upstairs.

We watched her go and then I turned to Hannah. "You sure you're all right?"

"I'm fine. Did your father actually do that to you?" she asked. "I'm really hoping you made the story up to distract me."

Embarrassed heat filled my face. I led the way back to the living room. Using my foot, I pushed the fold-out mattress back into the base and then replaced the cushions. I didn't want to get poked in the butt with a loose spring and get the same wound Hannah had, although I knew I was up on my tetanus vaccine because my sister made it her business to be in my medical business.

I sat on the couch and Hannah sat beside me. She tucked her legs beneath her and Dude climbed up on her other side, wedging her neatly between the two of us. I wanted to put an arm around her, pull her close, and comfort her, but I didn't. The line between us—of strangers owning a house together—was blurring with every moment I spent with her. It occurred to me if I wanted her to tell me why she was afraid of shots then I needed to be honest about my fear of heights.

"He did." I cleared my throat. "Among many other tough-love parenting choices."

"You were just a boy." Her face crumpled in distress.

"That's what men are made of—boys. Or so my father always said. How about you? Where did the needle anxiety start?"

She shook her head and then rested it back on the couch, staring at the ceiling. She didn't speak for a long moment and I thought she wasn't going to share her phobia origin story, but then she said, "Ninety shots."

I didn't move. I didn't breathe. I couldn't imagine what would require ninety shots—rabies?—but it was clear that whatever it was had changed her relationship with needles forever.

"My ex-husband and I tried for five years to get pregnant. In the end, IVF was our last chance. I had to give myself shots, lots and lots of shots. It became psychologically impossible. I know it seems like I should have gotten used to it and been able to jab myself no problem, but it just got worse and worse until it was my ex doing the jabbing and he wasn't happy about it. I should have known then."

Ex-husband. Hannah had been married. I tried that information on for size and realized I didn't like it, which was ludicrous. It wasn't my business if she'd been married multiple times before I'd met her. I just felt bad that she'd had love go wrong on her. She deserved better than that. I regrouped and refocused back on the conversation.

"You should have known what?" I asked, although I suspected I knew exactly where this story was going, given that he was her ex and all.

"When I didn't get pregnant, my husband left me. I hear he's remarried and has three kids, the first of which was conceived while we were still trying."

"What an asshole," I hissed through gritted teeth.

"Oh, it gets better," she said. "He blamed me and my inability to conceive for the divorce. He said he never would have cheated if I'd just gotten knocked up."

"Correction," I said. "What a fucking asshole."

"Oh, there's more. I got stuck with the outrageous IVF medical bills because the judge in our divorce case felt bad for my ex because my ex now had a 'real family' to support whereas I was single and clearly defective. Then there was a reduction in staff at the newspaper where I worked, so I was abruptly unemployed as well," she said. "It was not my favorite year."

"This makes working a job I loathe seem not so bad," I said. "I can see why you hit the open road. You probably couldn't put enough miles between you and the wandering wanker."

She laughed, which was what I'd been hoping for. From what I'd observed over the past few days, Hannah Spencer was kind, compassionate, funny, smart, and beautiful. She deserved so much more than the man who had done her so dirty.

"I debated buying a plane ticket to Europe but then I saw Buttercup and knew that the open road and the four hundred thirty-three national park sites of the United States beckoned. I've only managed to see about half of them." She rolled her head toward me. "By the way, thanks for distracting me so I could get the vaccine. It would have been ridiculous not to. I mean, lockjaw? It's so pre–Civil War."

"Right?" I mimicked her posture, slouching down and resting my head on the back of the couch. I turned to face her and reached up and gently tapped her lips with my index finger. "How would you eat?"

"Or kiss?" Her voice was breathy and messed with my brain chemistry, making me want to lean in and kiss her, but that would be taking advantage of her vulnerable state, wouldn't it?

"That would be tragic." I leaned in anyway, hoping she'd close the gap just so that we both knew the choice was hers. She did.

I didn't move, letting her take the lead. She pressed her mouth against mine and I clenched my fingers to keep from grabbing her and pulling her close. I wanted to. I wanted to feel her in my arms, pressed up against me. If I were being honest, I'd thought about it ever since she'd jumped off the dock to save me and even more so after our first kiss. I'd never met anyone like Hannah Spencer before and I knew she had the potential to wreck me, but I didn't pull away.

Her mouth was soft and warm. She shifted, fitting her lips to mine, knowing from our first kiss that we'd match up perfectly. We did. She opened her mouth and deepened the kiss and I lost the self-control battle. I simply had to touch her. I slid my hand up her arm, across her shoulder, and speared my fingers into the thick hair at the nape of her neck. I pulled her in closer and she responded by twining her arms around my neck.

The feel of her was everything. She was soft and sweet and warm and furry. *Furry?* I pulled back and a startled laugh burst out of me.

Hannah's brow creased in confusion and she blinked at me. "That's not the reaction I usually get when I kiss someone."

I put my fist to my mouth, trying to stop the laughter, before I said, "Well, do you usually have audience participation?" I pointed over her shoulder and she turned to find Dude hovering over her with his ears up.

"Dude!" she cried. "We have talked about this." She pointed to the recliners and the big beast turned his head as if he didn't see her then he didn't have to go. "Now, Dude."

Dude put his front feet on the floor and eased forward. Dragging his back feet, he stretched his full length as he slowly made his way to the chair, casting Hannah a reproving glance over his shoulder as if he'd been sent to the dungeon.

"Well, that was mortifying," Hannah said. "Sorry about the one hundred and fifty pounds of mood killer."

I glanced at the chair; Dude was obviously sulking as he'd turned his back to us. I glanced at Hannah, who looked as on edge as I felt. I tucked a strand of hair behind her ear and she leaned into my touch. "It would take a lot more than a pouting dog to kill the mood for me."

She tipped her head and studied me as if trying to determine if I was sincere. I held her gaze as I moved in, only closing my eyes when she closed hers right before my mouth landed on hers. There was a quick gasp of what sounded like relief in her throat and it lured me in. Knowing what I did about the past few years of her life, I was stunned by how sunny-side up she was, taking each adventure as it came—just her, Dude, and her T-shirt cannon.

Hannah pulled me close and I reveled in the feel of her pressed against me. She was all lush curves and soft skin. That coconut-lime shampoo of hers filled my senses and I knew I would never smell that combination again without thinking of her. The thought yanked me out of the moment like a car stopping short.

What was I doing? There was no future here for me or her or us. What if feelings got involved? The end of summer was our expiration date. Period. Full stop. Hannah had no interest in selling, and I had to sell to secure Charlie's future care. Crossing the line from housemate to hookup was a bad, bad, bad idea.

I eased my way out of the kiss. I pressed my forehead to Hannah's and said, "Hey, Spencer."

She leaned back and I noted her breathing was as erratic as

mine. Damn it, this would be so much easier if she felt lukewarm about me. It'd be a blow to the ego, but I could take it.

"O'Malley?" She must have sensed the change in my tone.

"It occurs to me that getting involved might not be a great idea."

She blinked and then made a face as if she smelled something bad. "Getting involved? Is that what you think we're doing?"

"Well, we were headed in that direction." My voice came out more defensive than I liked.

"No, we weren't," she protested. "I enjoy short-term flings here and there, but I don't 'get involved.' I can't."

"Why not?" I was perplexed. "Are you still hung up on the diddling dick?"

"God no!"

"Then why can't you 'get involved'?"

"Do I need to remind you that you just said 'getting involved might not be a great idea'?"

"No, here's the thing. I don't do short-term flings." My voice sounded growly. I tried to soften it, but I suspected she had some horseshit reason for not getting involved, and I wanted to hear her say it so I could clear it up for her. "Why don't you ever 'get involved'?"

"O'Malley, I can't have children." She spoke slowly as if I hadn't heard her before. "I'm broken, defective, a plowed field where seed can find no purchase, pick your descriptor. I have nothing to offer for the long term so I don't get involved. Not for more than a week or two at most. After that, feelings get involved and it gets messy."

"Who called you defective?" I zeroed in on the important bit and called it out. "Was it the fuckwit philanderer?"

She slumped back on the couch and blew out a breath. "Does it matter? It's the truth."

"I call bullshit on that." I picked her up under the arms. She let out a surprised yelp but didn't fight me when I moved her so she was straddling my lap. I skimmed my hands from her knees, up her thighs, along her sides, cupping her breasts ever so gently before I slid my hands up her arms to her shoulders, trailing my fingers along the sensitive skin of her neck.

She shivered at my touch and I felt invincible. To have this woman respond to my caress was some pretty heady stuff. I cupped her face and pulled her forward until she was almost lying on top of me.

"There." I softly kissed the center of her mouth. "Is." I kissed the left corner. "Nothing." I kissed the right. "Defective." I pulled her in and kissed her deeply, almost losing myself and forgetting to pull back. "About." This time I did go deep, parting her lips and sliding my tongue into her mouth. She let out a breathy sigh and again I had to drag myself back. I pulled away, leaving just a breath between our mouths and said, "You."

"Oh, Simon." It was the second time she'd said my name, and I loved the way her voice wrapped around it, making the syllables resonate with affection as if my name belonged to her and her alone.

She cupped my face and put her mouth on mine. The kiss was sweet and tender and I felt it plucking my heartstrings even while it made my groin throb with wanting her, all of her.

"You're very kind," she said. "But I am broken and there's nothing that can be done to fix it. It's taken me five years to put myself back together and accept that my dream of having a family of my own is never going to happen. I simply don't have the emotional fortitude to go through that again. Temporary is all can I offer and if you can't accept that then this"—she gestured between us—"can't happen."

She slipped off my lap then and with a sad smile she disappeared up the stairs to her room. Dude rolled over and stared at me as if to say he'd tried to warn me.

Well, hell. Now what was I going to do? Having Hannah believe such utter horseshit about herself was completely unacceptable. And the contrary part of me who thought he'd been noble about slamming on the brakes and not getting involved when we had two very different agendas about what to do with the house suddenly felt the need to prove to her that she was worth so much more than she believed. And if a fling was the only opportunity I'd have to show her the kind of love and support she truly deserved from a partner, how could I not take it?

Hannah

I took extra care getting dressed in the morning, which was stupid. The man had seen me half drowned, without makeup, and covered in dirt, dust, and cobwebs. Curling my hair and putting on makeup wasn't going to erase those images of me from his mind, especially as I was wearing a baggy T-shirt and shorts to finish tackling the decluttering of the attic.

Still, it was a sort of armor and I wasn't one to pass up anything that could give me a boost of confidence when facing the potential awkwardness that might exist between Simon and me now that we'd once again crossed the don't-kiss-your-housemate line. Why had I kissed him again?

Well, easy. Because he was smokin' hot and I liked him, I genuinely liked him as a person. I loved how he cared about Dude and his sister and . . . me. I felt as if I could tell him anything and there was no judgment, just support and understanding.

Of course he was the sort of guy who didn't do flings. That was just my luck. But maybe it was for the best. My potential to fall for him was great and did I really want to invite heartbreak into my life? No, I did not.

I tried to block out the memory of the feel of his mouth against mine and his fingers on my skin. It was a struggle, especially when I arrived in the kitchen to find him standing there barefoot in a pair of gray sweatpants and a white T-shirt that clung to his shoulders with his hair mussed as if he'd just woken up. Lorelei was seated at the counter, drinking coffee and eating a fried egg sandwich. Her dark hair was twisted into a knot on the top of her head and she was frowning at her phone as if it had done something to offend her.

"Mornin'," I murmured as I sidled toward the coffeepot. Dude had abandoned me in my room when I changed my outfit for the third time and was seated at Lorelei's feet, staring at her sandwich as if he might mind-command it to fall into his mouth.

"Mornin', Spencer," Simon greeted me as he lifted his coffee mug to his lips. He watched me over the rim and I felt his gaze boring a hole in my back while I poured a mug of black, bitter goodness for myself.

"I'm glad you're up so I could say good-bye." Lorelei hopped off the stool and handed Dude the last bite of her sandwich. His tail thumped loudly on the floor, clearly in gratitude while he swallowed the bite whole.

Lorelei rounded the counter and gave me a fierce hug. "Don't let Simon bully you."

"Wouldn't dream of it," I said. I stood patiently while she removed the bandage on my hand and gave it a quick examination.

"Who's picking you up?" Simon frowned at his sister.

"No one you know." Lorelei said it in a case-closed voice, which I found interesting. Were Simon and Charlie that overbearing about who their sister got involved with?

There was a knock on the front door and Lorelei jumped before quickly rewrapping my hand. "Damn it, I told him to wait in the car." She lifted her backpack and slipped it over one shoulder while grabbing her rolling cooler, which had her medical kit strapped to it.

"Him?" Simon followed her to the door. "Who him?"

"Not your business," Lorelei called over her shoulder. She tried to slip out and shut the door behind her but Simon blocked it with his foot. "Quit it, Simon!"

He ignored his sister, glancing over her head at the man leaning against the porch railing. He was tall and broad and ridiculously good-looking with wavy golden-brown hair that reached his shoulders.

"Don't embarrass me," Lorelei growled at her brother.

"Me?" Simon put his hand over his heart, the picture of innocence.

Lorelei glowered and strode across the front porch. The man shoved off the railing and met her halfway, holding out his hand to take her bag. She ignored him. "Chance, this is Simon and Hannah, and vice versa, okay, let's go."

Chance pushed his sunglasses up onto his head, revealing intense gray eyes, then held out a hand to me and then Simon. "I'd say I've heard a lot about you but I haven't."

"Likewise." Simon shook his hand and they both turned to Lorelei. She busied herself giving Dude a good-bye hug.

"Be a good boy." She smooched the top of his head and smiled at me. "Good luck . . . with everything."

"Thanks." I glanced at Chance and on a hunch, I said, "You, too."

She rolled her eyes. "Yeah, I'm going to need it." With that, she turned on her heel and walked around Chance and Simon, who pulled her into a half hug.

"See ya, sis." Simon kissed the top of her head and I watched Chance's eyebrows lift at the word "sis."

"Bye." Lorelei shoved off her brother and dragged her stuff down the steps to the walkway that led to a blue sports car parked in front of the house. "Come on, No Chance, we're going to be late and Tilly will worry." She stuffed her belongings into the back then settled herself into the passenger seat, slamming the door after her.

Chance sighed. He lowered his sunglasses and ran a hand through his hair. He glanced at Simon and said, "Your sister is my Aunt Tilly's night nurse and a royal pain in my ass."

At that, Simon laughed and clapped Chance on the shoulder. "Word of advice? Don't give her an inch, you'll never get it back if you do."

Chance gestured from where we stood to where she sat in the car and said, "I think that inch and a couple of yards have already been taken, but I appreciate the thought."

He strolled down the walkway as if intentionally making her wait for him. Judging by the hard stare Lorelei was giving him, she knew it, too. With a wave, Chance climbed into the driver's seat and they sped away. Even though the doors and windows of the car were closed, I could feel the tension between them all the way to where we stood.

"Poor bastard," Simon muttered.

"I'd think your sympathy would be with your sister." We turned to go back inside with Dude leading the way.

"Yeah, no. My sister is a heartbreaker of the first order," Simon said. "Growing up, I can't even count how many lovelorn guys showed up at our house, mooning over Lor. Charlie and I used to have to chase them off before Gramps saw them—for their own health and well-being."

"Lorelei doesn't seem like the sort of woman who strings people along," I said.

"She's not," Simon said. "But she has the ability to make you feel better about yourself without it feeling like she's blowing sunshine up your butt."

I laughed. "You mean she's sincere?"

"Yeah, but it's more than that. Her gift is that she makes you believe in yourself even when all the evidence points to the contrary." Simon opened the door and Dude bounded inside, leaving Simon holding the door for me. As I passed him, his voice was low and he said, "You share that ability."

I glanced at him, surprised by the compliment, and found his gaze holding mine with a look of tenderness that made my cold heart melt just a little bit.

"Thank you." It was one of the nicest things anyone had ever said to me but I didn't say that. Instead, I said, "I think I get it from Pops. As I mentioned, he was definitely a sunny-side-up type of guy."

"I fear I am more like Gramps." Simon's tone was rueful. "Always looking for the storm."

"Given that a tree went through our house, you're not completely wrong, O'Malley," I said.

"See? There you go making me feel better about being a salty old curmudgeon."

I smiled while I studied his handsome face. I didn't know how to break it to him but a curmudgeon was a thin-lipped, sneering sourpuss of an old man. This guy was nothing like that with his full lips, glinting eyes, arched brows, and strong jaw. Yeah, not a whiff of curmudgeon about him.

"Keep looking at me like that, and I'll have to kiss you again, Spencer." His voice had dropped to a low rumble and I felt it all the way to the soles of my shoes.

I was about to ask what was stopping him when Dude, obviously out of patience, came back through the door and gave me a hard nudge with his muzzle. I wasn't sure if he was rescuing me from my own stupidity or ruining a potentially hot moment. Either way he would not be denied as he plowed into me.

"Breakfast. Got it." I moved past Simon into the kitchen, feeling a pang of regret for what might have been.

Simon followed us and began to clean the kitchen while I fed Dude. As he unloaded the dishwasher, he asked, "What's our plan of attack for today? Finish the attic? Take on the bedroom closets?"

"What about your brother?" I finished my coffee and poured a second mug. I felt like I was going to need it today.

"As Lor said, there's no way of knowing when he'll show up," he said.

"You could call him."

"That's not how we roll."

I studied him over the rim of the mug. This was not my business. He was not my concern nor was his relationship with his siblings. Although the argument could be made that since I was trying to learn everything I could about Pops, then learning all I could about Gramps and his family was a part of that.

"Why do you suppose your brother is coming to see you?" I asked.

Simon shrugged as if to say he had no idea, but it was clear that he and Lorelei were not being fully transparent about Charlie. I supposed if he did show up at some point, we'd discover the why of his visit together.

"Do you think he's upset about you inheriting the house?" I asked.

Simon's head snapped up and he placed the dinner plates in the cupboard before turning to face me. "What do you mean?"

"Nothing." I shook my head. "It's just that some families can get pretty testy about properties and inheritances and whatnot."

"Not mine." His voice was sharp. I wondered whom he was trying to convince, me or himself.

"That's good." I leveled him with a firm look. "Because I'm not selling my half."

Simon heaved a sigh. "We said we wouldn't talk about it."

"I'm not talking about it, I'm merely updating you that my opinion hasn't changed." I grabbed an apple from the bowl I'd filled yesterday and my coffee mug and headed for the stairs. "We should try and finish the attic this morning as it's going to get too hot to be up there later."

"I'll be right up."

Dude glanced between us as if he knew we were at odds and wasn't sure which side he was on. As if there was any question, the person in the kitchen near the food had his loyalty and we both knew it. I patted his head and said, "Behave."

Dude lay down in the middle of the kitchen as if supervising Simon. I headed upstairs determined not to think about Simon or his kisses, especially when he told me I wasn't defective in his incredibly sweet way. I hadn't argued the point last night but the reality was that I felt less than because of my infertility and even while creating a pretty great life for myself, I hadn't managed to change that.

I pulled the folding stairs down and began the climb into the attic. Simon had found the string light switch in the attic and replaced the bulb. I dragged my feet forward in the darkness until I saw the string. I set my coffee down and tugged on the thin cotton cord. With a snap, the light came on and the shadows in the attic vanished. Electricity was a magical thing that I appreciated only when I didn't have it.

There was a large steamer trunk that had intrigued me last week, but I had gotten distracted by the piles of other things. I crossed over to it now, taking a bite out of my apple as I went. I switched on the flashlight app on my phone and ran it over the dark red-brown surface, noting that it appeared to be locked. Nuts.

The wood was scarred and scuffed, clearly the worse for wear, but it occurred to me that it was the perfect place to keep old memories. And it might not belong to either Pops or Gramps. It could be that the previous owners had left it behind like the bassinet and the snowshoes. Unless Simon and I were way off the mark and that stuff belonged to our grandfathers.

"I was thinking we should put everything out on the lawn."

"Ah!" I whirled around and there was Simon.

"Sorry. I should have coughed or something," he said.

I waved my apple at him. "No, it's fine." I took another bite to keep myself from saying anything else like how indecently hot he was in gray sweats and could he please put on normal pants.

He crossed the attic and knelt beside me, considering the trunk. "About last night—"

I took another bite of apple and shook my head. "No."

"No what?" he asked. "You don't even know what I'm going to say."

I swallowed and the apple chunks went down hard. "It doesn't matter. There's no need to talk about it."

"What if I disagree?" he asked.

"You? O'Malley? Disagreeing with me? Shocking!" I finished my apple and dropped the core into the trash bag we'd brought up yesterday.

"Are you done?" he asked.

I nodded at him.

"Great," he said. "Then hear me out."

"Oh, that can't be good," I said. "Nothing good ever starts with 'hear me out.'"

"I thought you were an optimist," he challenged me.

"I am, but that doesn't mean I don't know when things are about to get messy."

"I thought about what you said last night, and I've decided to take you up on it."

"I'm sorry?" I blinked. "What did I say?"

"You said you only do short-term flings." He held my gaze and then said, "So, I'm in."

My heart dropped into my feet and I felt immediately hot and dizzy.

"But you don't think getting involved is a great idea," I reminded him.

"Yes, but if we just have a fling we should be fine, right?" One of his eyebrows rose higher than the other in a look that straight-up called me out.

"You also don't do flings," I reminded him.

"You've caused me to reconsider." His small smile lit his eyes as he took me in, from the bandanna I'd tied on my head to protect my hair from the cobwebs to my baggy T-shirt and jean shorts.

I narrowed my eyes at him. "What? Why are you looking at me like that?"

He raised his eyebrows. "So suspicious. Maybe, Spencer, I'm looking at you 'like that' because I like you."

My treacherous affection-starved heart did a silly flutter in my chest. I held his gaze, trying to figure out if he was playing me and if so, for what purpose? Sex? Or did he think he could woo the house out from under me?

"You don't believe me." There was no surprise or hurt in his voice, just curiosity.

"It's not that I don't believe you, I just . . ." I shrugged. Running out of words was not a normal state of being for me, and it was definitely his fault. I was caught off guard and didn't know how to respond.

"Let me give you some empirical evidence. I like your fearlessness. For as long as I live, I will never forget that you jumped into the water to pull me out even though you were afraid of alligators."

"Still am." I shifted on my feet, trying to get comfortable with his praise.

"I like your laugh," he said. "It bubbles up from deep inside and then pops like a champagne cork."

"It's a loud one." I put my hand on the back of my neck, which felt hot.

"And I like the way you look at me when I kiss you." His voice dropped to a lower octave and my gaze was caught and held by his. I couldn't move. I couldn't breathe. "I like you, Spencer, I really do."

"Is it hot up here?" I ripped my gaze from his and fanned my face with my hands. "I feel like it's suddenly very hot."

"It's probably all of that shmoopy talk." A head popped up in the attic opening and I yelped. Roland pushed his ball cap back on his head and said, "Mornin'."

Simon's mouth lifted in that small smile of his and I noticed there was a wicked glint in his eye to accompany the lone dimple in his cheek. Meanwhile, I felt as if I were being embalmed in embarrassment.

"Well, this is mortifying," I muttered, and shot Simon a flustered glower.

Simon leaned close and whispered, "We'll finish later."

My mouth went completely dry. Forcing myself to look away from Simon and his killer dimple, I glanced at our surprise guest and said, "Morning, Roland, was there something we could help you with?"

"Not for me, no, I came because Be—" His gaze was diverted to something behind me. "Wow, is that Billy and Bobby's tandem bike? I always wondered what happened to it when they stopped riding."

"It was theirs? They really rode it?" I was completely charmed by the idea of Pops riding a tandem bike with his partner.

"They did, all over the OBX," Roland said. "Although Bobby was always the captain in front and Billy was the stoker in the back. We used to laugh when Billy would take his feet off the pedals and let Bobby do all the work."

I burst out laughing and Simon let out a huff of air that sounded almost like a full chuckle. "That tracks. Gramps would have to be the steersman."

Roland squinted at the bike. "It looks like it's in great shape, no rust or anything."

"It is." Simon held out a hand and pulled Roland into the attic. "As far as I can tell, it just needs new tires."

"I know where I can get some." Roland ran a hand over the frame. "That is, if you want to fix it up."

"Absolutely," Simon and I said together. Our gazes met and we exchanged a conspiratorial smile.

"Bring it on downstairs and I'll fix it today," Roland offered.

Simon looked thrilled by the prospect.

"Roland, did you need us for something specific or were you just stopping by?" I asked. I had a feeling the allure of our packed front porch was calling to him and I needed to keep him on task.

"Oh, yeah." Roland snapped his fingers. "Bebe sent me. Her water broke and she and Luke are about to head to the hospital, but their dog sitter is on vacation so she wondered if you'd keep an eye on Frank."

"Hospital? But she's not due for another two weeks!" I hurried across the attic to the opening. "Is she still at home?"

"Yes, Luke was trying to get her out the door, but she wasn't having it until she knew Frank would be okay," Roland said.

I glanced at Simon and said, "I'm going!"

"Right behind you!" He turned to Roland. "We're going to finish the attic today. If you and Zach want to help, we'll pay you."

Roland rubbed his hands together. "Deal."

I scurried down the ladder to the landing where Dude was napping. "Come on, boy, we're going to get Frank."

At his buddy's name, Dude perked up. We dashed downstairs. Dude in front and Simon brought up the rear. Bebe and Luke's house was halfway down our narrow neighborhood street. When we got there, Luke was outside, tossing a carry-on into the car and looking frantic.

"Oh, thank goodness," he said. "I can't get her to budge until Frank is settled." He ran toward the house, leading the way. "Bebe, they're here for Frank, let's go."

Bebe was sitting at her kitchen table, drinking coffee and thumbing through her phone. Frank hopped up and charged Dude as soon as he saw him. The two dogs started to run around the house with absolute glee. Simon opened the back door and they tumbled into the yard.

"We're happy to watch Frank for you, Bebe," I said.

She glanced up from her phone at me. "I don't think it's going to be necessary."

I exchanged a look with Luke. He crouched beside her chair and in a gentle voice said, "Frank will have a great time with Dude. And now we need to—"

His words were cut off as Bebe gasped and then shut her eyes, clearly in pain from a contraction.

"Babe, we have to go." Luke's voice was pleading.

"I changed my mind," Bebe grunted. "I don't think I can do

this." Her brown eyes were huge as she looked down at her husband. Her lower lip trembled.

"Yes, you can. You have Dr. Swan attending," he said. "You love her and she's not going to let anything happen to you." His voice was fierce when he added, "*I* won't let anything happen to you."

Bebe bowed her head, and I could tell she was petrified. As a woman who struggled with infertility, I had no idea what to say. *Be grateful you get to risk your life for a baby*? That seemed incredibly wrong. I thought about what I'd want someone to say to me if I was feeling overwhelmed and afraid.

"Bebe, I know we only met a few weeks ago, but here's what I've learned about you so far," I said. I gave her a half hug, resting my head on hers. "You have a huge heart, just look at how you love Luke and Frank." I felt her nod beneath my cheek so I kept going. "You are brave, so brave. Choosing to be a mother is one of the most courageous decisions a woman can make. And you are strong." I squeezed her muscled bicep. "You've been training for this your whole life. You were born to do this. You know it, I know it, Luke knows it, and your baby knows it. Now go get it done!"

To my surprise and delight, Bebe hugged me hard and then rose to her feet. "You're right. I am a badass. I can totally do this." She reached down and pulled Luke to his feet. She cupped his face and kissed him quick. "Let's go meet our baby."

Luke sagged with relief. He glanced over Bebe's head and mouthed the words, "Thank you."

"We'll lock up the house and take Frank to the cottage," Simon said as we followed them to their car, watching as Luke opened the door for Bebe. Simon handed Luke his phone. "Give me your cell number, then you can call or text us if you need anything."

Luke typed his number into Simon's phone and shot him a

thumbs-up. He hurried around to the driver's side. With a blast of his horn, they were hospital bound.

I watched them go, waving as their car disappeared. Feeling Simon move to stand beside me, I turned to share the exhilarating-yet-anxious moment with him and found him watching me with a tenderness that made my throat tight.

"Bebe's going to be okay," Simon said. "You heard Luke. She has an excellent doctor and you gave her a hell of a pep talk."

"It was the least I could do. It's not like a woman can change her mind once her water breaks," I said.

"Still, it can't have been easy for you to rally her after what you've been through." He pulled me into his side and kissed the top of my head in a gesture that was genuinely comforting. I felt seen and understood in a way I never had before.

"A few years ago, it would have been a challenge," I admitted. "But I've made peace with it and I'm grateful for the amazing life I've been given, which apparently includes a house in the Outer Banks."

"An attitude of gratitude. You are something, Spencer."

He turned me into his arms and I went. The immediate heat that flared up between us was just as intense as it had been the night before. His gaze was locked on mine as if he was trying to decide whether to kiss me or not, as if he was worried it wouldn't be received well. I didn't let him overthink it. I just stepped over the line. We hadn't really discussed the whole fling thing since being interrupted by Roland earlier, but I'd made my decision, and I felt the best way to tell him was to show him.

I twined my arms around his neck and pulled his mouth down to mine at the same time I rose up on my toes to meet him. His lips were soft but his mouth was firm, taking control of the kiss as soon as we touched.

This was not like the exploratory kisses of our previous encounters, this was a reigniting of the need and desire that had been cut short the night before. I had regretted leaving him the second I climbed off his lap and started upstairs, but my pride had refused to allow me to turn around. But now I had a second chance to let my attraction for this man consume me and I wasn't going to walk away this time.

I dug my fingers into his wavy hair and parted my lips as he deepened the kiss, licking my lower lip and slowly sliding his tongue into my mouth as if knowing that the slow siege would cause me to surrender completely.

His mouth moved from mine to trace a path along my jaw and down the side of my neck to nestle in the sweet spot he'd discovered the night before. I tipped my head back to give him better access and I could feel him smile against my skin.

I could have stood there and kissed him all day, but a *woof* interrupted and I pulled away to see Dude barking in the direction of the road. There was Frank, hauling ass as if he was reveling in his first taste of freedom.

"Oh, shit, we have a runner!" I cried.

"I got him, you lock up!" Simon ordered, and he took off running with Dude at his side.

Frank only got past the neighbor's house before Simon scooped him up and I sagged with relief. I locked the door and jogged down the driveway to meet them.

Simon cradled Frank with one arm in a football hold and then put his other hand on the small of my back as if he just needed to maintain contact. I didn't move away. If anything, I leaned into his touch.

I knew this was a dangerous game. We owned a house together and big decisions needed to be made. Simon O'Malley with his sweet smile, sharp wit, and stupefying good looks was definitely not a man I should be playing with . . . and yet, I simply couldn't resist him.

As we walked back to our house, I assured myself I could handle him. In fact, I couldn't wait to get started.

It was amazing how sorting everything from the attic on the front lawn was a clarion call to the entire street. The Fisks and their children showed up, keeping Frank and Dude busy chasing the littles around the backyard. Roland and Zach helped haul the last of the items down from the attic while everyone else helped us sort what was of value and what could be donated. I suspected the entire street needed something to do while we waited for news from Luke about Bebe.

"You all right, Spencer?" Simon asked as he caught me staring down the street at Bebe and Luke's house.

"Worried," I admitted.

"You're not alone," Simon said. I studied his face and saw the tightness in the line of his mouth. He gestured to our neighbors and said, "Every conversation is a variation on why we haven't heard anything yet. I think Stephanie and Monica are going to drive to the hospital if we don't get some news soon."

"I'll go with them. Heck, I can fit most of us in Buttercup and drive everyone myself," I said.

"That's a picture," Simon said. "We'd have to double up and I'd likely end up with Roland on my lap."

I grinned at the mental picture, and chided myself for even thinking of volunteering to sit in his lap. I was determined to behave myself and focus on the task at hand, which was the sea of items still to be sorted.

Simon ruined it however, as he leaned in close and said, “I desperately want to kiss you again but I’ll settle for getting you to go for a ride on the tandem bike with me.”

He pointed to where Roland had the bike propped upside down while he and Zach fitted wheels to it.

“No way,” I said.

“Way,” he countered. “Come on, let’s take it for a spin.”

“Fine, but I’m the stoker.” I realized as soon as I said it that it sounded like a sexy innuendo so I went with it and winked at him.

Simon hissed out a breath and his gaze dropped to my mouth. “Indeed.”

“Just to clarify, I call the back seat.”

“Is that so you can relax while I do all the work?”

I feigned an innocent look and fluttered my eyelashes. “I have no idea what you mean. I’m trying to be true to our grandfathers and keep a Spencer in the rear.” Did that sound sexy, too? Or was it this man who had just kissed me stupid who made everything seem like a proposition?

“Is that so?” The heat in his gaze could melt ice.

“Stop that.” I fanned my face with my hand.

“Stop what?”

“You know.”

His chuckle was low and deep and I felt it vibrate right down my spine. We strolled across the lawn, stopping by Stephanie, where she was sorting a box of baking tins.

“Hannah, Simon, you have some real treasures here. You could sell these online and make a nice profit,” she said. She was holding a stack of Bundt pans of varying sizes.

“Or the owner of the local bakery could take them off our hands for free?” I glanced at Simon and he confirmed the offer with a small nod.

Stephanie hugged the pans to her chest. Her gray bob was held back from her face by a wide pink headband and the sleeves of her white chef's coat were rolled up to her elbows, revealing muscled forearms. I suspected it came from years of kneading the bread . . . er . . . buns that her bakery was known for.

"You have to let me pay you," she insisted.

Simon shook his head. "Gramps and Pops wouldn't hear of it and neither will we."

With a grin, she turned and shouted at her husband, Mike. "Hon, look what I scored!"

He answered with an enthusiastic, "That's my girl!"

I felt a bubble of happiness float up in my chest. "I see why the grandfathers loved it here so much. I haven't felt a part of a neighborhood in years, since I was a kid, in fact."

Simon was studying the neighbors with a thoughtful gaze. "They were lucky to find this place."

"And each other," I added.

"Yeah." Simon tucked a stray strand of hair behind my ear and I got the feeling he wasn't talking about our grandfathers anymore.

"She's finished!" Roland approached us, wheeling the tandem bike beside him. "You ready to take her for a spin? Davis is watching the kids and dogs in the backyard. Zach went back there to make sure Frank stays put."

"Thanks." Simon took the front handlebars and held the bike steady.

"Oh, and don't leave without these." Roland handed us two dark blue bike helmets. Simon made a face but Roland said, "Your grandfathers always wore them."

"Fine." Simon strapped his on and I did the same. He gestured for me to climb on, so I lifted my leg over the middle bar and stood on my tiptoes while Simon did the same.

"Now what?" I asked.

"Let's get our pedaling in sync," he said. "We'll start on the right."

He moved his right pedal with the top of his foot until it was up and I did the same.

"On the count of three, we push off," he said. "One, two, thr—"

In my eagerness, I pushed off early, nearly tipping us over with my shift in weight.

"Whoa, whoa, whoa," Simon said. He grabbed the bike with one hand and me with the other, keeping us both from falling over. "Let's try again. We launch at the *end* of three, Spencer."

"Got it!" I could feel the amused gazes of our neighbors but I refused to be embarrassed even though Roland's shoulders were shaking with laughter.

I repositioned myself and waited while Simon counted down. On three, we pushed off together, heading down the road with only a few bobbles and wobbles. I had absolutely no idea how we were going to stop but that was a problem for end-of-the-ride Hannah.

We shot down the narrow lane. Simon looked at me over his shoulder and I tried to ignore how close we were, with my hands clutching the handlebar that was on each side of his seat, putting his butt right in the middle of my grasp. I kept my chin up, refusing to look.

"I think we've got it!" Simon said. He sounded uncharacteristically joyous and the smile on his face was so genuine, I suspected this was what he'd looked like as a boy—full of mischief and fun and enthusiasm. I remembered how Lorelei had said he hadn't always been so serious and I wondered if this was the real Simon. His exuberance was contagious. I grinned in return but then saw a car heading right for us.

"Car!" I shouted. I tried to steer us to the side but of course I had no steering capability.

“I’ve got it!” Simon said. “Don’t panic.”

Too late. Being a control freak, I was leaning hard to the right, trying to get us out of the way of the large SUV. Simon struggled to keep us upright but failed. My shift in weight sent us off the road and into the shallow brackish water, which I was certain contained hidden gators.

I let out a shriek just as our tires got sucked into the mud, stopping the bike abruptly and sending us both ass over teakettle into the water with undignified splats. The car came to a stop, but I ignored it as I stared up at the blue sky while lying in the stinky marsh mud.

“Spencer, are you all right?” Simon’s face was pale and his eyes wide as he crawled toward me.

I pushed up to my feet, letting the water and mud drip off me. I reached down and hauled him to his feet. His eyes scoured my person as if reassuring himself that I was intact.

“I’m fine. You?” I looked him over, relieved that he seemed fine, too.

“I think I swallowed an eel.” He cringed and made a gagging noise.

I jumped, grabbing him around the middle in a stranglehold. “Eels? Where?”

He chuckled and I realized he was joking. I shoved him hard and he slipped deeper into the mud, grabbing my hand and pulling me with him as he went. I slid into him and clipped him behind one knee, knocking him down and dragging me with him.

Simon was covered in mud with bits of marsh grass and stray leaves on his face and shirt. He looked like hell and yet still ridiculously attractive. I didn’t think about what I did. I was too annoyed. I scooped a fistful of mud and threw it at him. It hit him square in the shoulder with a very satisfying splat.

"Be careful, Spencer," he cautioned. "You might not enjoy where this leads."

I threw another gob of mud. This one landed on his neck.

He stared at me in surprise and then scooped up a fistful of his own. It occurred to me to move a beat too late and his ball of goo hit me right in the chest.

"Game on!" I grunted, and the next thing I knew we were tossing fistfuls of the marsh muck at each other. I scooted closer to him to make sure I didn't miss him when I slipped and reached out to save myself by clutching his arm, succeeding only in pulling him down with me.

"Oh, I see how it is," Simon said. He reached for me but I rolled away, not anticipating him grabbing my foot and halting my escape. When he tried to pull me toward him, he slipped and landed in the mud next to me. I sent a spray of water in his direction and he sent one back.

When Simon crawled by me, I climbed onto his back. He rose to standing, spinning in a circle, trying to dislodge me. I held on like a barnacle. I heard someone laughing. It took me a moment to realize it was me. It was—but it was also him and it was the most delightful sound.

Simon slowed his spin and reached behind, plucking me off his back and holding me high up in the air. My breath caught as he guided me in a slow slide down the front of his body, setting me on my feet but still holding me close.

This had to be the most ridiculous and still the sexiest moment of my life. I should have been mortified. Instead, I cracked up with more laughter. Every time I tried to pull it together, I made eye contact with him and we both erupted again. I laughed until my stomach cramped and then I laughed some more, hanging on him for support even though he was laughing, too.

Simon half carried, half dragged me to solid ground. I reached up and picked some marsh grass off his helmet and he swiped a gob of dirt off my cheek. We were grinning at each other like idiots.

"I can't remember the last time I heard you laugh like that, Simon." A man was standing by the side of the road, watching us. He was wearing jeans and a white T-shirt. His dark hair was long and unkempt, and he had a day or two's worth of stubble on his chin. When he smiled, a dimple appeared in one cheek and I knew exactly who he was.

I felt Simon stiffen in surprise. He slipped his arm around my waist and pulled me into his side as if to shield me. In a blink, his face became its usual emotionless mask and his voice perfectly even when he said, "Hannah Spencer, this is my brother, Charlie O'Malley."

Twenty

Simon

The look on Hannah's face was comically horrified. If I looked as mucked up as she did—and of course I did—then her dismay wasn't out of order. We must've looked like two creatures from the Black Lagoon. Totally worth it. I tamped down my smile, not wanting to give Charlie any emotion to misinterpret.

"Charlie, it's good to see you." I unclipped my helmet and let it dangle from my hand. Hannah did the same with hers.

"Is it?" Charlie asked. His eyes were guarded and I knew he was assessing, trying to figure out what the meaning behind my words was while trying to respond appropriately.

"Of course it is." Julian Quinto, Charlie's caregiver, came around from the driver's side of the car. "We talked about this, Charlie. You know how Simon feels about you."

"He loves me." Charlie nodded as if remembering an important detail. I smiled at him, encouragingly, even as my heart was smashed into a thousand pieces. I held my arms wide and said, "I'm your favorite baby brother."

A quick flash of recognition at the old joke lit Charlie's face and he stepped into my hug. "That's right." He smiled and there was a twinkle of the old Charlie in his eyes when he responded, "You're my only brother."

"Doesn't mean I'm not your favorite." I hugged him close and felt my throat get tight when he returned the embrace with a laugh. This easy affection wasn't always the case with Charlie.

"I hope it's all right that we just stopped by," Julian said. "Charlie wanted to surprise you."

"Happy to have you visit anytime." Julian and I exchanged a look and I knew that he knew that Lorelei had given me a heads-up.

"Were you surprised?" Charlie asked. His voice was high and he sounded more like a middle schooler than a thirty-seven-year-old man.

"Totally." I clapped him on the shoulder. "You got me, Charlie."

"And you got me!" He gestured to the mud on his T-shirt but he was amused rather than angry.

"I can loan you a clean shirt," I said.

Charlie turned around to face Julian and I glanced at Hannah. She was watching the interaction with gentle curiosity. No judgment, just clearly trying to put the pieces together. I could have kicked myself for not explaining it to her sooner. I hadn't really thought Charlie would show up so soon and, frankly, I'd been distracted by her.

"Told you, Julian." Charlie was laughing. "I told you I'd surprise him."

Julian raised his hands in surrender. "You were right, Charlie."

Charlie spun to face me. He was grinning but it immediately vanished when he spotted Hannah. His eyes narrowed in suspicion. "Who's she?"

I reached out and took Hannah by the arm, pulling her close to my side but leaving a small gap between us. "This is my friend Hannah."

Charlie's gaze darted to mine. "Friend?"

"Yes, actually, her grandfather was friends with Gramps," I said.

"Our Gramps?" Charlie's voice came out high and squeaky.

"Yup. Her Pops was Gramps's . . . fishing buddy."

"I miss him." Charlie's eyes filled with tears and his face crumpled. "Gramps used to come and play cards with me every Sunday, didn't he, Julian?"

"He did," Julian said.

"Do you want to see the house where Gramps used to go fishing?" I asked Charlie.

His eyes lit up and he nodded. "Yes!"

"It's the house at the end of the street," I said. "Number 81."

Julian nodded. He glanced at Charlie and said, "Think we can beat them there?"

Charlie looked from the car to our bike, which was still on the ground. "Totally."

He hurried into the passenger seat and Julian climbed into the driver's side. Julian sent me a wave as he slowly pulled back onto the road.

I picked up the bike and checked it over. Other than some mud on the wheels, it seemed fine.

"Do you want to ride or walk?" I asked Hannah.

She glanced down at the mud coating her shorts and said, "Walk?" She phrased it as a question but I wasn't going to argue. The idea of riding a bike while covered in mud had zero appeal. Plus, it would give me a minute to explain everything.

Ever since Lor had told me that Charlie was coming, I'd been debating how much to tell Hannah. Now that she'd met him, I didn't see how I could avoid telling her the whole story.

"About Charlie . . ." I began, but she interrupted.

"You don't have to explain anything to me," she said.

"I know, but . . . I want to." I was surprised to discover this was true. I rarely told anyone about my brother or his condition because it just hurt too much to talk about. But Hannah was different.

"He wasn't always like this." I started to push the bike with one hand on the handlebars and the other on the seat. Hannah moved to the other side and mirrored my position, helping to keep the bike balanced.

"What happened?" she asked.

"About ten years ago, he was in a horrible car accident," I said. "He swerved to avoid a deer, lost control of the car, and wrapped his Mercedes around a tree."

"Oh, that's awful."

"Yeah." I didn't go into the late-night call from my sister telling me what had happened or the frantic flight I made from New York City, where I'd been working with an author on a book. Instead, I kept it on Charlie. "He spent ten days in a medically induced coma as they tried to get the swelling around his brain down. When he woke up, he struggled with headaches, memory loss, his emotions, and the ability to do regular day-to-day tasks. The doctors said he'd suffered from a traumatic brain injury in the crash and it developed into posttraumatic dementia."

Hannah gasped and her brow creased in a frown. "'I'm sorry' feels like a pitifully inadequate thing to say, but I am so incredibly sorry." She let go of her side of the seat and put her hand on mine.

"Thank you." I appreciated the gesture and resisted the urge to stop walking and pull her into my arms for a hug.

"Is Julian his caregiver?" she asked.

"Yes, he's an occupational therapist with experience in helping patients with chronic traumatic encephalopathy. PTD presents similarly to CTE, and Charlie has made huge strides under Julian's care," I said. I hesitated and then added, "But it's not cheap."

Hannah nodded in understanding. I was unloading a lot of personal stuff onto her and Charlie was waiting for us. Also, I didn't want her to think I was trying to guilt her into agreeing to sell our house.

"Does Charlie live near here?"

"No, he's in a group home in Raleigh with four other men. They have similar conditions and needs and have created a found family there."

"I'm glad he's doing so well under the circumstances," she said. "I can't imagine how hard that was to go through for him and for all of you."

"It certainly wasn't the plan," I said. "Charlie was Gramps's right-hand man in his insurance business. It was the role he'd been born to and he took it on without hesitation. Charlie was going to do amazing things with the company."

"What was he like as an older brother?" Hannah tipped her head to the side, waiting for my answer as I sifted through a lifetime of memories.

"He's three years older than me, and he was my hero. Still is in many ways. I was happy to be his sidekick. I followed him everywhere and wanted to dress like him, act like him, and be just like him, but then our mom passed away from pancreatic cancer, and Charlie went away to college, and it was just me and Dad and Lor and everything changed."

"How so?"

"Without Charlie as buffer, my father was entirely too aware of me and the fact that I wasn't the charmer, the athlete, or the leader that Charlie was," I said. "My father didn't understand my love of art over football and it made life . . . difficult until my father decided he didn't want the responsibility anymore and turned Lorelei and me over to Gramps so he could start over in Florida without any baggage."

I felt Hannah's swift glance on the side of my face, but I kept my gaze on the road ahead. How much did I want to share? A part of me wanted to share all of it, every miserable moment of my home life from those years, but to what purpose? This conversation was about Charlie and it was best to focus on that.

"Needless to say, after the accident the one thing I could do for Charlie was to make sure he got the very best care, so I took his place in the business since Gramps had retired and I've been an insurance guy ever since. Given that Charlie's conservatorship became my responsibility after Gramps passed, it's all worked out for the best."

"That's . . . you . . ." Hannah's voice trailed off as if she couldn't figure out what exactly she wanted to say. "You're a good brother, O'Malley."

"Nah, that's just what you do for family," I corrected.

We reached the house. Julian was parked in front and I could see him and Charlie watching our neighbors as they sorted the stuff from the attic.

Zach was the first to spot us and his guffaw was enough to startle the birds out of the trees and set the dogs to barking. Dude ran at us at a gallop from around the side of the house. I wondered if he was upset that he'd missed the fun, but Frank was hot on his heels and Dude seemed happy to have his little buddy by his side.

"You know that bike wasn't built to ride *on* the water, Simon," Roland teased with a full belly laugh.

"That's why Monica and I don't have one of those," Davis chimed in. "I call them divorce bikes."

"That's because you'd try to boss me around and we both know how that would go," Monica retorted.

"Something like that." Davis waved his hands at us.

"Any word from Bebe or Luke?" Hannah asked.

"Minor update," Stephanie said. "She's dilated to four centimeters and holding."

Hannah nodded, absently patting Dude's head. Then she glanced at me and said, "I call first shower."

I had no chance to respond as she bolted into the house, leaving me muddy and dripping in the yard with our neighbors as my brother and Julian joined me.

"Another O'Malley?" Zach asked as he approached with his hand out while cradling an old brass lamp with his other arm.

"My brother, Charlie, and his friend Julian," I confirmed. I took a minute to introduce them to the rest of the neighbors. I watched Charlie closely. He nodded and smiled and shook hands, leaving the small talk to Julian. He looked shy and a bit nervous, so different from the boisterous charmer he once was.

Our neighbors had only nice things to say about Gramps but they didn't mention the nature of his relationship with Pops, for which I was grateful. If Charlie happened to talk to our father, I didn't want him to mention Hannah as anything more than my friend or that our grandfathers shared the cottage. It would invite too much trouble if my father decided he deserved a cut of the cottage and took me and Hannah to court.

"Come on." I parked the bike and led Charlie and Julian around the side of the house to the back. "I'll show you Gramps's fishing dock."

"I'll wait up here and give you brothers some time to yourselves." Julian sat on the steps of the back porch and took out his phone.

"Thanks." I appreciated the gesture. We crossed the lawn, which still looked untamed despite being freshly mowed. Charlie's face lit up at the sight of the dock and the boathouse.

Frank and Dude stretched out in a patch of sun in the middle of the lawn, panting, obviously recovering from playing so hard. We left them to it. Out on the dock the channel was calm with only a slight breeze stirring the marsh grass by the bank.

"Can't you see Gramps, sitting here in his broken old folding chair, puffing his cigar and drinking his whiskey, while fishing?" I glanced at Charlie. I had no idea what he remembered about Gramps. Sometimes it was everything and other times not. I felt a pain in my chest for all that my brother had lost.

"Hey, Simon, watch this!" Charlie yelled. Before I could process what he was doing, Charlie broke into a run and jumped high into the air, tightening himself into a ball before plunging into the water and sending up a huge wave.

It was a direct hit and I was drenched. Not a bad thing since it got a lot of the dried mud off me. I shook my head to get my sodden hair out of my eyes and stared at the water where Charlie had gone down. Oh, shit! Had he forgotten how to swim?

I kicked off my shoes while I pulled my shirt over my head. I emptied my pockets, dropping my phone and wallet as I ran to the edge. I jumped into the water just as I saw my brother hunkered by the edge of the dock—hiding!—while I sailed past him and hit the water in a belly flop that was definitely going to sting. I could hear Charlie laughing as I went under and I felt myself smile as the water closed over my head.

When I surfaced, I shot an arc of water at my brother and he dodged, still laughing. For a second it felt as if we were who we'd always been and my heart swelled.

"That cannonball was not funny, Charlie," I groused.

"Oh, yes, it was," Charlie argued. "You should have expected it."

"You're right. I should have." I swam back toward the dock. "But it's been a long time since we got up to no good together."

There was a cheerfulness in Charlie's gaze that caught me off guard. I narrowed my eyes at him, seeing him, really seeing him for the first time in a long while. His dark hair, so like mine, was longer and curlier. The lines that had bracketed his mouth and the beer gut he'd been rocking before his accident were gone. Clean living and a lot of physical therapy under Julian's care had erased years off him, so much so that I wondered which of us looked like the older brother now. I suspected it was me.

Before I reached him, Charlie let out a yelp and disappeared under the surface.

"Charlie!" I shouted. I swam faster. When I got to the dock there was no sign of him. I dove deep, checking under the dock. The water was muddy and weedy and I couldn't see a thing. Panic started to thump hard in my chest. I needed help. I powered to the surface to call Julian.

When I broke the surface, Charlie was sitting on the dock laughing so hard he was holding his sides. I didn't think, I reacted, slapping the surface of the water and sending a spray over Charlie, which only made him laugh harder.

"Damn it, Charlie, you scared the shit out of me!" I grabbed the side of the dock and put my hand on my chest where my heart was still racing.

Charlie popped to his feet and did another cannonball. He

looked so carefree and full of life that I couldn't be mad, not really. I treaded water, watching the surface for him.

Of course, Charlie came up out of the water like a shark on the Discovery channel and leapt on top of me, sending us both under the surface. I pulled away, putting some distance between us. When I broke the surface, he hit me full in the face with a wave of water.

Our gazes met, his grin was full of mischief, and his eyes twinkled like the Charlie of old. It was as if we were rambunctious teens again. I wished Lor was here to see this. Still, I was just so fucking grateful to have my big brother back even if it was just for a little while. Naturally, I sent a wave crashing over his head.

The battle continued as we maneuvered around each other. I dove under and tried to pull him down. He countered by diving deeper. We both came up for air and the splash battle commenced until we were both winded. I floated on my back while my lungs heaved. I felt duly schooled, given that Charlie was not breathing anywhere near as hard as I was.

"Are you two finished?" I turned to face the dock to see Hannah standing there, holding towels and shaking her head.

"Yes!" Charlie said. He turned to me. "Truce?"

We shook hands but it turned into another grappling match as we each tried to get the upper hand. We landed on the dock in an awkward splat.

"Lovely." Hannah dropped our towels on the dock and turned to go back to the house. Dude and Frank flanked her and she glanced down at them and said, "Thank you two for being such well-behaved boys."

"Was that directed at us?" Charlie asked. "I feel like it was."

"Yup, it was," I confirmed. "Hannah says what she means and means what she says." I watched her go, admiring the swing in her hips and the sway of her ponytail and felt the unfinished business between us stir to life.

I turned away to find Charlie watching me. The glint was still in his eye when he said in a singsong voice, "You like her."

Inexplicably, I felt my face get hot. I hoisted myself up onto the dock, trying to avoid his gaze.

"Is she your girlfriend?" Charlie asked.

In a flash, I felt exactly like I did when I was in middle school and he was in high school and he was teasing me about my biology lab partner, Priya Patel, who was a stone-cold fox by seventh-grade standards. I'd been so embarrassed I'd skipped biology for a week until my mother got a call from my science teacher wanting to know why I was at the nurse every fifth period.

With her extraordinary mother's intuition, Mom had parsed out what had happened and read Charlie the riot act. To his credit, Charlie felt bad about it and apologized. But my former friendship with Priya was ruined forever.

I glanced at Charlie and said, "Remember what happened the last time you teased me about a girl?"

Charlie's brow scrunched up in concentration. His eyes were worried when he said, "Don't tell Mom, okay?"

I stared at him for a beat. Did I remind him that Mom was gone? That we weren't kids anymore? I couldn't do it. Instead, I punched him in the shoulder like we used to and said, "Of course not. I'll always have your back, Charlie."

"And I'll have yours," he said.

It was a long-held promise among Charlie, me, and Lor. Out of the few things he remembered from our childhood, I was glad he remembered that.

Charlie climbed onto the dock and I handed him a towel.

"Are you dating her?" He rubbed his hair with the towel.

What to say . . . what to say. I decided on the truth without the full disclosure. "I'm hoping to."

"Only hoping?" Charlie's eyebrows shot up. "She seems nice. You should ask her out."

I bent over and dried my legs. I didn't want to think about how a real relationship with Hannah would be. She'd been very clear that she didn't do long-term and, truthfully, if I took away this cottage as a connection, I wasn't certain she would want to have anything to do with me.

"We'll see," I said. "I haven't known her very long."

Charlie nodded. "I met a woman at the library the other day. She had a cool tattoo of books going up her arm."

I studied Charlie's face. There was a faint pink tinge in his cheeks as if he was embarrassed, and I realized he'd been teasing me about Hannah because he had a crush of his own. He hadn't shown any interest in women at all since his accident and I felt a hopeful little flutter in my chest that this woman might see all the good in Charlie and maybe . . . then the panic set in. What if she didn't like Charlie? What if he pestered her and got into trouble? I took a slow breath, forcing myself to be steady.

"Does she work at the library?" I asked.

"She volunteers. Her name is Diana and she lives in a group home like mine."

Okay, then. "Are you going to ask her out?"

Charlie grinned, looking pleased with himself. "I already did and she said yes."

I clapped him on the shoulder. "Good for you. What does Julian think?"

"He likes her." Charlie glanced up to where Julian was throwing the ball for Dude and Frank. He waved at Julian, who waved back. "He said he'd drive us."

"Well, that's great, Charlie," I said. "Just . . . um . . . take it slow, you know?"

Charlie nodded. "I will. I know I'm not like I used to be. You know, comfortable around women and all smooth and stuff."

He didn't say it with any self-pity but it caused my heart to twist in my chest all the same. Back in the day, Charlie could have had any woman he wanted. He'd had it all—charm, looks, smarts, kindness, money—the women had flocked to him. Heck, not just the women. Everyone had loved Charlie O'Malley.

"So . . . um . . . can I borrow a suit?" Charlie gave me a hopeful glance.

"Is that why you came to see me today?"

Charlie shrugged. "Yeah, I knew you'd have some really good ones."

I felt a slow smile curve my lips. Borrowing a suit was such a brotherly thing to do. It made me feel ridiculously happy that he'd come to me.

"Of course, you can borrow whatever you want." I threw my arm around his shoulders and led him up to the house. Between me, Gramps, and Pops—if Hannah was okay with it—Charlie was going to have the best dating wardrobe a guy could want.

Unsurprisingly, Hannah took to the dressing of Charlie as if it were her job. She had him in and out of outfits—casual, formal, sporty—while color-matching his complexion to each shirt and blazer.

Most of our neighbors had gone home to await news of Bebe and the baby, but Zach and Roland joined Julian and me on the couch in the living room as Hannah trotted Charlie through for our opinions. Not that what we had to say mattered very much. Hannah and Charlie were in a full-on fashion mind meld. At one point I heard them laughing together in the bedroom and I was torn between delight that she and my brother were bonding so hard and straight-up jealousy that I wanted it to be me laughing with her.

I shook it off and turned to Julian. "This date, it's a good thing?"

Julian nodded. "It's a great thing. Don't worry. He's ready."

"Does my father know?" I had a slight paranoia that my father would try to use Charlie dating as a way to get the courts to give Charlie's conservatorship to him.

"Not from me and not from Charlie." Julian met my gaze and said, "You and Lorelei are the only people outside his fellow residents that he's told about Diana."

"And what's her story?" I asked. I didn't want to sound like a hard-ass but I didn't want Charlie to get hurt.

"She's your age, attractive, volunteers at the library and an animal shelter," Julian said. "But that's not what you want to know."

I stared at him and he sighed. "Because she's not my patient, I can tell you that she has autism. She manages very well in structured environments, which is why her caregiver and I will be accompanying Diana and Charlie on their dates to help them communicate their needs in a dating situation, at least for now."

"Her caregiver, huh?"

Julian glanced away. "It's purely professional."

"Right." I scoffed. Julian ignored me but I could tell by his smile that he was interested in the other caregiver. Good. Julian was a great guy. He deserved to be happy.

"All right, get ready. Here he comes!" Hannah came bounding down the steps with Dude and Frank on her heels. She clapped her hands to get our attention. Roland and Zach looked up from their phones while Julian and I straightened up.

"May I present Charlie O'Malley, wearing the latest in men's formal apparel . . ." Hannah moved to the side of the bottom step and we all glanced at the stairs. No one appeared.

"Charlie, that's your cue," Hannah hissed up the steps.

"Oh! Okay!"

Charlie, dressed to kill in my navy blue Canali suit with a white dress shirt open at the throat and wearing a pair of my brown Jimmy Choo loafers, strode down the stairs, looking so much like the Charlie of old that the sight of him was like being blasted back in time.

"Dang, you are one sharp-dressed man," Roland said.

"I'll say," Zach agreed. "Your lady's heart doesn't stand a chance."

"You think?" Charlie looked so shy and earnest as he glanced down at the suit that eight years ago wouldn't have meant anything to him other than another day at work. My throat constricted into a hard knot and I blinked back the tears in my eyes, not wanting Charlie to misread my emotion and be distressed.

"Oh, wait!" Hannah reached into her pocket and said, "Give me your wrists."

Charlie did without question. I watched Hannah fasten the mother-of-pearl cuff links that had belonged to her Pops, the same ones that had made her cry, to the cuffs of my brother's shirt and I felt my heart do a free fall right into her hands. I was so fucked.

I was about to excuse myself to go outside and regroup when the front door burst open and Stephanie stood there with a grin as wide as the sky.

"Bebe had the baby!" she cried. She threw herself into Roland's arms and he let out a whoop of joy. Zach was next and he peppered her with questions. "Is she all right? Is the baby all right? What did she have? Is Luke okay?"

My gaze shot to Hannah's. She had her hands pressed to her

mouth, as if bracing for any bad news and I was reminded of how fraught this must be for her. I didn't think about it. I crossed the room to stand beside her, giving her my unspoken support. She didn't look at me but leaned slightly against me.

Stephanie laughed and said, "Bebe's fine. The baby is perfect and a girl. And, yes, other than crying with joy, Luke is fine. He said Bebe pushed that baby out like a champ."

Hannah let out a relieved sigh and fell against me, wrapping her arms around my middle in a solid hug. I caught her close and held her tight, reveling in the feel of her body against mine.

A surprising surge of happiness thrummed through me as I thought of our new friends and their bundle of joy. Our friends. It hit me then that Hannah and I were making friends together. I couldn't remember the last time I'd had couple friends or if I'd ever had them. It was . . . nice.

"How long will they be at the hospital?" Roland asked.

"Overnight." Stephanie glanced at us.

"Frank is welcome to spend the night with us." Hannah glanced at me and added, "Or for as long as Bebe, Luke, and the baby need to get settled when they get home."

"Absolutely," I agreed. I glanced at Charlie and Julian. "How about you? Are you spending the night?"

"No, we have to get back to the house," Julian said.

"But we can stay for dinner," Charlie said. "Can't we?"

Hannah reached over and squeezed his arm. "We won't take no for an answer."

There it was again. "We." I really loved the sound of that.

Zach, Roland, and Stephanie departed, leaving Charlie and Julian as our sole dinner guests. Charlie was so excited about his date, we spent most of the meal going over proper date etiquette. Hannah let him practice pulling her chair out and coached him on how to compliment Diana without being inappropriate.

By unspoken agreement, neither Hannah nor I mentioned the true nature of Gramps and Pops's relationship or that they co-owned the house. I didn't think the shared ownership would matter to Charlie, but I didn't want him to inadvertently mention any of this to my father.

After dinner, I walked Julian and Charlie out to their car.

Roland had updated me on the status of the items from the attic. Charity donations had been taken by Roland and Zach to the local secondhand center. Items that were broken or no longer useful had been set aside for a run to the dump. And keepers, like the tandem bike, had been put away.

"I'll go start the car." Julian held out his hand and we shook. "Good to see you, Simon."

"You, too. And thanks for bringing Charlie for a visit."

"Anytime." Julian strode around the car with a wave.

Charlie and I stood silently for a moment. The clothes he was borrowing had already been packed in a box by Hannah and were in the back of the SUV.

"Will you be coming to Raleigh anytime soon?" Charlie asked.

"Not for at least a month," I said. "I have to deal with selling Gramps's place and all. But keep me in the loop about your date."

A faint pink tinged Charlie's cheeks. "I will. I promise."

"And if you need anything, you know you can call me or Lor anytime, day or night." It had been such a nice day with Charlie that I found myself reluctant to let him go.

"I know." Charlie pulled me in for a quick catch-and-release hug. "Simon, I think if you sell, you might lose more than just a house. It feels more like a home." He jutted his chin and I turned to see Hannah in the window with Dude.

The dog was standing on his hind legs with his front paws on her shoulders and they were . . . dancing? Her high ponytail swung in time to the beachy surf music she had playing on the wireless speaker she'd synced to her phone during Charlie's fashion show. I felt a wide smile curve my lips.

Charlie clapped me on the shoulder and said, "Go dance with your girl, bro."

It felt like something the old Charlie would have said. He didn't have to tell me twice. I strode into the house and paused in the doorway to the living room. Hannah was singing and Dude leaned his head back and howled in what I assumed was his harmony part. Frank sat on the couch watching the duo with his tongue hanging out. I crossed the room driven by the simple need, as primal as the need to breathe, to have this woman in my arms again.

I paused behind Dude and tapped his shoulder. "May I cut in?"

Dude woofed and hopped down, moving onto the couch, where he sat with his buddy, awaiting his next turn. I didn't have the heart to tell him I was not planning on letting go of this woman anytime soon.

Hannah

I felt my breath hitch when Simon slid his arm about my waist and pulled me close. I was caught off guard by his willingness to dance. Most of the men in my life to date, including my ex-husband, had not been comfortable on the dance floor. Afraid of looking like a fool, my ex had always refused and if I danced with my friends, he'd pouted. Needless to say, there had not been a lot of partner dancing in my life. I was prepared for the simple side-to-side swaying that most men preferred. To say I was wrong about Simon O'Malley was a colossal understatement.

He pulled me in tight and with our bodies just inches apart, he moved his hand to my hip and guided me into a seductive two-step—quick, quick, slow, slow, repeat—that included him spinning me out and reeling me back in.

"What was that?" I cried as I landed against his chest with all the grace of Dude pouncing on one of his toys.

"You might not be aware, being a New Englander and all, but any Southern man worth his salt knows how to dance—a two-step at the very least—or so my mama said when she forced Charlie and me to learn how to dance."

"I did not know that." My voice was breathy and it wasn't from exertion.

"Come on, there's not enough room in here." He took me by the hand and grabbed the wireless speaker as he led me out onto the back deck.

The sun was just setting and the sky was turning a soft orange sliding into a deep red at the horizon. Simon set the speaker on the railing and turned to me. He held out his hands and I took a second to take him in from his dark wavy curls and arching brows, to his warm brown eyes, square jaw, and full lips. It was unfair that he was so ludicrously handsome. He was tall and lean and when I took his hands and slid into his arms I immediately felt safe.

He held me close for just a moment, pressing his cheek to my hair. "Do you know what drives me crazy about you?"

"My refusal to sell the cottage?" I asked.

I felt his smile and he released me, putting one hand on my hip while taking my hand with the other. He began a slow two-step, guiding me effortlessly into mirroring his moves.

"No." He shook his head. "It's the smell of your hair. Coconut and lime. It's been driving me crazy since our first night at the cottage."

I was immediately flustered but tried not to show it. "Good to know I have a secret weapon when it comes to bending you to my will, O'Malley."

His small closed-lip smile plucked all my heartstrings as he spun me once, twice, three times until I felt as if I was flying within the safety of his arms. It was beautiful and I felt for the first time in a long time like the carefree girl I once was. He caught me gently and we moved slowly around the deck to the charming duet "You Look Like You Love Me" by Ella Langley and Riley Green.

"Do you know what drives me crazy about you?" I asked.

"My determination to sell the house," he said.

I shook my head. "No. It's that one dimple you get in your cheek on the right side when you smile."

He blinked in surprise, then his brow furrowed. "I don't have a dimple."

"Yeah, you do," I said. "And it's dead sexy."

He spun me again and I felt the night air whoosh past my face as the sky twirled by in a kaleidoscope of colors, peach and crimson and dusky violet. I laughed out loud with the sheer joy of it. And when I landed back in Simon's arms, he was grinning. It was big and bold and beautiful and his dimple winked at me like it was beckoning me in.

I reached up and gently let my finger run over the dimple that intrigued me so. He had just the one, not a matched set, as if his life didn't allow him to have that much joy, as if he was made of half happy and half sad. Weren't we all?

He caught my hand when I took it away and he placed it on his shoulder. He pulled my body into his and again I followed his lead, wrapping my arms around his neck. When he lowered his head to kiss me, I met him halfway. The awareness that had been building between us over the past few weeks was now all-consuming.

The only thing I felt was him. His scent, his touch, his warmth, all of it wrapped me in a cocoon where nothing else mattered. Not the house, not our grandfathers or their secret relationship, nothing but Simon and me was allowed in this safe space.

Then he kissed me and I couldn't even remember where we were or what my name was. Much like our dance, it started out quick, quick, and then slow. He kissed me, then nipped my mouth, and then slid his tongue across my lower lip, romancing me with his mouth just as he had when we danced.

I opened my mouth and he accepted the invitation without hesitation, but I wasn't willing to just follow this time. I wanted him to feel as wooed as I did. I slid my hands into his hair. He moaned, letting me know this was appreciated. I angled his head down so that I could kiss him as thoroughly as he'd kissed me. To my delight, he let me take the lead, moving his hands to my hips to steady me while I stood on tiptoe and sought out the taste of him with a single-mindedness that left us both breathless.

When I pulled back, his eyes burned with a heat that scorched. I had done that to him. Me. It was heady stuff.

"I know I said we shouldn't get involved." Simon brushed a lock of hair out of my eyes. "And while I'm not normally a short-term guy, I'll take whatever you're offering, Spencer, because I want to be with you for however long you'll have me, assuming you still want this."

Want this? My god, I was sure I'd die if I didn't have him right now.

"Take me to bed, O'Malley." My voice was husky and rough with need.

His dimple flashed and he lowered his head until his mouth was next to mine. "I thought you'd never ask." Then he scooped me up as if I were a dainty little thing, which I was not, and carried me into the house. Dude was asleep, belly-up on the couch, and Frank was curled up beside him. I thought Simon would put me down and we'd walk up the stairs, but no. He carried me up to the landing and wasn't even breathing heavy when we reached the top.

"Which room?" he asked. We looked at each other and I said, "Yours," at the same time he said, "Mine."

We were in accord. Somehow it just felt wrong to do the wild thing in the bedroom our grandfathers had shared.

Simon carried me into his room and kicked the door shut behind him. Once inside, he shifted me in his arms so that I slid down his body until I was standing in front of him. He reached up and brushed a lock of hair that had slipped from my ponytail out of my eyes and the gentleness of the touch made me ache for so much more.

I quickly pulled my hair tie loose, letting my hair fall down around my shoulders. Simon reached out and let the strands slide through his fingers. Then he pulled me close and lowered his lips to mine.

His kiss was slow and soft as if he knew he had all night and he planned to use every moment of it. A biting fierce need inside of me rose as he kissed me, plundering my mouth with his tongue, running his lips down the side of my neck, while his hands slid up my sides to cup my breasts, which had become unbearably sensitive.

When he broke the kiss, I reached for the hem of his T-shirt. It was a crazy sort of madness that drove me as I pulled it over his head. I needed to touch him, to run my hands along the taut muscles of his chest and abs. I found myself resisting the urge to rub myself all over him as if I were a cat—this was not a reaction I could ever remember having for a half-naked man at my fingertips before.

"Easy, Spencer." Simon captured my hands, holding them out to my sides while he kissed me. "We've got all night and many orgasms to go. Pace yourself."

"Many?" My voice was something between a squeak and a whisper.

"Three at the very least," he promised. Oh, my.

I was only surprised I didn't immediately melt into a puddle of goo right there. I blinked at him and he chuckled low in his throat. His hands slid down my sides again to the bottom of my tank top.

As if he was savoring unwrapping a present, he slowly inched my shirt up, revealing my skin bit by bit. Then he kneeled in front of me and kissed the skin as it was exposed, moving ever so slowly up to my breasts, which were already tight in response to his nearness.

The blood was pounding in my ears. I was hot and there was a frantic fluttering feeling inside of me that demanded to be released. I plowed my fingers into his hair and tilted his head back so he could see the need on my face.

"Spencer, that might be the sexiest look any woman has ever given me," he drawled. Then he pulled my shirt over my head as he rose and scooped me up in his arms. In three steps he crossed to the bed and dropped me onto the covers. Thank goodness, if I was going to fall into an abyss of pleasure, I didn't want to attempt it while standing.

He climbed up beside me and stretched out, resting one very large hand on my abdomen as if to keep me in place while he continued kissing me, as the other speared into my hair, cradling the back of my head. When I slid my hands over his shoulders and pulled him closer, he grunted approval and his hand began to explore every inch of me while his mouth took mine, kissing me with a skill I'd never experienced before.

I could feel the hard calluses on his palms roughly rub along my skin as he slid his hand from my ankle, over my knee, along the inside of my thigh, where he paused to squeeze the throbbing juncture between my legs. I bucked against his hold, looking for relief, but his fingers moved on, caressing my hip and sliding up my side until he reached my breast, now clothed in just a bra.

In seconds, his fingers undid the front clasp and my breasts spilled out. I was amply built all over thanks to the aftereffects of the hormones I'd taken while trying to get pregnant, but I refused to let my mind go to a place where I felt less than for being curvy.

Still, I glanced at Simon's face, trying to determine how he felt about my body.

He used one finger to slide over my exposed nipples and my back arched. He breathed one word before he lowered his head and sucked the aching tip into his mouth. "Gorgeous."

My entire body flushed and I didn't know if it was the pleasure from his touch or the happiness from his praise or a combination of both. I just knew that never ever in my thirty-two years of aliveness had I ever wanted anyone as desperately as I wanted Simon O'Malley right now.

"Now, O'Malley," I groaned as he moved his leg between mine, pressing his weight against my heat-slickened core.

"No." He continued to tongue my nipple, then he sucked one between his teeth, giving me a jolt of pleasure-pain that almost made me come without even taking off my shorts.

This was simply not fair. It was as if he'd been given a manual on exactly how to touch me but I knew that wasn't it. What Simon had that no other man in my romantic life did—not my ex or my many flings—was the power of observation. When I arched my back in response to his touch, he noticed and he doubled down. If my breath caught in my throat, he registered the response and used it against me to elicit more gasps and sighs.

I refused to let him be the only one skilled at this dance, however. I loosened my grip on his shoulders and let my hands skim down his arms, moving to his sides and very purposefully tracing the defined muscles of his torso until I reached his waist, where I didn't hesitate but used one hand to grip his hip and the other to cup and squeeze the hard length of him beneath his shorts. The hiss he drew through his teeth might have been the most satisfying sound I'd ever heard. It was my turn to chuckle.

Simon captured my hands in his and held them by my side while he nudged my legs farther apart with his knee and settled himself in the cradle of my thighs as if he planned to be there for a very long time. He let go of my hands and started kissing me again, but this time both of his hands were busy, alternately tracing my curves with gentle fingers and kneading my ass while hauling me closer. Thought ceased. All I could do was feel.

By the time I felt him unbutton my shorts and slide my remaining clothes down my legs, I felt as if my insides had liquefied. More. I wanted more and more and more of him, touching me, kissing me, slipping inside of me, I was more ready than I'd ever been. Simon, however, had other ideas.

As he tossed my shorts and undies over his shoulder, he shifted until his mouth was at the juncture of my legs. I sucked in a breath when I realized his intent. My ex had never enjoyed oral, either giving or receiving, and so I had always felt awkward when a guy headed down south. I rose up on my elbows and started to protest, but Simon grasped me under the knees and yanked me back down, putting my legs over his shoulders as he moved in on me. I could feel his hot breath against my tender skin and I lost the will to fight. If this was what the man wanted to do, far be it from me to get in his way.

His lips moved up my inner thigh and I melted. His teeth nipped my clit and I arched as exquisite sensations rocketed through me. I was so close I knew if he open-mouth kissed me I was going to explode into an orgasm of cataclysmic proportions. Instead, Simon slipped one finger inside and gently pumped. It felt amazing. Then he added a finger and I was sure I saw stars. Then he kissed me, stroking my clit in a firm circular motion with his tongue while his fingers kept up the pressure and I let out a moan as the orgasm crashed over me in blissful waves of sensation. I felt as if I were a star exploding across the night sky. Simon didn't stop stroking with his tongue or his fingers until my orgasm finished with one final shudder.

He moved back up my body with predatory grace. The wicked dimple flashed in his cheek as he smiled with supreme male satisfaction. When my gaze met his, he said, "That's one."

I laughed. It came out low and throaty as if I were some sexy siren and not a woman who lived in her van with her dog. Then again, why couldn't I be both? Simon had laid me bare, literally, and it was time to do the same to him.

I reached between us and unfastened his shorts, pushing his clothing down past his jutting erection—well, hello—and over his firm backside to his thighs, where I used my feet to push them down all the way. I put my hands on his hips and pushed him up so I could take in all of him from his sculpted physique, to his beautiful face and crown of wavy hair. Had I ever been with such a perfect male specimen? No. Unequivocally, no.

"Why are you so perfect?" I asked. "Tell me you have a bunion somewhere."

He choked out a laugh. "What?"

"Dandruff," I said. "Please have dandruff."

"Sorry, no." He was still smiling as he leaned in to nuzzle my neck.

"A hairy wart?"

"Nope."

"There has to be something wrong with you," I protested. "It's simply not fair for you to be this handsome, smart, sexy, and kind. Come on, give me something."

"Why?" he asked. "I'd say we're perfectly matched."

I shook my head at him. "Um, I know you're in bed with a naked woman and that could make a guy temporarily mentally impaired but we are not the same." I gestured between us.

"Of course we are," he said. "You are exquisite."

I'd have argued the point but he swooped in and kissed me and I lost the thread of the discussion. I hadn't thought I could queue up for another orgasm so fast, but there I was, clinging to him and touching him everywhere my fingers could reach. I wanted to memorize every rippling muscle, I wanted to draw him—which was weird because I couldn't draw—still, I felt this need to seek out every inch of his skin and memorize the feel of him beneath my fingers. When I moved my hands up his thigh he stilled. I didn't.

I stroked his cock in a firm grip and I heard him mutter under his breath just before he grabbed my hand and redirected it to his pecs.

"Careful there, we don't want to have an early discharge," he drawled, and I felt a rush of power. Did I do that to him? Me?

I rolled out from beneath him and pushed him onto his back. I climbed on top of him, straddling his hips until his cock was pressed right where I wanted it. I swear I could feel it pulse against my opening and I felt a flutter of another orgasm building. I bracketed his head with my hands and said, "Now, Simon, I need you now."

At the use of his first name, his nostrils flared and he grabbed a condom from the nightstand and made quick work of sheathing his length before he grabbed my hips with his hands. I reached down and guided him to my entrance. The clenched muscles of my previous orgasm resisted him just enough to make his entry a delicious stretch that caused even more sensations to swamp me.

He slid in so gently, as if to be certain I was ready. Heck, I was so ready I wanted to bite something—him. Instead, I spread my knees and lowered myself onto him with a decisive drop. He hissed at the sensation of me squeezing him and his eyes shut as he went perfectly still as if fighting for control. I didn't want him to have any control. I straightened up and grabbed the headboard in my hands and moved up and down, establishing a vigorous rhythm as I chased down the sweet sensation that was beginning to swell inside of me.

Simon let out a grunt of satisfaction and reached up to cup my breasts, his thumbs flicking my nipples as I kept up the pace. I felt his hips stiffen and I knew he was close. I wanted him to lose it just as I had and I wanted to be the one who drove him right over the edge. I reached behind me to cup him at the juncture of his legs and he arched his back as if he was about to climax, but no. Instead, he gritted his teeth and rolled us over until I was under him again.

"You are a wicked woman." He drove into me and I arched, trying to get closer as I felt the beginning of my orgasm sparkle in my peripheral vision.

I wanted to shout his name, knowing it would push him over the edge, but I'd lost my powers of speech as the swirling desire dragged me under and all I could do was tighten my core, waiting for the release to break over me.

As if he was right there with me, Simon lifted one of my legs and drove more deeply into me. Then he lowered his mouth to my ear and whispered, "I swear I could happily drown in you, Hannah."

It was the first time he'd used my first name, and it sent a shiver down my spine, which detonated my orgasm and I felt my body clench and release around him as the pleasure rippled through me.

"Simon." It came out as a multisyllabic moan and Simon responded by thrusting into me once, twice, three times and then he was in the same whirlwind of sensation I was. We clung to each other as we rode out the waves. When it finally stopped, Simon rolled to his side, taking me with him.

I was draped half across him and as limp and sated as I'd ever been when I felt him kiss my hair as he said, "That's two."

I awoke hours later and slipped away to shower. I was just rinsing off the bodywash when Simon slipped into the shower with me. I wish I could say it was his fault but it was me. I was the problem. The sight of the hot water sluicing down his muscular form behooved me to soap the man up from top to bottom and he let me. When he turned me around to face the wall and slid into me from behind, well, it was the quickest foreplay to orgasm of the night.

When my legs would have given out, he wrapped his arms around me, pulling my back to his chest. He nuzzled the sweet spot at the curve of my shoulder and growled, "That's three."

The man positively swaggered when we left the shower and, honestly, I couldn't begrudge him a bit of it.

Simon

The scent of coconut and lime filtered into my sleep, rousing me and not just into a state of awake. I reached across the bed, seeking the woman who had slept in my arms all night but all I found was a fistful of cold sheet. Hannah was gone.

I sat up and glanced around the bedroom. Had I dreamed last night? I leaned over and sniffed her pillow. No, there was the scent of her shampoo clinging to the cotton. She had definitely been in my bed. I adjusted my situation and pushed the covers back. I grabbed my clothes and pulled them on while I moved across the room. I had no idea why the need to see her felt so imperative but it did.

I heard humming coming from the kitchen at the same time the scent of hot coffee hit my nose. It took me a moment to recognize the song she was humming as the one we had danced to the night before. She sounded happy and I realized the Hannah I had come to know was not one to sing in the morning and definitely not before breakfast. I decided it had to be the three orgasms that had put her in a good mood, because they'd certainly worked for me. I smiled when remembering her coming apart for me repeatedly. A guy could get addicted to that sort of response.

I paused in the doorway to watch her standing in front of the stove cooking something that smelled like home with notes of vanilla and cinnamon. She had her hair up in a messy bun and she was barefoot, wearing a faded purple T-shirt with a national park logo on the front and a baggy pair of linen shorts. She was beyond a doubt the sexiest woman I had ever seen.

Dude and Frank were sacked out at her feet and she paused in her singing to lift the frying pan off the stove. "Okay, guys, watch this."

The dogs' ears perked up as she shook the pan back and forth. "And now for the flip!" she announced, and she jerked the frying pan. I watched as a pancake flew up in the air, flipping end over end as it went. Hannah moved the pan to catch it, but the pancake never came back down. Instead, it adhered itself to the ceiling with Hannah and the dogs staring at it with matching looks of disappointment.

"Well, that underwhelms." Hannah reached for a spatula to scrape it off the ceiling but even on her tiptoes she couldn't reach.

"Need a hand?" I stepped into the kitchen and she started.

A faint pink blush tinged her cheeks and she waved the spatula at me. "I . . . uh . . . was starving so I decided to make apple cinnamon pancakes but . . ." She glanced up. "There have been some technical difficulties."

"You don't say." I took the spatula and the pan from her hands and scraped the pancake off the ceiling and into the pan.

"Thank you." She primly took back her cookware and dumped the pancake into the trash while I used a wet sponge to get the batter residue off the ceiling. I was trying to read her. She looked nervous. I wondered why. Was she second-guessing last night? She'd disappeared down here before I woke up. Was she avoiding me? There was only one way to find out. I steeled myself for whatever she'd decided.

"I managed that stack over there if you're hungry." She put the pan in the sink and waved the spatula at a pile of pancakes on the counter. She didn't make eye contact and her face was still pink. Was she feeling shy? This was surprising for many reasons, not the least of which was the fact that there wasn't an inch of her body that I was not intimately acquainted with now.

"I'm starved." I didn't move. I merely held her gaze and let her see that I was not talking about pancakes.

"Oh . . . my." Her voice was decidedly breathy, and I smiled. There she was. I reached out and grabbed the spatula, using it to pull her toward me.

She sighed when our bodies met and I reached behind her to pull her even closer, locking her in a hug where her head fit perfectly against my shoulder and I could rest my cheek on her hair. Last night with her had been amazing—flirty and fun, sexy and salacious, and tender and touching. Hannah was lush and curvy and sexy as hell and I knew I would never get over how perfect we were in bed, but this, this was even more dangerous because holding this woman in my arms like this was the most at peace I'd felt in years.

She leaned back to study my face and I wondered if my emotions were easy to read. I wasn't ready for that much exposure. I lowered my mouth to hers. I paused just an inch away and she rolled up on her toes and closed the distance, tossing the spatula aside as she looped her arms around my neck. Her lips parted ever so slightly as our mouths met and I took it as an invitation to deepen the kiss. The taste of her was a seductive blend of coffee and cinnamon and I wanted to devour her. I reined in the impulse, barely. When I set her back on her feet, her eyes were half closed and I flexed my fingers on the soft skin of her lower back where her T-shirt had lifted before releasing her.

She shook her head, then glanced about the kitchen as if realizing where we were.

"Well." She cleared her throat and gestured to the coffeepot. I felt my lips curve up as an unfamiliar surge of happiness filled me. I could get used to befuddling this woman with kisses. I poured myself a cup and took a seat at the counter.

Hannah switched off the stove and slid onto the seat next to me. She pushed the butter and syrup at me, while I loaded a plate and set it in front of her before I served myself.

Her eyes widened and she seemed surprised by the gesture. She reached out and squeezed my arm as if she just needed to touch me again. "Thank you."

I felt a tenderness thrum inside of me. Ninety shots. I hadn't forgotten her horror of needles or the reason why. I knew I didn't know her or her relationship with her ex well enough to make assumptions, but I didn't think it was a stretch to assume that a man who would cheat on his wife while she was going through months of fertility treatments was also the sort of selfish prick who had never put her first—not even when it came to serving food.

For the rest of our time in this summer share, I promised myself she would always come first. Starting with our plans for the day.

"I was thinking after we take Frank home, assuming his parents are ready for him, we should visit a few more places that Gramps and Pops enjoyed," I said.

Hannah turned toward me. She had a bite of pancake in her mouth and her expression was surprised. Through her mouthful, she mumbled, "Really?"

"Yeah," I said. "I think you're right. We should take the opportunity to get to know this place that they loved so much."

"That would be amazing," she said. "I was talking to Stephanie and she said before Gramps got sick they rode their bike into town just about every afternoon and stopped at Beach Buns and the coffee shop and then they walked the pier." She paused and I saw a shadow of grief pass over her face. She blinked her eyes quickly as if fighting back tears and her voice was just above a whisper when she said, "I was thinking if we ride their bike into town, we could re-create their time together and maybe I could feel Pops with me. I miss him so much."

"Of course." I put my arm around her and pulled her into a hug. "I really love that idea. I'm sure I'll hear Gramps laughing if this bike ride goes as well as our first attempt."

She snorted and wiped her tears away with the back of her hand. "Thank you. This means a lot to me." Then she grinned and sent me a wicked wink. "Plus, I have an excellent view from the back seat."

"Ha!" I let out a surprised laugh.

"I'll bet you didn't suspect I had an ulterior motive." Her twinkling blue eyes met mine and I felt a gear shift, like sliding from neutral into drive, and I knew she was waking up some dormant part of me that had been on cruise control for far too long.

"And now I'm going to have to add *devious* to the list of things I'm learning about you." I raised one eyebrow, giving her an assessing glance.

She laughed, and it felt like a win to help her move through her grief and find some joy. I could almost feel my chest puff up, I was so pleased to be able to help her.

The self-protective part of me was metaphorically standing under the streetlights, waving his arms to let me know the bridge was out. But it was too late for warnings. I was already attached to

this woman. I wanted to deny it. I told myself I was just interested in learning more about Gramps's life here as his will had dictated, but we were cruising up on four weeks of time spent in this cottage, meaning our required two months were half over. With only four weeks to go, it suddenly felt as if there wasn't enough time to learn all that I wanted to about Gramps's life or about . . . her. The truth was I was way more interested in spending time with Hannah but, yeah, learning about the grandfathers would be cool, too.

I picked up our plates and headed for the sink. Hannah joined me and we washed the dishes together as if we'd been doing this for years instead of weeks. I crouched down to shelve the newly dried pots only to find there wasn't much room in the cupboard. How two grown men had accumulated so much cookware, I had no idea. I was thirty-six and owned a total of three pots and one frying pan.

"You stuck down there, O'Malley?"

"So, it's O'Malley again?"

"In the daytime." She stared down at me with a sassy smirk.

"Are you assuming that Simon only shows up at night, Spencer?" I grabbed her hand and tugged her down to sit on the floor with me, pulling her close until our bodies were flush. I leaned forward and kissed her. It was like a balm. I had the crazy feeling that nothing could touch me if this woman was in my orbit.

"I think Hannah is making an appearance." She made a soft sound in her throat and pulled me in closer, opening her mouth beneath mine and tunneling her fingers into my hair.

I kissed her until I couldn't breathe and then I kissed her some more. I was just about to haul her to her feet and lead her upstairs when a blast of hot breath and a cold snout nudged their way between us.

With a yelp, Hannah and I pulled back to find both Dude and

Frank wedging in between us. Dude had a crocheted pot holder in his mouth, which he dropped into Hannah's lap, while Frank climbed onto my lap, demanding pets.

"I think the chaperones have arrived." I dutifully scratched the pug's belly and he shut his eyes in ecstasy while his tongue slid out the side of his mouth.

Hannah laughed and patted Dude's head before she glanced down at the pot holder. "Oh."

"What is it?"

She gently picked up the colorful square and flipped it over, studying it as if it was more than something to grab hot things with. I waited, watching a parade of emotions cross her face.

"I crocheted this for Pops when I was away at summer camp when I was fifteen because I missed him so much." She sighed. "I can't believe he kept it all these years."

She held it up and I admired the stitching while I pictured a younger version of her, crafting a gift for her Pops. It made my heart ache.

"He obviously loved you very much."

Her smile was small and her eyes sad. "It's just so hard. I miss him so much. I was filming at Arches National Park when my dad called to tell me that they thought it was a matter of days. I had to drive straight through, running on caffeine and panic. I slid into Pops's room right as he took his last breath. I grabbed his hand and said, 'I'm here,' but he didn't come back and I don't even know if he knew I was there." A tear slid down her cheek and I reached up and caught it with my thumb. Her voice was little more than a sob when she said, "I never had a chance to say a proper good-bye."

I pulled her close and let her cry it out on my shoulder. I could feel the fabric of my shirt getting damp and didn't care. She could soak me through with her tears and I'd be grateful just to be there to ease her pain if I could.

As if sensing the solemnity of the moment, Dude lay down beside her and plopped his head in Hannah's lap while Frank remained in mine. Somehow it felt right to be in this tangle of human and canine as Hannah worked through her feelings.

"Sorry, for some reason my emotions are extremely close to the surface today." Hannah sniffed and pulled back to meet my gaze.

"Three orgasms will do that, or so I've heard," I teased.

She laughed and pushed halfheartedly at my chest. "Quite proud of that, aren't you?"

"Not gonna brag, but I think it was some of my best work." I shrugged.

"I'll say it was." Her voice dropped to a husky whisper and I felt a flash of heat hit me low and deep.

"Careful, Spencer, or we'll never make it out of the kitchen."

"Would that be so bad?" She twined her arms around my neck and pulled me close. Her mouth moved across mine with a seductive sweetness that lured me in on every level. I could have kissed her for hours, days, or possibly weeks. But I also wanted to know that she was okay. I remembered my initial depression after Gramps passed. I forced myself to keep busy at work, never allowing the grief in. I wished I could grieve with the abandon that Hannah did. I'd locked down the pain so hard in the days following Gramps's death that I had yet to cry and sometimes, I just felt completely broken inside.

I eased out of the kiss, cupped her face in my hands, and took a moment to appreciate her half-lidded swollen-lipped dreamy expression and damn near lost my purpose. Instead, I shook my head like Dude when he came out of the water, cleared my throat, and said, "Are you okay?"

She sighed and leaned into me, her head fitting perfectly against my shoulder. I rested my cheek on top of her head and it felt as if we'd been engineered to fit just so.

"Thank you for asking," she said. "I will be. I know you didn't get to say good-bye to Gramps, either. Have you made peace with it? Does it get easier?"

"I think it's easier for me because his last words to me were to get it together and go live the life I wanted. A nice kick in the pants, which felt like an appropriate last conversation coming from him," I said.

Hannah chuckled and I knew it was because she had come to know Gramps through me and she could understand what I was saying, just as I understood how much it hurt her not to have had that same sort of moment with her Pops.

"Of course, I couldn't just pitch my responsibilities and pursue my dreams," I said. "But I did take his words to heart, and I am trying to live up to his expectations."

"I'm glad you had that time together." She hugged me, resting her head on my shoulder and I kissed her hair, inhaling the soothing scent that was uniquely hers.

"Come on, let's get out of here." I glanced at the clock. "Luke texted that he and Bebe were leaving the hospital this morning. We can walk Frank home so he can meet his new sister."

Bebe was tucked into a recliner in the living room while Luke was in the kitchen making her a sandwich. Hannah was seated next to Bebe, listening as she told the story of Luke almost passing out while holding her in place for the epidural.

"It's a very large needle!" Luke yelled from the kitchen.

Bebe and Hannah exchanged a knowing look and I was struck

by how normal it felt to be here in this moment right now. I had a feeling of belonging that was so unexpected it caught me off guard. I glanced down at the little human bundle in my arms.

Were newborns always this tiny? She barely filled both of my hands. Why were they entrusting me with this itty-bitty little being? What if I dropped her? I stood perfectly still, terrified I might trip. I studied her thick eyelashes and tiny nose and her wizened little face. She was so defenseless, I felt a primal urge to slay dragons for her if it was required . . . or was she? What the little one lacked in size, she made up for in volume. One moment she was deep in dreamland and the next her tiny little limbs twitched and her face scrunched up as she began wailing.

"Um . . . Luke . . . Bebe . . . Hannah . . . help."

Bebe turned toward me and held up her hands. I gently lowered the baby into them and released a breath I hadn't known I was holding.

Baby girl settled into her mother's arms as if she knew that was exactly where she was supposed to be. Hannah reached up and took one tiny little fist between her thumb and forefinger.

"She is perfection." Hannah and Bebe studied the tiny one with matching awed smiles. Hannah rose to her feet and said, "We'll let you settle in. Call us if you need anything. Dude is always happy to have Frank come and play."

"Thank you." Bebe reached up and squeezed Hannah's hand and then mine. "I'm so glad you two are our neighbors. Bobby and Billy were two of the first people I told that I was pregnant. Having you with us just feels right."

We walked home with our fingers interlaced. It was a meandering walk. We didn't rush. We let the ocean breeze gently nudge us toward the cottage. There were boxes upon boxes to be sorted and I wondered what we'd discover next about our grandfathers.

I glanced at the woman beside me and was hit with the realization that if I had inherited this cottage all by my lonesome, without anyone to meet the neighbors or share the discoveries with, there was no way I would have appreciated the life Gramps had carved out for himself here. But because Hannah was here and I was seeing the relationship between Pops and Gramps through her eyes, I was much more invested.

I squeezed her hand. "Thank you."

Hannah turned to me in surprise. "Context?"

"This." I gestured to our cottage at the end of the street. "Would have been infinitely more difficult without you."

She tipped her chin up and hugged my arm to her side. Her smile was full of affection and understanding and I couldn't remember the last time I had felt this connected to another person.

"So, what you're saying is you like me."

My gaze moved over her face from her bright blue eyes and upturned nose to her wide generous mouth. My voice was gruff when I said, "I definitely like you."

Hannah

Simon said he definitely liked me but I was afraid it was more than that for me. I was falling for him. I didn't want to. I didn't want to be the first one to fall in love or—oh, horror—the only one to fall in love. But how was I supposed to resist a man holding a tiny baby? I supposed I could blame it on my system never fully recovering from the hormones I'd had rocketing through me when I was trying to conceive, but I suspected that wasn't it. I was smitten with Simon O'Malley for better or worse. If we had only this summer, so be it. I was going to enjoy every second of my time with him before we went our separate ways.

"You know, I was thinking." Simon let go of my hand and looped his arm around my shoulders, pulling me up against his side. "On our bike ride to town, we should stop by the beach where our grandfathers first met."

"Do we even know where that is?" I asked.

"Yes, because I called Tim Larson this morning and asked."

"Tim from the Scoop? Did he ask you about painting the mural again?" I asked. What I didn't tell Simon was I'd looked up his children's book. It was a retelling of classic fairy tales. The artwork was colorful and chaotic and his style would be absolutely perfect as a larger-than-life mural on the side of the building. I would have badgered him to do it, but I wanted to respect his position that he was done with art even though I disagreed with that choice with every fiber of my being.

"No. He started to talk about it, but I redirected him, a skill I have honed when talking with Charlie when he gets caught in a conversational loop."

"And what did you learn?" We walked up the steps to our front door together. Our front door. I tried not to get too enamored with the sound of that. Dude was standing in the living room window and started barking a greeting as soon as we stepped onto the porch.

"It's only a little ways past town. I figured we could poke around town, check out the library and community center, and then press on to the beach. We can make a day of it. It'll be fun." He paused to examine my face as if I needed to be talked into such an awesome plan.

"Let's do it." I glanced up at the brilliant blue sky and knew I'd go anywhere this man asked me to . . . unless it involved selling the cottage. I pushed the thought away. I didn't want to think about that right now. All I could hope was that if he spent enough time here in Cape Split, he'd become too attached—to the town, the cottage, me?—to sell.

"All right, change into your bathing suit and beach clothes and meet me out front in ten," he said. "Oh, and can Dude come with us? Is it too far for him?"

"No, in fact, if we don't bring him, he'll be deeply hurt."

"Excellent," he said. "I love that dog."

And that right there was when my heart went splat as I fell for the man completely.

Dude trotted beside the bike as Simon and I wobbled our way to the beach. We were a little bit better than we'd been the first time, but I suspected it was because I was too tired from the night before to try to steer from the back.

Maybe it was the memory of triple orgasms, but when I looked at Simon in his bicycle helmet with his eyes shielded by a pair of aviators, I felt my heart rate pick up. The man was just irresistible. Good thing I had to hold on to the handlebar or I might have gotten handsy with the steersman.

Dude occasionally veered off the path to chase down a scent. Simon would whistle and Dude would come bounding back with his ears flapping, his tongue hanging out, and a happy bounce in his step. I laughed and glanced at Simon to share the moment and found him already watching me over his shoulder. The intensity of his gaze caused my body to flash hot, and a delicious fluttery feeling hit me low and deep. I hadn't felt this sort of all-consuming attraction in forever and I reveled in it.

It occurred to me that this could be the solution to our problem. If Simon fell as hard for me as I was falling for him then maybe he would begin seeing the cottage as *our place*. Yes, it was a huge *if*, but I had a few weeks to hope for the best.

As we approached town, Simon guided us down Main Street. Dude stuck to the sidewalk while we stayed in the bike lane. We parked in front of the library, an old brick building that was two stories tall.

"We should get library cards," I said as we stood outside with Dude.

Simon looked as if he was about to ask why when Monica Fisk exited with her three tykes in tow.

"Simon, Hannah, hello," she began but the children shouted over her, "Dude!"

And just like that, Dude and the kids took off, scampering across the lawn that was enclosed by a short wrought iron fence.

"Are you going in?" Monica asked. "I can watch Dude for you. It'll be good for the kids to run around a bit." She set the large bag of picture books she carried onto the park bench and sat next to them as if relieved to have a minute of peace.

Simon and I exchanged a look. "Thanks, Monica. We'll be right back."

"Do not hurry," she ordered as she relaxed back into her seat.

Simon and I entered the library and I was instantly entranced by the scent of books. The building had two wings, one side was the adult side and one was the children's. The noise from the children's side was cheerful chaos. In front of us was a wide curving desk with two women working behind it. One was middle-aged with a head of gray hair with purple streaks and the other looked to be in her early twenties with glasses and a wide welcoming smile.

"Hi, how can I help you?" she greeted us.

"What's required for a library card?" I asked.

The young woman told us we needed a proof of local address for a permanent card, which neither of us had, or if we wanted a temporary card for the summer that was available, too. Much to my surprise Simon signed up for a card with me and we spent a pleasant half hour investigating the collection.

When we were leaving, the librarian with the purple streaks in her hair waved us over. "Hi, I was entering your information in the system, when I noticed your names. Are you related to Billy and Bobby?"

"Billy." I pointed to myself.

"Bobby." Simon did the same. "We're their grandchildren."

"Of course." She nodded. Her eyes took on a shimmer and her lips were pressed tight. She forced a smile and said, "The reporter and the illustrator, your grandfathers spoke of you both quite highly. In fact, we have your book here, Mr. O'Malley, but I checked and all copies are out."

"That's very nice of you," Simon said. He looked embarrassed so I quickly changed the subject while making a mental note to put the book on hold for myself.

"Were our grandfathers frequent patrons?" I asked.

"More than that," the librarian said. "They were members of the Friends of the Library and volunteered to work every book sale. Billy always said they did it to get first dibs on the good stuff."

I smiled as that sounded exactly like Pops.

"I was very sorry to hear of their passing," she continued. "I'm Linda Tolliver. If ever you need anything, please come and see me."

"Thank you, Linda, that's very nice of you," Simon said.

She smiled and then handed us two postcards. "These are Friends of the Library applications. If you just use the QR code and fill out the online form you'll be all signed up."

"Thank you," Simon and I said together. We left the library with a wave, not speaking until we were outside.

"Did we just get muscled by a librarian?" Simon asked.

"And how," I said, and then laughed.

"Let me guess," Monica said as we joined her. "Linda got you to join the Friends."

We both held up our cards and Monica tipped her head back and guffawed. "That woman is a marvel. If she ever decides to run the world, she'll have it sorted in a week."

Dude spotted us and ran across the grass as if he hadn't seen us in years. He flopped at my feet with his tongue hanging out and Monica sighed as she rose from the bench. "Ah, well, break time is over. Come on, kids."

"But, Mom . . ." the oldest, who had flopped on top of Dude, started to protest.

"No buts except the one on top of your legs that had better be headed to the car if you want ice cream from the Scoop for dessert tonight," Monica said.

All three children fell in line, holding hands, as they speed-walked to the car. Monica smiled at us and said, "Never underestimate the power of ice cream." She waved as she jogged after the kids.

"No truer words," Simon said.

We ambled through town and I was struck by how idyllic life seemed here. Oh, sure, I knew people still had bills to pay, health crises, bad breakups, and dental appointments. I knew it wasn't a utopia but at the same time, I could see why Pops and Gramps had made this their special place together.

By the time we got back on the bike, it was late afternoon as the day had gotten away from us. We were cruising past the shops when Simon turned his head toward me and said, "I need to make a stop."

He steered us to a bike rack in front of Stephanie's bakery, Beach Buns. The name still cracked me up. Dude sat beside me while I took off my helmet and settled it on the handlebars.

"Where are we going?" I asked.

"Nowhere," he said. "I'm waiting for someone."

I eyed him curiously. Now I was intrigued. Outside the bakery was a bowl of water for dogs and Dude helped himself. While he was slurping away, Stephanie came out of the bakery with a large tote bag and handed it to Simon. "Here you go, Simon, I got everything you asked for."

"Hey, Hannah," Stephanie greeted me. She leaned over and gave Dude a big old hug. "Who's my sweet boy, Mr. Dude?"

Dude's tail thumped the ground in response and when Stephanie handed him a dog biscuit, he let out a snuffle of approval before it disappeared into his mouth and was gone in two bites.

"Good appetite." Stephanie patted his head in approval. A bell rang in the shop and she headed back inside. "Duty calls. Have fun on your picnic!"

Simon handed me the tote bag, and I peeked inside and saw sandwiches, iced tea, and some baked goods that looked equally delicious and lethal—to my hips, not that I cared.

"A picnic?" I glanced at him. "Better watch it, O'Malley, the way to my heart is most definitely by way of a sandwich."

Instead of looking terrified by the prospect as some men would, Simon simply smiled that knee-wilter of a closed-lip expression of amusement that highlighted his lone dimple. He kissed my head as he walked past. "You need to raise the bar, Spencer. You should hold out for a whole pizza with all the toppings, at the very least."

I laughed, not informing him that after last night he could have all of me for a lone grape.

Simon took the bag and settled it on the bike in front of him. We climbed aboard and pedaled through town, turning down a winding road to a modest-sized beach nestled into a cove. We were the only ones there. I was thrilled. Having Simon and Dude all to myself on a beach was perfection, and I didn't want to share.

We walked to the edge of the water. I kicked off my shoes and let the sand slip between my toes. Dude ran ahead with his nose to the ground, taking in all the smells.

Simon picked a smooth spot and set down the tote bag. From a smaller duffel bag that I hadn't noticed, he unfurled a beach blanket and Dude's Frisbee. The man had thought of everything.

The sun was warm, the breeze was cool, and the sound of the waves soothing as the water rushed to meet the sand only to slide away as if it couldn't figure out how to stay.

Simon handed me Dude's Frisbee and I flung it down the beach. Dude set off at a gallop to catch it. He missed and chose to stomp on it as if drowning it before he snatched it up in his jaws and trotted back to me, looking quite pleased with himself.

"Now, if what Tim said was accurate, this was the spot where my Gramps met your Pops, or at least it's in the vicinity." Simon spread his arms wide, gesturing to the cove.

"What do you suppose was the first thing they said to each other?" I asked.

"Knowing Gramps, it was 'Hey, get out of my spot!'" Simon said in a gruff voice that I suspected was a spot-on impression of Gramps.

"To which my Pops would have said, 'Make me.'"

"Oh, that wouldn't go well." Simon picked up the Frisbee that Dude dropped at his feet and sent it sailing.

I watched my big boy run down the beach, kicking up sand in his wake, and tried to imagine the two young men in the picture we'd found in Gramps's duffel bag, standing here vying for the best fishing spot almost sixty years ago.

"Do you think it was love at first sight?" I asked.

Simon turned to face me. "From the way Tim described it, I don't think so."

I nodded. "But there had to have been something. A spark, a connection, a feeling—something must have happened between them to start as enemies and end up as lovers."

Simon looked pained.

"Does it bother you that they were young lovers?" I asked.

"No." He shook his head. "It's contemplating Gramps's love life, whether it was a woman or a man he was with, that has me feeling . . ." His voice trailed off as if he couldn't find the right word.

"Embarrassed?" I offered. He shook his head. "Grossed out?" He shook his head again.

"Acutely uncomfortable?"

"That's it!" he yelled, and held up one finger. I laughed, relieved that he was being honest and that he had humor about it. "It's like walking in on your parents doing the wild thing. Awkward."

When Dude returned and dropped the Frisbee at his feet, Simon took it and sent it flying low into the waves, much to Dude's delight.

"Is it because he's your Gramps?" I asked.

Simon reached for my hand and pulled me into his side. "Yeah. I mean, I know I'm here because he and Granny conceived my dad, and my mom and dad conceived me, but I don't like to think of any of them being . . . you know."

"Intimate?"

He shuddered.

"Simon O'Malley, after last night, I wouldn't have thought you to be a prude," I teased.

"I'm not," he said. "It's just he's Gramps, you know?"

"No, I don't," I said. "Old people enjoy sex."

Simon clapped his hands over his ears and sang, "La la la la."

I laughed and pulled his hands away, stepping fully into his arms.

"What about Lor and Charlie?" I asked. "Does the thought of either of them being in a relationship make you acutely uncomfortable?"

"It hasn't been an issue with Charlie until recently, but I trust Julian to oversee things, so no," he said. "But Lor? Yeah, growing up Charlie and I strongly encouraged her to join a convent."

"What about that guy Chance who gave her a ride home?"

"Poor bastard is aptly named as he doesn't stand a chance," he said. "None of them ever do."

"Why do you suppose that is?"

"Because she has a terrible father, so her trust in men—aside from me and Charlie—is as thin as a dime." His tone was rueful when he said it as if he wished he could have protected her from whatever hurt their father had caused. "You know the whole debate about whether a woman would choose to run into a strange man or a bear in the woods? Meaning which would she feel safer with?"

"Oh, yes." I nodded. "My girlfriends and I have had many a conversation about it."

He narrowed his eyes and studied me and said, "I'm betting you'd choose the strange man."

I blinked. "What makes you say that?"

"Because despite being married to an asshole, you clearly have good relationships with your father and grandfather."

"That's true," I said. "And, yes, I was one of the women who would choose the strange man despite my crummy ex."

"My theory is that women who come from homes with horrible fathers choose the bear," he said. "Lor said she'd choose the bear every single time."

That theory made sense and I took a moment to think about the friends I'd debated it with, and Simon was right. The ones who were staunchly bear had terrible fathers, so for them the first and most important man in their life failed to make them feel safe, so why would any man be viewed as safe? Of course a bear seemed the better choice to them.

"At least she has you and Charlie," I said. "I'll bet that matters more than you know."

He shrugged, unconvinced, and I couldn't let that stand. I

looped my arms around his neck and pulled him down so I could kiss him. Simon clutched me close and when I ran my tongue across the seam of his lips, he dug his fingers into my hair, holding me still while his mouth opened for mine and I plundered him like I was a pirate seeking treasure.

When we parted with a need to breathe, I glanced up at him, taking in his extremely sexy gaze and slightly swollen mouth, and I couldn't help myself. "Do you think Gramps and Pops made out here, too?"

His eyes snapped to mine with a look of horror and I laughed, dancing away from him, keeping just out of reach as he strode after me. When he got too close, I turned and began to run. Dude barked and joined me as we sprinted down the beach. I only got fifty yards when two arms scooped me up from behind and I was lifted into the air.

Simon dragged me out into the waves, dangling me over them. I wrapped my arms around his neck and clung like a barnacle on a rock. If I was going in, he was going with me.

"You are in deep trouble, Spencer," he growled. This sounded like a hot proposition to me, so I wrapped my legs around his waist and pulled him in tight against the juncture of my thighs. Simon let out a hiss and I knew I'd gotten his attention.

"Exactly what sort of trouble would that be?" I whispered in his ear before gently biting the lobe and tugging it with my teeth.

"Hannah! Simon!" A shout sounded from the beach and Simon turned with me still in his arms to see Roland, with Zach and Taylor, striding toward the surf with Dude beside them.

Simon let out a small groan and lowered me until my feet were in the water. "Their timing could not be worse. Cover me."

He moved me to stand in front of him, and I realized from the feel of him pressed up against my lower back that he had an issue.

There was a splash and I glanced over my shoulder to see that he had dunked himself. He shot back up out of the water with a shudder, and I glanced down at his bathing suit. "Problem solved?"

"Don't look at me like that or it won't be for long." He grabbed my hand and pulled me ashore.

"Hey, neighbors," I greeted our friends. "Are you here for a swim?"

"Not tonight," Roland said. "We're on nest watch."

I glanced at the barren beach, wondering where a tree might be that would have a nest.

"Not a bird nest," Taylor said, correctly interpreting my glance. "A turtle nest."

"Here?" Simon glanced around the sand.

"Up above the waterline, where the marked-off area is." Roland gestured to the section closer to the seagrass that was taped off with wooden stakes and a sign. "Our volunteer group marks the nests when the mother turtle comes ashore and then we start watching them at night when we think the littles are about to hatch.

"We try to assist the baby turtles on their trek to the ocean, by making certain there's no light pollution to disorient them, or predators, human or animal, who might disturb them on their journey."

"Oh, no, we'll get Dude out of here," I said. "I don't think he'd mean any harm but we don't want to have him get overexcited with baby turtles in the area."

"If you want to stay with the guys, I can take Dude home with me. I'm only here to help them with the gear. My mom and I did the watch last night and I'm exhausted," Taylor said. "You can pick him up later or tomorrow or whenever."

Simon and I exchanged a look. Simon's eyebrows were raised and he said, "I've never seen a turtle hatch, have you?"

"No." I shook my head. "But I'd love to if it's no imposition."

"Imposition?" Roland scoffed. "We're going to put you to work."

"I'm in." I turned to Simon. "You?"

"Absolutely." He jogged over to our stuff and scooped it up, giving Taylor Dude's Frisbee.

"Be a good boy." I kissed Dude's big, blocky head and he trotted off with Taylor as she hyped him up about going to her house.

"He's really just leaving me," I said.

"In all fairness, she did say 'car ride.'" Simon handed me our blanket while he carried the tote bag as we strode toward the area where Roland and Zach were setting up to wait.

"Yeah, I'll always lose to a ride in the car."

Under Roland's guidance we set up amber lights so we could see the nest in the coming darkness. He explained that the newly hatched turtles were drawn to the white of the waves on the beach or the moon's reflection on the water, which was why they used amber lights so as not to send the hatchlings in the wrong direction.

Simon was given a plastic shovel to flatten the sand from the nest all the way to the water so the baby turtles had fewer impediments on their journey. Zach took the other shovel and the two of them set to work.

Roland removed the net that had been placed over the nest. "To keep predators out."

Using the camera on my phone, I shot B-roll of the sign, indicating that the spot was a turtle nest. I framed Simon behind the sign. He was small and blurry, as I intended, but I could still see his muscles bunch as he and Zach worked, and I wanted to have footage of him. I opted not to examine the need too closely.

"Do you think they'll hatch tonight?" I asked Roland.

He shrugged. "Nature isn't on the clock. They're due, but it might be tomorrow night or the night after that."

"Is it always at night?"

Roland unfolded the chair he'd brought with him and plopped into it. "Usually. The mama comes ashore at night and the babies are born at night. I read it's an instinctual thing because there are less predators at night, also it's cooler and she has to do a lot of digging."

I spread our blanket beside Roland's chair and noted that the sun was beginning to dip and would set soon. I glanced at the nest area, hoping tonight would be the night.

"So, are you two a thing?" Roland bit into the apple he'd taken out of his cooler and pushed his well-worn baseball cap back on his head.

"Are you asking about the status of my personal life?" I stalled.

"Not me." He shook his head. "I mind my own business."

"Uh-huh, I noticed that about you." My voice dripped sarcasm and Roland wheezed out a laugh.

"An old man has to have hobbies," he defended himself. "Mine is gossip. So, are you?"

I met his curious gaze and shrugged. "I can give you a solid maybe."

"Pfft." He shook his head. "If that man doesn't put a lock on you, he's an idiot."

I was flattered but wanted to defend Simon when we inevitably went our separate ways. "It's complicated."

"No, it isn't." Roland gestured to Simon, who was standing at the water's edge, talking to Zach. "Either you want him in your life or you don't."

"I barely know him," I protested.

Roland pointed his half-eaten apple at me. "That clinch in the water we came upon was not the I-barely-know-you kind."

My face immediately heated up. "Okay, fine, there is an attraction but I can't . . . I'm not . . ." I lost my words. Not a common occurrence for me, but I just didn't know how to explain to this older gentleman, of whom I'd become very fond, that I was not a long-term-relationship prospect.

"Is this because you couldn't get pregnant with your ex?" he asked.

I sucked in a shocked breath as if he'd just pulled a gun on me. "How do you know about that?"

"Billy blabbed. He was worried about you." Roland took another bite of his apple.

I nodded. That sounded like Pops. "Does everybody in Cape Split know?" I asked.

Roland shifted in his chair. "Not *everyone*."

I turned and stared at the waves. I didn't know how I felt about this. Strangers knew the most vulnerable part of me. I expected to feel violated, instead, I felt oddly relieved. My new neighbors, who were becoming my friends, already knew my most painful personal struggle. So the endless "Don't you want to get married and have kids?" question that had started as soon as I turned twenty-five and had dogged me ever since wouldn't be happening here. Phew.

"Any sign of the turtle boil?" Zach asked as he and Simon joined us near the nest.

"Boil?" I asked.

"They call it that because it looks like the sand is bubbling when the babies start popping out," Roland explained, much to my relief. He pointed to the taped-off area. "But the sand is definitely indented. I think it'll be soon."

Simon and I exchanged an excited look. He grabbed our tote bag and sat down on the blanket beside me. He handed me a paper-wrapped sandwich. "We should fortify."

I realized I was starving. I unwrapped the paper and found a club sandwich inside. I bit into it as if I hadn't eaten in a week. Simon handed me a can of iced tea while Zach set up his chair next to his father's and they unpacked their cooler.

The four of us ate in companionable silence as the breeze picked up, signaling that the tide was coming in. Zach pointed to the waterline that was getting closer. "This is good. The turtles won't have as far to go if they hatch at high tide."

As the sun disappeared behind the horizon and the sky shifted from golden to purple to completely dark, Zach and Roland entertained us with stories about Pops and Gramps. They had volunteered with the turtle rescue outfit as well.

Roland told us about the time an unfortunate ATV rider came cruising down the beach while Gramps was on watch. "It must have been about ten years ago." Roland scratched his chin. "Me, my wife, Jeanie, Billy, and Bobby were all on duty. ATV guy came cruising through and we warned him away but he took it as a personal challenge." He paused to shake his head. "The next thing I knew Bobby took the dope off his ride with a flying tackle and Pops hopped on and drove the ATV right to the police station. The driver had to explain how he'd had his ass handed to him by a couple of old men and then had to do community service."

"Sounds like they were quite the dynamic duo," Simon said.

"They were good men." Zach held up his soda and we all clinked cans. I took a long sip, hoping to ease the sudden knot in my throat.

"Um, Roland, I think something's happening." Simon gestured to the sand. Sure enough, it was shifting and moving, looking just as Zach had described, like it was starting to boil.

"Oh, it's happening!" Roland hopped up from his seat. "Okay, we have to make sure they go in the right direction and we need to take count."

The amber lights that we'd set up on stands illuminated the depression and I crawled closer with my phone to film the moment. Simon was beside me while Zach and Roland moved to each side of the nest, ready to redirect any hatchlings that went the wrong way.

"This is amazing," I whispered to Simon. I turned and his face was just inches from mine and he looked as excited as I felt. I reached out and grabbed his hand just because I had to touch him. He squeezed my fingers in return and we both turned back to the nest.

The sand was churning and moving more swiftly now. A little button of a head popped out of the sand and I felt my heart flutter in my chest from the sheer wonder of it. *Baby sea turtles!* I checked to make certain I was filming and then turned back to the nest. A second head popped out of the sand and then a third. A little flipper appeared and I watched as the first baby turtle covered in sand pushed out of the nest and began to flail in the churning dirt, trying to find his path.

"Come on, little one," Roland coaxed. I remembered that he was the critter whisperer and I wondered if he could even talk the baby turtles into doing what he wanted.

More turtles appeared, popping up out of the sand. "There are so many," I cried.

"A mama turtle lays about one hundred eggs and they all hatch at the same time, give or take," Zach said.

"One hundred?" I was amazed and awed.

Our first hatchling had found the flattened path to the sea and he was using his front and back flippers to scurry his way toward the ocean. There was a determination in him that made me want to clap and cheer as if he were competing in the Olympics.

Watching him, I was overwhelmed with a sudden feeling of

protectiveness. I wanted to scoop him up, he'd barely fill my palm, and protect him from the deep, dark ocean in front of him, which seemed entirely too big and scary for a little fella who was the size of a coaster.

"What happens to them in the ocean?" I asked. More and more babies were following the first one as the nest became a churning mass of itty-bitty turtles all climbing out of the sand.

"They'll go into a swim frenzy," Roland said. "It'll last for a day or two to get away from the shore and predators. They'll reach the ocean currents, which will take them deeper into the ocean to places like the Sargasso Sea, where they'll live in relative safety during their juvenile years."

I filmed the line of turtles marching to the sea, staying off to the side as I followed them. Zach was stationed by the middle of the path and he was counting the babies with a pad and pencil, making hash marks as each one passed him.

I squatted down by the water's edge and watched the first of the turtles propel themselves into the waves. The water pushed them back up the beach but they were undeterred, continuing to chase the water that would take them away. It was incredible to watch but still my fear for their little lives remained. My anxiety must have shown because Simon crouched down beside me and put his hand on my back and said, "They'll be all right."

I shut the video off on my phone and pocketed it. I turned to face Simon, knowing my worry and doubt were etched on my face.

He sighed and pulled me close, giving me a half hug and placing a kiss in my hair. "This is one of those moments that you have to trust the universe, Spencer. And whatever you do, do not get attached."

I pulled back and studied him in the amber light with his ridiculously long eyelashes, his dark hair that curled in the humidity, his square jaw and full lips, and I thought how it was entirely too late for his warning.

My post about the baby turtles went viral. Taylor, my number one fan in Cape Split, made certain that everyone in the village saw it. I had taken out the original sound and narrated over the video the facts that Roland and Zach had taught me about the turtles. One particularly poignant shot of a lone little guy being swept out to sea by a wave I narrated by describing this time as the "lost years" of juvenile sea turtles where they headed out to sea and, other than sightings in the Sargasso Sea, no one was exactly certain where they went. My voice cracked in the narration, giving the piece an honest bit of emotion that I decided not to edit out.

I had set up the post with links to the local rescue outfit that Gramps and Pops and most of the residents of Cape Split worked with and according to Roland, their donations were enjoying a healthy spike. I liked to think that would help more sea turtles survive and thrive.

Simon and I fell into a routine over the next two weeks where we spent our mornings working on the house, either decluttering or fixing something that needed it, our afternoons either exploring the Outer Banks or working our jobs, and our nights naked in bed together. I knew it wasn't wise to let it go on so long, but I felt as if I could never get enough of him and our required two months of living in the cottage would be over in just two weeks.

Decisions were going to have to be made and soon. We didn't talk about keeping or selling the cottage, and as far as I knew neither of us had changed our minds. At least, I thought I hadn't.

When I considered Charlie and Simon's responsibility for him, I understood why selling the cottage was important to Simon. It would give Charlie financial stability should anything happen to Simon—although I couldn't bear to even think about that possibility.

Unfortunately, the time Simon and I spent here caused me to become more attached to the place than ever. But Charlie . . . I cared about him, too, and I wanted to help do whatever was best for Charlie and for Simon. If I thought selling the cottage would bring Simon joy, I wouldn't hesitate for a second, but I didn't think it would. In fact, I feared that losing this place would hurt Simon; he'd become so much more relaxed over the past few weeks than the man I'd first met. I suspected his Gramps had left the cottage to him specifically to give Simon the same sort of escape from his responsibilities that Gramps had enjoyed. I wished I knew for certain.

Simon had turned the dining room into a temporary office, a place I actively avoided because . . . bat. I could hear him talking to clients and I wondered how a man who had illustrated such a delightful children's book could bear to spend an hour talking to his boss about the fluctuations in premium rates and how he believed they should adjust their pricing strategies accordingly.

Feeling restless while Simon worked and Dude napped on the couch, I wandered upstairs to the main bedroom as Simon and I had moved into the guest bedroom. The locked steamer trunk I'd found in the attic was now here, pushed up against the wall. No one had been able to unlock it and Simon and I had agreed not to get rid of it until we saw the contents.

I doubled back to the kitchen and examined the junk drawer for any implements that might work to pick the lock. A cake tester, a flathead screwdriver, and a metal meat skewer. I returned to the bedroom and began to try to pry the round face of the lock with the screwdriver. No luck. I tried the other items as well and it still didn't budge. Next, I tried inserting the flathead into the keyhole. I jiggled it, angling it down a bit. The inner circle depressed under pressure and I tried to turn the lock. It moved! I turned it ninety degrees and then pulled forward, leaving the screwdriver in the keyhole. The faceplate of the lock dropped forward. The trunk was unlocked.

"Simon! Dude!" Neither of them came running. Darn it.

I popped the latches and pushed the lid up and gasped. Inside were stacks of drawing pads, art supplies, and several paintings carefully wrapped. I reached for the first one. I hesitated. Should I? Of course I should. The trunk was a part of the house and we had to go through everything. Should I wait for Simon? Who knew how long he'd be on the phone? I forged ahead. I slid my finger under the masking tape and gently pried the paper off the piece.

I knew right away whose work it was. Simon's. The painting was done in his usual explosion of color that swept the viewer right into the piece. It was a whimsical painting of a young woman, climbing a circular staircase up to the clouds. I recognized Lorelei as the model immediately and I was amazed at how much depth the piece had. I wasn't even afraid of heights and I felt my palms sweat at the fall she would take if she plummeted off the staircase.

I'd seen the illustrations from Simon's book on the small screen of my phone but holding his work in my hands and seeing the colors and control in every brushstroke was pure magic. The man was so talented. How could he have quit?

I unwrapped the next piece and the next until they were scattered all around me in a riotous circle of whimsy and color. How had Gramps gotten all of Simon's artwork and why was it hidden in a trunk in the attic? It should be on every wall of the house.

I reached in and plucked out a sketchbook. I flipped through the pages of pencil drawings, many of which were the starting point for the paintings around me. I heard footsteps outside the bedroom door and started. Fearing Simon would consider this an invasion of his privacy, I debated tossing everything back into the trunk and pretending I hadn't gotten it open. I shook off the thought. I knew deep in my heart that he needed to see this.

"Sorry, I heard you call but I was stuck on the ph . . ." Simon's voice trailed off as he took in the sight of me seated in the middle of all his paintings. His gaze darted from one piece to the next as he took it all in.

"I got the trunk open." I didn't know what else to say.

"How?" he asked.

"Flathead screwdriver." I held it up.

He nodded and stepped slowly into the room as if he were leery of land mines.

I scooted to the side to make room for him beside the trunk. He picked up the nearest painting. It was a woman with a sweet smile and long deep purple hair, wearing a pale blue sundress, walking three frogs on leashes on a pond covered in lily pads. It had all the fantastical elements of Simon's other pieces but I suspected this one was more personal. I noticed that two of the frogs wore bow ties while one had a bow on its head. Was this their mother walking Simon and his two siblings?

"Your mother?" I whispered.

He ran his forefinger down the profile of her face and nodded. "Yeah."

I was silent, watching him examine each painting as if he was reacquainting himself with long-lost friends. When he looked up at me, his eyes were damp and his voice was rough. "I thought I got rid of all of these."

"What?" I gasped. I couldn't even wrap my mind around doing such a thing.

He blinked a few times as if he could dry any tears before they fell.

"When I chose to take the job at the insurance company, I packed up every piece of my work and tossed it in the dumpster behind my apartment." He lifted one of the sketchbooks and studied the corner. "If I'm not mistaken, that's a blob of dried ketchup, at least I hope it is."

"Why . . ." I had no words. I couldn't fathom doing such a thing to all these magnificent pieces. "Please explain."

"I was really freaked out about what happened to Charlie and couldn't imagine doing anything as frivolous as art while he was fighting for his life," he said. "I was terrified for my brother. Gramps, Lorelei, and I—we didn't even know if he'd get his ability to speak back in those early days."

The fear and grief in Simon's eyes made my heart hurt.

"I think I was in the dealmaking phase of things. I thought if I gave it all up and devoted myself to making certain that Charlie had the best care then he'd be all right. I wouldn't lose him like I'd lost my mother and essentially my father, although good riddance to that one."

He pressed the heels of his hands to his eyes as if he could push back the feelings. "You're going to think I'm a jerk, but if I'm being completely honest, a part of me needed to cut art out of my life so I could be the person Charlie and Lorelei, who was still in nursing school, needed me to be. I'd dreamed of being an illustrator my entire life and knowing that I wouldn't have time for it anymore hurt too much, so I chucked it all. In hindsight, I might have been a tad dramatic."

"I still don't understand," I said. "Why couldn't you keep art in your life?"

"I just didn't want it anymore." Simon shrugged. "Artists talk about their muse, you know, the thing that inspires them?"

I nodded. I felt stomach-sick thinking about all he had been through and what it had cost him.

"When Charlie got into that accident on top of my mother dying and my father abandoning us, I just didn't have it in me anymore," Simon said. "Creating had always been my escape from the real world but at that point in my life, there was no escape."

"You're a good brother, Simon O'Malley." I took his hand in mine and laced our fingers together.

"I would do anything for my siblings." Simon met my gaze. "Anything. I think of it this way: If the house was on fire, and I had to choose between saving my siblings or my paintings, I would choose my siblings. It's a no-brainer."

"Of course, but that's not what happened," I countered. I wanted him to see that his art mattered. That he could find it in himself again.

Simon's brown eyes were filled with stark honesty. "That's exactly what happened—metaphorically. I mentioned that my father left after my mother passed away? He took her entire life insurance and left us with nothing. Gramps took care of us, finished raising us, and then Charlie stepped up and took care of me and Lorelei, making sure I got through school. Then when Charlie was injured, I looked at it as my turn."

"But surely, your father—" I began but he interrupted.

"Tried to take over the conservatorship for Charlie from Gramps so he would have access to Charlie's disability money. When Gramps passed and left the conservatorship to me, my father tried to get his sticky fingers on that and our inheritance from Gramps, too, which Lorelei and I both agreed was to be put in a trust for Charlie."

Fury—swift, hot, and intense—lit up my core. If his father was here in the room with us, I thought I'd probably take a swing at him. Simon didn't seem to feel the same. He released my hand with a quick squeeze and reached into the trunk and pulled out a stack of sketchbooks. He began to flip through the pages and I studied his profile, trying to parse out how he was feeling.

He reached into the trunk again and came back with a note on an index card. Scrawled in the worst handwriting I'd ever seen, it read: *Simon, I left you this house and kept your work here for you to find when you were ready. I hope you learn from my choices. Choose happiness, Simon. Don't give up what you love most or you'll live a life of regret. Find a way to live your life so that you have room for both your responsibilities and your passions. Let the people who love you, help you. And always remember who you are. Love, Gramps.*

"That crazy old man must have dumpster dived all of my work out of the trash." Simon's words ended in a sob.

A tear dropped onto the note. I reached over and put my arms around his middle, hoping to offer him some comfort. He responded by pulling me in even tighter and lowering his face to the curve of my neck. I felt his tears soak my shirt just as I'd done to him over that ridiculous pot holder.

I ran my hands up and down his back, trying to soothe the grief that was silently pouring out of him. From his stories about Gramps, I had already grown fond of the old man, but now, this gesture to his grandson caused me to love the supposedly crotchety old man whom I would sadly never get to meet.

Simon

It was the first time I had cried about losing Gramps. And it seemed that once the tears started, I couldn't stop them. Normally, I would have been shamed by my loss of control. But it was different with Hannah. In the weeks I had come to know her, she had given me something that no one in my life could—I was safe with her. I could be vulnerable with her.

The coconut-lime scent of her hair washed over me in a soothing wave. I pulled her in even tighter, reveling in her softness, her warmth, and the feel of her hands running up and down my back as she comforted me. It was working. Slowly the knot of grief in my throat eased and I could breathe. I gave her a final squeeze and let her go even though I knew I would prefer to stay in her arms permanently, if given the option.

"Thank you." My voice was hoarse.

"Anytime." She reached up and brushed my hair off my forehead in a tender gesture that made my throat ache all over again. She leaned forward and brushed her mouth against mine. "It's good to let the sadness out every now and then."

I nodded. I couldn't deny that I felt lighter in that moment than I had in months. Would I have cried if I'd been alone in this house with the trunk? Probably not. But having Hannah here, also grieving her Pops, made my grief feel less overwhelming.

While I sat there regrouping, taking in the work I had done so many years ago, Hannah went back to the trunk, sifting through the items as if looking for something specific. She came up with a blank sketchpad and a pack of pencils and turned to me with her eyes alight. "Do me."

I blinked, panicked at the thought of what she was asking. I tried to divert her. "Here and now? Okay, but Dude is right downstairs and the door is open."

She laughed and it trickled down my spine like a musical waterfall. "Very funny. I meant draw me." She thrust the materials at me, giving me no choice but to take them.

"I . . . it's been . . . I don't . . ." I stammered. I hadn't drawn anything more than doodles during long boring meetings in years.

"Listen, we're more than halfway through our summer share, and I want something to remember you by. If you're uncomfortable drawing me, draw Dude. I would love that."

At her assertion that this situationship was headed toward an ending, I felt my chest constrict. With each day that I spent with her, I had a harder time imagining a day where I didn't hear her singing the same three lines of a song on repeat, or smell her shampoo, or hear her call Dude to come and eat. Her life was becoming entwined with mine and the fact that I didn't mind at all and rather wanted our lives to be enmeshed should have scared me stupid. Instead, I welcomed it. All of it.

"My work is . . ."

"Charming? Whimsical? Fantastic?" she asked, her blue eyes

twinkling so brightly I was certain I could see stars in them. There was my first image.

"All right," I said. "I'll *do you* on one condition." My voice dropped on "do you" and she actually shivered. I lowered my gaze to the pencils in my hand so I didn't pounce on her right then and there.

"What's the condition?" she asked, and then whispered, "Please let it be sexual favors."

I let out a surprised laugh and she grinned. I leaned forward and kissed her firmly on the mouth. "Behave."

"Trying my best," she whispered against my lips. "I swear."

It was my turn to shiver. I held her gaze and said, "The condition is that you don't get to look at the piece until I'm done."

She looked like she would balk, but I lifted my eyebrows in a *this is not negotiable* look and she sighed very dramatically.

"Fine. Have it your way," she said.

"I will." I put aside the pad and pencils. "Now off with your clothes."

"What? I am not posing nude." She put her hand over her chest as if trying to cover herself. "No one needs to see that."

"Correction." I rose to my feet and grabbed her hands, pulling her up with me. "I need to see it, all of it, especially if I'm going to *do you*."

"I'm never going to hear the end of that unfortunate phrase, am I?" she asked.

"No." I ducked low and caught her in an over-the-shoulder fireman's hold.

"Simon! I'm too heavy. Put me down," she protested.

"No, you're not and, no, I won't," I said as I strode across the hall to the other bedroom. "I need some time to study my subject if I'm going to *do you* properly."

I heard her snort-laugh and I felt myself smile. I set her down on her feet when we reached our bedroom. All teasing aside, I wanted her to feel equal control in this situation. I stepped back, giving her space and was completely unprepared when she pounced.

I caught her when she launched herself at me. It was a real hardship as I was forced to cup her backside with my hands while she wrapped her legs around my waist, buried her fingers in my hair, and kissed me until everything went fuzzy and I started to see spots.

"Bed. Now. O'Malley."

"Yes, ma'am." She didn't have to ask me once.

I kicked the door shut behind us so that Dude wouldn't feel the need to investigate any noise he heard coming from the room, because if I had it my way there was going to be an awful lot of noise, preferably her begging me for more and crying my name out in that insanely sexy way she had.

We staggered to the bed and dropped on top of it without breaking the kiss. She tugged at my clothes while I yanked on hers, our fingers got tangled, and we both laughed. The need to be skin to skin with her was all-consuming. I wanted to bury myself deep inside of her soft warmth and escape all the grief and anger I'd been carrying for what felt like years.

Hannah squirmed out from under me, taking my shirt with her. Before I could catch up, she had my shorts whisked off, leaving me in just my briefs. Not gonna lie, it was oddly exhilarating to have such enthusiasm coming at me from a person who didn't want anything from me except sex. Wait a minute.

Suddenly, as flattering as it was to be wanted, it also felt incredibly important to me that I meant more to her than being a sex toy in human form. I caught her around the waist and rolled her beneath me, catching her hands with mine so as not to be distracted by her questing fingers.

"Real talk," I said.

"Now?" Her blue eyes were heavy lidded in a seductive look that almost made me lose my focus.

"Yes." My tone was firm.

She went still then her eyes narrowed, blasting away every bit of sexy siren. She pulled her hands from mine and braced them against my chest and asked, "Are you married, O'Malley, because if you are, so help me . . ."

"No!" I was appalled at the thought of being a cheater. "It's nothing like that. Why would you even think that about me?"

"Sorry." She winced. "I might have some trust issues."

"Understandable." I brushed a lock of hair from her face. The thought that her ex had done such a number on her made my jaw tighten and I wished I'd been around to protect her. I hoped for his sake, I never ran into the guy because I didn't think I'd be able to keep myself from planting my fist in his face.

"Hey." Hannah cupped my face and brought my gaze to meet hers. "What are you thinking?"

"I won't hurt you like that," I said. It wasn't what I'd planned to say. I'd planned to confess that this was more than sex for me, that I had feelings in play, but I didn't have the balls to go there if she wasn't ready for that sort of confession. I couldn't demand more from her than she was willing to give and I didn't want to make things awkward between us.

Her eyebrows lifted and she nodded. "Is that it?"

"That's it," I confirmed.

She watched me for a beat and I knew she'd figured out that I was going to say something else but had done a last-minute pivot.

"You can trust me, too," she said. I didn't know if she meant I could trust her with whatever I'd been about to say or if she was just parroting me to comfort me. It didn't matter. I'd take all the comfort I could get.

"I know." I leaned in and kissed her. And then because I wanted to lighten the mood, I said, "Now, about that drawing. I think I want to start here." I nuzzled the curve of her neck and she let out a sexy gasp that made my cock twitch. I pulled her T-shirt over her head and slid my lips across her skin until I reached the fancy lace of her bra.

I leaned back to take her in, her dark hair spilled across the pillow, her kiss-swollen lips, and her hands sliding up my bare arms, her fingers wrapped around my biceps as she tried to pull me closer. She was glorious.

I unfastened her bra and let her generous breasts spill. Whoever said that a boob that was more than a mouthful was a waste was an idiot. I cupped her breasts and flicked her nipples with my thumbs, alternately pinching them and then soothing them with my tongue. I glanced up at her face, took in her rosy blush, and I could swear her pupils dilated. I did it again and again until she arched her back, grinding her head into the pillow as she made the sexiest pants and then broke down to pleading.

"Simon, I need more," she gasped.

"What sort of more?" I moved my lips down her torso, over her belly, stopping at the waist of her shorts. It took only moments to unfasten them and slide them down her legs. When I glanced down, Hannah Spencer was deliciously naked from head to toe and the sight of her made me so hard, I could have drilled through concrete.

"You. I need you. Now." There was a determined light in her eye that should have warned me, but my brain had only one thought going on a loop in my head. *Hannah. I belong to her and she belongs to me.*

Caught up in my own epiphany about us, Hannah was able to tackle me to the mattress with little to no resistance. She made quick work of my briefs, grabbed protection from the nightstand, and then she was straddling me, sliding down on top of me as if I was the answer to every question she had ever asked.

My hands grabbed her hips, but she took them and wrapped my fingers around the wrought iron bed frame. With a look that made my blood heat, she said, "Behave, Simon."

So fucking hot! I gritted my teeth to keep from coming right then and there. I watched as she rode me, taking over our mutual pleasure in every possible way. Relentlessly, she brought me to the peak of release and then slowed it down, keeping my orgasm just out of reach. It was the most delicious torture. Absolute exquisite pleasure-pain as she brought me to the point of orgasm and then denied me again and again and again.

I was sweating and panting, my abs and ass tight and ready to come when she stopped right on the tip of my penis as if she knew, she knew it would drive me completely mad. She looked down at me through a tumble of wavy hair and I was certain I had never seen anything or anyone this beautiful in my entire life. This was how I would draw her but that would be just for me.

"Hey," she whispered. "What are you thinking?"

I was thinking that I was in love with her, deeply, passionately in love, and there was no way I was ever going to get enough of her—not today, tonight, tomorrow, or ever.

Instead, I let go of the headboard and grabbed her hips. I rolled us until she was beneath me and then I plunged inside of her with a force that made her cry out and I felt her orgasm hit as she convulsed around me. It wasn't enough. It would never be enough. I put my thumb on her clit and rubbed it in circles that sent her into a thrashing frenzy where she was almost sobbing from the pleasure as her orgasm crashed over her again and again.

When her shudders eased, I rose up onto my knees, lifted her hips, and drilled into her once, twice, three times, and then my own orgasm fired up the back of my legs, tightened my balls, and swelled my cock until I felt as if it was being physically wrung from me.

I braced myself to keep from collapsing on top of her, marveling that I was lucky to survive such an intense climax. I pulled her in close, wrapping myself around her and burying my nose in her soft hair where the smell of lime and coconut soothed me. I was almost asleep when Hannah spoke.

"That's one," she said with a throaty laugh, and I found myself smiling, feeling a soul-deep contentment cover me like a blanket.

Our final days took on a rhythm. We sorted a little, repaired a bit, volunteered for baby turtle watch a few times, visited with our neighbors, but mostly, we spent every available second together. When Hannah worked on her content for her social media accounts, I usually caught up on office work and checked in with Lor and Charlie.

Lor was still working for the woman Chance had called his aunt, but if Chance was a part of things, she never said and refused to answer when I asked. *Sisters!* Charlie had his date with Diana and they were going on another one. Julian had assured me that Charlie and Diana were well matched and taking it slowly. When I asked Charlie about it, he changed the subject. *Brothers!*

They both asked me about Hannah and I told them she was fine. I did not tell them that we had moved into the spare bedroom and that Dude now slept sprawled on the bed in the main bedroom or that I couldn't decide what my favorite time of the day was anymore. Was it waking up and finding Hannah beside me? Was it laughing or crying with her as we went through the possessions our grandfathers had accumulated over the years? Probably it was when I made love to her and found her looking at me with her twinkling blue eyes and wide grin. A guy could get lost in a smile that big. Of course, I said none of those things. *Siblings!*

I was sitting on the back deck, working on my sketch of Hannah. I hadn't drawn anything in years but as soon as I put my pencil to the pad, the remembered image of Hannah looking down at me through her tumble of hair with an expression of such complete love that it had taken my breath away then did so even now as my pencil filled the page with it.

"Holy shit! You're good, like, really good."

I jumped and glanced behind me to see Roland standing there. He was in his usual ball cap and T-shirt, but his eyes were riveted on the page as he took in Hannah. I slapped the sketchbook shut, grateful that I had decided to draw her from just the collarbone up instead of including that glorious bust of hers.

"Thanks, Roland." I wiped the pencil residue off my fingers with a cloth. "How are things with you?"

"Funnily enough, I was just talking to Tim Larson about you," he said. "Specifically, about your artwork."

"Oh?"

"You know he's looking to have a mural painted on the side of the Scoop," he said.

"He mentioned something about that," I said.

"You should do it!" Roland said.

"My art days—"

"Zach, Luke, come here!" Roland called out over me.

"They're here?"

"Bebe told Luke to quit hovering over her and the baby. Tossed him right out the door, so we're going fishing and wanted to know if you want to come."

"Um . . . sure." Hannah and Dude wouldn't be back from her

latest project for a couple of hours. It was cool to have neighbors ask me to join them. In my life in Raleigh, I didn't have time for anything more than outings that involved trying to woo big corporate clients. Plus, it would be good for me to get away from the cottage, where it felt as if bits of Hannah existed in every room I entered. I missed her even though she'd been gone only a few hours, which was something else I'd never experienced with a romantic partner.

"You find him, Dad?" Zach cried.

"Back here!" Roland hollered in return.

Around the corner of the house came Zach and Luke. They were laughing and chatting about Luke's new baby and whether Luke was ever going to let her date or not.

"Of course I will," Luke said. "After I teach her how to knock a handsy boy out with one shot to the chin."

"That's the way." Zach raised his hand and Luke slapped it in a high five.

"There's been a change of plan," Roland announced.

"What?" Zach cried. "Why?"

"Because we need to talk Simon, here, into being the one who paints the mural on the side of the Scoop."

Both Zach and Luke glanced at me in confusion and I shrugged. If they assumed Roland was having a mental episode, far be it from me to disabuse them of that notion.

"Look at this!" Roland snatched up my drawing pad.

"Hey!" I cried, but he danced out of reach.

Holding it up so the others could see, he started flipping through the pages. "He's actually really good."

"You don't have to sound so surprised," I said. "I know Gramps bragged about me to anyone who would listen."

"Yeah, but I actually saw you creating this," Roland said as he tapped Hannah's portrait. "It made it much more accessible."

Luke and Zach flipped through the pad. I tried to tell myself their opinions didn't matter, that these were just crude sketches I'd been doing as warm-ups to painting again, but still I felt a tight twisting in my gut.

It was the same nervousness I'd felt when my book came out. The only opinion I'd never worried about was Gramps's. He'd always gassed me up, making me think I was the next J. C. Leyendecker. Damn, I missed Gramps. I felt my eyes grow damp. Ever since I'd cried out my grief in Hannah's arms, it was like the spigot on my tears had been turned on. I shook my head, now was not the time.

"Hypothetically, if you were going to do a mural, what would it be of?" Roland asked. "Big bowl of ice cream?"

"Obviously," I said. "But it'd have to be reflective of Cape Split, too. The people, the landmarks, the history. It's a monumental task, which is another reason why I passed on the opportunity."

"You can't pass," Zach said while still studying my sketches.

"Excuse me?"

Zach glanced up and said, "If you don't do it, Tim is going to hire Damian Shapiro." Both Luke and Roland let out groans.

I stared at Zach. "And?"

"He's not a local artist," Luke said. He took out his phone and did a quick search.

"He has no connection to the Outer Banks at all," Roland said, sounding outraged. "How can he possibly paint a mural in our town if he has no connection to the Split?"

"Why would Tim hire him then?" I asked.

"Because he's available and has been badgering Tim to let him do it for *years*," Zach said.

"You have to save our community, Simon, it's as simple as that," Roland said.

"I'm not sure I qualify any more than Shapiro," I said. "I've only lived here for a summer."

"That's more than the other guy," Roland argued.

"And your family has been here for decades, making you a legacy," Zach said.

"You're literally grandfathered into the community," Luke added.

The three of them were staring at me and I wanted to stand firm in my no, but I couldn't seem to force the words out. I thought of my afternoon with Hannah and Dude at the Scoop and couldn't bear the thought of an outsider leaving their mark on that big wall.

The picture of Gramps and Pops in front of the Scoop flitted through my mind. I wondered what Gramps would think of me doing the mural for the Scoop, but deep down I knew. He'd be so damn proud. It hit me right then. The mural was what I could do to honor him.

"Come on, Simon," Luke cajoled.

"Say yes," Zach badgered.

I turned to Roland. "All right, let's do it. Let's see if Tim still wants this mural. One thing, though, promise me you won't let Hannah find out."

"You don't think she's going to notice a fourteen-foot-high painting?" Roland asked.

"Before it's done," I said. "Promise me you won't tell anyone that I'm doing it until it's finished."

The three exchanged curious glances and then spoke together. "Promise."

Hannah

I was breaking my own rules. Simon and I had been romantically involved for more than two weeks and had now known each other for six. It was time to break up with him. Every single fiber of my being was against this horrible idea but I also knew that I was falling hard for Simon O'Malley and the longer we were a thing, even if it was just for the remainder of our time in the cottage, the more likely I was to get hurt. And I desperately didn't want to get hurt.

And it wasn't just me. Dude had a man crush on Simon that was ridiculously adorable. Wherever Simon was, Dude wanted to be. Feeling the same way, I understood my dog completely.

Dude and I took a seat on the beach where we were filming some van life content. I'd gotten so many wonderful shots of the big boy playing in the waves, I'd have plenty to edit later into a piece about the beauty of the Outer Banks beaches.

I thumbed through my phone looking for the contact I needed. Nana's name came up and knowing that she should be back from her cruise as of a few days ago, I pressed dial.

"Hannah-Banana, how are you, dearest girl?" Nana answered on the second ring with our shared nickname, which always made me smile.

"I'm good, Nana-Banana, and you? Recovered from your trip yet?"

"Not even close. It'll take me another week, at least. Has your father sent you the pictures yet?"

"He sent a few whenever he got good Wi-Fi," I said. "I especially liked the one of you and Grandpa George riding camels in Marrakech."

"They spit. Camels, I mean. Did you know that?" Nana said it like she was still surprised, and I laughed. It was so good to hear her voice.

"I had heard that they do but only if they like you," I said.

"Liar." Nana barked a laugh but quickly sobered. "Now tell me what's wrong."

"Why do you assume something's wrong?" I sifted some sand through my fingers. "Can't I just call to check in?"

"Because you don't call to check in, you text," Nana said. "If you're calling, it's because something is bothering you. Out with it."

I hesitated.

"And because you're calling me and not your parents, I have to assume it's about Pops."

"I didn't know who else to call," I admitted.

"You found out about Bobby." It wasn't a question.

"You knew?" I gasped.

"Of course, your grandfather was my best friend."

"Why didn't anyone tell me?"

"It wasn't my place to tell you," Nana said. "There were circumstances—"

"His partner's family?" I interrupted.

"Yes." She sighed. "Your Pops so wanted you to be a part of their lives but . . ."

"Gramps's son is an asshole who would have made their lives miserable?" I asked.

"Have you met him?" Nana asked.

"No, but I'm sharing the house with his son, who is nothing like him." My tone came out fiercer than I intended and I cleared my throat. "His name is Simon and . . ."

"You care for him." Again, it wasn't a question.

I watched a group of sandpipers dart in and out of the water. As they scurried away from an incoming wave, I found their frantic run very relatable. Was that why I'd called Nana? Was I trying to outrun my feelings for Simon?

"I do, but we're not serious. We've agreed to clean out the house together and at the end of two months, we'll decide what we're doing with it." I paused and then added, "I want to stay but Simon wants to sell. He's offered to buy me out and then sell it on his own."

"Why?" Nana asked.

"Why what?"

"Why do you want to stay? Why does he want to sell?"

"I love it here. It feels like home," I said. "But Simon wants to sell, because he has responsibilities and the money from the sale would help with that."

"Oh, that's a tough one. What have you been doing to change his mind . . . other than sex?"

"Nana, I would never," I protested. "Any sex that's happening is because the guy is smoking hot and I wanted it."

"That's my girl." Nana laughed. "That being said, sometimes sex offers thick men some clarity of thought. I'm just saying."

This time I laughed. "I have just two more weeks until we agreed to make our decision."

She was quiet for a moment and then she said, "Your grandfather and I were very happy together, you know that, right?"

I felt the ocean breeze tug at my clothing while Dude snored on my bare feet. I thought back to the grandparents who had loved me unconditionally since the moment I'd arrived in their world. They had been happy together.

"Despite that love, we weren't meant for each other. Your Pops had already given his heart away, and he would never love me like he loved Bobby. When Pops discovered Bobby had been widowed, he spiraled into a real crisis. Stay with me and the family we'd created or follow his heart."

Her voice was gentle but I could feel the old emotions in it. My throat got tight and my eyes damp. I couldn't imagine how confused she must have felt. "What did you do?"

"I told him to follow his heart," Nana said. "Because, honestly, Hannah-Banana, I deserved better than second place in someone's life. I wanted first place for myself."

"And you found Grandpa George," I concluded.

"I did," she said. "*If* you find that love with Simon—the selfless love that I have with George, that your parents have, and that Pops found with Bobby—hang on to it with both hands, Hannah. Not everyone gets to find the love of their life and if you let it go, you may not get a second chance."

Truth. Nana spoke the truth that I knew deep in my heart but was reluctant to acknowledge. Was Simon the love of my life? Judging by the way my heart jackhammered around my chest cavity at the mere thought of him, I suspected he was. But was I his? Or was I exactly what I'd told him I was—just a short-term situationship?

The need to see him was sudden and swift and all-consuming. I ended the call with Nana and gathered my things. "Come on, Dude, let's go see our guy."

We arrived home to find Simon sketching away in his notebook. He hadn't let me see any of his work and I was burning with curiosity but a deal was a deal. I would see it when he was finished.

Still, I was human and I crept up behind him, hoping to catch a glance but he slammed the cover shut and tossed the pad onto the table with his pencil. Then he scooped me about the waist and pulled me into his lap.

"I missed you." He didn't give me a chance to respond as he kissed me with a raw hunger that made my insides liquefy.

"I missed you, too." I gasped when he broke the kiss.

Dude, not to be neglected, nudged his way into the embrace. I slid off Simon's lap and watched as he rubbed Dude's ears and scratched his neck just the way he liked. Dude thumped his back foot in response and melted into a doggy puddle at Simon's feet. I knew exactly how he felt.

Unable to keep from touching him, I leaned over the back of his chair and hugged Simon from behind so as not to interrupt Dude's pets. Simon turned his head and kissed me quick.

"What's all the affection for?" he asked. "Not that I'm complaining."

"It's nothing." I shrugged. "I just want to hang on to you with both hands."

We exchanged small smiles and I knew Nana would approve. Simon was definitely a man worth hanging on to.

Simon was up before the sun the next morning. I heard him moving around the room and felt him tuck my bare feet under the covers as if he was concerned that they'd get cold. He kissed me on the forehead and I heard him slip from the room.

The man had kept me up all night—in the most delicious ways—but after a day spent filming outside and a night spent in his arms, I was exhausted.

I awoke to the feel of the bed dipping and assumed it was Simon, returning. A big black snout nuzzled my chin and my eyes flew open to find Dude staring down at me. I closed my eyes but he wasn't having it. He began to push me with his nose as if trying to roll me right out of the bed.

"Dude!" I cried as I prevented a fall by planting my foot on the floor. He cocked his head to the side in feigned innocence. "Don't give me that look. I know you know better."

He jumped off the bed and bolted for the door.

"Fine. I'm coming." I shoved aside my covers and staggered out of the bedroom. When I reached the kitchen, Dude was sitting by the back door, his tail thumping against the wall. Clearly, he had to go outside *right now.*

I opened the door and he bolted outside. There was no sign of Simon on the dock, the deck, or in his makeshift office in the dining room. The light on the coffeepot was on and beside it was a piece of paper torn from Simon's sketchbook. It was the first note I'd ever gotten from him and I was intrigued by his very precise handwriting and charmed by the sketch of Dude he'd made in the corner. I laughed at the dopey expression Simon had captured so perfectly.

Good morning, darling, (I could practically hear his drawl speaking the endearment)

Coffee is made. Dude has been fed and let out multiple times. Don't let him fool you.

I have to go work on a project but I'll be back later this morning.

X, Simon

I traced the sketch of Dude with my finger. My lips curved up as I glanced out the window and saw Dude lying in the grass, playing catch with himself, tossing the ball in the air and letting it drop into his mouth. Ridiculous. It occurred to me that this was the first house that Dude had ever known and I wanted this permanent patch of grass for him as much as I wanted it for myself.

It occurred to me that I had changed so much since I'd first arrived in Cape Split. It was the longest amount of time I'd spent anywhere in over five years. I'd been outrunning my grief over my marriage and my career for so long, it had become a lifestyle instead of a coping mechanism and it hit me that I didn't want that life anymore. The community I'd found here had allowed me to flourish, making friendships for more than a day, working on stories—like the one about the sea turtle habitats—that went deeper about conservation than just a thirty-second clickbait video. It felt as if I was finding myself again and it was the magic of this place that allowed me to do so.

I took my coffee out onto the deck and sat facing the dock. The heat was already beginning to rise and I could see the surface of the water in the channel ripple as a breeze blew across it. I watched an egret launch into the sky and heard the songbirds chatter in the trees. I tried to picture where I would put a vegetable garden and decided it'd be along the east side of the yard, running from the house to the marsh, because that had the best light for growing. The thought of sharing something like that with Simon gave me a thrill. I wondered if I could ever get him to consider making this place home.

Abruptly, Dude jumped to his feet and started barking. Before

I could call him, he bolted around the side of the house to the front. Dude was harmless but he didn't look harmless when he was barreling down on a person. Fearing that a neighbor was about to have the snot scared out of them, I set down my coffee and bolted back through the house to the front door.

I yanked it open just in time to see Dude growling at a man in a navy blue suit with a perfectly trimmed head of silver hair. He held out his hand to ward off Dude, and the sun glinted off the snazzy Rolex he had strapped to his wrist.

"Dude, enough!" I ordered. For once Dude listened and he stopped growling and sat, staring at the man as if he'd pounce at my command if needed. It was very reassuring. "Sorry about that. Can I help you?"

The man looked me up and down. It wasn't in a predatory way, thankfully, but it was definitely an assessment of my worth and judging by the way his lip curled ever so slightly, I was found lacking. Okay, then.

"It was my understanding that Simon O'Malley owns this house," he said.

A million thoughts flashed through my mind. Who was this guy? Why did he want Simon? If Simon had known he was coming, he would have told me, wouldn't he? Was Simon in trouble? Should I lie for him? Instead, I shrugged, giving him nothing.

My years as a journalist had taught me that people don't like silence. When interviewing someone, I gave them plenty of time to fill the air, getting much more out of them than I would if I hammered them with questions.

"Your name?" he asked.

"Since you're the one who is looking for someone, maybe you should give me your name first," I suggested.

"You think you're clever, don't you?"

“Not really. I’m just a woman trying to survive in a misogynistic world,” I said. “It makes a gal cautious.”

The man’s curled lip actually twisted into a sneer. He gestured to the cottage. “This house belongs to *my* family. I suggest you leave before I call the police.”

That was unexpected. I studied him. His face was flushed as if he had a low simmering anger burning inside of him constantly looking for an outlet. How would he know to look for Simon here, but then declare the house was his family’s? That sort of toxic narcissism reminded me of the stories Simon and Lor had told me about . . . their father.

I returned his scrutinizing look. “Mr. O’Malley, I presume?”

Simon

The mural was going to be spectacular assuming I hadn't lost my skills, which admittedly was a pretty big assumption. I'd stayed later than I intended but Tim and I had a lot to discuss about the design and the colors. Mostly, he was letting me do whatever I wanted but he had some solid ideas for customer engagement and promotion of the Scoop. We'd also worked out a price for the mural that was going to make the idea bubbling in my brain potentially feasible but I still had to work out some details.

Finding that trunk full of my work from Gramps had unlocked something inside me. And Hannah, having Hannah encourage me, had sealed the deal. I wanted to be an artist again. I'd missed it as if I'd lost a part of my soul. Providing for Charlie and Lor had become my number one priority and I had no regrets, but now, as Lorelei had pointed out on her visit, they were doing all right and maybe, just maybe, I could take back my own life, too.

I maneuvered my Jeep down the narrow dirt road to the cottage. I saw Davis Fisk teaching his oldest how to ride a bike. We shared a wave and a smile and I thought about my condo in Raleigh, where I didn't know my neighbors because the hours I kept made it impossible to ever meet anyone, and I realized that I didn't want to leave the Split. I wanted to stay here with Hannah and Dude and build the life of my dreams. I could make art again and Hannah could keep doing her online content or maybe go back to being a journalist. If Tim was right and my mural painting could be developed into a business, I could make enough money to pay for Charlie's care, while getting back into the illustration game.

Quit. The. Business. Those three little words felt like a key unlocking a jail cell. It felt as if a weight that had been pressing on my chest for eight long years had finally been lifted.

This was all because of Gramps. In his note, he had said to choose happiness. For the longest time, happiness hadn't even been on my radar, but being here and becoming a part of this community, having the time to create and find my passion again, I could see it. This summer at the Split had changed me and I didn't want to go back to the way I was. I wanted to stay right here in this place and time with the woman I loved.

I glanced at the seat beside me. I had impulsively picked up two blue hydrangea plants for the pots on either side of the cottage's front door. Hannah had been making the house more of a home with little touches here and there, like new bath towels and vases of fresh-cut wildflowers from the neighborhood that she gathered on our walks. She'd mentioned replacing whatever had died in those front porch planters, and I'd seen the hydrangea and the deep blue petals of the flowers reminded me of her eyes. I debated how I could tell her that without sounding like I was completely besotted with her. Yeah, I was just going to have to own it.

I pulled up to the house, excited to see my woman—yes, she was mine even if she didn't realize it yet—when I noticed the silver

Bentley with Florida plates parked in front. My heart dropped into my feet. *Oh, shit!*

I jammed the car into park and jumped out, not even bothering to shut off the engine. Fear was coursing through me as I realized Hannah was at the mercy of my father. I knew he wouldn't hurt her physically. My father never laid a hand on any of us. His cruelty came in the form of words and neglect. So help me, if he said one rotten thing to her, I would lay my hands on him and make him regret it.

"Hannah!" I ran up the walkway to the house and there she was, standing on the top step like a queen with my father looking up at her from the base of the steps. Her arms were crossed over her chest as if in challenge to my father. She was fantastic!

My father whipped around and glared at me. "Where have you been?"

"Working." Not a total lie.

His gaze moved over me, taking in my cargo pants, work boots, and ratty T-shirt. "I find that difficult to believe."

I glanced from him to Hannah. How much had they spoken? Did he know who she was? Hannah must have sensed my unease because she patted her thigh and Dude left his spot where he'd been staring down my father—good dog!—and trotted up the steps to her side. Our gazes met and she shook her head ever so slightly, indicating that my father didn't know who she was.

"I'll let you talk in private," she said. And then she went inside without another word, closing the door behind her.

"Really, Simon?" my father snapped.

"Really what?" I asked.

"That." My father waved his hand at the house. "You have a woman and her dog here with you in my father's house?"

And there it was. I turned away from him and rolled my eyes.

I'd been in such a good mood before he arrived. I walked back to the Jeep I'd left running, reached through the open window, and switched the engine off. My father didn't move from his place in front of the house. I had no doubt he wanted to be invited in. Not gonna happen. I wasn't letting him anywhere near Gramps's sanctuary.

"I'm disappointed in you, Simon," Dad said in his usual disapproving tone. "You should have informed me about my inheritance."

I mimicked his stance, shoving my hands in my pockets. A good place to put them to keep from strangling him. "There was no need, because it's not yours."

"I am Robert O'Malley's son." It was a declarative statement.

"But not his heir," I said. "I am."

"You can't cut me out." My father checked the time on his Rolex as if he'd expected to have already won my acquiescence by now.

"I don't have to," I said. "Gramps already did that."

"I'll take you to court."

"Really? You're going to sue me for my inheritance?"

"If I have to." Dad brushed some imaginary lint off his sleeve. "And I'll win."

"Doubt it," I said. "Because only half of the house was left to me. The other half belongs to someone else."

"What are you talking about?" Dad dropped his hands and balled his fingers into fists while a deep frown marred his forehead.

"Oh, you didn't know?" I asked. My tone was feigned curiosity with subtle notes of smug. "Then you aren't aware that Gramps bought this cottage with . . . a friend."

"Friend?" My father scoffed. "If you're referring to that limp-wristed TV whore—"

"Don't." I reached forward and grabbed my father by the lapel of his suit, lifting him until he was standing up on his toes and we were nose to nose. "Say. Another. Word."

"What? You think I didn't know that my own father was—" I halted his words with a rough shake. He snapped his head toward the house as if he'd just put it together. "Is that who that woman is? The granddaughter of the queer who turned your grandfather?"

"No one was turned," I snapped, releasing him. I was disgusted with him and myself for losing my temper. "They were soulmates who were lucky enough to find each other again and have a second chance."

My father recoiled, horror on his face, and then he stepped forward with his teeth bared and fists still clenched. "You listen to me, Simon. This house will be mine and you will get it for me. I don't care if you have to fuck that woman into signing it over to you. You'll do it or I'll come after you and have you removed from the conservatorship of your brother."

"That's it!" I'd never wanted to hit another human being as badly as I did right now. "Time for you to leave, old man." It was a cheap shot to his vanity but still satisfying.

"What did you call me?" Dad snapped, jutting his chin forward.

"You heard me." I grabbed him by the elbow and began to escort him to his car. I hadn't planned to throw hands with my father but the minute he'd insulted Gramps, he'd lit the match, and when he mentioned Hannah and Charlie, he burned it all down.

"Not another fucking word." I half dragged, half carried him to his Bentley and then shoved him toward his car. "Get off *my* property *now*."

"You're going to regret this, Simon!" Dad shouted. "I don't care who owns this property with you. I will file a partition action for full ownership and take it away from you and your little friend."

"Sorry, old man, but I'm not a kid and you can't take the ladder from the tree house and leave me alone in the dark anymore."

Dad looked as if he was going to take a swing at me. I braced myself. If he wanted a fight, I'd give him one. Before he could make a move, Dude came bounding out of the house, snarling with an impressive amount of teeth showing.

My father scrambled to get into his car. He just made it. Still, Dude jumped up, putting his paws on the driver's side window and dropping a nice splat of drool on the glass.

"Dude!" I called him off, not to protect my father but rather to keep my father from hurting the dog. Dude barked a few more times and pushed off, coming back to stand beside me.

My father hit the gas and sped away, leaving a cloud of dirt behind him.

"Not for nothing," Hannah said from behind me. "But what an asshole."

I spun to face her. Before Hannah could read my expression, I cupped her head and pulled her in close, kissing her with a fierceness that made my hunger for her flash through me like a bolt of lightning. I hated that she'd had to deal with him.

"Don't let anything he said bother you." I leaned back to study her face. "He's a miserable man who's never cared for anyone but himself."

"Is it true about Charlie? Could he do that?" She cupped my face in her hands, her eyes studying my expression, looking for the truth.

"No," I said. "Don't let him rattle you. He's the very definition of a—"

"Shit stirrer," Hannah supplied.

My lips twitched. No one nailed descriptions quite like Hannah. "Yeah. That."

"Okay." She nodded. Then she hugged me tight and I pressed my head to her hair and wrapped my arms around her. I would not let my father use Charlie as leverage, and I wouldn't let him take the place Hannah and I were making into a home away from her . . . from us.

Hannah

It was one thing to agree not to let his father get to me, it was another to block out the voice that whispered in my ear whenever Simon wasn't by my side. It was needy and gross and I hated it, but as I trimmed the overgrown azaleas that lined the garden bed in front of the porch, I kept hearing his father's words.

I don't care if you have to fuck that woman into signing it over to you. You'll do it or I'll come after you and have you removed from the conservatorship of your brother.

It was so vulgar and nasty. It made my skin crawl. It made me feel as vulnerable as I'd felt the day I discovered my husband had impregnated his assistant. That had been such a cliché, it should have been laughable, but it had devastated me. And my husband displaying my inadequacies at divorce court had broken me completely.

Did I believe Simon had started a relationship with me to romance the house out from under me? No. But was I completely certain? Also, no. How could I be when I knew that he'd tossed away his dream career as an artist to provide for his brother? He was toiling in a job he hated for a steady paycheck so that Charlie received the care he needed and so that Lorelei had been able to get her career underway. Sleeping with me to woo me into selling my share of the house to him was a small sacrifice compared to the artistic career he'd given up.

And if Simon wasn't using me, if he meant it when he said not to worry that his father would cause him problems, well, that was equally disturbing. I'd done an information deep dive on Robert O'Malley Jr. He was, to put it mildly, a piece of work.

Judging by the simple internet search I did, Robert O'Malley Jr. was a litigious nightmare. He sued everyone from his dog groomer for a bad haircut on his dog to his local dry cleaner for missing pants and even the town council of his Florida hometown for not raising the speed limit after he got a ticket. Given that only 5 percent of civil cases go to trial, and that most of Robert's did go and he lost, I was amazed he had enough money to threaten to sue Simon. But perhaps his financial hardship was why he was so hungry to get his hands on our house and on Charlie's conservatorship. I wasn't even family and I would fight this guy with my last nickel to protect Charlie and my home.

I stood and pressed my fist into my lower back. Being hunkered over the bushes had tightened my muscles. I glanced at the hydrangeas in the pots on each side of the front door. The cheerful sight of the blue blossoms lifted my spirits a bit. I'd been touched when Simon had given me the plants last week and told me that the blue reminded him of my eyes. Also, he'd known the dead plants in the pots had bothered me and the fact that he'd bought something for the house felt like a positive sign. It was that sort of thoughtfulness that made the insecure part of me shut up. Simon was a good guy. He wasn't like my ex. I was sure of it.

Except, he'd been disappearing every morning before I woke

up and returning hours later only to jump into the shower right away. Suspicious, right? When I casually asked him where he'd been, he always said he was working on a project. When I asked what sort of project, he changed the subject.

We were well past my self-imposed limit of two weeks for being involved. The smart thing to do would be to break things off now before one of us—meaning me—got hurt. But I wasn't feeling smart at the moment. I was feeling stupidly head over heels in love with Simon O'Malley and there wasn't a damn thing I could do about it.

I wiped the sweat off my brow and decided to shower and then take a walk over to Bebe's to visit her and baby Ava. Luke had returned to work and Bebe was beginning to get her rhythm with motherhood, taking to it like a bird to flight. It had become our habit to get together in the morning and let Dude and Frank run around while we visited over sweet tea with baked Brie and fig jam bruschetta.

I hurried through my shower and threw on a sundress and sandals. I wanted loose clothing to let the heavy humid air flow through. Dude waited patiently on the couch for me and the minute I said, "Let's go see Frank," he let out a *woof* and trotted to the door.

I pulled it open and almost crashed into Charlie, who stood there with wide eyes, hugging his middle. He looked terrified.

"Charlie, hi, how are you?" I asked.

"I'm in trouble, Hannah, big trouble." His soft brown eyes, so like Simon's, were huge, and I felt my nerves flutter in my stomach. He started to pace the length of the porch, so I stepped outside with Dude to join him. "I need Simon."

"Have you tried to call him?" I asked.

"I don't have my phone."

"Okay, I'll try." I pulled my phone out of my pocket. Simon and I had exchanged numbers at his insistence the first time I went out to work on my online content. He'd said he'd be my in-case-of-emergency contact if anything happened to me. I'd never needed to call him, we generally just texted, and I hoped it wasn't weird now. His phone went to voicemail on the fifth ring. I left a message asking him to call me and ended the call.

Charlie sat on the porch steps where Dude plopped down beside him and put his head in Charlie's lap. Charlie absently stroked Dude's ears while staring out at the front yard.

"I left Simon a message." I leaned against the porch railing. "Do you want to talk about it?"

"I ran away." Charlie stared at the toes of his shoes, not meeting my eyes.

"What? Why?" I cried. "What did Julian say?"

"He wasn't there." Charlie glanced at me. "Bob, the night counselor, was there and he's a stickler. The police were there, too, so I had to go."

I took a long steadying breath. I didn't want to cause Charlie any more distress than he was already feeling but I needed more information. "Can you tell me why you ran away?"

Charlie shook his head. I saw tears well up in his eyes and his face flushed a deep shade of red. This expression was one I knew all too well. Shame.

I sat down beside Charlie so that he was nestled between me and Dude. "Charlie, there is nothing that you can tell me that will make me not like you. You're safe with me."

"Promise?"

"I promise." I really hoped I wasn't lying.

"Okay. Well, I wanted to show Diana how much I like her," he said.

I waited, letting him choose his words, even as I felt my stomach constrict. What if he had done something inappropriate or offensive or worse? Where the hell was Simon?

“So, I bought her flowers,” he said.

I waited a beat. “Well, that’s nice.”

“And I snuck into her room to surprise her with them.”

“Oh.” That wasn’t good.

“But she wasn’t there.”

“Okay.” Maybe he left them behind and this was a nothingburger.

“I left them in her room with a note.”

“Well, that seems thoughtful.”

“But I really wanted to know if she liked them.”

“Understandable.” I started to sweat.

“So, I waited until it was dark and I climbed up the side of her house.”

“Oh, dear.”

“And knocked on her window.”

“Oh, boy.”

“Except I got confused and it wasn’t her window.”

“Oh?”

“It was the night counselor’s window.”

“That’s unfortunate.”

“She screamed and hit me with a shoe.”

“Are you okay?” I put my hand on his arm.

“I’m fine. It was a slipper.”

“Oh.” My voice sounded faint even to my own ears.

“I ran all the way back to my house but the cops were waiting for me,” he said. “So, I ran away . . . to here.”

“Charlie, Raleigh is three and a half hours away,” I cried. “How did you get all the way here?”

“I hitchhiked.”

A wave of dizziness washed over me. So many horrible things could have happened to him. I reached over and hugged him, reassuring myself that he was okay.

"Charlie, listen to me," I said. "You didn't do anything wrong. Certainly nothing that would warrant the police. It was just a misunderstanding."

"Really?" I felt the tension in his shoulders ease.

"Absolutely. Simon will be home soon and I'll bet he can get this all sorted and everything will be fine." I hugged him again.

"You should be careful not to make promises you can't keep, Ms. Spencer."

I glanced up to see Simon's father standing there. Dude left Charlie's side to move down the steps in front of us. He started to growl and I put my hand on his back to calm him. He'd always been an excellent judge of people.

"Dad!" Charlie cried, and jumped to his feet.

"Sit down, Charlie." A look of disgust passed over his father's face. Charlie sat down, looking chastised, and I felt a visceral need to punch his father right in the face.

"What do you want, Mr. O'Malley?" I used his last name just as dismissively as he'd used mine.

"You know what I want," he snapped. Then his eyes narrowed. "You care for Simon, don't you?"

I didn't answer as it was none of his business, besides "care for" was an anemic way to describe what I felt for Simon.

"Don't bother denying it. I saw it on your face the other day when you looked at him." He took a deep breath and said, "Charlie, I need to speak with Ms. Spencer. Go wait in the car."

"But I want to see Simon," Charlie said.

"I'm here to take you back to the group home, you don't need Simon," Mr. O'Malley said. Charlie sat frozen. "Now, Charlie."

"Bye, Hannah." Charlie stood and I did, too, giving him a quick hug.

"Call Simon the minute you get home," I said. I was feeling very ill at ease. I didn't like anything about this, and I had questions, lots of questions.

"I will." Charlie climbed into the back of his father's car as if he knew he wasn't allowed to sit in front with his father.

I turned to Mr. O'Malley. "If he doesn't call . . ."

"He'll call." He waved a dismissive hand at me. "I'm taking him home. What could I do with him?"

"How did you know he was here?" I asked.

"Where else would he go?" he countered. "The home called me when he ran off because they said they couldn't get in touch with Simon or Lorelei—not very good care of their brother, if you ask me."

"I didn't ask. You're not here for Charlie," I said. "What do you really want?"

"This cottage, for starters," he said. "I'm tired of Florida and ready for a change."

"It's unfortunate that the cottage belongs to me and Simon."

"Does it? It belonged to *my* father and the right of succession . . ."

"Is irrelevant because it also belonged to my grandfather."

Mr. O'Malley began to pace, clearly not wanting to acknowledge my point.

"I'll make this simple, Ms. Spencer. You can either have Simon or this house but you can't have both. Because if you keep your half of the house, I'll be forced to use this incident with Charlie—stalking a defenseless woman, attempting a break-in, committing assault on a caregiver, and running from the law—to petition the court to take his conservatorship from Simon and turn it over to me."

"They won't do it," I said.

"Of course they will," he argued. "I'm Charlie's father and when he got himself into trouble, who was there to make things right? Me. Who failed him? Simon."

Dread began to thrum its cold fingers in my belly. I couldn't believe what I was hearing. This man, who had abandoned his children as teens, actually thought a judge would put him in charge of Charlie's health and well-being because he was his father and he happened to field one call? A tiny voice inside of me whispered that it could happen, and I was immediately terrified.

"You're beginning to get it." Mr. O'Malley continued pacing. I glanced at the car and saw Charlie watching us with an anxious expression. I forced a smile that felt brittle and turned back to Mr. O'Malley. I was about to argue with his assessment of the situation when he said, "How do you think Simon would feel about you if he knew you had the means to stop my takeover of the conservatorship but chose not to? Spoiler: It won't go well for you."

"I think it's time for you to leave," I said.

"I'm going. Think about what I said. All you have to do is sign your half of the house over to me, for a fair market price of course, and Charlie will go back to his safe little life and I won't challenge Simon for the conservatorship." He pulled a folded packet of papers out of the inside pocket of his suit coat.

"You can't be serious," I said. "You're actually going to leverage my feelings for your son to steal his inheritance right out from under him?"

Mr. O'Malley stared at me as if I were the stupidest person he'd ever encountered. "I can assure you that to get what I want I would do much worse."

"Fine." I held out my hand. I had no idea what I was going to do, but it had to be something brilliant to get us all out of this mess.

"I thought you'd see it that way." Mr. O'Malley handed me the sheaf of papers. "I'll be back tomorrow."

What a bastard. Simon had hypothesized that his father was either a narcissist or an asshole. At the moment, I was certain it was the latter.

Charlie rolled his window down as I approached. I leaned in and said, "Don't you worry. Simon and I will take care of everything. I promise."

As I watched them speed away, I was consumed with a fury I had never felt before. This man was not going to win. I didn't know how but I was not going to let him hurt his children ever again.

Simon

I parked the Jeep in front of the house and jogged up the steps. There was a spring in my step that I hadn't felt in years, and I found myself smiling all throughout the day for no apparent reason. I used to wake up, lie in bed, and dread the day. Now I was up before the sun and eager to be working on the mural. I felt whole again and I owed it all to Hannah.

"Spencer!" I called out. "Where are you?"

I paused in the living room. Usually, she and Dude met me out front. I'd gotten used to seeing her wearing her floppy straw sun hat, a streak of dirt on her cheek, and wielding her gardening shears. Maybe she'd moved to the backyard where I knew she was planning a vegetable garden and a chicken coop. She was still lobbying hard for chickens.

I strode to the sliding screen door and saw her sitting at the patio table. The breeze was tugging long strands of her hair out of the messy knot she'd fastened it into at the nape of her neck. Her profile was lit by the early-afternoon sun and I knew I could stare at her all day.

Dude heard me or smelled me or something because he jumped to his feet and began to bark a greeting. Hannah started and turned toward the door. Her face was pale and her eyes sad. It was then that I noticed a thick stack of papers being held down by her coffee mug.

I slid open the door and stepped outside. It hit me then, a sense of foreboding, like the air when the summer humidity is too thick to breathe and you know a storm is coming.

"What's wrong?" I felt my chest tighten with unease.

"Do you remember when you told me that if you had to choose between saving your art or Charlie, you would always choose Charlie?"

I nodded. "But I—" I began but she kept talking.

"It's one of the things I admire most about you."

"I adm—" I started to say but she interrupted.

"No." She held up her hand in a *stop* gesture. "I wasn't fishing for a return compliment."

"But I—"

"You don't have to say anything back," she said.

"Am I going to be allowed to finish a sentence?" I crossed the deck to where she sat and pulled her to her feet. I stared down at her, trying to figure out why she looked so devastated.

"You just did." She glanced away as if it was too hard to look at me. I felt my lips twitch at her sass, relieved to see my Hannah was still in there.

I cupped her face, trying to get her to look at me but she still wouldn't meet my eyes. "What happened?"

"I've made a decision." She ducked her head, pulling it out of my hands. "I'm selling my half of the house to you."

I blinked. If she'd slapped me, I couldn't have been more stunned. "The fuck you are."

Her face snapped up and her mouth formed an O. I would have

laughed at her comical expression of shock if I wasn't so frustrated that she'd made this out-of-the-blue decision without talking to me.

Dude, sensing the tension between us, came over and nudged his way into our huddle. Absently, I patted his head. "It's okay, buddy, I just have to talk some sense into your mama."

"Don't bother." Hannah shook her head. "I won't change my mind."

I narrowed my eyes at her. She'd mentioned how I'd said I'd choose Charlie over my art. Clearly something had happened and I'd bet my last nickel it had to do with my father and his threat to fight me for Charlie's conservatorship.

"Those papers?" I gestured to the table. "I assume they're from my father? What happened, Hannah? Talk to me."

She tipped her head back and her voice was thick when she spoke. "You've given me so much over the past few weeks. I don't know if I can adequately tell you how much you've repaired the damage that was done to my self-esteem during my marriage. You healed me, Simon."

"This sounds like the beginning of a breakup speech." My throat was tight.

Her smile was sad. "I told you I don't do long term."

"This isn't just a summer fling." My voice came out harsh with fear and desperation. "Not for me."

She shook her head, dismissing my words. "Your father . . ." She paused. ". . . made me an offer that I'm not interested in, but it did give me the idea that I could sell my half of the house to you, as you requested before, and you can then do with the cottage what you will."

"No." I shook my head. "I call bullshit on this idea. You're sinking roots here—literally, planting gardens. You can't suddenly be willing to walk away."

She said nothing, but I could see her lips tremble.

I gripped her upper arms and held her steady. "You love this house and this community. You've made yourself a part of it. Now tell me what my father has done to make you walk away from this . . . from me."

"If I don't sell him my half of the house, he'll take Charlie's conservatorship away from you," she said. "I can't see any way around it, other than to sell the cottage to you."

"What?" I rocked back on my heels. "How could he possibly think he stands a chance—"

"Some things have happened." Hannah told me everything then, about finding Charlie outside. About the poor and terrifying choices Charlie had made and about my father showing up, ready to swoop in and steal our home away from us, leveraging Charlie's conservatorship to do it. When she was finished, she looked so defeated and sad. I wrapped her in my arms and hugged her tight. I was furious and wished I had punched my father the day he'd shown up here. But perhaps I would still get my chance.

When I released her, I put my hands on her shoulders and said, "You need to listen to me. I'm not going to allow you to give up your dream of living here because my father is a miserable son of a bitch who thinks he's going to destroy our lives again. He's my problem, not yours."

She glanced up and met my gaze. I brushed her hair back from her face and resisted the urge to kiss her. Good thing, because she narrowed her eyes and said, "What have you been up to, O'Malley?"

"What do you mean?" I widened my eyes in what I hoped was an innocent look.

"I thought you wanted to buy my half of the house, but now you say you don't want me to *give up my dream of living here*? You've been disappearing for hours every day and you say 'it's work,' but

I've heard that story before. I've tried to be patient, but no more. What's going on?"

I felt like a fish on a hook and almost started wriggling. This was not how I pictured this moment going down. I'd had crazy visions of a tandem bike ride to the Scoop and champagne on ice waiting for us, with all our new friends gathered as I declared my feelings, but when Hannah met my gaze for a nanosecond and then glanced away, I saw it. The vulnerability in her eyes caused by the betrayal from her bastard of an ex. He'd taken her self-worth and even though she'd said I'd repaired the damage, I realized that now was the moment I was going to have to prove beyond any doubt how I felt about her.

I took her hand and said, "Come on."

"But—"

"No 'buts.'" I patted my thigh. "Come on, Dude. You might as well see this, too."

"See what?" she asked.

"Nope. I'm not saying another word. You've already ruined it."

"Ruined what?" she asked. I opened the door to the Jeep and she sat on the passenger seat while Dude hopped into the back.

"Wait and see." This time I couldn't resist and I kissed her quick and shut her door.

The drive into Cape Split was short. While I'd wanted to wait and show her when the piece was done, it was almost there and honestly, I was nervous and excited and a little sick to my stomach about her reaction. Maybe it was best to get it over with now and if she hated it, I could paint over it.

We found a parking spot down the street from the Scoop. Hannah was looking at me with one eyebrow raised in question, but Dude was just happy to be invited. He walked between us with his ears up and his tail wagging.

I stopped Hannah before we got to the patio. "Close your eyes."

"Excuse me?"

"Close your eyes," I repeated. "Don't worry, I'll make sure you don't trip."

"What's going on, Simon?"

I held her gaze. "Do you trust me?"

"Yes." She said it without hesitation.

"Then close your eyes."

With one more suspicious glance, Hannah closed her eyes and I guided her onto the patio. There were several groups of people enjoying ice cream and they watched us, no doubt wondering what I was up to.

I positioned Hannah exactly where I wanted her and then stepped to the side. "Open your eyes."

Her eyelids fluttered open and she took in the mural that I had been working on every morning for the past week and a half. I held my breath, waiting for her reaction. As she took it in, her mouth dropped and her eyes got wider and wider. When she turned to face me, I could see a sheen of tears in her eyes.

"You did it!" she cried, spreading her arms wide. "You painted the mural!"

"It's not done yet," I said. "I wanted to surprise you when it was finished, and I had all these plans, and things I wanted to say to you about how I feel about you, but given the circumstances I figured I'd better show you."

I gestured to the wall. Tim and I had agreed upon a concept for the mural that would look like a bunch of photographs scattered across the wall. I had done them in a more realistic style than my usual, but with a few fantastical elements thrown in, as it was my thing. The photos were replicas of ones I'd gathered from our friends and neighbors and a few from Tim Larson as well. I'd painted him and his father serving ice cream, Gramps and Pops fishing, and Luke and Bebe with baby Ava having a picnic in another.

Hannah's eyes took in every picture. When she saw the one of Gramps and Pops, she let out a sob and put her hand to her throat. When she looked at me, the tears in her eyes started to fall.

"Oh, Simon."

I felt my heart do a backflip in my chest. There was nothing I wouldn't do for this woman when she said my name just like that.

"Hey, that's your dog!" A little boy ran up to the wall and patted the photo that wasn't finished yet. "See?"

Hannah glanced to where he pointed and her hand moved to cover her mouth as she gasped in surprise. This photo was of her running on the beach with Dude at her side. Her hair was flying and I could almost hear the laughter coming from her wide smile. And there on the side of the photo was the back of the man she was running toward with so much love in her eyes. Me.

Now the tears ran down her face. I stepped in front of her and wiped the tears away with my thumbs. "Now do you see? I love you, Hannah Spencer. I. Love. You. And I don't want to sell our home. Not now, not ever."

"Oh, Simon O'Malley." Hannah sobbed and leapt up, grabbing me in a hug that strangled. "I love you, too, and while I'm glad we're not selling, I need you to know that whenever and wherever I'm with you, I am home."

And just like that, I was crying, too.

I heard several people laugh and I knew we were making a scene and I didn't care one bit. I leaned down and kissed her and I knew she was right. I would never feel as at home as I did when I was with Hannah.

I broke the kiss and hugged her tight, wanting to savor this happiness to the last drop. It was then that the note Gramps had written to me came back to me: *Remember who you are.* Finally, I thought I did.

Hannah and I enjoyed ice cream cones while taking in the project that had been consuming me. Hannah was quick to notice the fantastical elements I'd worked into each picture. The fish Gramps and Pops had caught were wearing Hawaiian shirts. Baby Ava wore a dress made of butterflies. The ice cream that Tim and his father scooped had comical expressions. And the beach Hannah ran on was littered with starfish that watched her as she ran past.

Tim and I had agreed to create one photo as a backdrop for tourists to take pictures of themselves to post to their social media. I'd painted a sandy beach with rolling waves and a sea serpent at the horizon. The frame listed my name and had the social media handle for the Scoop.

Hannah shot a video of herself and Dude jumping into the picture and I had no doubt it would be featured on her platform. I found it hard to believe that I, the guy who resisted social media stuff, was now weaponizing it to help me win the biggest fight of my life. Taking on my father and winning the conservatorship of Charlie once and for all.

"Your father is coming back tomorrow to get my answer," Hannah said. She was draped over my chest, delightfully naked, and she shivered when I trailed my fingers up and down her spine.

We'd left the Scoop and come right home. Our need to be together after confessing our feelings had been all-consuming. Making love to Hannah had always been one of the most spectacular sexual experiences of my life, but with the addition of those three little words, *I love you,* it became next-level.

"And we'll tell him no," I said.

"What about Charlie?" she asked. "We can't let your father use him like this."

"We won't, because I have a plan."

Hannah tipped her head to the side and her eyebrows rose. "I'm listening."

And so I told her. I gave her the option to bow out if she wasn't up for a confrontation, but my woman was all in. I hadn't thought it was possible to love her more, but in that moment when we were united as one in the fight for the life we wanted, I fell even harder.

Hannah

I was nervous. Not because I was afraid of Robert O'Malley Jr. but because I desperately didn't want to mess this up for Simon and Charlie. I sat on the front porch while Simon sat inside the house with the window open, listening.

Dude was outside with me just because he preferred to be outside, but it also made me feel better to have him nearby when O'Malley arrived. Not that I thought he'd hurt me, but one never knew how a privileged man would handle being denied what he wanted.

"Hey, Spencer," Simon whispered through the screened window.

"Yeah?" I leaned back so I could hear him.

"I think we should get married."

"What?" I spun around to stare at him through the screen, except the light wasn't in my favor and I couldn't see him. Not even his outline.

"Marriage. You and me."

"Is this really the time to talk about this?" I asked.

"Say yes, Hannah," Roland said from his hidden spot behind the crape myrtle.

"You should," Luke agreed. "Bebe and I were just saying we haven't had a wedding on the Split in forever."

"I make an amazing wedding cake, not to brag," Stephanie said.

"She does," her husband agreed.

My phone rang, mercifully ending the conversation. I glanced at the display. It was Bebe. "Hi," I answered.

"He's on his way. The Bentley you described just passed our house."

"Thanks." I ended the call. And then spoke to Simon and the neighbors hidden all around us. "Bebe says he's almost here."

"Good," Simon said. "We'll talk about our wedding later."

I let out an amused and somewhat exasperated sigh but didn't say anything as the Bentley stopped in front of the house. Robert got out in an impeccable charcoal gray suit and shiny black shoes. Dude growled low in his throat but I put my hand on his back to let him know it was okay.

I had the papers he'd given me the day before on the table beside me. I hadn't signed them.

Robert came up the steps and crossed the porch. I didn't get up but I did gesture to the vacant chair across from mine.

"Ms. Spencer." He inclined his head as he sat.

"Mr. O'Malley." I tipped my chin up.

"I assume you've made the correct choice."

"Actually, I have some questions," I said.

A quick frown flitted across his face before his mouth curved in a smile that didn't reach his eyes. "Such as?" he asked.

"You told me I had to sign my half of the house over to you or you would try to take Charlie's conservatorship away from Simon even though the incident you're using to do so was clearly a misunderstanding," I said. "You know Charlie wasn't going to hurt anyone. He just wanted to see if Diana liked the flowers he'd brought her."

Robert tipped his head back. "Your point?"

"How can I trust that you won't do it anyway?" I asked. "After all, any man who can use his disabled son for leverage to gain a property would likely just do it again if an opportunity presented itself. So, if I'm giving up my inheritance to keep Simon as Charlie's conservator, I want reassurances."

"You're not 'giving up' anything." Mr. O'Malley leaned back. He crossed one leg over the other, looking entirely too smug. "You'll be duly compensated for your half of the house."

"But how do I know you won't threaten Simon with this misunderstanding about Charlie?" I persisted. "How do I know you won't try to take Simon to court over Charlie's conservatorship if Simon doesn't sign over his half of the house to you?"

"I don't have to threaten Simon with anything," Mr. O'Malley said. "I am the heir to my father's estate, all of his estate. I will file a partition action and Simon's half of the house will be given to me by the courts as it should have been all along."

"Except it won't." Simon stepped out of the house. "Hannah isn't selling her half of the house to you and I'm not letting you take mine, either."

Simon's father rose from his seat. His nostrils flared and his face became flushed. "I was under the impression you weren't here."

"Because I wanted you to believe that, which is why I hid my car." Simon approached his father, stopping until he was just out of reach. "Let me tell you how this is going to go. You're going to walk away and you're never going to bother us again."

"Ha!" Mr. O'Malley scoffed. "The hell I will. I want what's

rightfully mine and that is Charlie's conservatorship money and this cottage."

"It was never yours and it never will be." Simon nodded. "Thanks to Gramps and Pops, there is no way you can take it from us."

"It's her, isn't it?" Simon's father waved a dismissive hand in my direction. "She's convinced you that you can take me on and win, but you can't. You don't want to give me the house now? Fine. I'll take control of your brother's conservatorship and reallocate the funds to buy my own property. After all, it's what I deserve as my father's only child."

"I will never let that happen." Simon shook his head.

"Neither will I." Lorelei came around the side of the house to stand beside Simon. "Charlie's conservatorship will never be under your control."

Simon put his arm around his sister's shoulders.

"You called your sister in on this?" Mr. O'Malley looked incensed. "Are you seriously hiding behind a woman?"

Simon looked at him as if he were incomprehensible. "Hiding behind . . . ? What is wrong with you? Lor and I are a team and we're infinitely more qualified to take care of our brother than you are."

Mr. O'Malley glowered at his children. "You think you can keep the conservatorship from me? What judge would allow that? I'm Charlie's father. You two were MIA when he was in trouble the other day and I'm the one who stepped in and took care of things."

"By using the situation to coerce me into selling my half of the house to you," I said. "Leveraging your son's well-being for your own gain makes you a shit guardian."

"Stay out of this!" Simon's father snapped.

"Hey, watch how you talk to my future wife!" Simon retorted.

"Wife?" Mr. O'Malley looked like he'd swallowed a bug. "I've had enough." He frowned at me. "Since you refuse to see reason, I'll move forward with my attorney to have the conservatorship switched to me. Remember this is all on you. How do you feel about your wife material now, Simon? She's willing to let you lose your conservatorship for a piece of property."

"Do you even hear yourself?" Simon asked. "Hannah has done nothing. It's you who's made threats about Charlie's care."

"There's not a judge in the state who'd believe you against me." Mr. O'Malley took his phone out of his pocket.

"Oh, I think I know a judge or two." Vincent Cosmo stepped out of the house, where he'd been waiting with Simon. "In fact, I went to law school with Judge Talley, who presided over the switching of the conservatorship from Simon's grandfather to Simon."

"Who are you?" Mr. O'Malley asked through clenched teeth.

"I'm the estate attorney for your late father, and I think Judge Talley would be fascinated to hear how you've used your threat to take away the conservatorship from Simon to try and coerce Hannah into selling her inheritance to you."

"That's not what's happened," Mr. O'Malley lied. "Besides, it's your word against mine and these three are in cahoots to try and screw me out of what's rightfully mine. How much are they paying you to lie for them?"

"That's not true, but you have brought up an interesting point—without witnesses this could become a case of your word against theirs," Vincent said.

"Exactly." Simon's father pointed at him. "And you will lose."

"Hmm." Vincent rubbed his chin. "It's a good thing we have witnesses, then."

Luke and Roland popped up out of their respective hiding places as did Stephanie and Mike. Roland sent Robert a powerful stink eye and said, "I heard every word. You should be ashamed of yourself."

"I guess we'll see you in court, Dad." Simon stared at his father in a look that was so cold I was surprised Mr. O'Malley didn't get frostbite.

"You'll regret this." Simon's father stormed off the porch.

"Doubt it," Lorelei called after him.

As soon as the Bentley peeled off down the road, we all let out a collective whoop of triumph. Even Dude tipped his head back and howled.

"We did it!" Lor hugged her brother and high-fived a bemused Vincent.

Luke and Roland joined us on the porch and Stephanie and Mike came around the side of the house and she said, "This calls for champagne and sticky buns!"

Everyone trotted inside, but when I would've followed, Vincent caught my arm and said, "Can I have a word, Hannah?"

I glanced at Simon to see if he knew what this was about but he shrugged. Then he clapped Vincent on the shoulder and said, "Thanks for your help. I'll meet you both inside."

The screen door swung shut behind him with a bang.

"Is something wrong?" I asked. "Did I break a law I'm unaware of?"

"No." Vincent shook his head. "When your grandfather wrote up his will, he gave me two letters. One I was to give to you if you sold the house, and the other was for if you decided to stay." He reached inside his sport coat and withdrew a business-sized envelope. It was thin but I recognized the handwriting on the outside. Pops.

My throat got tight and my breathing shallow as I took the envelope. "I don't understand, why two? And where's the other one?"

"As Mr. Spencer explained it to me, he wanted you to make your own decision about the house," he said. "The other letter per his instructions will be destroyed."

I glanced down at the envelope. This was so very Pops, prepared for any contingency. I nodded and said, "Thank you."

"I'll give you your privacy." Vincent excused himself.

The door shut behind him and I slid my thumb under the envelope flap, working it gently open so as not to tear it. Inside was one sheet of fancy writing paper. I took it out and unfolded it.

It read:

My dearest Hannah,

Congratulations on your new home. I hope you'll be as happy here as I was. You've been running for a long time, trying to escape your pain. You deserve a peaceful place to rest and heal. Cape Split was that special place for me. It's where I met the love of my life and later where I found him again.

I know you must be hurt and angry that I didn't include you in my life here. Bobby's situation was complicated, and I had to protect him and his family. I hope you understand. I bought this house because it was one Nana and I had rented when you were a little girl.

Do you remember our vacations here, you riding your bike on the wraparound porch, pretending to be a race car driver, until Nana said you were making her dizzy? It was those memories that kept you here with me even when I couldn't share this part of my life with you.

I am so proud of you, Hannah. Choosing to stay here in Cape Split tells me that you are ready to embrace life again. There is something magical about the Outer Banks.

There's no place like it in the world, and I think that choosing to stay means you're ready. You're ready to live fully and completely again.

A tear splattered onto the page and I sobbed. I paused to let out the grief that had bubbled to the surface, then I took in a slow breath and wiped my eyes before I continued reading.

No life is without challenges, Hannah, but if you find your community, and can surround yourself with people who will care for you as you care for them, then the challenges become much easier. I left this house to you, and asked you to live here for two months, hoping you'd find your community here as well. Know that whenever you stand on the dock, stroll the beach, enjoy ice cream, or watch a storm roll in, I'm with you in spirit.

All my love, Pops

P.S. I know you're sharing the house with Bobby's grandson. I don't know how you two have worked out the house share, but I want you to know that I met Simon at Bobby's funeral and I liked him. I liked him a lot. He reminded me of his grandfather and it occurs to me that you could do a lot worse. This is where your Nana tells me to mind my own business. Fine. Be happy, Hannah, however that manifests for you.

I burst into tears and hugged the paper to my chest.

"Hey, darling, are you all right?" Simon stepped out onto the porch.

I couldn't speak so I thrust the letter at him. I fanned my face and tried to pull it together while watching him read.

When he reached the end, his face crumpled and he looked up at me and asked, "He was at the funeral?"

"Yes, and apparently, he liked you . . . a lot." The sobs took over then and Simon opened his arms and held me while I cried.

It took me some time to pull it together. When the worst of my crying jag was over, I pulled away to tuck Pops's letter back into its envelope and faced Simon.

"I'm glad Pops was there. It's bothered me that they weren't together at the end," he said.

"I felt the same way," I said. "But I think everything worked out the way it was supposed to."

"I think so, too," Simon said as he tenderly tucked a lock of hair behind my ear. "By the way, I came out here to tell you that you handled my father perfectly. Thank you."

I put my hand on his face, cupping his cheek and admiring the sheer goodness of him. Never mind that his father was an awful person, that altercation had to have been difficult for Simon. "You were incredible."

"Couldn't have pulled it off without everyone here." He gestured to our friends in the house and then threw his arm around my shoulders as he guided me toward the door. "Now, about our getting married."

I rolled my eyes. "You know how I feel about marriage. I don't want to tie you down to someone who can't give you children."

Simon stopped walking and waved his hands at Dude, who was staring at us through the front window. "We have a child."

I burst out laughing. "In dog years, he's older than we are. What are you really saying, Simon?"

"I'm saying I don't care if we don't have kids. All I want is you.

You are everything to me. You are the reason I've found myself again, and I don't want to give you up. Not now. Not ever."

My eyes flooded. Simon became a blurry watercolor image. I blinked frantically but the tears rolled down my face until I was a drippy mess . . . again. I swiped my face with the backs of my hands, trying to get it together.

"You don't have to agree to marry me," he said. "Just tell me you want this. Tell me you want to build a life with me here in Cape Split as much as I want one with you."

I sniffed. No one had ever loved me like Simon had over the past few weeks and I believed him. I believed that I was enough for him. My throat got tight and a little sob bubbled up. I steadied myself by leaning against him. I knew he wouldn't let me fall. This was my moment. The moment everything I had ever longed for was mine for the taking. I desperately did not want to mess this up.

"I have some conditions." I turned toward him, put my hands on his chest, and stared up into his dreamy brown gaze.

"Conditions?" He leaned down and kissed me quick. "Such as?"

"Chickens."

He closed his eyes and I couldn't tell if it was exasperation or amusement or both. Probably both. "How many?"

"Four, no, six, maybe ten."

Simon took my hand and led me toward the house.

"And I think some goats would do wonders on the lawn."

"Goats?" His voice came out sounding strangled.

"Just picture them scampering around in pajamas," I said. "That would totally go viral on our social media account."

"*Our* account?" he asked.

"Yes, the artist and the writer on their mini farm in the Outer Banks. We'd crush that." I might have been going too far but it was such fun to tease him.

“Oh, of course. Anything else?”

“A baby cow. Every woman needs her own cow.”

“Of course she does,” he agreed. He stopped in front of the door and said, “If chickens, goats, and a cow will get you to stay with me forever and ever then so be it.”

I grinned and threw my arms around him. “Then, yes, you just got yourself a life partner!”

A whoop sounded from inside that I suspected was Roland but as Simon leaned down and kissed me, our world narrowed to just the two of us. I knew I’d finally found the life I was meant to live and I owed it all to the two men who fell in love as teens and when the chance came their way again, they grabbed on to love with both hands and never let go.

Acknowledgments

One of my earliest childhood memories is running on the beach in the Outer Banks, chasing my brother, who had a toy boat that I decided I wanted. I can still feel the sand between my toes and the waves tickling my feet as we laughed and played until we passed out for nap time on a beach blanket. I remember another trip where I climbed up to the top of the Cape Hatteras lighthouse and felt quite proud as my brother was too scared to do it. I lived off that feat of bravery for months. My mother, Susan McKinlay, is the one who dragged us to North Carolina for family vacations and in doing so gave me all these wonderful memories, so it is her and her wanderlust that I have to acknowledge first and foremost. Thanks, Mom!

As for this particular story, I also want to thank my late uncle Brian McKinlay. He spent the last years of his life, with his partner, running a daylily plantation in North Carolina, and his brilliant and hilarious emails to me about his daily life informed much of the story.

And now for the nuts and bolts. I want to thank my team at Berkley—Kate Seaver, Amanda Maurer, Christine Legon, Kaila Mundell-Hill, and Kim-Salina I; as well as the team at Rotrosen,

Christina Hogrebe and Jessica Errera. I am so fortunate to work with such brilliant, creative, incredibly hardworking editors, publicists, marketers, and agents. Best team ever!

Much appreciation to Vikki Chu for this spectacular cover and the book designer Kristin del Rosario for making this book an actual work of art.

Shout-out of gratitude to my personal assistants. You'd never see me online without the support and talent of Jenel Looney, Maddee James, and Christie Conlee. They make my socials and website worth visiting.

Lastly, my fam—I am ever grateful for Chris Hansen Orf, love of my life, and our Hooligans, Beckett Orf and Wyatt Orf. Without the three of you and your unwavering support, I don't think I'd have the confidence or the stamina to be a writer. Love you all forever and ever.

The Summer Share

Jenn McKinlay

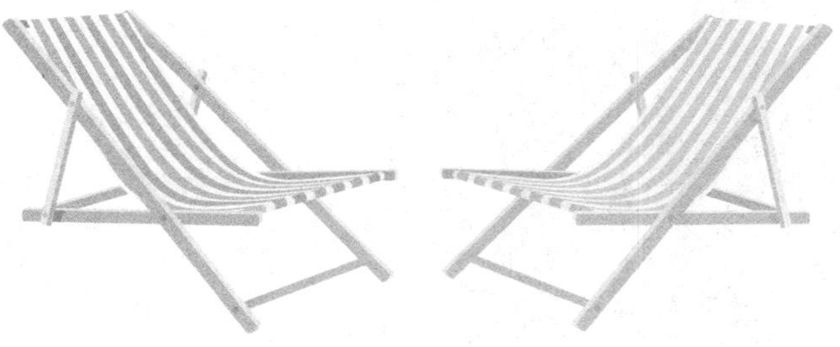

READERS GUIDE

Questions for Discussion

1. How did you feel about the alternating chapters—Hannah's and Simon's—with each told in the first-person point of view? Do you feel that this perspective gave you a deeper insight into the characters? Why or why not?

2. There's a "meet-cute" tradition in rom-com storytelling. Discuss Hannah and Simon's "meet-cute." What was your reaction when Dude knocked Simon into the water?

3. What are some of the moments—large and small—that made you like Hannah and Simon? What made them perfect for each other? How did they change and grow during their time together in the cottage?

4. What would you do if you inherited half of a seaside cottage with a total stranger? Would you want to sell it or keep it? Why?

5. Why do you think Gramps and Pops left the cottage to Simon and Hannah specifically, rather than to other family members?

6. Simon said, "The two things we've lost as individuals navigating the world largely through our phones are our privacy and our time." What do you think of this observation? Would you want to be a content creator like Hannah? Why or why not? Why do you think the van lifestyle worked for her for so long, but doesn't anymore?

7. How did Dude, the Great Dane, help reveal aspects of Simon's and Hannah's characters?

8. Simon has two siblings, while Hannah is an only child. In what ways are they each shaped by these familial roles? How do their family dynamics inform their decisions?

9. Hannah thinks that Simon's lone dimple is a symbol of the fact that he's half happy, half sad. "Aren't we all?" she thinks. Is she right—are we all half happy and half sad?

10. In what ways did the story surprise you, and how did it make you feel?

11. Over the course of the novel, Hannah and Simon find happiness, even while navigating their grief over the loss of their grandfathers. Who are some of the people in your life who have helped you find happiness through difficult times?

Keep reading for an excerpt from
Jenn McKinlay's novel

Witches of Dubious Origin

Questions for Discussion

1. How did you feel about the alternating chapters—Hannah's and Simon's—with each told in the first-person point of view? Do you feel that this perspective gave you a deeper insight into the characters? Why or why not?

2. There's a "meet-cute" tradition in rom-com storytelling. Discuss Hannah and Simon's "meet-cute." What was your reaction when Dude knocked Simon into the water?

3. What are some of the moments—large and small—that made you like Hannah and Simon? What made them perfect for each other? How did they change and grow during their time together in the cottage?

4. What would you do if you inherited half of a seaside cottage with a total stranger? Would you want to sell it or keep it? Why?

5. Why do you think Gramps and Pops left the cottage to Simon and Hannah specifically, rather than to other family members?

6. Simon said, "The two things we've lost as individuals navigating the world largely through our phones are our privacy and our time." What do you think of this observation? Would you want to be a content creator like Hannah? Why or why not? Why do you think the van lifestyle worked for her for so long, but doesn't anymore?

7. How did Dude, the Great Dane, help reveal aspects of Simon's and Hannah's characters?

8. Simon has two siblings, while Hannah is an only child. In what ways are they each shaped by these familial roles? How do their family dynamics inform their decisions?

9. Hannah thinks that Simon's lone dimple is a symbol of the fact that he's half happy, half sad. "Aren't we all?" she thinks. Is she right—are we all half happy and half sad?

10. In what ways did the story surprise you, and how did it make you feel?

11. Over the course of the novel, Hannah and Simon find happiness, even while navigating their grief over the loss of their grandfathers. Who are some of the people in your life who have helped you find happiness through difficult times?

Keep reading for an excerpt from
Jenn McKinlay's novel

Witches of Dubious Origin

Keep reading for an excerpt from
Jenn McKinlay's novel

Witches of Dubious Origin

One

“Package for you, Zoe.” Bill Reed, my coworker at the Wessex Public Library, dropped a thick padded envelope, clearly holding a book, onto my desk. I glanced up at him. I was the reference librarian. He was acquisitions. Generally, book purchases went right to him.

Bill shrugged at the confusion on my face. “I know, but it’s addressed to you and stamped *Personal.*”

I glanced at the brown envelope. Sure enough, there was the stamp in an imperative shade of red right above the handwritten name *Zoanne Ziakas*—my name—and the library’s address. Weirdly, there was no postmark or stamps or anything to indicate it had been delivered the usual way through the post office.

“Be careful opening it.” Bill’s eyes narrowed behind his wire-framed glasses. “It could be—”

He paused. Clearly his imagination had run out or he was hesitant to say *bomb* or *poison* or whatever nefarious thing could possibly be stuffed into a nine-by-twelve-inch padded envelope. Bill had the pasty complexion of a man who’d spent his adult life under fluorescent lighting. He was in his fifties, happily married to his wife, Meredith, of thirty years. They had two kids in college and spent most of their time dreaming about retirement. There wasn't much that disturbed Bill, so I was surprised by his unusual caution.

"Could be what?" I prodded.

"I don't know." He ran a hand over his thinning hair in a self-soothing gesture. "I just have a bad feeling about it."

"It's probably a catalog from a publisher or a library supply company that got misdirected to me," I said. Although, when I studied the loopy script of my name written in felt-tip pen, I felt the hair on the back of my neck prickle, and a flutter of alarm tickled my insides. I knew this handwriting. It was my mother's.

No, it couldn't be. My mother had passed away a month ago. There was no way she could have addressed this envelope from beyond the grave. It was just an unfortunate coincidence. Shaking off the unsettling feeling, I grabbed my scissors and sliced the envelope open. It didn't explode. No plume of poisonous smoke was emitted. Instead, out fell a thick black book encircled with a half-inch metal band that was engraved with a series of interlocking lines similar to a Celtic knot. The band latched into a decorative hexagon on the front cover. Fancy.

"Well, that underwhelms," Bill said. He appeared visibly relieved. "Looks like a journal of some sort. You were right. It's probably a promo item from a publisher."

I set the book down and glanced into the envelope. There was no note explaining what the book was, no flyer, nothing. I put the envelope aside and picked up the book. I pressed on the hexagon, thinking that might open the band. It didn't work. I tried turning the hexagon. It didn't budge.

"It's a pretty pricey item for a promo," I said. "Especially since I can't open it."

"Do you want me to try?" he offered.

"Go for it." I handed him the book.

Bill did the same pressing and twisting that I had. He tried to tug on the band but it was secured too tightly to give him any leverage. He handed it back and I returned it to its envelope for safekeeping.

"What we have here is a very decorative paperweight," he concluded.

I laughed. I opened my desk's bottom drawer and dropped the book inside. "I'll look at it later."

Bill headed back to his office, and I returned to my weekly report, forgetting all about the strange black book.

October was my favorite month, when the sticky humidity of summer departed and jeans-and-sweater weather returned. As I walked the half mile from the library to my cottage, I reveled in the chilly temperatures, the scent of wood fires on the air, and the satisfying crunch of leaves under my feet.

The village of Wessex, where I lived and worked, was nestled between the Appalachian Trail and the Housatonic River, in the northwestern corner of Connecticut. It was a small community known for the private boarding school that resided on the west side of the river. I had attended that school before leaving to go to university in New Haven and then doubling back here to the only place that had ever felt like home.

As soon as I stepped inside my cottage, I slipped into my pajamas while I microwaved a big bowl of mac and cheese. I flicked on the television and scrolled through the streaming channels until I found a mystery series I had yet to watch. I preferred the British ones because I loved that the actors and actresses in them looked like real people, as opposed to American television shows, where everyone looks like a supermodel pretending to be a real person.

I was halfway through my bowl of cheesy goodness and a third of the way through the first episode when I heard a thump on my front porch. I paused the show and stopped chewing, listening intently. Living in Wessex, where everyone knew everyone, I wasn't as worried about crime as I was about a neighbor dropping by to chat. It wasn't that bad things didn't happen here—of course they did—it was just that it was very rare, and usually the person who did the crime was known for having a dented moral compass, so it wasn't a big surprise.

Thump!

The noise sounded again, only more forcefully. Putting my bowl down on the coffee table, I shoved my chenille throw aside and crossed the room to the front door, switching on the outside light. I peered out the side window that looked onto the porch before opening the door. If it was a rabid raccoon looking for food, I didn't want to get into it with him. The porch was empty.

Just to be certain everything was all right, I opened the door and poked my head out. I glanced from side to side, seeing only my large potted geranium on one side and my small wicker table and two chairs on the other. Satisfied, I went to close the door and glanced down at the doormat. I gasped. Placed on the center of the mat was the same envelope that Bill had delivered to me at work. But I knew I had left it in my desk drawer. What the hell was it doing here?

I glanced around the porch to see if someone was lurking in the shadows, playing a prank on me. It wasn't really Bill's style—he was more of a dad-joke type of guy—but he was the only person who knew about the book, so logic dictated it had to be him.

"Not funny, Bill!" I called into the darkening evening. There was no answer. No one was there.

I picked up the envelope and pulled the book out, experiencing the same twinge of unease I'd felt before. A flash of green lit the porch as the envelope was immediately engulfed in emerald flames. I yelped and dropped it. In seconds the envelope was gone, leaving no ash or smoke behind. I examined my hand and noted that the weird neon fire hadn't even felt hot.

I glanced out at the street, making certain no one had seen what had just happened. Ever since my childhood, unexpected magic had always made me anxious.

I took another look around the porch and yard before I went back inside, then locked the dead bolt. I studied the aged volume more closely. It was a shade of black so matte it seemed to soak up light. The edges of the pages were jagged and uneven. And the book's hexagonal metal latch was rusted from humidity or lack of use, I couldn't tell which. I brought it to the kitchen, thinking I could open it with a knife.

Not wanting to lose a finger, I chose a butter knife. I slid it under the decorative metal band and tried to pry it loose. The metal didn't budge. I tried to pop the hexagon with the blade as well, but it held fast. I set down the utensil and glanced at the door. If it wasn't Bill who had dropped the book off and made the envelope go *poof* . . . nope. I refused to go there.

The pin pricked my finger and blood beaded up out of the wound. I yelped and dropped the pin. Drops of blood dripped from my middle finger and I pressed my thumb to the tip to stop the flow. Had I just stabbed myself with a pin . . . *on purpose*? I blinked. I glanced down, noting that I was wearing my pajamas.

Relief whooshed inside me. It was okay. It was just a dream. An awful, stupid, painful dream. I shook my head, trying to wake myself up. It didn't work. It couldn't . . . because I was already awake.

I glanced down at my kitchen counter, where small splats of blood marred the smooth surface. The battered old book that I had tucked into my shoulder bag earlier sat on the granite beneath my pricked finger.

Shit! I had almost bled on the book. I spun away from the counter and rinsed my finger in the sink. What the hell had just happened? Sleepwalking? Night terrors? Had I actually pricked myself with a pin? *Why?*

Grabbing a paper towel, I wiped the blood off the granite. I rinsed off the pin and returned it to the container I kept in the utility drawer at the end of the counter. I threw the towel in the trash and stood, staring at the book in confusion. What was the book doing on the counter when I was certain I had put it in my bag?

Insistent whispers sounded at the edge of my mind. Like shadows that faded as the sun rose, the words weren't quite loud enough for me to make out, but I knew. I knew without a doubt that those whispers had been in my dreams and that they had instructed me to stab myself with the straight pin. I glanced down. Goose bumps raised on my forearms as I gazed at the black book. I ran an uninjured finger over the cover, half expecting it to be absorbed into the black leather, as if it could pull me in just as it seemed to soak in the light. It didn't and I lifted my hand and noted my fingers were trembling.

I'd had a strange feeling about this mysterious volume from the moment I'd first touched it, and I knew of only one person who might be able to help me.

Author photo by Hailey Gilman

Jenn McKinlay is the award-winning *New York Times*, *USA Today*, and *Publishers Weekly* bestselling author of several mystery and romance series. Her work has been translated into multiple languages in countries all over the world. She lives in sunny Arizona in a house that is overrun with books, pets, and her husband's guitars.

VISIT JENN MCKINLAY ONLINE

JennMcKinlay.com

JennMcKinlayAuthor

McKinlayJenn

Learn more about this book and other titles from *New York Times* Bestselling Author

JENN McKINLAY